OUT OF THE ASHES
KNOXVILLE FBI - BOOK FOUR

LIZ BRADFORD

Copyright © 2024 Liz Bradford

All rights reserved.

Stand on the Rock Publishing LLC

liz@lizbradfordwrites.com

Lizbradfordwrites.com

Print ISBN: 978-1-960692-02-3

Cover Design by Emilie Haney at EAH Creative https://www.eahcreative.com/

Comprehensive Edit by Teresa Crupmton at AuthorSpark, Inc. authorspark.org

Copy Edit by Sharyn Kopf https://sharynkopf.wordpress.com/

Scripture quotations are taken from The Holy Bible, English Standard Version. ESV® Text Edition: 2016. Copyright © 2001 by Crossway Bibles, a publishing ministry of Good News Publishers.

Scripture quotations may also be taken from the *Holy Bible,* New Living Translation, copyright © 1996, 2004, 2007 by Tyndale House Foundation. Used by permission of Tyndale House Publishers, Inc., Carol Stream, Illinois 60188. All rights reserved.

Scripture quotations may also be taken from Holy Bible, New International Version®, NIV® Copyright ©1973, 1978, 1984, 2011 by Biblica, Inc.® Used by permission. All rights reserved worldwide.

This novel is a work of fiction. Names, characters, businesses, places, events, locales, and incidents are either the products of the author's imagination or used in a fictitious manner. Any resemblance to actual persons, living or dead, or actual events is purely coincidental.

No portion of this book may be reproduced in any form without written permission from the publisher or author, except as permitted by U.S. copyright law.

To you, dear reader.
Wherever you are, whoever you are,
Jesus loves you.
Put your hope in Him
because
Hope in Jesus is never *false*.

Isaiah 43:1-3
...Fear not, for I have redeemed you;
I have called you by name, you are mine.
When you pass through the waters, I will be with you;
and through the rivers, they shall not overwhelm you;
when you walk through fire you shall not be burned,
and the flame shall not consume you.
For I am the Lord your God,
the Holy One of Israel, your Savior...

2 Peter 5:10
And after you have suffered a little while, the God of all grace, who has called you to his eternal glory in Christ, will himself restore, confirm, strengthen, and establish you.

Chapter One

July

Aurora sat on the floor in her bedroom in the mountain house playing with the doll her daddy had given her for her birthday.

Auntie, not Aurora's real aunt—she was just another in a long line of women Daddy made take care of Aurora—sat nearby. "You know, Aurora, today is your half birthday." This Auntie was different. She liked Aurora, and Aurora liked her.

"What's that mean?"

Auntie's smile was kind, even if a little sad. It didn't make sense to Aurora that a smile could be sad, but Auntie's was.

"It means it is halfway between your sixth birthday and your seventh birthday."

Aurora held the doll with black curly hair in front of her and talked to it. "That must mean it's yours too." Aurora hugged the doll to her chest.

Auntie picked up Aurora's stuffed unicorn and played with Aurora. She loved Auntie. She took care of her and had fun with her.

A car made a noise outside.

Daddy's home!

Excitement shot through Aurora's whole body.

Auntie dropped the unicorn and took a quick breath in. Her eyes grew wide. "Stay in here, Aurora. I'll come back up later." She kissed Aurora's head and ran out the door.

Aurora jumped up and skipped to the window. The curtains were open so she could see the mountains, but she went to the side and hid. Careful to not be seen—she knew better than to get caught—she peeked out from the corner of the window.

When he got out of the car, his face was red. *Daddy looks angry.* He slammed the door.

Aurora gasped. She slapped her hand over her mouth. *I hope he didn't hear me.*

Auntie came outside. She was breathing so hard her chest went up and down. "Can I do anything for you?"

"You can explain to me how this stupid situation happened. I've lost her again!" Daddy said a very bad word and kicked the tire.

"You don't have her mother?"

Aurora bit her lip. Mother? Was that why Daddy had left in such a good mood this morning? He'd been looking for Mommy for all of Aurora's life. She'd overheard him and Auntie talking a couple of months ago after he brought Aurora back from France. He said he'd found Mommy but hadn't been able to bring her home. So why wasn't she home now?

Daddy said another bad word and leaned back against the car. "I was supposed to meet that lowlife Ronan—I had everything he asked for, and she agreed to come with me for real this time."

Auntie stepped closer to Daddy. "What happened?"

"They didn't show for the exchange." Daddy's fists were angry balls by his sides. "I called, but his phone was off. I spoke to a few of my contacts, and they said they'd heard a rumor the FBI had killed him." Daddy crossed his arms. Aurora didn't understand the look on his face.

Auntie walked up next to Daddy and put her body against his. "You'll find her again. You've gotten this close; she couldn't have gone far. But for now, let me take care of you."

Daddy let Auntie slip under his arms.

Aurora felt sick to her stomach. She didn't know much, but something inside her didn't want Daddy touching Auntie like that.

Every auntie she'd ever had always put her body against Daddy's. It wasn't right. Aurora wanted Mommy and Daddy to love each other. And most of the time Auntie didn't look like she wanted to be touched by Daddy.

Aurora backed away from the window and crossed to her nightstand. She picked up the picture frame and traced her finger on the only picture she had of her real family.

It was from the day she was born. Mommy looked really happy, but there was something else in her eyes Aurora didn't quite understand. It was the same look she'd seen in all of her aunties' eyes when Daddy pushed them into his bedroom.

Aurora sat on the edge of her bed. Would Daddy come see her tonight or would they forget about her? She didn't get to be with Daddy very often now that school was off since he worked so far away in Knoxville, and they were staying in the mountains. But she'd hoped to see him tonight. Maybe she still wouldn't have time with him until Saturday again. She wished she knew her days of the week better so she could be sure when that would be. Maybe she'd get that down when she started first grade next month.

She looked at the picture again.

Mommy had the same dark eyes and hair as Aurora. Their skin was a little darker than Daddy's. Would she get to meet her mommy one day?

Chapter Two

SEPTEMBER

The late-afternoon storm dropped a deluge of rain as Morgan stepped out onto the porch of Jacqui's mountain house. She'd been staying here for the last two months, but she'd move into the little travel-trailer Gio bought them when Dylan and Jacq returned from their honeymoon. Although by the time they got back, Morgan and Gio would be off on their own grand adventure.

Her heart shook. Adventure? Yes. But she was scared, terrified even. Meeting Gio's parents in person? Seeing her family again for the first time in more than thirteen years? At least she had Gio and, more importantly, Jesus.

She propped her shoulder against the post at the top of the stairs and gazed across the clearing. Two-and-a-half months ago, she'd danced in that clearing and experienced true freedom for the first time ever. That freedom and her life may have been severely threatened, but Ronan was dead and would never threaten her again.

Still, the devil's voice tried to convince her she'd never be free. Just because one pimp was dead didn't mean there weren't another million out there who would jump at the chance to enslave her. Only Ronan was dead, not any of the other pimps who had sold her again and again. And not the tricks who had paid another man to have access to her body.

That was the past, though. She had to move on.

Today held hope. Healing. Peace.

Lightning filled the sky.

Peace even in the midst of the thunderstorm.

The thunder cracked.

She had planned to apply the final coat of paint inside the trailer today, but the humidity was intense. The little AC unit would have to crank entirely too much to dry the paint anytime soon. It could wait until tomorrow. Gio would be here then, and he could help, as much as his knee let him.

Her phone dinged, indicating motion at the gate, and her nerves lit up like they'd been struck by lightning. She backed toward the door and pulled out her phone, opening the surveillance app as fast as she could.

Gio!

Her heart bounced. As much as she wanted to run straight to him, the rain held her back until he parked in front of the house. Then she disregarded the downpour and bolted for Gio. He opened the door, and before he was even out of the car, her arms were around his neck.

He pulled her close and released a contented sigh. "You're exactly what these weary eyes needed to see," he whispered into her hair.

"You too, Mr. Crespi."

He chuckled, but the heaviness in his spirit wasn't hard to miss. She pulled back. "You okay?"

"Inside first? You're getting soaked."

"I guess I can't argue with that." She grabbed his bag from the backseat and offered her arm.

Despite the two-and-a-half months that had passed since he took a gunshot to the knee, he still struggled to walk. Thankfully, he wasn't too proud to take her support.

As quick as Gio's knee would allow, they made it inside out of the rain, just before another crack of thunder shook the entire house. Sometimes being closer to the heavens up on the mountain wasn't a good thing.

Once inside, Gio spun her toward him and brought his face to hers. Their lips met in a tender but passion-filled kiss, nearly knocking her off her feet.

But it was over as fast as it started.

She giggled, and he walked away, leaning heavily on his cane.

They really were going to get married, weren't they? She couldn't wait. She followed him into the kitchen, where he fixed himself a glass of tea, but his normal smile was nowhere to be found. "What's wrong, Gio?" Had someone from her past appeared?

"Remember that boy the team has been looking for?"

She nodded, trying not to reveal on her face that she noticed he said "the team" and not "we" again. Desk duty was a slow death, and she hated it for him.

"Matt and Aliza found him and extracted him."

Joy filled her. "That's amazing. Why aren't you more excited?"

"Two months he was missing, and during those months, the boy went through hell." Gio closed the fridge and turned toward her. "Four or five tricks a day."

Morgan winced. The boy was only nine years old.

"It makes me so angry."

"Did your sketch of the kidnapper help?"

"Thankfully, yes. It's a miracle we found him at all. But he should never have had to endure that."

She closed the gap between them and slid her arms around Gio's waist. "We pray for him and praise the Lord for the successful rescue."

"But it's so much bigger."

She nodded. "So big."

Gio stroked her hair. "Can we ever do enough?"

"Honestly, no. It's too big for you and me, but nothing is impossible with God. That's what *you* keep telling me."

His smile returned. "Exactly. We keep fighting this, obeying God, and helping those who have escaped find Jesus and life on the other side."

"You got it." The biggest question was one she'd avoided asking for a few weeks now since his knee wasn't improving as expected. But his lack of healing was the exact reason she needed to ask the question. If he wasn't ever cleared for full duty again, was he thinking of an alternative? It was only the two of them now, so maybe she should just ask. "Any idea what that looks like at this point?"

"I'm surprised you haven't asked sooner."

"I didn't want to push."

"We should talk about the possibilities. I'm not sure if I will go back to full duty."

"But you still want to be on the front lines of rescuing people?"

"I do."

"You could go to the private sector."

"Maybe, but we need to pray about it. I know your heart is to be here as Jacq opens the home, and I don't want to be far."

"Good, because I don't want you far either, but let's see where God directs us." Morgan laid her head on Gio's chest. As broken as she still was, she wanted more than anything to help others find new life outside the trafficking world. Hers and Gio's dreams coupled nicely, so she had confidence God would use them together, wherever, however He saw fit.

Gio slid his shoes back on. Getting through the Nashville airport security was a nightmare. Why was everyone traveling on a Thursday morning in the middle of September? And the TSA agents had decided to be extra thorough with everyone.

"So much for having plenty of time for a leisurely stroll to the gate." Morgan tugged her backpack on and grinned.

Her smile lifted his heart, but getting to their gate on time was going to push him to speeds he wasn't sure he could manage. Before the injury it wouldn't have even been a worry, and while the pain wasn't as extensive as it had been even a month ago, the knee just didn't want to function correctly. He couldn't run or ride a bike. On good days he could pull off the elliptical or rowing machine. Today was not a good day. He had probably done too much the last two days helping Morgan finish remodeling their trailer. It looked amazing, though, and would be a perfect little home until their house could be built.

Morgan slid her hand around his elbow. "We can see if we can get a ride on one of those tram things."

"I'll be fine. Pain isn't bad. We'll just have to keep moving."

She raised her eyebrows. "Don't be stubborn."

"I'm not. At least I'm not meaning to be; let's just go."

She nodded, and they walked down the terminal toward their gate.

Morgan did a good job of masking her nerves, but they'd had many honest conversations about this trip. She was ready, even if she wasn't sure she was.

His parents were ecstatic they were coming. His mom's health made it too difficult for them to travel, and he'd begged her to stay home after he got shot. She wanted to make the trip, no matter how challenging. She'd agreed not to come only after he'd promised to visit as soon as he was able.

His mom was going to love Morgan, even if Morgan didn't think it was possible. She slid her hand down his arm and intertwined their fingers. Why had God blessed him with such a fantastic woman? Her wounds were still healing, and would be for a long time, but she loved fiercely, and that made him love her even more.

He squeezed her hand. "You're awfully quiet."

She smiled at him. "My thoughts haven't changed. They keep repeating, like a scratched CD, over and over again. I'm truly looking forward to meeting your parents and then to seeing Nate, but what if ..."

"They all love you, Morgan. Plus, I'll be right by your side."

"And that's the only reason I agreed to any of this." She swept her arm toward the gates ahead of them. "Which gate are we headed to again?"

Gio looked down the concourse. "That one. What do you know; we made it on time." *And I didn't fall once.*

Maybe he was improving.

"I should make a pit stop before we get on the plane. There's the little girl's room."

"Not a bad idea. Maybe we'll even have time to grab a snack. I haven't heard our flight called yet."

"Perfect." She came up and touched her lips to his.

He stood there frozen in time for a moment while she went around the corner into the women's bathroom.

A man bumped into him, knocking him out of his trance.

"Sorry, man."

"It's okay." Gio's knee buckled, and he leaned heavily on his cane in order to not hit the ground. Frustrated words pooled in his mind. Keeping them inside, he stepped carefully toward the restroom.

A few minutes later he limped out, his knee still unhappy about the guy who had bumped into him. Gio glanced around for Morgan. For a woman, she could be surprisingly quick in the bathroom. He didn't see her.

The concourse was filled with people. But no Morgan.

His breath caught, and his heart thundered. Surely she would have beat him out.

People milled about all over the place. Their stomping feet and screeching conversations pounded in his ears. *Where is Morgan?*

Maybe she was still in the bathroom. He didn't want to consider any other alternatives. She wouldn't leave, of that he was certain. Wasn't he? Yes. He shuffled to the entryway of the women's bathroom. "Morgan?"

No sound returned.

A hand dryer turned on, and a moment later a middle-aged woman came out.

"Is there anyone else still in there?"

She gave him a glower. "A few, I suppose." After rolling her eyes, she walked away.

"Morgan?" he called into the bathroom again. His attempt at keeping the fear out of his voice fell flat.

"Gio?" She edged around the corner.

"What's wrong?"

"I'll ask you the same in a minute." She snuck out of the bathroom. "Don't think I didn't catch that expression. When I came out I saw *him*." Morgan didn't look at Gio; instead she searched the crowd. "There." She turned back to Gio and buried her head on his shoulder.

"Who? Where?"

"Duke. He's across the way between the two gates."

"There are a bunch of men in that area. I need more info."

She pulled the hood of her sweatshirt over her dark curls and turned. "Shoot. I don't see him now." She took Gio's hand and tugged him into the stream of travelers. Stopping halfway across the concourse, she sighed. "I swear it was him."

"I don't doubt you for a second. Do you think he saw you?"

She shook her head. "I can't believe he'd ignore it if he did, though he's also not one to just abandon what he's doing. But ..." She glanced around frantically, her hand shaking in Gio's.

"Morgan." He tugged on her hand. "Look at me."

She peeled her eyes away from her search and met his gaze.

"You're safe. He doesn't stand a chance against me and"—he tapped the floor—"my trusty cane."

She turned fully toward him and ran her hand around his side. Her smile returned as the fear faded.

"It's been months. He's probably moved on, right?"

"I don't know why he wouldn't have." Her eyes grew distant again.

They both knew a man like Duke wasn't going to abandon his obsession so quickly, but somehow lying to themselves about it made the reality of not knowing his real name easier to swallow. They knew which hospital he worked at but still couldn't identify who "Duke" was.

Not that it necessarily mattered. Gio had nothing to peg on him to prosecute. He wouldn't actually be able to arrest the man who had bought his fiancée like she was a commodity to be sold. Other than her testimony, they had no evidence.

But Gio would find something to lock the man away on. Once they discovered his true identity, even if it was on something like tax fraud, Gio would put him behind bars.

Chapter Three

Morgan stepped into Gio's arms, running hers between his pack and his back. When she saw Duke, everything in her mind crashed like a multi-car pile-up. But Gio held her steady in the midst of the storm. *Jesus, what if Duke saw me? Do I need to be afraid of him? Or does he not really care about me now?*

She should laugh at herself. Duke had been entirely too fixated on her and willing to give Ronan anything he wanted.

A shudder coursed through her body.

Gio kissed her head.

Another call to board came across the intercom, so she stepped out of Gio's embrace. "Let's fly far away from here."

"That's a great idea. Trust me, Duke doesn't want to mess with my mom."

Morgan laughed. According to Gio, his mom was a petite woman who fit in just fine with his dad's Italian family. Morgan could almost see Mrs. Crespi going after Duke with a rolling pin. He wouldn't stand a chance.

With that mental image, they moved toward their departure gate.

But Morgan continued to check over her shoulder.

She'd seen Duke. Without a single doubt, it was him. But had he spotted her? Did he get on this plane?

Fresh fear made her feet unable to move.

"Miss?" The gate agent held out his hand.

She snapped out of it and handed the man her boarding pass. With concerted effort she put one foot in front of another as they walked toward the plane. If Duke was there, she had no doubt he was in first class. That would require walking past him to get to their regular seats.

"Morgan?"

She met Gio's eyes.

"Don't worry. If he's there, I'll punch him in the face."

She couldn't contain the laugh that erupted. The passengers around her probably gave her weird looks, but she didn't care. This man beside her was perfection.

They made it to the plane, but once they walked on, her amusement vanished. Hand firmly planted in Gio's, she let him lead her to their seats. If she spotted Duke, she'd give Gio's hand a tug.

But Duke wasn't there.

They arrived at their seats and tucked their backpacks into the overhead compartments. Gio gave her the window seat and settled in next to her. She laid her head on his shoulder. Her emotions wouldn't stay at bay, though, no matter how hard she fought them. Tiny sobs escaped.

Gio took her hand with both of his. "You are safe and free."

She loved that he reminded her of that every day. She needed to hear it as often as possible. "Thank you."

"I got you. And, more importantly, Jesus does too."

"Yep." Another sob shook her body.

"Jesus, give us peace, and help us not to fear, but to walk in faith that You are leading and guiding us. Prepare us for what lies ahead. Help us bring justice and freedom for others too."

"Amen." She took a breath, settling the sobs, and lifted her head. "Time to focus on the future, not the past. You really think your mom is going to like me?"

"I know she will." He leaned his head back and smiled.

Morgan pushed herself up and kissed his cheek.

His smile grew.

She intertwined her fingers into his and looked out the window. She was hopeful about meeting Gio's parents and praying she would never have to run into or even see Duke again.

The car pulled to a stop in front of an adorable, stucco house. Morgan's heart spun like a plate let loose by a professional spinner. It was time to meet Gio's mother.

The ride from the airport with Gio's dad had been delightful. He was Gio plus thirty years. Kind, a little goofy, as long as he didn't take himself too seriously, and reliable. It had only been a thirty-minute drive, but Morgan was already certain those descriptors fit Leo Crespi.

He'd picked Gio and Morgan up outside of baggage claim. His smile was as bright as Gio's, despite the sadness deep in his eyes, the sadness that comes with the intense grief of losing one's child.

The passenger door opened beside her, and Gio offered his hand. His eyebrows fluttered comically, easing her nerves a teensy bit. She took the offer up, and once they'd retrieved their bags from the trunk, made their way to the front door.

Morgan half expected Gio's mom to come bursting out to meet them, but she didn't. Morgan adjusted her backpack and took a deep breath as Leo unlocked the door.

Gio mouthed, *You'll be fine.*

Morgan's cheeks grew warm. She'd been caught in her nervousness. *But what will Mrs. Crespi think of this former harlot? And Gio loves his mom and values her opinion. What if she doesn't approve of me?*

The door opened, and Gio took Morgan's hand, leading her inside.

An older woman in capris and a flowing flowery top came around the corner leaning heavily on her cane. She braced her hand on the back of the couch and raised her cane toward Gio. "On guard."

He laughed out loud, tightened his grip on Morgan's hand, raised his "sword," and met his mother's in the air.

As quickly as they'd been raised, both canes went back to the floor, and the two embraced.

"Oh my dear, Giovanni!" Sarah Crespi hugged her son with all her might.

Emotion caught in Morgan's throat. This was the first time Gio's mom had been able to hug him since he'd been shot. And she'd already lost one son. That was enough.

Leo winked at Morgan.

Her smile in response loosed the tears that had pooled in her eyes.

Gio's mom released him and turned to Morgan. She shoved her cane into Gio's chest and extended her hands to Morgan. "Morgan. I've always wanted a daughter. Welcome to the family."

Morgan bit her quivering lip and walked into the woman's waiting arms and heart.

Mrs. Crespi held Morgan firmly until Morgan loosened her grip. It was a hug like no other. That of a mother who truly loved.

Mrs. Crespi grasped Gio's forearm while still holding Morgan. "I bet you two are starving. I've been in an Italian family long enough to know you feed people when they are traveling. Dinner will be ready any minute."

As if on cue, a timer went off in the kitchen.

"See?" She took her cane from Gio and led the way.

Gio slid his arm across Morgan's shoulders. "And why were you nervous?"

She elbowed him in the side.

Leo said, "Go help your mom. I'll put your suitcases in your room. Morgan, you get the guest room. Gio, we set up an air mattress in the study for you."

"Thanks, Dad."

Morgan smiled. Separate rooms was new to her, but it was the way it should be until they were married. Though they hadn't even decided yet when that would be.

They went into the kitchen, and Gio immediately jumped in, lending a hand as if he did it every day. Morgan helped as given the opportunity. In just a few minutes, homemade mostaccioli, salad, and garlic bread were on the table.

They all sat, and Leo led them in a prayer full of thanksgiving for Gio and Morgan, their safe trip, and God's miracles in both of their lives.

Morgan didn't know what to think other than that these people were amazing. She understood from Gio his parents didn't always get along so swimmingly, even on their best days, but her family had never been so kind and joyful. They weren't filled with the light of Christ like the Crespis.

With the first bite of mostaccioli, Morgan was convinced the food in heaven would all be Italian. She looked up at Sarah, who sat across the table, and said, "This is amazing. Will you teach me how to make it one day?"

Sarah almost dropped her fork. "Of course, dear. I would absolutely love that."

Around a large bite of noodles, Gio said, "I would love that too."

They all laughed.

Dinner continued until Morgan was so full she thought she'd burst.

Instead of getting up as soon as everyone was done, the four of them lingered at the table and continued to talk about life and faith. They didn't ask her a ton of probing questions like some people might, and she appreciated it. She had a very short part of life she actually wanted to talk about.

Sarah tapped her husband's arm, and he nodded. A request had been made, but not a single word had passed between the two. Was that what it was like to be married to the same person for forty years? It was beautiful.

Leo left the table but returned shortly with a small box in his hand. "We have something for the two of you." He met Gio's eyes. "Your mother wanted to get you a cane with a sword in it, but I told her it would be too hard for you to take it on the plane."

Sarah shook her head, equally amused and annoyed by her husband. "Not the sword, the derringer. The handle was the gun."

Gio laughed. "Either one wouldn't get far through TSA."

Morgan loved this family more by the minute.

Sarah's face turned solemn. "In all seriousness, though."

"Mom, gifts aren't necessary."

"I know." She looked at Morgan. "And I understand you aren't keen on getting gifts, so I hesitated, but I think—I hope this is different enough." Sarah took the box from her husband, who was now sitting again, and opened it. "These rings were my parents'." She turned the box toward Morgan and Gio.

A very simple set of white gold rings, two plain bands, and a tiny solitaire engagement ring rested in the box.

Morgan didn't know how to respond. She and Gio had talked about getting something just like this because she wanted to have something, but the draw of "things" was part of what made leaving the trafficking life so challenging. She looked at Gio, whose eyes sparkled with amazement. His expression told her exactly how to feel. This was an honor.

She nodded at Gio. He lifted the solitaire from the box and held it up.

Sarah said, "I know it's nothing fancy. But it was all my dad could afford. They struggled in many ways over the years; finances were just one."

Gio held the ring where Morgan could see it better and said, "Granddad was a pastor who loved Jesus with all he was. And

Grammy kept him pointed toward Jesus at all times, much like you remind me to keep my eyes on Him."

"A beautiful couple with beautiful rings." Morgan smiled at Sarah.

She asked, "Will you accept them? Mom and Daddy would be thrilled to have them passed to you."

Morgan nodded, her throat too tight with emotion to allow any words. She lifted her left hand to Gio.

"You'll still have me as your husband?"

She nodded a little more enthusiastically this time.

He slid the ring on. It fit perfectly.

Sarah clapped and squealed.

Morgan slid her arms around Gio's neck and his went around her middle. They really were going to get married.

He loosened his grip and pressed his lips to hers.

His mom giggled.

They joined his mother's amusement. Morgan felt more loved than she could ever have imagined. Could this actually be real? Did she need to prepare herself for the other shoe to smack her upside the head?

Jacq watched the man on the plane four rows ahead of them and across the aisle.

Knocking her elbow off the armrest between them, Dylan whispered, "Stop staring."

"He's no good, Dylan."

He sighed. "We have three hours left of our honeymoon, and you are already back in work mode. How are you going to survive not being an FBI agent?"

"You really think those kids are his?"

This time Dylan's sigh was more of a humph. "No. But we literally have nothing to go on other than they don't look like him. Could be an uncle or a federal agent, for all we know. We can't assume every man walking around is a trafficker."

"Of course. The man across the aisle isn't."

"Are you sure?" Dylan glanced over her head.

Jacq almost laughed out loud. The man had been writing his Sunday sermon the entire flight. Not only had she read his laptop screen, his Bible was tattered and the commentary equally well used. Not that you could rule out anyone, but this man at least pulled off the devoted Christian look.

"Okay, fine, you're probably right about him." He took her hand in his. "Keep an eye on the guy; just don't stare."

"I can handle that." She slid a little lower into her seat. The flight was another twenty minutes. "I can't wait to see Harper. Don't get me wrong—this time with just the two of us was amazing—"

"No need to justify that statement. I'm looking forward to seeing her too."

They were ready to be a family of three and eventually more, but one day at a time.

The rest of the flight was uneventful. The man with the two kids did nothing suspicious, other than look distinctly different than the two children, who appeared to be from Central America. The man, though, was without a doubt of northern-European descent. But who was she to judge? He could easily be their father or adopted father or uncle or any other such legit reason for traveling with them.

When it was time to disembark, Jacq tried to gauge her speed so she could get as close to the man with the kids as possible, and Dylan was right there with her.

The man slung a backpack over his shoulders, but the children had no belongings. Red flag.

Should she try to talk to one of the kids? If they didn't speak English that would say loads. But they kept their heads down. Another red flag.

She waited for a third, but it didn't present itself. Maybe she was just imagining it.

As soon as they were in the terminal of the small Knoxville airport, she lost sight of the man, despite her determination to keep tabs on him in case there was something else to spot.

Dylan put his hand on her shoulder. "It'll be okay. Let's focus on getting home to Harper."

She smiled up into her husband's freshly tanned face.

Husband. Dylan was actually her husband. She was now Mrs. Harris—Nope, Mrs. Harris would always be Dylan's mom. She was now Jacq Harris. She wondered how long it would take her to adjust to it.

When she married her first husband, Sean, they'd had a much longer dating and engagement period, and she had practiced being Jacqui Sheppard plenty before the day came. But with all the craziness of the last six months, this was nearly the first time she'd really thought about the fact her name had changed. When was she actually going to make it to the Social Security office to make it official? And the DMV?

As her mental to-do list grew, they made their way down the escalators to baggage claim.

She wished she'd had the chance to see Morgan before she and Gio headed off to visit family. But the best flights didn't line up for that ... the couples didn't even pass through the same airport.

Jacq's phone dinged. She retrieved it from her pocket. "It's Morgan!"

She opened the text message. No words, just a photo. A simple solitaire diamond on a white gold band on Morgan's ring finger.

Jacq squealed and turned the phone to Dylan. "I guess it's officially official."

"Excellent. I didn't think they were going to get an engagement ring."

Another text came through. "It's Gio's grandmother's."

"That's awesome. Tell them congratulations again."

She sent the message, adding she'd call tomorrow.

At the bottom of the escalator, Jacq squeezed Dylan's hand. "I need to run to the restroom."

"Go. I'll get the luggage."

She turned in the opposite direction from Dylan.

When she exited the bathroom, she saw a little shadow duck around a trash can behind the escalators. Was that a child?

Jacq scanned the area for a person looking for somebody and walked toward the trash can. She pulled a small bag of mixed nuts out of her purse and pretended she was picking through them and throwing some away.

"Are you hiding from a bad man?"

There was a little sniff.

She repeated the sentence but in Spanish.

A shuffle.

She tried in Russian. She'd be out of languages if this one didn't work. But it was all she could say in Russian—that and a few other random words she'd picked up working trafficking cases over the years.

The little face of a dark-haired girl appeared. "Sei tu poliziotto?"

That was not Spanish or Russian. Accent didn't sound French. "Police?"

"Sì?"

"Sí." She tried Spanish again. "Soy policía. ¿Estás en peligro?"

"Sono in pericolo." The girl's eyebrows wrinkled in confusion. The language was close but not the same.

Jacq stuffed the bag of nuts back in her purse, pulled out her phone, and opened Google translate. She met the girl's eyes. "Italiano?"

She smiled and nodded.

Jacq spoke into her phone. "How do you say 'I can keep you safe' in Italian."

The phone spoke the sentence.

"Sei sicuro?"

Jacq didn't understand the words, but she understood the questioning in the girl's eyes and nodded, opening her arms.

The girl stood and came around the trash can. At her full height, Jacq guessed she was nearly ten years old. Older than her scared eyes had indicated as she'd hidden behind the trash can. She stepped close to Jacq.

She put her arm around the girl. "Do you speak any English?"

"Molto poco ... little."

Jacq nodded and used hand motions to indicated her meaning. "Who were you hiding from?"

"Qualcuno che stava cercando di vendermi." She shook her head. "Trafficker."

Jacq's stomach dropped. How was that an English word this child knew? "Man or woman?"

"Uomo—man."

Jacq nodded and ushered the girl toward the women's bathroom. At least if her trafficker was a man, he'd hesitate for a moment to look for the girl in here.

Once in the restroom, Jacq held up her phone. "I need to make a call." She called Dylan and explained as concisely as possible. He said he'd get airport security and meet them there. Jacq hung up and used her phone to figure out how to ask the girl her name.

"Nicoletta."

Jacq placed a hand on her chest. "Jacqui."

The girl wrapped her arms around Jacq's middle. And Jacq hugged her back. *God, help us keep her safe and find her trafficker.*

Chapter Four

Dylan walked toward the bathroom as he hung up with airport security. They were sending someone to meet Dylan and alerting the rest of the security team. It was possible the man would ask for help finding his missing "daughter."

Dylan then sent a text message to the rest of their team. *Landed in Knoxville. Jacq found an allegedly trafficked girl. Requesting backup. Need Italian interpreter.*

A security guard arrived near the bathroom at the same time Dylan did. He introduced himself and shook the man's hand. Could they trust him? Dylan hated to doubt people, but trafficking was rampant, and he had no doubt some people who were supposed to be good guys really weren't. Their former colleague Lawrence had proved that.

Dylan stepped closer to the women's entrance where he could see around the first corner. "Jacq?"

She moved around the second corner, a girl a bit younger than his niece clinging to Jacq's side. He smiled at the girl, but she didn't return the smile. How many men had abused this child? It made him sick.

He looked her in the eye, and even though there was a chance she wouldn't understand, he said, "You are safe."

Her lips curled up ever so slightly. She'd caught his intent.

The security guard tapped Dylan's arm with the back of his hand. "We have a man in his late thirties looking for his niece who he says doesn't speak English."

"That's got to be him." Dylan glanced back at Jacq. "Any notable descriptors?"

The girl's finger went up, as if she'd figured out what he was asking. She tapped the inside of her left forearm. "Ha un tatuaggio dell'orologio."

He shook his head. He didn't understand.

She came to him and gestured at his arm. Coming even closer, she touched his tattoo.

"Tattoo?"

She pointed again and then to his watch, making a motion of spinning around.

"A clock tattoo?"

She shrugged.

"I think I understand."

Jacq pulled out her phone and asked it how to say "clock tattoo."

The girl nodded emphatically when she heard the response.

Dylan touched the girl's shoulder. "I'll get him." He turned and left with the security guard. On the other side of the escalators a man talked to another guard.

The first man raked a hand through his hair. He was sweating and clearly distraught. When he put his arm down, a clock tattoo on his left forearm showed. His gaze met Dylan's, and his eyes widened.

Did he recognize Dylan? It wasn't a mutual recognition, but he'd been made.

The man backed away from the guard. As soon as Dylan was within ten feet, the man turned and bolted.

Dylan groaned and ran after him. "Stop! FBI."

The man shoved a group of people out of his way, throwing a piece of luggage over in an attempt to trip Dylan. But Dylan hurdled the fallen suitcase and continued his pursuit without slowing.

The suspect jumped onto the edge of the baggage conveyor, then onto the top. He risked a glance back at Dylan before he jumped down the other side.

Dylan mimicked the man's movements and made it over the conveyor with as little trouble. Before he jumped down he made mental note of the best path.

"FBI. Stop!"

The man didn't even look back. He wove between confused and panicked travelers.

Dylan wished he could pull his gun, but his first priority was keeping everyone safe. His second was apprehending the suspect. Plus, he had no reason to believe the man was armed. If they'd just gotten off a plane, he would have been through security, so while not impossible, it wasn't likely he was armed with even a pair of toenail clippers.

If only there weren't so many people in the way.

The man aimed toward the door that led to the parking garage.

Dylan busted through the door five seconds after him. He was gaining on the guy.

A car pulled up and a door opened from the inside, but no one got out.

The man grabbed the door and jumped into the vehicle. The car sped away before he could even close the door.

Dylan focused on the car. Newer model. Black Toyota Accord. License plate: Tennessee P51 0. The car turned, and he missed the last two.

He punched the air.

How did that guy know he was a federal agent? Ronan had had pictures of their team, but had he shared them with other traffickers in the area before he died? If so, it would make their jobs much more difficult.

His phone rang. Matt Olsen. "Hey, Matt," Dylan said.

"I'm here. Where are y'all?"

"That was fast. I'm outside of baggage claim. The suspect just fled."

"Call in the description to KPD."

"Will do. Jacq is with the victim in the women's bathroom in baggage claim."

"I'll head there."

They hung up, and Dylan phoned in a BOLO to the local police.

Gio pushed himself up out of the pool, turned, and sat on the edge. Apparently retiring in Arizona required a pool in the backyard. But he wasn't complaining. Swimming was the one exercise he could do to work his whole body without the fear of falling. His knee actually seemed to like the cool water.

He watched Morgan swim back and forth across the not-very-long pool, which was helpful for her learning how to swim. After the river, she had become determined not to be afraid of the water. He was so proud of her.

"Good morning." His mom brought him a cup of iced coffee and placed a second one on the little table between the lounge chairs. "It's the perfect morning for a swim."

"It really is. Can't do this in Tennessee this time of year."

"I bet not." His mom looked like she was thinking hard about something.

"Join us."

"Well, I'm not going to swim. But maybe I'll dip my toes."

Gio jumped up and snagged a thin chair cushion and set it beside the pool and helped his mom lower herself to sit.

"Thank you. Your knee is doing well this morning, I see."

He hadn't even thought about using his cane. "It's weird like that."

Morgan swam over. "Good morning, Mrs. Crespi."

"Please dear, don't be so formal. It's Sarah, unless you want to call me *Mom*, but that is entirely up to what you feel comfortable with."

Morgan smiled. "Mom. I like that." She moved closer and put her arms on Gio's legs before darting away.

He wanted to laugh. She did this kind of thing all the time: became affectionate, then questioned herself as to the appropriateness.

Amusement danced in his mother's eyes, even though she tried concealing her grin with her hand. She'd caught Morgan's action.

Morgan grabbed a floating lounger and climbed up onto it. Gio drew it closer with his feet.

"How are you doing this morning, Morgan?" Mom asked.

"I slept better than I expected."

"Don't sleep well in new places?"

"It's not that. I can sleep anywhere." She went on to tell Mom about spotting Duke at the airport.

Gio was pretty sure he would catch a fly, but he couldn't close his gaping mouth. He had not expected her to open up to his mother so much.

"I can't even imagine. I'll be praying. And don't hesitate to tell me if there is anything I can specifically pray for." The expression in his mother's eyes shifted, but he couldn't quite identify it.

They chatted about plans for the home they were assisting Jacq in starting for women who escape trafficking, and the mission to help them embrace their freedom in Christ while preparing themselves for entering the real world. But as they talked, his mom increasingly seemed like she had something on her mind.

When the conversation lulled, Gio called her on it. "Mom, is there something you're not telling us?"

She sighed and set her hand on Gio's. "I know you told me this topic is off limits—"

"Mom." Gio's pulse thundered. He'd only given her one topic she absolutely should not bring up: children. They weren't ready to talk about it yet. His heart still hurt too fresh at the idea they would never have children of their own, and the guilt on Morgan's face when it came up hurt even more. It was not her fault.

They would need to work through it. They would see a specialist and confirm, but they first wanted to come to terms with being confident they would embrace God's will above all.

"I'm sorry, Gio and Morgan. I want you to know I am praying for you both as you face the challenge of wondering if you will ever have children."

Gio watched Morgan. She was hanging onto his mom's every word and fighting to keep her emotions suppressed.

"But as I was reading First Samuel, about how Hannah pleaded with God for a child of her own. I felt it impressed on my heart to tell you a family is in your future, and to not give up hope."

Gio pressed the heel of his hand into his eye.

Morgan, with a catch in her voice, said, "I want to believe you, but I don't want to live in a place of false hope."

"Morgan." His mom reached out for her hand. She floated closer and took it.

"Hope in Jesus is never false. Trust Him, and we pray. He does big things when His people pray. And Morgan, you are His child. He loves you and wants to shower you with good things. That doesn't take the hard of this world away, but you know that better than most. Remember, if I know how to give good gifts to my children, how much greater does our heavenly Father? He is the giver of every good and perfect gift."

Tears flowed down Morgan's face and mingled with the chlorinated water. She slid off the raft into the water, and he did the same off the side of the pool. He pulled her into his arms.

His mom placed a hand on each of their heads and prayed for them, for their future family, whatever that looked like, and the ministry of rescuing others from trafficking God had called them both to.

Gio's heart swelled. God was in charge of everything. He had rescued Morgan and would use them both in ways Gio was certain he couldn't imagine.

Jacq tapped her thumb against her side as she paced the FBI field office lobby, waiting for the social worker to bring Nicoletta. It was already noon, and they should be there any minute. The social worker, who spoke Italian, had stayed with the girl at the hospital last night. Other than some scarring from previous trauma, a few fresh bruises, and being slightly malnourished, Nicoletta was in good health, all things considered.

The goal for today was to see if Nicoletta could help them identify any more players in the trafficking ring, to get her whole story, and then, above all else, to find her family so she could go home.

A car pulled into a guest-parking spot. The social worker and Nicoletta were here.

"Patience, my darling," Dylan said.

She turned to see Dylan holding three-year-old Harper. It had been late last night by the time they'd made it to his parents' house to pick her up. They woke this morning to Harper jumping on Dylan and calling him "Dylan-Daddy." Harper had never met her biological father as he had died in an apartment fire before Jacq even knew she was pregnant. It seemed perfect for her to call Dylan *daddy*.

Therefore, they'd brought her with them to the field office this morning. Not exactly protocol, but they needed to be with their daughter just as much as they needed to catch a bad guy.

Dylan said, "Harper and I are going to get lunch while you talk to Nicoletta. We'll bring you something back."

"Thank you." She reached out for Harper, who jumped from Dylan's arms to hers. "I love you, kiddo. Be good for Daddy."

She giggled.

"You like the idea that he's your daddy now?"

She nodded.

Jacq nuzzled and kissed her little girl. "Good. Have some good daddy-daughter time, but not too much fun without me."

Dylan laughed and took Harper back. "We'll try not to. Praying for you as you talk to Nicoletta."

She mouthed, *Thank you.*

Nicoletta and the social worker walked into the lobby.

Dylan moved toward the door and Harper waved at Nicoletta, who shyly returned the gesture.

"Your daughter?" Nicoletta asked in forced English.

"Sì," then Jacq added in English with hand motions, "We'll go upstairs and talk."

They took the elevator to the third floor, then went to an interview room designed for witnesses and victims' families. It was set up much like a living room with couches and chairs, a few toys, and plenty of paper and crayons.

The social worker and Nicoletta took one couch and Jacq took another.

Before they could even say a word, the door opened again, and Jacq's co-worker Aliza Blake came into the room. Since Gio, their usual artist was out of town, Aliza would be able to do any sketches, but she also had a knack for connecting with kids. The fact she was raising her nephew and two nieces, one of which was nearly Nicoletta's age, definitely helped.

Aliza started the interview. "Tell me about your family, Nicoletta."

The girl's face drooped.

Jacq winced. Apparently, that wasn't a good topic.

Aliza moved to the floor and slid a stack of paper and crayons to the girl across the coffee table. "These really aren't the greatest for drawing, are they? Let's use my pencils." Aliza opened her art kit.

Nicoletta's eyes widened. She joined Aliza on the floor, and they both started doodling.

They let the silence hang for a few moments. Before too long, Nicoletta said, in broken English, "My family died." In Italian, she added they had died in a car accident, and she and her sister had ended up in an orphanage—until a man claimed to be their uncle and took them away.

Jacq caught the word for uncle. "He was not your *zio*?"

Nicoletta shook her head. "He brought us to America."

Aliza asked, "What happened once you were here?"

The social worker interpreted the question and then the answer.

"He kept us, along with a bunch of other kids, in a basement and brought us out for parties. At one of these parties, another man said he had a better place for me, so he took me away from Bianca."

Nicoletta continued to draw while she talked, showing zero emotion save the increasing intensity of the line of graphite as she drew.

Everyone waited for Nicoletta to tell them more. Jacq didn't want to push her, but the more they learned about this girl, the more she might reveal about the men who did this to her.

"At the first guy's house I stayed in line because Bianca told me to, but without her I started acting up. I hated what was happening to me. So I fought back. That just made it worse, but I didn't learn. They finally started threatening my sister. Said they'd kill her if I didn't start doing what I was told. That shut me up, but then ..."

Her words trailed off giving the interpreter a chance to catch up. Nicoletta's breathing became intense.

Overtop the beautiful landscape she'd been sketching she drew a distorted devil face. "I refused a request from a trick. It was too nasty. And I spit in his face when he peed on me." Her entire body shook violently.

Jacq wanted to pull the girl into her arms and soothe her pain.

"My master, as he called himself, said he was done with me. He called and told them to kill Bianca. He hung up and said he'd take me back to the boss who would do far worse to me."

"So he brought you to Knoxville?" Aliza asked.

Nicoletta nodded. "And with Bianca dead, I had no reason to keep listening to them. So I ran. They've done their worst."

The interpreter translated as Nicoletta laid her head down on the table and sobbed.

Aliza put her hand on the girl's back.

Nicoletta looked up and met Jacq's eyes. There was a longing in her expression. Without processing what she was doing, Jacq opened her arms. The girl stood and vaulted over the table, crashing onto the couch and into Jacq's arms.

Oh Jesus, help this little girl! She needs more than I can give her. More than anyone on earth can. Heal her, and help us catch the monsters who did this to her.

She held the girl for a long time and prayed over her.

Eventually Nicoletta lifted her head. "The FBI catches bad guys? Can you catch these men?"

"We sure will try. Can you help us by telling us what they look like?"

Aliza held up her pencil. "I'm pretty good at using this. But I'll need your help."

Nicoletta nodded. "Anything for Bianca."

The girl didn't leave Jacq's side but stayed close. Aliza rendered a sketch of the man with the clock tattoo that brought Nicoletta to Knoxville and of the "uncle" who stole the girls away to the States and kept them caged like animals.

Chapter Five

Fifteen-year-old Bianca tucked the covers up tightly around Aurora and left the room. The little girl had fallen asleep on the drive to the mountain house late Friday evening. Bianca didn't understand why they were there. The plan had been to stay in town this weekend. The change in agenda was sudden, so something must have happened.

She walked out of Aurora's room and found the girl's father—Dean—waiting in the hallway.

"Lock it."

Bianca nodded and flipped the lock into its latch. Was Bianca going to get locked in her room too? Anything was possible. Some nights he wanted her with him, while other nights she was no more than Aurora's nanny. Bianca preferred that to be her only role in this household. She turned back to Dean.

He lifted his arm and draped it across Bianca's shoulders. His cologne drifted to her nose. It smelled nice. At least he wasn't gross like some of the men she'd been sold to in the past. She really shouldn't complain. Dean had taken her in as his own and stopped letting her be a selection at parties. And at least he was attractive, even if he was three times her age.

They walked downstairs to the living room. Someone knocked on the front door.

"Sit. I'll get it." Dean nudged her into the living room before crossing to the entryway.

She sat in the wingback chair, resisting the urge to curl up in it.

Dean opened the door and three men she'd seen before entered. She didn't know any of their names, but they had been around from time to time, normally making deliveries.

"Where is it?" Dean completely skipped hellos. Every vein in his arms and forehead looked like they would explode.

The man, who had a clock tattoo on his arm, lifted his hands up in front of himself.

This was not going to go well. Any time someone tried to defend themselves against Dean, they paid.

"I can explain," said the man with the clock tattoo.

Dean stepped forward and gripped the man's neck, shoved him against the wall, and lifted him off his feet. "You weren't about to tell me you lost the package, were you, Mick?"

Bianca sank deeper into the chair, wishing she could disappear. She hated being around when Dean lost his temper.

Mick didn't answer.

Dean lowered Mick and straightened the shoulders of his shirt. "I'm sure you can get it back. Right?"

"The FBI was there."

Dean's back went rigid.

"But I will. I'll figure it out. I shouldn't have come here empty-handed."

Dean jabbed his index finger into Mick's chest. "You'd better. Because if you don't, if you screw up one more time, then—do you remember what happened to Carlos when he made a mess of things?"

Mick nodded with wide eyes.

Bianca pulled up her legs and hugged them. That was not a hallow threat from Dean. She remembered Carlos. When someone wronged Dean, they suffered the most agonizing death imaginable. She'd only seen it once in her time with Dean, and she wished she never had.

Her insides shook like Pompeii must have when Vesuvius erupted. She'd rather go back to Italy and live inside a volcano than in Dean's house.

Saturday came too quickly for Morgan. She hadn't wanted to leave Gio's parents. It was the safest she'd ever felt, not just physically, but emotionally and spiritually above all. As they'd left for the airport to catch their flight to Ohio that morning, Sarah—Mom took them by the hands and prayed for them again. She then admonished them not to feel like they needed to wait to get married until she was able to travel.

"I will be there in spirit," she said, "but wouldn't mind attending via a video call."

Morgan smiled and leaned back in the passenger seat of the rental car as Gio drove down an Ohio highway. Their flight had been uneventful, and time with his parents had been considerably better than she could have ever imagined. It actually made her less nervous about the next two days with her family. Although the nerves hadn't gone away entirely. Even if this went terribly, though, they had Gio's family, and that was all she needed. Any of her family they connected with would just be a bonus.

Multiple calls with her brother over the last few months had proved he was in her court. But she hadn't talked to her mom once. Would she be there this weekend? Who else would be there?

Gio touched her arm. "Are you okay? You're biting your lip."

"Sorry."

He glared at her.

She'd done it again. Apologized for behavior that didn't need it. He was pointing the lip thing out to encourage her to stop because he loved her, not because he wanted to control her. "I love you."

"I love you too." He took her hand. "What's bothering you?"

"Not knowing who will be there. Why did we agree to this? Why can't we just see Nate and his family? I don't want to do this whole homecoming thing. It's stupid. I don't even know these people."

"Tell me how you really feel." He winked.

She chuckled and leaned her head back against the seat. "I feel like it's a mistake."

"You can't know that."

"I didn't say 'know.' It's a gut thing. I thought you were supposed to be the one with the intuitive gut. What's yours saying?"

"Don't ask questions you don't want the answer to."

She laughed out loud. "That good, huh?"

He shrugged and turned off the highway.

Fifteen minutes later they turned down the long driveway of her aunt and uncle's farm. It was beautiful and quaint. The smell of smoked meat on a grill seeped in through the vents. But the closer they got, the higher Morgan's anxiety rose.

God, help me. Calm my nerves. Help this to go better than I fear it will. They are family, after all.

Gio pulled to a stop, parking among a half dozen other cars in front of the house.

"What are they going to think of me? What do they already think?"

"Does it matter? Isn't what God thinks the most important?"

She pressed her lips together. Gio was right.

Nate walked out the front door. He looked exactly the same as he did last time she saw him more than thirteen years ago, except for the crow's feet at the corner of his eyes and the gray streaks in his dark hair.

The breath caught in her throat. Her big brother.

All the lies her pimps had yelled in her ears over the years bombarded her mind. *Your family doesn't want you. You're a filthy rag. Your brother would be ashamed of you. He doesn't want to talk to a whore like you.*

She was frozen in her seat.

Gio opened her door. "Are you okay?"

"So many lies." She stared at nothing ahead of her.

"Replace them with truth. You are wanted. There is no shame in Jesus. Your brother loves you and wants to see you, talk to you, be a part of your life."

Gio knew the right words because this wasn't the first time. It was no mystery to him what was going on in her mind. He touched her cheek and nudged her face toward his. "I love you. I'm right here with you."

She nodded and slid out of the vehicle.

"Morgan?" Nate stood about eight feet away wringing his hands.

"Nate." She took a few slow steps that turned into a full run until she slammed into her brother's chest.

"It's really you. You're alive." He held her at arm's length.

"It's me. And I am."

"I thought I'd lost you forever. It's like you've risen from the dead."

"Feels that way to me too."

"Gah. It is just so good to see you in person again. I'm sorry I gave up all those years. If it wasn't for your friend Jacqui ..."

"We owe Jacqui a lot. She didn't give up on me. Neither did this guy. Nate, this is my fiancé, Gio."

Gio came up beside her and shook Nate's hand.

"Thank you for your part in helping my sister."

"She's the one who saved my life." Gio's grin nearly melted her away.

"It was mutual saving. You're the one who pulled me from a burning building."

Nate shook his head. "Are you two keeping score? See who can save the other the most? Because I advise stopping that and living a nice quiet life."

The three of them laughed and moved toward the house. Nate introduced them first to his wife, Mandy, and two kids, Josiah and Felicity. Then he smoothly introduced Gio to the rest of the family, so Morgan didn't have to feel weird if she didn't remember someone. They'd talked about this beforehand, and Nate pulled it off so slickly there was no way anyone suspected.

It worked. Nate introduced an aunt and a cousin who Morgan didn't recognize, but as soon as Nate said their names, memories clicked together. The years had not been good to those two family members.

Dinner was served not long after they arrived. Gio stuck close to her side as they filled paper plates with a true Midwest barbecue. They found a spot to eat sitting on a bench along the back of the deck.

Morgan's Aunt Sondra, whose house they were at, sat down with them. "It's so good to have you here, Morgan. I wish you would have come home sooner. We've worried about you over the years."

Should she say she would have visited if she hadn't been enslaved by evil men? That would probably be too much, so instead she smiled. Well-meaning people often said things they didn't fully understand.

Aunt Sondra continued, "I really thought your mom was going to come today."

"Really?" Morgan hadn't actually expected her. A slight bit of her had hoped she would, but the reality was her mom had never truly forgiven her for putting her stepdad in jail. As if somehow it was Morgan's fault he had raped her.

"I talked to her yesterday. Maybe she'll show up yet."

Morgan shrugged. She didn't have the heart to tell her mom's sister she'd be fine without seeing the woman she hadn't talked to in longer than she'd been missing.

The conversation shifted to how her aunt and family had been doing, and before too long Morgan found herself and Gio chatting with other relatives.

But try as she might to engage in the conversation, watching Nate interact with his children captivated her attention. She wanted to spend more time with them, not all these other people.

Three hours later, Morgan was still chatting with everyone except Nate, and now even Gio wasn't at hand. He'd run inside, but when he was on his way out, her uncle had caught his attention and was talking incessantly.

Nate and one of their cousins had started a bonfire, complete with s'mores.

Morgan made one for herself, then leaned against the fence by the barn while she ate it. She needed a little bit of space from people for a few minutes. She believed in her heart these people had good intentions, but the number of comments that made her uneasy had grown unbearable. They varied in degree of distastefulness—everything from jabs at Gio's cane to "You only fell in love with him because he rescued you" to "What are you going to do for a real job?" to the one that got her riled the most: "Thirteen years of partying couldn't have been so bad."

Maybe she was just tired. Either way, she was done with the party, and it seemed like they had only gotten started.

The smell of cheap beer assaulted her nose, and her cousin Jan's husband, Don, came up beside her from the other side of the fence and leaned his forearms on the top of it. "How much?"

"Excuse me?" Surely she didn't hear him correctly.

"How much do you charge? We can slip away into the barn here, and no one would notice."

Was he seriously asking what it sounded like? She swallowed the bile that rose in her throat. "You have got to be kidding." She pushed herself off the fence.

"You're a hooker, aren't you?"

If she had a drink, she'd splash it in his face.

"Fifteen minutes should be fine. I'll pay you twice your normal rate for fifteen minutes."

She backed away, staring at him. "No. Absolutely not."

"Really? You're going to keep playing the reformed card? Once a whore, always a whore."

A dagger to the heart. She spun around and tried to zip up any reaction. She had to hold it in.

Chapter Six

Gio scanned the yard for Morgan. He was still talking to her uncle on the deck, but the need to find her was growing more urgent.

He spotted her by the bonfire; she was headed toward them. Good.

Gio smiled at her. "Hey."

She looked up and met his eyes.

His stomach flipped over. Something was not right. He put his arm across her shoulders—they were shaking.

"I'm tired. I'd like to head to bed."

Her uncle said, "I'll have Sondra show you to your room."

"Thank you." Morgan barely glanced at her uncle.

Gio wanted to ask her what was wrong, but it would be better to talk about whatever it was away from others. They walked through the house and retrieved their luggage before Sondra found them.

"Up this way," she said.

They followed her up the narrow stairs and down the hallway. Sondra stopped in front of a room at the end.

"You two are in here. It's only a double bed, but I'm sure you love birds don't mind snuggling."

Gio tried to contain his frustrated grunt. The assumptions people made were infuriating sometimes.

Morgan said, "We aren't married yet. We need separate sleeping arrangements."

Sondra's eyes narrowed. "What? Really? I just thought ... I'm sorry, but there isn't anywhere else. Everyone is crashing here. Don and Jan are across the hall; Nate and his family next door."

"I can sleep anywhere. A couch, even a chair."

"All taken. Sorry, kids, but you'll have to get cozy. This is the twenty-first century after all. Good night, you guys." Sondra turned and walked away.

Morgan darted into the room.

"Are you okay?" He followed her in but didn't close the door.

She shook her head and dropped to the bed before reaching her hand out to him.

"We should just get married. And definitely should not have come here before we did."

He closed the space, tossed his cane on the bed, and sat beside her. "I can go out to the car. You know I can sleep anywhere."

"No!" She gripped his arm.

"It won't bother me."

"That's not it. I don't trust Don."

"Your cousin Jan's husband?"

She told Gio what the man had suggested and what he had called her.

Rage set Gio's blood on fire. "That—" He went to stand.

"No." Her grip tightened. "You can't."

"Do you want to leave?"

She nodded. "I don't know where to go. But I don't know if I can stay here. I mean, I don't want to abandon everyone. I should get to know them again. I guess you could sleep on the floor. But I don't want him to hurt you."

He wrapped his arm around her. She buried her head against his neck. Hot tears dripped onto his collar.

"There you guys are."

Gio glanced at the door. Nate.

Concern filled his eyes. "Is everything okay?"

Gio shook his head.

Morgan lifted her face and wiped it. "Jan really married a piece of work."

Nate nodded and came into the room. "Don has been a jerk since she started dating him eleven years ago."

"Jerk is a nice way to put it. He propositioned me."

"He did what?"

She told Nate what had happened.

His face turned bright red. "That—that—I'm gonna—He's gonna wish—" He turned toward the door and muttered something about ground beef.

"Nate, don't." She stood.

He spun back. "I won't stand for it, Sis. I will defend your honor. Gio can't because of his job, but I have nothing to lose." He was gone.

Morgan grabbed Gio's cane off the bed and handed it to him, and they followed Nate down the stairs and out the back door.

By the time they were on the deck Nate was by the fire, face to face with Don. He pulled back and punched the brute square in the eye.

Curse words flew, and Don swung back at Nate.

Others came and pulled them apart. Morgan's uncle's voice thundered, calling them to the deck.

He asked, "What on earth is going on?"

Nate answered, "This pig came on to my sister."

"She came on to me, like the whore she is."

Gio wrapped his arm around Morgan's waist.

Jan came out of the kitchen door with a bag of ice in her hand and offered it to Don. Morgan ripped it out of her hand and gave it to Nate, who put it on his knuckles, then turned to her uncle.

But before she could defend herself, her uncle said, "I think you all need to leave."

"Gladly," Morgan said. "I don't want to stay in a place that makes light of the trauma in my life. A place where I'm not safe to be the true me, the new me. He"—she pointed at Don—"tried to proposition me. Don't believe the lies he said. Jan, you didn't choose well. I'm sorry for you. If he treats me like this after just a couple of hours, I can't imagine the trauma you experience at home. Seriously consider leaving him."

She turned and walked into the house, letting the screen door slam. Gio and Nate had no choice but to follow her. And they didn't hesitate.

Gio couldn't be prouder of his fiancée. She was completely unaccustomed to standing up for herself like that , but this spunk showed who she truly was.

He started up the stairs behind her, but she turned and said, "I'll get the bags. The adrenaline is coursing with such intensity I could probably carry the car."

"If you're sure."

She nodded and disappeared.

Nate gripped his arm. "I can help if she needs it."

"Aren't your kids asleep?"

"Multiple trips won't hurt. Stand guard?"

Gio nodded.

Nate's wife came down with their youngest in her arms, keys dangling from her fingers.

"Let me help you." Gio took the keys and opened the front door, then followed her to the car.

"Thank you. Do you mind staying here with Felicity while I run back up?"

"Not at all." He kept an eye out for trouble, worried someone would cause more problems. Thankfully, no one did, and little Felicity stayed asleep.

Nate's wife came out with their son and strapped him in the car. Shortly followed by Morgan and Nate.

Morgan put down their bags and turned to Mandy. "I'm so sorry about all of this."

"You do *not* need to apologize. Let's put it this way: I didn't want to be here much more than you did, but I was here for you and Nate. You two leaving means I *get* to leave."

Gio asked, "The question is, now what? It's quite a drive for the two of you to go home this late, right?"

Nate suggested they find a hotel with a suite, adding, "You two will have your chaperones, and I get to spend more time with my sister."

Mandy nodded. "That sounds perfect. Maybe an indoor pool too or at least a park nearby? How about I look for something while we drive?"

They all agreed and left.

In the rental car, Gio reached over for Morgan's hand. She took it, but hers was still shaking.

Before he could even ask, she said, "I'll be okay."

He prayed that was true. He hated that her family had turned out to be so rotten to her. Some of them seemed like they had the best of intentions, but clearly others did not. He prayed for them all as he drove down the dark Ohio road.

Morgan rolled over in bed, a sliver of light from the window cascading down upon her face. The sound of the TV and giggles from the conjoining rooms told her she'd slept later than anyone else. It had been eleven-thirty last night before they had pulled into the parking lot of the hotel Mandy had found them. She wasn't able to find a hotel with a two-room suite but instead found two conjoining rooms—a girl's room and a guy's room. The four adults had stayed up entirely too late talking in hushed tones to avoid waking the kids, but it was exactly what they had all needed after the experience with their extended family.

Rolling onto her back, Morgan squished the pillow beneath her head and processed. During that late-night conversation, she'd asked Nate about their mother. He'd told her Morgan was safe. Mom had expressed thanksgiving and excitement, but it had ended there. Nate had given her Morgan's number and asked if he could pass her number to Morgan, but she'd said *no*, she'd reach out when she was ready. She'd been invited to last night's reunion but had only told Nate she'd think about it.

Should Morgan just write off her mom, or reach out and try to restore their relationship? She wasn't a fool who thought everything would be magically restored. God could do it, but that didn't mean He would. Some things would have to wait until eternity to be mended fully.

She rolled to her side then sat up with a glance at the clock, but instantly disregarded the numbers. It didn't matter. No one was going to harp on her for sleeping. They would be glad to see her whenever she made her way into the other room.

No one was demanding anything of her and abusing her if she didn't meet those demands. She was living her own life. It was so hard to learn. She'd been telling herself the same thing every day for months. How long was it going to take for these ideas to stick? She stood and stretched.

Boom. Josiah's cry pierced the quiet.

Morgan's vision tunneled, and the hotel room disappeared.

She couldn't distinguish what her ears were hearing and what was in her head. Cries, screams, all muffled. Children. Not just one little boy.

Fear. No, terror filled her.

She needed to get away. Where was she? What was happening?

She stumbled forward and caught her hand on something. It was smooth, but it fell and she crashed to the floor with it. It was rough.

Her lungs felt like they were caving in on her. *Air. I need air.* It wouldn't come.

The voices seemed to become more distant. But then they were back again.

"Morgan."

Was that her name? It sounded so strange.

"Morgan." A hand gripped her arm. "Are you okay? Look at my eyes, Morgan."

Her vision cleared, but she still couldn't breathe.

"Morgan. Take a deep breath." Strong warm arms, safe arms, wrapped around her.

She obeyed.

"That's it. Again."

Another breath. Her heart let off the gas of her pulse. She relaxed into his arms. Gio.

Another deep breath brought in the scent of his body wash. She was home. Wherever they were, she was home in his arms. *Jesus, help. Thank you for Gio.*

The hotel. Her brother, his family, his son.

"Is Josiah okay? Did he get hurt?"

"Just a little bump from jumping off the bed," Nate said.

She finally was able to fix eyes on her brother and then Gio.

The little table next to the armchair was lying on its side. Rug burn graced her knees.

"What happened?" she asked.

"I was going to ask you the same thing." Gio nudged a loose strand of hair from her face.

"I was getting up, and I heard the crash and Josiah cry." Her vision tunneled slightly.

"Morgan, stay with me."

She blinked and shook her head. "Was that a flashback?"

"Maybe. Of what?"

"That's the thing I don't know. Children crying. A darkness. I was scared." She shook her head again.

Nate asked, "How could you have a flashback and not remember?"

She pushed up from Gio's arms but didn't leave his side. "I have nearly a year's worth of time I don't remember."

Gio, who didn't seem to have his cane, helped her off the ground.

Mandy popped her head into the room. "Everything okay?"

Morgan half nodded, half shrugged. "I was going to ask you that."

"He's fine. Nothing a little ice won't fix." She came fully into the room. "They're watching a cartoon."

Nate touched Morgan's arm. "I'd like to know more about that missing time."

A dry chuckle escaped. "You and me both."

Gio was standing heavily on his good leg.

"Let's sit." Morgan took her spot near the head of the bed and pulled a pillow onto her lap.

Gio stayed close, and Nate and Mandy sat on the end.

"It's weird to have a blank gap in your memory," Morgan began. "It's different than forgetting or losing periods of time from childhood. With that you can say, well, I lived here, went to that school, whatever. But with this I distinctly remember living in Miami, where I'd been for a while with this one guy who used drugs to control us. He kept it well regulated, but he'd bring us to parties sometimes where the drugs flowed a little more freely, and frankly, it was nice to not be too aware of what was happening at those."

Nate cringed.

"But I remember that time clearly; well, as clearly as a junkie can. He was pretty awful, and as much as I'd like to forget it, I can't. I remember spring break, early March. Another stupid party. But my next memory is February—Valentine's Day, the following year."

"And you're sure about those?" Nate tilted his head.

"Positive. But that Valentine's Day I was in Nashville with a guy who had promised to make me a star. He took me out for dinner—that's why I remember it was Valentine's Day—but instead of wooing me for the night, he said it was going to cost a lot to make me a famous singer, so I needed to start earning some cash."

"Another pimp," Mandy said.

"Exactly. But that year is missing. As much as I ask myself 'what happened?' I can't remember anything."

Gio rested his hand on her knee. "When did you notice that time frame was missing?"

"Pretty soon after."

"Does that mean it was even worse?" Nate asked.

Morgan shrugged. "That's what my counselor has suggested. We've had so much else to work through, we haven't touched the lost memories yet."

Gio's hand on her knee grew more intense. "If you're getting flashbacks, it might be time to explore them."

She leaned back against the headboard. "I was afraid you were going to say that. After the intense fear I felt during that little episode ... I don't know if I can." She stared out the gap in the curtains, and silence hung. "But I want answers."

Chapter Seven

Monday morning Dylan leaned back in his desk chair at the FBI field office. Nicoletta's "uncle" had to have used fake IDs to bring the girls into the States because there was no record of either Bianca or Nicoletta ever entering the country.

The license plate had been a dead-end so far.

Aliza's sketches of the man with the clock tattoo and the "uncle" were also proving unfruitful.

It seemed the only positive out of the whole situation was Nicoletta was safe. She'd been placed in a secure home designed for survivors—much like the one Jacq and he were opening up in the mountains.

"Any luck?" Jacq crossed the bullpen and leaned over his desk.

"Is this the face of a guy who's found what he was looking for?"

She gave him a fake cheesy grin. "In other news, everything is set for the fundraiser in three weeks. Church is booked, catering is ordered, and invitations are being sent."

"Excellent." This project was only going to be possible with generous hearts being won over to the plight of the survivors.

Their supervisor, Warren Bridges, walked out of his office. "I have a special request of you guys." He came around to Dylan's desk. "I have a friend from Honduras who has been working a case there of two missing children. He has reason to believe the alleged kidnapper has brought the brother and sister to the States. Since we've already been searching the video footage from the airport, let's see if we can find these two as well. It's a long shot, but pray someone finds them before it's too late."

Warren handed a folder to Dylan.

He opened the cover. Staring back at him was a boy and a girl. Only five and eight.

Jacq came around, looked at the photographs, and slammed her hand on his desk. "I told you."

Dylan's lungs seized up. Jacq was right. These were the kids they had seen on the airplane.

Warren questioned Jacq's outburst.

"We saw them. They were on our plane, and I'll prove it." Jacq zoomed over to her desk and clicked away at her computer before finally declaring she'd found what she was looking for. "They are here in Knoxville. At least they were on Thursday night."

Dylan wanted to kick himself. They'd been right there. If they had approached the situation maybe those kids would be safe now.

But Nicoletta. If they hadn't gone to baggage claim when they did, would they have missed her?

"How much is our little airport a hub for this evil?" Jacq asked.

No one answered. No one wanted to think about how trafficking happened everywhere they turned.

Jacq cast the surveillance footage of the man up on the screen.

"That's the guy," their fellow-agent Matt Olsen said.

"Obviously. He's there with the kids."

"No," Matt said. "It's the guy who was driving the car the other guy got in." He sent another picture up to the screen.

"Were the kids in the backseat then?" Dylan's stomach turned in on itself.

Matt shrugged. "Can't tell from any of the traffic cameras."

Warren crossed his arms. "Were you able to identify either of these men?"

Matt shook his head. "Fake addresses on their driver's licenses. We really need to figure out who in the DMV is getting these official licenses through with fake addresses."

"But we have names?" Dylan hoped they would have at least something.

Matt put their licenses on the screen. "Assuming they aren't fake, as well, they are Mick Tirrell and Justin Wester. Both of them are squeaky clean. Not even as much as a parking ticket on their records."

Dylan memorized their images. He would find them. But how?

And the other *how* was: how did Mr. Clock-tattoo know Dylan was a fed even before he introduced himself? He had a feeling this case was going to get more frustrating before—if ever—it was resolved.

Home sweet home. Morgan opened the door to their trailer and was assaulted with fresh paint fumes. They'd faded some, but not entirely. She hauled her suitcase up the steps and inside.

Gio came in behind her. "I absolutely love what you've done with this space."

"It's not too much?" She'd picked a soft yellow for the walls.

"Nope. It looks more like a home and less like a factory model."

"That's what I was going for."

They'd removed the original table and couch that had filled the slide and put in a regular table and love seat that made the space feel more open.

She set her suitcase by the bedroom and turned around to Gio. She closed the gap between them and slid her arms around his neck. "While I'm excited to have a space of my own, I'd like to share it with you sooner rather than later."

His hands roamed her sides and back. "You aren't the only one."

She lifted herself to her toes and met her lips to his. There was no manipulation. No ulterior motive. No gross feeling. The kiss was genuine.

As she ran her fingers through his hair, their bodies grew closer.

Passion ignited her entire being. She wanted more, but they couldn't. Shouldn't. How could a kiss that felt so right still not be right?

She pulled out of the kiss and peeled her body away. "I'm sorry."

Gio's breathing was rapid. "Me too." He escaped to the bathroom, and she heard the faucet turn on. He was probably splashing his face.

"Waiting is hard." She sat in a chair at the little table.

He came out and took a seat across from her, extending his hand across the table. "But worth it."

"So you say." She shot him a coy look and slipped her hand in his.

"You don't believe me?"

She chuckled. "I know it's true. It feels so special this way."

"Your body may be healed from all the trauma you experienced. But it goes deeper than the physical."

She nodded.

"Don't get me wrong, though. If there was a good reason to get married tomorrow, I wouldn't hesitate."

"Temptation isn't a good enough reason?"

He laughed. "Touché." He ran his thumb across the back of her hand.

How did such a tiny action send so much electricity through her body? Especially when she'd learned to disassociate during sex. What would intimacy be like with this man who set her ablaze with a simple look, let alone a touch?

"Your mind is wandering."

Heat rushed into her face.

"Keeping it pure, I see."

"That's not fair." She gave him a fake pouting face.

"I'm not sure about that." He stood and took a cup out of the cabinet and filled it with water. "Want some?"

"I'll take a La Croix from the fridge. Please and thank you."

He handed it to her, and as she opened it, her phone rang.

"It's my counselor." She answered it.

"Hi, Morgan. It's Jolene. How are you doing? Did the weekend go well?"

"Hey. Yes and no. Lots of long stories we'll definitely need to talk about tomorrow."

"Tomorrow," Jolene's voice became weighted. "That's why I'm calling. I just found out your insurance is saying you've reached your max number of visits."

"What? I can't stop seeing you yet. I had a flashback yesterday. I think my memories from that lost period are resurfacing, and I don't know how to deal with that on my own."

Gio got his laptop from his backpack and tapped away.

"Oh Morgan. We still have a lot to do, but I don't want you to end up in debt either. I've been trying all day to figure out how to cut the bill so I can keep seeing you, but the center won't allow it. And per my contract, I'm not allowed to see anyone outside of the center."

Gio said, "Put it on speaker." He could probably already hear Jolene anyway.

Morgan tapped the button. "Jolene, Gio is here. I've put you on speaker."

"Hey, Jolene. Is it correct the Bureau's insurance covers an unlimited number of sessions for agents and family members?"

"Yes. If you were to put Morgan on your insurance, it would be covered. But I'm not sure if you'll be allowed to."

"Unless we get married."

A slight chuckle came across the speaker. "True, true. I bet you two are looking for an excuse to get married sooner rather than later, aren't you?"

Morgan bit her lip. "You're not wrong."

Gio slid his laptop aside and leaned on the table, a serious expression stretching across his face. "You know where Morgan is in her healing better than most, maybe even better than we do. Would you give your blessing on a quick marriage?"

"Oh Gio, you can't put me in that spot."

"I'm not looking for you to say we'll have an easy road; we know that's not our lot."

"If Morgan's memories are returning in flashbacks, it may be better if she's not alone too often. You'll be able to help her orient to the present. You have also both expressed your commitment to one another."

Morgan asked the question again, "So is that your blessing?"

"Yes. But whenever you two run into the difficulties you know are coming your way, don't hesitate to come in together."

Gio's smile reached across his entire face.

"And I expect an invitation. Just kidding."

Morgan laughed. "Oh you'll get one, don't worry." She clapped her hands, more elated than she'd ever been before. Gio was actually going to be her husband. Soon! "I've got a wedding to plan."

The sun dipped low in the sky, adding more orange and pink to the fall landscape. After a week and a half of whirlwind wedding planning, Gio stood in the middle of the clearing on top of the mountain, in the very spot where Morgan had dropped to her knees and let freedom wash over her. He stood between Dylan and their pastor.

The folding chairs lined up on the lawn were filled with their team from the FBI, Aliza and kids, Gabe along with his parents and sister, Jolene and her family, a few friends from church, Nate and his family, and a laptop with Gio's parents streaming in. It was a small gathering, but that was all they needed.

Everyone was settled, and soft music played in the background. Jacq came out of the house and descended the steps and then down the aisle before taking her place opposite Dylan. Next, Harper ran out and made everyone laugh just as much today as at Dylan and Jacq's wedding three weeks before.

Once Harper was beside Jacq, Gio looked back at the house. A radiant Morgan stood on the porch.

He could hardly breathe. To be sure he'd stay steady, he shifted his cane without taking his eyes off of her.

As she walked down the aisle, the most intense sense of déjà vu came over him. This was the exact scene he'd dreamed of so long ago. It really had been a vision of the future, now the present. And it was coming to life.

They had spent hours praying for their marriage, Morgan's continued healing, and God's leading. And they would keep praying and following God. He'd already brought them so far.

Morgan beamed. They had debated if someone would give her away, but nothing fit. Sure, Nate would have been honored to walk with her, but the restoration of their relationship was so new. Ultimately, she decided God was the only one who was able to give her to Gio, and that was why she carried a small Bible along with her bouquet.

When she reached him, he stretched out his hand. Her slender fingers slid into his, and they turned toward the pastor.

At the point in the service where they exchanged vows, Morgan pulled two slips of paper out of her Bible. She handed one to Gio.

He began reading. "Gio, the man who has pointed me to Jesus over and—"

Morgan pulled the paper from his hands. "That's not the right one."

A ripple of laughter reverberated through the clearing.

"Try this one." Morgan's voice danced with amusement.

He took the proper slip of paper and read his vows to Morgan. He promised to always point her to Jesus, to stand by her side no matter what came, no matter how hard the healing would be. Thick or thin, better or worse, plenty or famine. His commitment to her was unwavering, and with God on their side, they could face all He'd prepared for them.

Gio had barely been able to get the words out loud enough for anyone but her to hear, but it didn't really matter if anyone else heard him. His commitment was to her and God.

His throat hurt from holding back his tears, but Morgan's probably didn't, as her tears flowed freely.

She then read her vows to him. In the vows, she poured out her heart. She addressed how broken she knew she was, but God was healing her. Marriage wasn't going to be easy for them with her past, yet it was clear God had brought Gio into her life not just to help her break free from the trafficking life, but also to lead her back into the arms of her Savior. She promised never to run from him or their problems. To be open, honest, and faithful.

His face was as wet as hers by the time she finished.

The pastor pronounced them husband and wife and gave Gio the cue he'd been waiting for.

He shifted closer to Morgan, but his knee collapsed beneath him.

Chapter Eight

MORGAN CAUGHT GIO BEFORE anyone else could notice he'd fallen and made it look like they'd just swooped in for a whoop-worthy kiss.

By the time they pulled out of the kiss, Gio had regained his knee. "Not exactly how I imagined that first kiss. But thank you."

"You catch me all the time; the least I can do is return the favor. Literally." She went in for another kiss, which garnered another round of applause.

It was so strange to have people cheer for her to kiss. But this really was different. This man was now her husband.

Morgan took Gio's arm, and they proceeded into the group of their friends and family where hugs and congratulations were in ample supply.

She kept waiting for the other shoe to drop. For something to swoop in and destroy her perfect day. Surely a flashback would take over at any minute and ruin everything. But nothing bad happened. The ceremony had gone off without a single flaw.

No broken guitar strings. No delayed flowers. No missing or late guests. No internet issues preventing Gio's parents from being present.

She had given Gio the wrong vows, but that was just hilarious, and the ceremony proceeded without further hitch. Surely something should have gone wrong.

What if the cake was bad? Or if she spilled punch on her dress?

Jacq leaned close to her. "Stop worrying."

"What?"

"It's all over your face."

Heat rushed through Morgan's body.

"Everything is going well; relax and enjoy it."

Morgan hugged her friend. "Thank you."

"That's what friends are for. Now go flirt with your husband."

Morgan released a tiny squeal. Gio was her husband! She slid over next to him and tucked herself beneath his arm.

After a short while, everyone made their way to the house where refreshments were served, and the cake was eventually cut.

As the sun set, a bonfire was lit, and they danced under the stars.

Gio held her close and whispered in her ear, "Just because it's our wedding night, doesn't mean we have to—ya know."

She giggled. "Have sex? Isn't that part of why we rushed the date?"

He leaned back and peered deep into her heart. "I don't ever want you to think I'm 'getting something from you.' We can take it as slow or not as you want."

"Or not." She went up on her toes and kissed him.

He gently nudged her away. "We're still in public."

"Then tell everyone to leave." She stifled a yawn.

He laughed. "In time, my dear."

Eventually they said goodbye to everyone, and as Dylan, Jacq, and Harper went into their house, Gio led Morgan into their tiny little home.

Finally, she wouldn't have to sleep alone in this little trailer.

After covering a yawn, she tugged Gio to a stop. "And how would you like it, my dear husband?"

"Nope, that's not how this is going down."

Her heart stopped. "What do you mean?"

He drew her close. "You take the lead. This isn't about how I want it. This is about us. As a married couple, it is an act of worship."

Worship? Anything done for the Lord was worship. Even this?

"Morgan, I also don't know what I want yet, other than to be close to you."

He stroked the side of her face with his fingertips.

Her entire body tingled.

"I'll meet you in the bedroom. I'm gonna make a pit stop first."

They parted ways.

In the room, her exhaustion started catching up with her, so she lay on the bed to wait for him. But not long after her head rested down, she slipped into slumber.

She was aware of Gio coming into the room and chuckling. She tried to open her eyes, but they wouldn't obey.

Gio climbed onto the bed and wrapped his arms around her. "Just sleep. I got you."

She snuggled deeper and, in the comfort of her husband's embrace, let sleep win.

Somehow Morgan was aware she was asleep, but everything before her seemed so real. Where was she? She knew the hallway she was tiptoeing down. But why?

She turned another corner, heart racing like she'd just run the length of Florida without stopping. What would he do if he found her sneaking around? She didn't understand him. Some days he wanted her to feel like this place was her home, but then she'd wake up, and the door to her room would be locked with her inside.

She had heard something strange and had to find the source. It was possible a bobcat or something had gotten into the basement. Or heaven forbid, an alligator.

She shuddered. Alligators were the worst, second only to angry pimps.

But that life was behind her now.

Yet here she was sneaking around again. She never was very good at following rules.

The sound pulled her down another hallway. Why was this house so big?

The sound changed. Now it sounded like crying. Who would be crying? No, not just someone, a child. There weren't any children here.

At the end of the hall, there was nothing but a bookcase, but the muffled crying was coming from behind it.

She ran her hand along the sides. It wasn't just a regular bookcase. Putting her back against the side she tried to move it, but it wouldn't budge.

There must be a secret lever to open it.

She searched the shelves until she found a small lever hidden beneath a book.

Opening it would be a bad idea. He'd likely kill her. No, wasn't he different than all the other men she'd ever encountered? Not really. The last few months had proved that. Just because he didn't sell her didn't mean he was any different. He still acted like she was his possession.

The cry again.

She had to know what was going on. There were too many secrets, and she was tired of it.

She pulled the lever and the bookcase slid open, revealing another wall. No, another door. It was large and solid.

She turned the handle. Another hallway. Four doors. Three on one side, like they were small rooms, and a fourth on the left. The crying came from the middle door on the right.

For whatever reason, she felt compelled to open the left door instead. She unlocked the outside bolt and pulled it open.

Inside the room, which ran the length of the hallway, at least a dozen bunkbeds lined the space and even more pallets lay on the floor. All filled with children of every skin color and age, down to a toddler.

Children?

She stumbled backward and into *him*.

She screamed and spun from his arms.

The door across the hall opened, and a burly man shoved a boy toward them.

She threw up in her mouth. What was going on?

He tossed the boy into the large room and locked the bolt. "You shouldn't have come down here."

She looked up. His face went from distorted to focused. Duke! She screamed again.

"Morgan!"

She jerked awake, breathing heavily, forehead drenched in sweat.

The room was dark, but she could sense Gio. His hand gripped her arm.

"Are you okay?" Gio turned his bedside light on.

She was still in their trailer, still in her wedding dress. Her entire body shook.

"Morgan?"

She sat up beside him. She couldn't get her voice to work. A half-empty water bottle sat on her bedside shelf. After taking a long swig, she turned back to Gio. "It was just a dream."

"Just a dream wouldn't make you scream bloody-murder like that."

She curled up in his arms and told him what she had seen. "But the kids probably have to do with that case you guys are working. And Duke ... clearly I'm still afraid of him."

"What if it was something more?"

"How could it be? Sure, it felt real. Some of the details don't make sense. Florida? The alligators fit; I really am afraid of those."

"The boy crying. Like the last flashback you had?"

She sank a little deeper against Gio. Maybe it was connected. But it seemed so disjointed in her brain. "I'm probably just putting random things together. Dreams do that after all, right?"

"They can." Gio kissed her head. "But let's pray for clarity."

She nodded against his chest. "I'm scared to, though. I don't want that to be anything remotely related to a memory. It's too disturbing."

Gio ran his hand along her arm and prayed out loud. The Holy Spirit washed over her, bringing peace. Still, the images of the nightmare did not fade. They were as fresh as if they were a memory from yesterday, not some passing dream. But she would cling to the peace and to the Spirit who brought it.

Gio finished his prayer for his bride and kissed her head again. He couldn't imagine the terror she'd felt from that dream. But while she was having such a terrifying dream, he was having one of his own. And it was the opposite of terrifying. He couldn't tell her that.

She shifted against him.

"How about some tea? And perhaps get in something more comfortable than our wedding attire?" he whispered.

"I've wrinkled the dress something horrible, haven't I?"

He shrugged.

She turned her back to him. "Unzip me?"

He pulled the zipper down and didn't even try to stop himself from watching her stand and drop the dress. His cheeks warmed as she changed into a sleeveless nightgown.

"Show's over. Are you gonna stay in your button-up and slacks?"

He took the shirt off and chucked it at her.

Her laughter dispelled the lingering darkness from her dream.

She left the room, and he quickly changed into a pair of shorts and a T-shirt.

He exited and leaned up against the counter to watch Morgan fill the tea kettle.

"You can come closer, you know."

He walked up behind her and settled his hands on her hips and kissed her neck. "I like this marriage thing."

She giggled and placed the electric kettle on its base and flipped the switch to *on* before spinning in his grip.

He took in every inch of her face, but he already had it memorized. He'd had it memorized since his first dream about her years ago.

The dream he just had revisited his mind. How did he tell her about it? His mother's words echoed in his mind. *Hope isn't false if it's in Jesus.*

Morgan's fingertips slid into his hair beside his temples. "What's going on in here?" She tapped his head.

"You weren't the only one who had a dream in the last hour."

"Oh?" She tilted her head to the side.

"Mine was a good one. Though I'm confused by it."

"Tell me."

He nodded. He didn't want to keep any secrets. They got their tea and sat on the sofa. Morgan stretched her legs across his lap, and he rested his arm across the back of the couch. Consummation definitely needed to happen before morning.

"Was it another dream about me?"

He ran his hand along her lower leg before resting it on her knee. "I don't think so. Although the person in my dream looked exactly like you. But she was only six or seven, maybe eight."

"A little girl?" Morgan sighed and tears instantly brimmed in her eyes.

"Maybe I shouldn't have told you."

"Tell me more. What other senses did you get from it? Any other details?"

"She was wearing a purple headband." He stared into the distance, trying to pull the dream to the forefront of his mind. "She had longing in her eyes. But I'm not sure why."

"Can you sketch her?"

His heart swelled at the idea. "I can try. Then you can tell me if it is just you as a child."

She jumped up and retrieved his sketchpad that contained all his sketches of Morgan from the years of dreaming about her. After handing it to him, she grabbed his pencils.

As she sipped her tea, he worked on the sketch, closing his eyes frequently to recapture the image.

He rarely added color to his images, but the purple of this little girl's headband demanded to be shown.

When he returned the purple to its case, he studied the sketch until Morgan set her tea cup down.

"May I see it?"

He turned it.

She gasped, and her hands flew to her mouth. "Oh she's beautiful. Definitely not me, though. What do you think this means?"

"I don't know. I don't want to put words in God's mouth. But maybe it means what my mom said about putting our hope in the One who holds the future." Gio retrieved his pencil and added the date to the bottom of the page.

"You know, Jacqui joked with me that we shouldn't pray for a miracle pregnancy to happen too fast since we got married so quickly." A smirk toyed with Morgan's lips.

"What would people think?"

"I thought you were the one telling me I shouldn't care what people think."

He set the sketch pad on the floor and pulled Morgan against him, finding her lips with his.

As she kissed him back, she giggled. She pushed him away, jumped to her feet, and extended her hand.

He slid his into hers, allowing her to pull him to his feet and toward the bedroom. He'd never felt so alive.

Chapter Nine

Gio walked into the church carrying a box of pamphlets about the future home for trafficking survivors. It had been a week and a half since he and Morgan had gotten married. He wish he'd been able to take some time off of work to settle into marriage more, but he was out of leave. They were already dreaming up a nice honeymoon for after the new year. Only three months away.

They were off to a good start. Given her past, they'd had a few challenges to overcome when it came to intimacy, but they were working through them slowly, and neither one of them minded the practice.

He walked into the fellowship hall where they were hosting the fundraiser. Morgan and Jacq had done an amazing job of decorating and arranging the centerpieces on the tables. The room was ready for the event, which started in about twenty minutes.

"Hey, Jacq, where do you want these?"

"On that table by the door."

He set them out and slid the box underneath.

Jacq came up to him and gave him a hug. "Morgan was struggling a little. Maybe you can give her a pep talk?"

"I can do that." He squeezed his friend's shoulder and left the room.

But where had his wife gone off to? It didn't take much searching. He went straight to the kitchen and found her pulling a pan of something that smelled like heaven out of the oven.

She glanced up, and a smile took over her face. "Hello, my husband."

"Hey." He closed the space and pecked her lips with a kiss. He didn't dare let it be more. "You doing okay?"

"Nervous about sharing." She turned off the oven and set the oven mitt on the counter. "Part of me is excited. I know we're going to be doing such important work. But I feel like an impostor. Many people stuck in trafficking have it much worse than I did. Did you know the average life span of someone being trafficked is only like four years? I was trafficked for the better part of thirteen years. How did I make it out so well? But at the same time I still feel incredibly broken. It took a lot from me. But I'm being selfish. I have my life; I have you."

"Everyone's experience is different."

"But Eddie." She choked back a sob.

His brother's story fit her statistic. Only a few years of trafficking drove him to commit suicide. "I don't know why God shielded you from all the devastation that could have filled your life, but I praise Him that He did. He gave you a second chance."

"Yeah, and I plan to use it to help other people have a second chance too."

"Exactly."

"And it starts tonight by sharing my story with a bunch of strangers. God's got this."

He smiled at his wife, who'd given herself the pep talk he'd planned to. "I love you, Morgan Crespi."

She giggled. "I still love the sound of that."

"I hope you do for a long time."

"I will. Now, off with you. I need to finish this, and you need to start welcoming potential donors."

"Sure I can't help you?"

"You'll just make us both even later."

"Can't resist my rugged—"

"Stop it." She gently nudged him.

Leaning heavily on his cane, he pulled her against his body, kissing her with every bit of passion he dared, given their lack of privacy.

He released her, leaving himself reeling. "I love you."

"That is one thing I do not doubt at all. Love you too. Now, go."

He turned. "Going."

Guests were arriving and entering the fellowship hall. He nodded at one man to walk ahead of him.

Jacq tossed Gio a lanyard with his name and role in the organization. Not that "staff" was very specific, but no one knew exactly what any of their roles would be in the long run. For now, Dylan's and Gio's tags could say "liaisons with the FBI," but their roles as agents would be kept to a minimum during these fundraising events.

Gio mingled and introduced himself to several people, before Dylan called him over to where he was talking with a tall, good-looking man in an expensive suit.

Dylan said, "Dean, this is Gio Crespi. His wife will be one of our speakers this evening. Gio, this is Dr. Dean Rockefeller."

Gio extended his hand. "It's nice to meet you."

"Likewise. I'm impressed with what I've heard so far. Looking forward to finding out if I can back your project. Thank you for the invitation."

Maybe they stood a chance of getting significant donors tonight. They'd set a modest goal, but if a man like Dean contributed, they may blow that goal off the mountain.

Morgan finished the pastries and arranged them neatly on the platter. One of the women from church came in and took the platter to the fellowship hall.

Morgan glanced at the clock on the wall. *Shoot.* She was already ten minutes late. But at least the first little bit was scheduled for mingling. She didn't mind missing that.

For as much as she'd always thought herself an extrovert, she really was not a fan of chit-chat. It seemed so contrived anymore. She understood its purpose. You can't dive into deep issues until you get a feel for a person, but still.

And tonight was different. She was the survivor sharing her story. Sure, not everyone would know that at this point, but it would probably come out in the first few moments when someone asked her what her role would be in the home or what drove her to this work.

She wiped the counter and tossed the dishcloth into the dirty-rag bin. How many times she'd been tossed into the dirty-rag bin herself. But God had taken her from that bin, washed her with His own blood, and He was mending her rips. That's why she was doing this. To give that same hope she'd found to other women, to other survivors.

Dusting the remnants of powdered sugar from the front of her slacks and blouse, she sucked in the confidence God provided her and marched out the door toward the fellowship hall.

Once inside, she greeted a group of people with a warm smile and an "I'm so glad you're here."

She glanced around and caught Gio's eye. He was standing, talking to a few people, including a man just as tall as Gio and Dylan who had his back to her. Her husband waved her over.

She excused herself from the group she was with and strolled toward him.

"This is my wife, Morgan." Gio slid his arm across her shoulders when she reached him.

The man turned.

The world stopped. Her breathing, her heart, all the voices in the room. All stopped.

In front of her stood the only man left in the world she feared.

Duke.

Her legs gave out.

Gio's hand moved to her waist and kept her upright.

"Morgan, is it? It's nice to meet you." He extended his hand.

How was she supposed to respond? Slap his hand away? Kick him? Spit in his face? She sure wasn't going to shake his hand.

She gripped Gio and searched the crowd for Dylan. He was across the fellowship hall. But hadn't they already talked about how they don't currently have anything substantial to arrest Duke on? It was pointless.

"Morgan?" Gio's voice wavered. He recognized her fear.

She couldn't do this. "I'm so sorry." She let go of Gio and ran from the room.

Chapter Ten

GIO COULD DO NOTHING but watch his wife disappear, away from this man he'd introduced her to. Who was he? Why did he strike such terror in Morgan? Gio could only assume it meant Dean Rockefeller wasn't exactly as he led them to believe. A john? A pimp? Something worse?

"I apologize that I scared your wife away. I can't even begin to understand what would have elicited such a reaction. Do you suppose I remind her of someone from her past life?"

Dean's cool confidence in wake of Morgan's reaction set off more alarms not less.

Gio said, "I suppose that's possible."

Dylan came over cautiously. "Is everything all right?"

Dean said, "I seem to have upset Mrs. Crespi. I didn't mean to. I'm so sorry."

Gio didn't know what to say. *Arrest this man* came to mind, but he didn't know what the charge would be. "Excuse me. I'm going to see if I can find Morgan."

Dylan nodded and engaged Dean in further conversation.

As Gio picked up his pace, his knee yelled at him but didn't give out until he had exited the fellowship hall. He braced himself on the wall, thankful he didn't fall.

Where had Morgan gone this time? He hobbled to the kitchen but didn't find her.

The pastor turned a corner. "Hey, Gio."

"Have you seen Morgan?"

"Not sure it was Morgan, but I saw someone headed into the youth room. Might want to check there."

"Thank you."

He went to the youth room as quickly as his legs would carry him and pushed open the door. He didn't see anyone.

"Morgan?"

No reply. He walked around the space until he realized one of the cabinets wasn't quite closed all the way. He crossed the room, sure to make enough noise in the hope he wouldn't scare her if she was indeed in the wardrobe.

He nudged the door open. Her tear-streaked face tilted up at him. The terror in her eyes crushed his soul.

She scooted over to make space for him inside the cabinet where costumes from last year's Christmas program hung.

He wrapped his arm around her. "What happened?"

Her whole body trembled.

"I'm guessing he's somehow connected to trafficking, isn't he?"

Her eyes grew wide. She audibly swallowed before she finally found her voice. "That was Duke." She buried herself against Gio.

"Oh Morgan!" He tightened his arms, hugging her even closer. He didn't know what else to say.

"He found me. What do I do? Did you see the smug expression on his face, acting like he didn't even know who I am? I can't go out there and tell my story in from of him." A few choice words slipped from her lips. "Sorry."

"No need to apologize. He is a bad word to the nth degree."

"But what do we do? I don't know what he wants from me. But I'm more afraid of him than I ever was before. Maybe it's that dream. Yeah, that's probably it. I can't hold that against him."

"Morgan?" He waited until she looked up at him. "Maybe we should confront him."

"And show all our cards?"

"What cards? I'm not sure we have a hand to show. We can at least tell him we don't want the money he's clearly ready to throw at a trafficker."

"I don't know."

"Let me call Dylan."

She nodded.

He pulled out his phone and called his closest friend.

Dylan answered. "He's already gone. Made a big deal about feeling bad for upsetting Morgan and left."

"I bet he did. You'll never believe who he is."

"I can only think of one person who would strike such fear in Morgan. I'm gonna go out to the parking lot and see if he left completely."

"I'd appreciate it."

They hung up. Gio pulled Morgan against his chest, holding her for a long time.

Later that night, Gio opened the door at the field office and held it for Morgan before handing it off to Dylan. Once Gio had flipped the switch that controlled half of the lights on their side of the large office, he took Morgan's hand. She'd done such an amazing job at the fundraiser. It had taken a while for her to pull herself together after seeing Duke, but the encounter had invigorated her even more to tell her story.

She'd radiated the change God had worked in her life and spread that hope to all who attended. They had raised more than twice their goal for the evening. Everyone was floating after the event, but by the time they reached the field office, they were all firmly back on solid ground, and the weight of Duke showing his face sank them a little deeper.

They had to figure out who this guy was. But, Gio questioned, to what end? They had nothing on him. Maybe they'd find something, though Gio doubted it. They would look, but Gio wouldn't be surprised if Dean Rockefeller came up surgically clean.

Gio pulled out his chair, took a seat, and turned on his computer. Morgan slid onto the corner of his desk. Dylan and Jacq went to their desks and booted up their computers.

Gio leaned back in his chair. "Before we divide up tasks, it might be good if you"—he placed his hand on Morgan's thigh—"refreshed us on all you know about Duke."

She nodded slowly, then more quickly. "Want me to write stuff on the white board?"

"That might be helpful, and as we find things, you can add to it."

Dylan dashed across the room and pulled out the white board from the corner. Now that Sabrina wasn't on their team, they didn't seem to use it as often. He said, "There's no marker."

Gio grabbed one from his desk drawer and tossed it to Morgan, who now stood beside the board in the center of the bullpen.

Across the top Morgan wrote "Dean Rockefeller aka 'Duke'" with a thick line beneath. "Duke is just the nickname I gave him when Ronan brought him to me. When we met, something seemed off, but I couldn't pinpoint what. He wore his wedding ring and later mentioned something about his wife, so I know he's married." She wrote "married" as a bullet point along the side of the board.

She met Gio's eyes, and he thought she would bolt again. The pained expression in her eyes bit at his insides. He hated making her think about this disturbing man.

Gio nodded at her. "Keep going. Doesn't matter how disjointed things seem, that's how brainstorming works. We saw him at the hospital."

She turned back to the board and wrote "works at hospital" as a new bullet point. "And that explains how he was able to get the meds that helped me detox from the heroin. We also know Ronan was terrified of him. Like he always said, it was because Duke had such deep pockets, but it was more than that."

She added "deep pockets" and "strikes fear in traffickers."

Jacq asked, "Where did he ... where were your ..." She threw her hands in the air. "I don't know how to word that question with Gio in the room."

They all laughed at Jacq's flustered expression.

But Morgan turned her back to Gio to answer Jacq. "I know what you're trying to ask. Mostly at that hotel downtown where you rescued Natalie. But occasionally at his house."

Dylan asked, "Do you remember where that house was? I mean, it might come up in our search, but there's a chance it won't."

"Up in the mountains. I drove out there at least once, and that's where he took me to detox, but I'm not sure I could get back." She wrote "mountain home" on the board.

She capped the marker and turned back to Gio. "That's it. I'm not sure what else is important."

Gio motioned her closer. "Then we dive into our search. Jacq: public records. Dylan: criminal records. Morgan and I will hit the internet."

She ran her hand across his shoulders. "Wow, high-tech FBI."

"It's amazing what you can find out about a person on the internet. Kind of scary really."

They all went headlong into their work. Morgan pulled Aliza's chair over and sat close to Gio as he entered "Dean Rockefeller" into the search engine.

They were able to find basic information, such as a home address in town, a business address, Dean's role as a doctor of internal medicine at one of the major local hospitals, his education. They found a few articles he'd been mentioned in, regarding helping patients or donating to an organization.

"This is interesting," Jacq said. "According to public records, he only has a house here in town. A relatively modest, upper-middle-class home in a nice neighborhood. No mountain home."

Morgan crossed her arms. "Then whose house was that? Maybe it's in his wife's name?"

"I'll search marriage records next and see if I can find her. But he also lived in Miami for a while."

Morgan's hands fell to her lap. "What? Huh."

Gio squeezed her knee. "What is it?"

"Is it possible I really did meet him before? He made it sound like I should remember him."

Jacq said, "He was definitely in Miami, where it looks like he was a doctor at a major hospital for a few years."

Gio didn't want to say anything. Still, ideas ran through his mind about how it could all connect. But Morgan needed to reach some of those conclusions on her own without his influencing it.

Dylan looked up from his computer. "I've got nothing as far as criminal records. He's clean. But not too clean. He has one speeding ticket from fifteen years ago. That's it."

Morgan stood, went to the board, and added the new information. His date of birth, education, the home address Jacq found, work details. They were developing a profile of this guy, but so far nothing pointed to him having a connection to any trafficking beyond being a sleazy john.

Maybe if they caught him soliciting a prostitute they could get him put away for something. But with his status at the hospital and the connections Gio could only imagine came with his wealth, he'd probably get barely anything more than a slap on the Rolex.

So why did Gio have such a grating feeling in his gut there was something much more sinister behind the doctor's coat?

Chapter Eleven

Morgan capped the marker and set it back in the white-board tray. It was kind of fun to play detective with her friends and husband, but at the same time, the focus of their search sent chills through Morgan's whole being.

She didn't want to hate anyone, but the way this man had used and tried to manipulate her made *hate* something she was going to have to fight. The image of his face in her dream shot back into her mind. She shook it loose.

"You okay?" Gio's voice was soft and comforting.

She gave him a half nod, half shrug.

"What on God's good earth?"

Jacqui's exclamation caused Morgan to spin so fast she nearly lost her balance. "What is it?"

"I found his wife. You aren't going to believe this."

Morgan walked over to Jacqui's desk.

Jacqui turned her computer. "Meet Evangeline Rockefeller. Her license is expired, but is it just me or does she look familiar?"

Morgan stared at the picture. The woman looked eerily like Morgan—definitely her doppelganger. Not the same, though, as she was clearly more Mediterranean in descent versus Middle Eastern like Morgan's grandfather.

Gio's hand came to rest on the small of Morgan's back.

She jumped.

"Sorry." He didn't move his hand.

She stepped closer to him. "That's weird."

"That may explain his fixation with you," Dylan offered. "Perhaps he has a type."

"I guess so." Morgan hugged herself. Knowing Duke's wife looked so much like her creeped her out in an entirely new way. Not that she could pinpoint why, but the expressions on everyone else's faces confirmed she wasn't alone in that feeling.

A giant yawn escaped from Morgan before she could catch it.

"Maybe that's enough for tonight?" Gio shifted his cane.

Jacq glanced at her watch. "Good golly, yes. I'm glad we've found what we have, but bed is a really good idea."

Gio nodded. "We made good progress, even if we didn't find a clear reason to hang him."

"Yet." Morgan tried to fill her voice with hope and confidence. "Maybe I can lure him into tying that noose himself?"

Gio's hand tightened around her waist. "Absolutely not. I don't want you to have to go anywhere near him again."

She turned toward him. "I know. Neither do I, but I want him to pay for what he's done." She looked to her friends.

Jacq shook her head. "I'm with Gio on this one. Right now our objective is to protect you from him should he pose a threat. Then, and only then, do we arrest. If we dig deeper and find something to prosecute, you better believe he'll go down."

"But not for buying me." It wasn't a question. She knew he could never actually be convicted for those crimes. The burden of proof was too great, and the evidence bag was empty.

They packed up and left.

Fifteen minutes later, Morgan walked through the door Gio held open and into his old apartment. Jacq and Dylan had headed to Dylan's parents' home to sleep since it was after midnight, and Gio had suggested they not drive up the mountain either.

She flipped the light switch. "You know, it might not be a bad idea to keep this place so you can crash close if you're on a case late."

"That's assuming I ever go back to full active duty." He rapped his cane on the floor and closed the door, locking it securely.

She turned toward him and took the cane from his hand. "You will." She tapped the handle to his chest. "You are the strongest man I know."

He wove his hand into her hair, giving her a half-smile. "That doesn't mean my knee will recover."

"One day at a time, anyway. I still think the apartment might be worth keeping." She handed him his cane and turned.

He grabbed her hips and drew up against her back, sliding his arm around her waist. "But I can't handle the idea of sleeping away from you for a single night." He tickled her neck with kisses.

She giggled. "As long as there isn't something else going on, maybe I can meet you here. Help you wind down from the intense cases."

"You know how to get me."

She leaned into his kisses before turning and meeting his lips with her own. Being married was more fun than she had ever expected. This man didn't kiss her neck because he'd paid for her or because he wanted to get something. He loved her, and she felt it through her entire being.

After a few minutes of enjoying his sweet kisses, Morgan slipped away to get ready for bed. Despite being on desk duty, Gio still had to be back at the office at eight in the morning. More fun would have to wait for tomorrow.

They both changed and brushed their teeth with brushes they'd left there last time they'd crashed at his old apartment. Once ready for bed, Morgan crawled in beside her husband and tucked herself against him.

He stroked her arm as he prayed for them like he did every night.

After he said *amen*, Morgan still couldn't fall asleep. She'd come face to face with Duke again. She almost wished she hadn't freaked out so badly. If she hadn't, perhaps she could have given him a piece of her mind. And a length of rope. Maybe this would be over then.

Instead, she had to live with the idea he was still out there, and now he knew she was still in Knoxville too. She shuddered.

Gio stirred and tightened his arms around her. "I will do everything in my power to keep him from hurting you."

"How did you know what I was thinking?"

"Because I'm thinking about it too. I'm regretting not going to that meeting you heard Ronan set up with Duke."

"You couldn't. You were recovering from a bullet wound."

"But ..."

She put her finger on his lips. "No. If I'm not allowed to say 'what ifs,' neither are you. We'll take each moment as they come and follow God in them all. He's got us. And even if we can't get Duke or Dean or whatever you want to call him—"

"Bad word."

She chuckled. "Exactly. Even if he never gets his just desserts here, he'll get them in eternity."

Gio kissed her forehead. "Precisely. It's God's job to avenge, not ours."

She snuggled even deeper against her husband and let God's peace fill her soul, and her mind finally surrendered to sleep.

Jacq settled into her desk Wednesday morning, thankful they'd slept in town. Having breakfast with Harper this morning had been delightful. The girl was going to give her gray hair, but at least Harper was funny.

The muffin Jacq had eaten for breakfast was not sitting well though. She hated heartburn. And she was bloated. What on earth had Dylan's mom put in those muffins?

She tried to ignore the discomfort and dove into work. She wanted to keep looking up information about Dean Rockefeller, but that wasn't official case business, so it would have to wait for free time. Right now she needed to once again—as she did every week—run the names of the two men from the airport. They'd found nothing about them for the last four weeks. It was probably pointless now. Nicoletta's trafficker could be back in Colorado where they'd flown in from, and the two kids and their trafficker could be anywhere in the States or overseas.

She put Mick Tirrell's information first through law-enforcement databases, then she ran his credit report. Mr. Clock-Tattoo was still completely off the radar. If he had flown back out of Knoxville or any other airport, he'd used a fake ID. Unfortunately, they hadn't been able to discover any aliases for him.

Justin Wester's turn. They had no aliases for him either. These guys had their butts covered. Either they were smart, or someone very smooth managed them. She put Justin through the databases first just like with Mick. Once again, she came up with nothing, so she ran his credit activity.

But this time there was a new line. A new charge. She squealed.

Dylan, Gio, Matt, and Aliza all raised their heads.

Dylan asked, "What is it?"

"It would appear Mr. Plane Boy has used his credit card at a place here in Knoxville. He hasn't left."

Aliza's eyes widened. "Maybe the kids are here too."

Hope surged through Jacq.

Dylan's face didn't look as hopeful. "I wouldn't jump to that so fast. They could be anywhere. Good chance he was a middle man."

Jacq sank back into her chair. Dylan was right, but she didn't want to believe it. Maybe there was still a chance they were nearby. Those two precious children had to be nearby somewhere, maybe in Knoxville.

Matt asked, "Where was the transaction?"

Jacq checked. "A gas station on the southeast side of town."

Dylan stood. "Let's go visit and see if they can shed some surveillance on this trafficker."

Jacq joined him. "That's a great idea."

Aurora skipped down the hallway, swinging her doll beside her. She stopped. Daddy's office door was open. It was never open. She skipped straight into the room.

His back was to her.

He slammed his briefcase on the desk and said a very naughty word.

She froze like Anna did at the end of her favorite movie, *Frozen*.

He shoved stuff off his desk. Pens flew through the air and spilled all over the floor.

A little squeak came out. She covered her mouth.

When Daddy was mad, she didn't want to be anywhere nearby.

"Bianca!" He shouted for Auntie.

Aurora bristled. She hated it when he yelled like that.

His face got all twisted up, but then he put on a smile and looked at her. Why was he faking being happy to see her?

"Sorry, my little sugar. I didn't mean to frighten you. Come here." He sat on the sofa and opened his arms to her.

Fear shook her stomach, but she walked slowly toward her father.

"How was school today, sweetheart?"

She stopped right in front of him. "Good. I got to feed the class fish."

"Excellent. Do you like first grade?"

She nodded. She didn't dare tell him the boys were mean and the girls meaner. He might get angry and hurt them.

He fixed her headband. "You do know purple doesn't match your dress?"

"That's what Auntie said, but it's my favorite." She wore it every day she could.

He shook his head. "You've always looked beautiful in purple, pumpkin."

"Thanks, Daddy."

Auntie ran into the room. "I'm so sorry, sir. Dinner is just about ready."

Aurora raised her hands. "I washed them."

"And didn't come right back to the kitchen."

"I wanted to say *hi* to Daddy."

Daddy patted her arm. "Run along to the kitchen. I'm going to talk to Bianca."

"Okay." Aurora kissed his cheek and walked out, hugging her doll close. She hoped Daddy didn't hurt Auntie because Aurora came into his office when he was angry. It wasn't Auntie's fault he'd left the door open.

Aurora stopped outside to listen. She could get in big trouble if they caught her, but she wanted to know what he was angry about.

Daddy said, "Clean up this mess. You're supposed to keep an eye on her."

"I'm sorry. I told her to come right back after washing her hands."

"Just don't let it happen again. She doesn't need to be frightened. There's going to be a big party this weekend. Will the new kittens behave?"

Kittens? Aurora always wanted a kitten.

Bianca answered, "I believe so. Will Aurora and I be at the mountain house this weekend?" Her voice sounded weird, like a tight rubber band.

Aurora hated being at the house when Daddy had a party. It meant she got locked in her room, and Daddy would give her sleepy medicine. She didn't like the sleepy medicine; it made her feel weird. But if there were kittens …

"I'm not sure yet. I could use your help with the kittens, but I'd rather have Aurora here. Some of that will depend on what happens between now and then. Last night I saw Angel. She's here in town. I will bring her home this week." Daddy's voice had changed like he was happy, but he kind of sounded like a bad guy too.

A shiver passed through Aurora, and she ran to the kitchen.

Chapter Twelve

On Thursday morning, Morgan arrived just on time for her eleven o'clock counseling appointment. She was grateful to be able to see Jolene twice a week without having to worry about whether she could afford it.

"Good morning, Morgan."

"Hey, Jolene." Morgan sat in her usual spot on the couch across from Jolene's chair.

"How are you doing this morning?"

"Eh. The last couple of nights' sleep hasn't been great." She filled Jolene in on running into Duke Tuesday evening. "I knew he worked at the hospital, but now I have a name. Not that it changes anything. The team wasn't able to find anything on him."

"So he definitely works at the hospital?"

Morgan nodded. "Dr. Dean Rockefeller. He's an internist."

Jolene's face lost a little color. "I know him." She looked off into the distance as if she was trying to reconcile what Morgan had told her with what she knew of the man.

"Maybe I shouldn't have told you his name."

Jolene met Morgan's eyes. "It's all right. I know many people aren't all they claim to be. It disgusts me how many people don't think twice about paying for sex. But let's not dwell on that. On Monday, we left off with the idea of digging for those lost memories. Are you ready for that?"

Morgan sat up a little straighter. "I think so. I'd rather face them with you where we can work through it right away instead of having them burst forth in the middle of something else."

"That makes sense. Get comfortable, and let's go back to what you do remember before the blank time. Maybe we can walk into it some."

Morgan kicked off her tennis shoes and crisscrossed her legs on the couch. Tugging a throw pillow onto her lap, she drove her mind back to her days in Miami. She had been there for years.

"This pimp was actually not near as bad as the one I was with in DC. He didn't run me ragged. But his favorite thing was parties. He'd keep us locked up all week, then bring us out for them. After one too many girls tried to run, he started shooting us up with heroin before we'd go."

"Think about some of those events."

It was all a mess of memories. But she could remember several different houses—mansions really—where the parties were held. She focused in on the last one she could remember ...

Morgan struggled to walk up the wide stone steps of the mansion. Her skirt was too tight, and the heroin too fresh in her system.

"Get moving," Rusty snarled at them before turning to the entrance and changing his demeanor. When the door opened, he declared, "The party is here!"

He stepped aside and ushered the girls in.

Men loitered all around, many of them very young—college age perhaps. It was spring break for some schools, wasn't it? But not all of them were college students. Regardless of age, the men gawked at the girls.

They were expected to spread throughout the house and patio and pool area out back. They were also to come on to the guys, paying special attention to the men who seemed to have more money. The girl who earned the most would get to sleep in the real bed in the basement they called home, instead of the lousy bunks with thin mattresses.

Morgan didn't care enough to fight for the bed. She'd rather sleep on the floor than have sex with any of these men. But she put on her fake smile and strutted through the living room.

One of the college boys smacked her butt as she walked past. She turned toward him and resisted the urge to spit in his face. Instead, she leaned over him, placing her hand on the couch behind his shoulder, her low-cut dress leaving nothing to his imagination. "You like it rough?" She'd gladly beat him to a bloody pulp if that's what he'd like.

"You're old." He shoved her.

"Fine." She walked away. Rusty would probably want her to fight for him, but there were plenty of younger options for the boy. And if Rusty knew how many times she'd heard the *old* line, he'd probably put a bullet in her head. Although there were still enough men who wanted an "experienced woman" of twenty-five.

She continued her jaunt around the room, past more ogling eyes. Until one of the men decided she was worth taking upstairs.

As she left the room, she caught the eyes of a tall, handsome man. Her heart seized. Something about the way he looked at her. It was as if he actually saw her.

She shot him a pleading expression, but he didn't act. He let her be led upstairs.

Twenty minutes later, she came back down the stairs feeling compelled to find the man with hair the color of bronze.

She spotted him out on the patio with a glass of something hard and strolled straight to him. He was rich—she could tell just by the way he carried himself—and more importantly, he'd looked at her differently. She wasn't sure if it was a good thing, but different was in and of itself better, even if it really wasn't.

He swung his leg over the lounger so he could straddle it and patted the seat in front of him. "Join me."

She lowered herself, ignoring the soreness the last man had caused.

The rich man studied her and brushed a strand of hair from her face. "You are absolutely stunning." His voice was thin like he needed air.

He meant it. Was this his first time with a group of prostitutes? No, he had the confidence of a man accustomed to this world. What was his deal?

"I'm Dean. What's your name?"

Morgan pulled her mind out of the memory. She couldn't breathe. Was her brain playing tricks on her? She stared at Jolene.

The counselor waited for her.

"Was it really him?"

Jolene said, "I can't tell you that, but it seems like it's possible."

"I know he expected me to remember him a couple of times along the way. But why didn't he act more surprised when I didn't recognize him the first time at that hotel earlier this year?" She hugged the pillow to her chest. "I don't understand."

"You're probably going to need more memories before you do. Did it end there?"

Morgan searched for the memory of that night over seven years ago.

She'd ended up spending the entire rest of the night with Dean. He had wooed her, and when he'd finally led her upstairs, he had taken his time and had refused to let her go back down.

When Rusty rounded up the girls at the end of the party, he yelled for Morgan. Not that he called her that. She ran down the stairs, and Dean followed.

"You've been with the same guy this whole time?" Rusty's ears grew red.

Dean came up behind her. "Is that a problem?"

Rusty shrank back. "Of course not, sir. I'm sorry. I didn't realize." He met Morgan's eyes. "In the van."

She moved to obey, but Dean caught her arm.

"I'll see you again."

She nodded, not sure how to feel about that. She was almost flattered, but something about him scared her. Maybe it was his intensity. Or maybe it was the way Rusty shrank back.

The memory faded. Morgan was shaking.

"Morgan, you're in my counseling office."

She met Jolene's gaze. "I know. But that left me with a creepy feeling. Did I see Dean again after that, before Knoxville? I can't remember."

"It's okay. That was a recovered memory, wasn't it?"

"Yeah, I had no idea I'd been with him before. Is it possible I'm just superimposing him into the memory?"

"Do you think that's what you are doing?"

Morgan considered it. "No. It was a real memory."

Chapter Thirteen

Gio sat at his desk as usual and checked his watch. Morgan should be leaving Jolene's office at any time. He'd felt an especially heavy need to pray for her during today's appointment. He was anxious to hear about it, but he would have to wait until after work.

Yesterday, Jacq and Dylan had gone to the gas station where Justin had used his credit card. The company that owned the station had agreed to send the surveillance footage their way, but they hadn't done so until about ten minutes ago. The clerk at the station had not interacted with the man since he hadn't come into the store.

They each took a camera view and searched for the time stamp of when the credit card was used. Gio moved the video on his computer to the correct time and watched a black pickup pull up to the pump. He had the suspect's picture in an always-on-top window in the corner of his screen.

A man exited the truck and looked around. Gio paused the video when the man was most facing the camera. Even though he didn't look directly into the lens there was no question this was the guy they were looking for.

"Got him." He reported the make and model of the car to see if some other angle could catch the license plate.

Now they knew what pump he was at and, more importantly, the car he drove.

Gio resumed the video and watched the truck. There was a passenger in the vehicle, but his face was obstructed by the visor.

Jacq crossed the room and watched with Gio. "Come on, lean forward."

Gio added, "Or put up the visor."

The person did both.

"There!" Jacq slapped Gio's shoulder.

Gio paused the video and took a screen shot.

Jacq said, "Send it to me, and I'll try to ID him." She reached for the top side drawer of his desk. "Do you mind?"

He dropped his voice. "Heartburn again?"

"A little bit. But I was going for the Tylenol too, if that's okay."

"Headache?"

"Just overall not feeling like myself."

"You did seem a little cranky this morning."

She narrowed her gaze until it turned into a glare. "It's a good thing we're friends."

"I wouldn't have said it otherwise."

She shrugged and poured herself the two medications she needed. "I'll feel better when we have this guy locked up and those kids rescued."

"Me too." Gio squeezed Jacq's elbow.

Dylan shouted from across the room, "I've got the license plate."

Jacq returned to her desk, and Gio sent her a message with the picture of the passenger. If they were able to identify that person, they might have a chance of talking to him and thus locating Justin.

Morgan drove back to the apartment after stopping at Chick-fil-A for some nuggets and a chocolate milkshake. Part of her wasn't at all hungry after walking through those memories. But she needed to eat and something about chocolate soothed her soul a bit.

At a stoplight she dipped a nugget into the sauce and popped it in her mouth. As she chewed, she glanced in the review mirror. Was that Duke's stupid-expensive car?

She shook her head. No way. Why did her mind play such tricks on her?

She popped another sauce-covered chicken nugget before the light turned green.

Once she arrived at the building, she finished her nuggets before getting out of Gio's—their SUV. For now, they were only driving one car. She'd been bumming rides and borrowing cars for months, and she didn't mind one bit. She loved picking up Gio from work when they were in town.

Walking up the steps, milkshake in one hand, she glanced at her phone. Too many hours until she had to get Gio. She needed a hug and his gentle reassurance that he'd stick with her whatever her memories revealed. She opened the phone app and clicked on his name. No, she shouldn't call him yet. She switched to the texting app.

Deciding to wait until she was inside, she slid her phone back into her pocket. She juggled her keys until she found the right one and tried to poke it in the slot.

"Hey." A familiar masculine voice boomed behind her.

She jumped and dropped the keys. *No!* She didn't want to turn around; she wanted it to be another trick of her imagination. No one was there, right?

"I finally found you." Duke was beside her.

His cologne smelled as good as always, but a new memory threatened. She shoved it aside. Now was not the time for a flashback. She had to stay in control.

She was as frozen as her milkshake, though. *God, help me.* Turning, she stepped away from him. She couldn't reach for her keys.

He might take the opportunity to knock her out or something. Should she scream?

"Angel, I don't understand why you keep acting this way around me. We've had such good times. I want to take you home."

"My name is not Angel, and nowhere with you is home. Please leave."

"Right, it's Morgan? Is that your real name? For all the years I've known you I can't believe you never told me."

"Years?" She shook her head. It didn't matter. But what if he could fill in her memory?

"You really don't remember. I can't believe you'd forget me. I honestly thought it would have come back by now." He moved in closer until her back was against the railing over the steps. But he kept his face in the shadows.

"It's starting to come back."

"Come with me, and I can help you remember." He lifted his hand to her.

She wanted to remember. Why was she so tempted by his offer? "No. I will in my own time. And if I don't, that's fine."

Duke's eyes flashed with fire. "You really should come with me." He gripped her arm, almost making her lose her hold on her milkshake.

But wait. He always wanted her to come willingly. Maybe that was the key to her safety right now.

"I don't want to. I want to be at home with my husband. You need to leave before I call the police." How was her voice not shaking as much as her insides were? She slid her phone out of her pocket.

He picked up her keys. "Angel—"

"That's not my name, Dean." *Jesus, keep me strong and steady. Make him leave.*

"Let me change your mind." He placed his hand over hers—the one that held the milkshake—and stepped closer until his face was right in front of her.

She couldn't breathe. But she tried to move her thumb on the phone. She just needed to get Gio.

Chapter Fourteen

Gio searched for the truck passenger's home address. Jacq had found his identification pretty easily. The search results popped up. They had their man. Or at least someone who clearly knew the man they were looking for. "I've got an address, and it's actually legit."

"Oh good." Jacq shoulder's dropped. "I wish you could go with us."

He waved his hand toward her. "Don't worry about it." He wouldn't tell her it crushed him to have to sit here and wait for them to bring someone in to interview.

His phone dinged with a text message. Morgan. His heart lifted. At least his spirits were renewed constantly by the woman he loved to call his wife.

But the message made no sense.

"What's wrong, Gio?" Jacq asked.

"Text from Morgan, but it's random words that make no sense."

Jacq all but flew across the room. "Show me."

He handed her the phone.

"She tends to use the swipe-to-type feature. I bet her finger was in the wrong place."

"Then what's she trying to say?"

"I have no idea."

He took the phone back and called Morgan. It picked up after one ring, but she didn't say hello. There was a muffled sound on the other side. Then in the distance he heard his wife's voice say, "Go away. Leave me alone."

Morgan!

He stood, grabbed his cane and bag, and turned toward the door.

"Gio! You didn't drive." Jacq ran back to her desk.

Phone still pressed to his ear, listening for any clue from his wife, he waited by the door. Dylan joined Jacq and the three of them sped out of the office and down the stairs, not willing to wait for the elevator.

The voices on the other end were muffled, and he couldn't make out what was being said. She hadn't spoken directly to Gio, so he didn't want to bring attention to the fact he was on the phone. Though everything inside him wanted to call out and tell her he was on his way. Not that they knew where she was.

Jacq was on her phone. "Matt got Morgan's location."

Good. Someone had thought of it.

"No!" Morgan screamed.

As they ran outside, Gio heard a thump on the other end of the line, as if the phone had hit the ground, followed by a scrape, a clang, a long pause, another thump, and then the line went dead.

What happened to my wife?

Dylan drove with excessive speed, and they arrived at Gio and Morgan's apartment in record time.

Gio flew out of the car. Their SUV was in the parking lot. He half-hobbled half-ran to the building and spotted Morgan's phone, cracked, on the ground. That must have been the final thud he heard.

He struggled up the steps, Jacq passing him as she ran.

He missed being able to take the stairs two or three at a time. He needed to get to his wife, if she was up there.

"Morgan!" Jacq called.

Gio hobbled around the corner. Morgan sat against the wall beside their door, Jacq beside her.

Morgan's eyes met his, and a smile softened her frightened features.

Jacq asked, "Was it Dean? Which way did he go?"

Morgan nodded and pointed the opposite way they had come up. Jacq stood and ran, so Gio took her spot.

"Are you okay?" he asked. "Did he hurt you?"

"He tried to convince me to go with him. It shook me up. And he killed my milkshake."

The foam cup was crushed, and chocolate shake dripped down her hand and arm.

"Let's get you inside and cleaned up."

She nodded, and they stood. "Where are my keys?"

They both looked around. No keys in sight.

"Duke had them."

"If he stole your keys, we can press charges."

Morgan's eyebrows contorted. "Ooo, a reprimand."

He ran his fingers into her hair, his hand cupping her face. "But we could arrest him and figure out what else he's been up to that might get him more time."

She leaned into his touch. "If only."

"Hey, guys." Dylan appeared from where Jacq had run and dangled a set of keys in front of them.

Morgan left Gio and walked toward Dylan. "He must have realized he had them and ditched them. So much for stolen property being his downfall." She took the keys.

Gio let out a breath. "This time." He wanted to reassure Morgan they would get Dean for his crimes, but it was getting harder to believe it.

Morgan said, "Guess he spotted the tracking tag."

Gio chuckled. He'd almost forgotten they put the tracker on them after Morgan lost her keys twice within a week after they got married. She'd made him put one on his phone too. If only Dean had taken the keys.

She raised her milkshake-y hand.

Gio unlocked the door.

The three of them went inside, and while Morgan cleaned up in the kitchen, Jacq joined them. "He's long gone."

Morgan said, "I figured he would be. He was gone before you got here." She chucked her to-go cup in the trash, eyes welling with tears.

Gio crossed to her and took her in his arms.

"I just wanted a milkshake." She dropped her head against his collarbone, and a moment later his shirt was damp.

"I'll get you a new milkshake." He held her a little tighter. The tears weren't for the milkshake. Not entirely. He guided her to the couch.

Dylan said, "I'll go get all of us milkshakes."

Gio wanted to ask her for all the details of what Dean said to her and how her counseling session went, but she was good at talking to him. She would tell him when she was ready. For now, he simply held her.

Jacq took a seat and remained quiet as well.

After about five minutes, Morgan lifted her head. "I remembered the first time I met Duke—Dean." She told them about her counseling session.

Every time she talked about her past, Gio's entire being ached. He hated that she ever had to live like that. So much stolen from her.

She continued, "I know you've told me to keep my awareness up. I knew better, but he caught me off-guard."

He ran his hand up and down her back. "It's okay."

She went on to tell them Dean said he would help her remember what she'd lost, that she only needed to go with him.

Anger flared up in Gio, heating his veins. Given the opportunity, he'd punch Dean right in his pretty little nose.

Jacq asked, "Why did he leave? Did he notice you'd called Gio?"

Morgan shook her head. "I don't think so. I accidentally dropped my phone when he squeezed my milkshake. I just kept telling him I wouldn't go with him, and I didn't want to have anything to do with him. He was about to bring me into the apartment to change my mind. But his phone rang, and then he left."

She turned more toward Gio and toyed with the button on his shirt. "I don't know that I want those memories, and I definitely don't want him to help me bring them back. Never."

"You don't have to convince me. You know I'm right here with you, memory or no memory."

After delivering the milkshakes, Dylan and Jacq left Gio with Morgan and went to the address of the man who had been pictured with Justin. Matt had continued doing research and discovered Justin and Ron were cousins and Ron lived with his mother. With any luck, the mother would be the one home when Dylan and Jacq arrived.

Dylan glanced over at his wife. Her eyes were closed, lips drawn tight, and head against the seat.

"What's wrong?"

She rubbed her face. "This headache just won't go away. I'll be fine."

"You've been having those a lot the last few weeks. Is being married to me that horrible?"

She let out a strained giggle. "Not that at all. I don't know what the deal is."

"Do you need to see a doctor?"

"No, they really aren't that bad; at least they haven't been until today. If it continues, I'll get it checked out, but I really doubt it's worth worrying about. My mom gets headaches all the time, and it isn't anything."

"If you say so." Fear surged in his heart. What if something terrible was going on? No, he couldn't think like that. It was just a headache.

He pulled up in front of a middle-class, split-level home. "Ready?"

Jacq shrugged but got out of the car.

He joined her on the sidewalk, and they headed to the front door where Dylan knocked.

Someone hollered from inside. "Just a minute."

What sounded like clanging of dishes and then shuffling of feet came in response before the door opened, revealing a portly older woman.

"Hello, ma'am, I'm Special Agent Dylan Harris with the FBI, and this is my partner, Special Agent Jacq Sheppard. Is this the residence of Ron Steube?"

The woman's pudgy face frowned. "That good-for-nothing boy-man is my son. He lives here most of the time. My name is Peggy by the way. Come on in. I'm sure the FBI has more questions than should be answered standing on the front stoop."

She led them into a small living room and motioned for them to take a seat. "Can I get y'all anything? Coffee, lemonade?"

Jacq smiled. "No, thank you."

The woman looked to Dylan.

He shook his head. "We appreciate your hospitality, but we're fine. Is Ron here?"

"Nah. He left for some big shindig this weekend. His cousin is trying to help him get a job or something."

"His cousin? I'd like to show you a surveillance image of your son." Dylan pulled up the image from the gas station on his phone and showed it to Peggy. "Is this the cousin?"

"Yep, that's my son and his cousin, Justin. What trouble have these two gotten themselves into this time?"

Dylan wanted to laugh, but silently wondered why more hadn't shown up on their background checks.

Jacq answered, "We're looking for Justin too. We have a few questions for him regarding an incident at the airport last month, but we haven't been able to track him down."

"Was it something to do with kittens? I overheard them talking about that. Don't know why anyone would need to take kittens on an airplane. Aren't there enough strays everywhere that need homes? Good gravy, I can't imagine having a kitten flown in from somewhere else."

A sick sensation grew in Dylan's gut. She had no idea what her nephew was involved in.

Jacq asked, "Ma'am, do you have any way of contacting your son or nephew?"

"No, they didn't tell me where they were going, but said it was work related and weren't to be disturbed. I guess they're having some sort of corporate retreat."

Dylan nodded. "If you do hear from either of them, please don't let them know we were here. We need to talk to them but don't want to scare them."

"You aren't going to tell me what this is about, are ya?"

"I'm not at liberty, ma'am, but it is important we speak to them as soon as possible. Would you be willing to let us know when they come around again?"

"That I can do. If they're doing anything illegal, please remove them from my home. I have enough trouble on my own. My grandson, Ron's sister's boy, comes over here regularly, and I want to keep him safe."

"Do you know where Justin lives? The address on his license isn't current."

"Here, there, everywhere. He keeps talking about buying a house but says he needs to do a few more jobs before he can pull that off."

Unfortunately, Dylan was pretty sure what kind of house she was talking about—one to hold his trafficking victims.

Friday afternoon, Morgan and Jacqui strolled up the walkway to a modest two-story home, where a family was fostering the young girl Jacq had found in the airport. Morgan was excited and nervous to meet the girl, but Jacq had insisted Morgan could be exactly what Nicoletta needed.

Morgan's emotions were still pretty raw after yesterday though. In addition to everything else, she'd had another flashback last night as she and Gio were getting ready for bed. What angered her was that she couldn't actually remember anything from the flashback. Just a moment of fear—no, terror—filled her. She wasn't even sure what triggered it. She and Gio had been talking, and he went into the bathroom while she sat on the bed in the apartment she'd told Gio she wasn't sure she wanted any longer. Then Duke flashed in her mind. Nothing more.

She'd freaked out—air wouldn't come—but Gio did. He coaxed her out of the panic and held her. He was so good to her. He prayed over her and led her straight to God's throne.

Could she be that support for Nicoletta? *God, please help me be what You want me to be for her. Bless this time with her. Bless this girl and let her know You love her.*

Jacqui knocked on the door.

The foster mom opened it and ushered them into the living room, where a ten-year-old girl with gorgeous black hair in braids sat at a coffee table, sketching. Nicoletta's smile grew when she saw them.

"Jacqui!" She jumped up and hugged her friend. "My English is better since you found me at the airport. Been working lots on it." She then shyly turned to Morgan.

Jacqui said, "This is my friend, Morgan. She's the one I was telling you about, the one who's been through some of the same kinds of things you have. I think you two will get along very well."

Morgan gave the girl a warm smile. "It's nice to meet you."

"You too. Can I show you some of my pictures?" The girl's accent, while very heavy, was beautiful.

"I would like that very much." Morgan joined the girl on the floor. "What's your favorite thing to sketch?"

"I think the word is landscapes?" Nicoletta held up a picture of a beach scene.

"That is stunning."

She showed Morgan a few more sketches of landscapes. One she identified as the mountains where she had been living most recently, and another she said was from the area near the orphanage in Italy.

"I'm not very good with people yet. I can't get the faces right." She handed her a picture of a young girl.

"I think it's very good. My husband is also talented with a pencil, especially with faces. I bet he could teach you a few things if you would like."

Nicoletta's face lit up. "Really? He would teach me? I would like that very much."

"So would he." Morgan noticed a sketch of a man and picked it up. It was more of a caricature, but something familiar about him unsettled Morgan's stomach. "Who's this?"

"The man that brought us from Italy to America. He said he was our uncle."

"Does drawing help you process what happened to you?"

She nodded. "This one is better of him."

Morgan's stomach flopped. No one else would probably identify it, but she was certain it was Duke—Dean Rockefeller. Why would he have played the part of an uncle? And brought Nicoletta and her sister to the states to traffic them? But maybe her mind was playing its normal games.

Morgan tried to keep her hand from shaking. "Hey, Jacqui."

Jacqui looked over from where she was chatting with the foster mom.

"Does the man in this sketch look familiar to you?"

Jacqui walked over and took the paper from Morgan's outstretched hand. "Kind of has a familiar look, but I can't place him as anyone in particular."

Morgan sighed. "No worries." She was probably wrong. She settled back into talking with Nicoletta.

"'Uncle' took more interest in my sister, Bianca. She was beautiful." Nicoletta smiled at Morgan. "You actually remind me of her." The smile faded, and Nicoletta's gaze drifted off. "I miss her."

"Jacqui told me."

"I'll never know what happened. If she's truly dead, her body will be gone forever—they would never let it be found."

"I know. Those people are ruthless."

"Morgan, I like you. Maybe you could be my sister. You could never replace her, but I need a sister."

Morgan put her arm around the girl. "I'm honored. But I'm old enough to be your mother."

Nicoletta leaned into Morgan's embrace.

She stared down at the girl. Could this girl be the answer to her and Gio's prayers?

Chapter Fifteen

AT SIX P.M. ON Friday, Gio exited the elevator into the FBI field-office lobby with Dylan. They'd spent the day investigating the work-history of Justin and Ron. They had come up with no current employer for either. Not that Gio had expected they would. If these men were truly trafficking children, that wouldn't show up in any employment record.

He and Dylan chatted about nothing of consequence. Their wives were supposed to be getting back to the office at any moment after visiting Nicoletta for the afternoon. Gio sent up another prayer for the girl and also prayed she and Morgan had been able to connect.

Because the October evening was beautiful, air crisp and cool, they waited outside. And they didn't have to wait long. After they pulled up, Morgan hopped out of Jacq's sedan, and Dylan took her place.

Jacq said, "See you guys later."

They all waved goodbye. Gio turned to Morgan and embraced her. "How did it go?"

"Swimmingly! That girl is amazing. Resilient and so sweet."

"Wonderful."

They walked to their SUV, and Morgan grew quiet. He held the door for her, and the thoughtful look on her face made him curious. He went around to his seat but didn't start the car. "What is it?"

"Two things." Morgan took a breath so deep her shoulders and entire chest rose and fell. "Do you think we could adopt Nicoletta?"

His heart shot skyward. "I honestly don't know, but it might be possible. The adoption process has a lot of steps, but we can look into it. We don't really have room in the trailer, but—"

"We could keep the apartment. There's a second bedroom."

"That or we could get a new one." He wanted to add *so Dean doesn't know where we live*. But that seemed unnecessary. Plus, he'd found it in the first place. What's to say he wouldn't be able to find a different one?

"I fell in love with her today. She's an incredible young lady. She needs to know people can love her for who God made her to be."

"Sounds like someone else I know."

Morgan giggled.

"And number two?"

Her countenance shifted.

"I take it I got the good news first."

A dry laugh escaped her beautiful lips. "I think the guy she said claimed to be her uncle is Duke—I mean, Dean."

Gio couldn't quite believe his ears. "What makes you think that?"

"The sketches she drew. The facial features aren't quite right. She said she struggles to draw people. And Jacqui didn't recognize it as Duke, but I'm sure of it."

"Perhaps we need to pursue that line with her more. We've focused on whom she escaped from. Aliza did a sketch of the 'uncle,' but we didn't take it much further since he wasn't in play at the moment."

"I'm sure it's him. Maybe I'm just reading my own stuff into it, but—"

Gio reached over and placed his hand on his wife's shoulder. "It's worth pursuing. If he is the 'uncle,' we'll have him for more. We'll prove it and put him away for good."

"This might just be the thing. But Gio, if he's trafficking children ..."

"Then it could be possible that dream you had is not a conglomeration of things, but a memory."

"Maybe." She sank into the seat.

If that was true, Gio's desire to bring the man to justice increased by tenfold.

Saturday evening, Bianca sat on the edge of Aurora's bed in the mountain house and held out the cup of medicine to the little girl. "You have to take it."

Aurora screamed and shoved Bianca's hand away, and she almost dropped the cup.

The door swung open and Dean's voice boomed through the room. "No screaming." His face fumed but morphed to sickly sweet as he walked toward them. "Aurora, how many times do I have to tell you? Obey Auntie."

Aurora's bottom lip quivered.

Bianca gripped her hand.

Dean pointed at Bianca as he glared at Aurora. "Obey her." He turned and left the room.

"Come on, Aurora. Don't get us both in trouble." Bianca lifted the cup to the girl again.

"I don't wanna. I want to go back to the house in Knoxville. I don't want to be here."

Bianca kept her voice low. "I know; I don't either. But your dad wanted me here tonight, so here we are. Just take the medicine and sleep, kiddo. Trust me, you want to sleep as soundly as possible."

"Are you going to bed too? Does Daddy give you medicine to sleep?"

"Sometimes." But Dean's mood was such that Bianca was pretty sure she'd have to be at the party. Even worse, at the "business" meeting before the party. How she wished she could take the medicine herself and sleep through what was about to happen.

Aurora finally swallowed the liquid. She gave Bianca a hug and laid down.

Bianca pulled the covers up over the girl and kissed her forehead. "Sleep well, little one." She turned to leave, and Aurora grabbed her hand.

"Bianca? Will you be okay? Is Daddy going to hurt you?"

Her insides shook, but she forced a smile. "Of course not. Don't let worries fill your head." She tapped Aurora's temple. "I'll be fine."

Bianca turned and fought the dread filling her stomach. Dean rarely actually hurt Bianca physically. But if the "meeting" went like Bianca feared, Dean would need "comforting" afterward. A shudder rocked Bianca's body as she pulled Aurora's door shut. As much as Dean hosted parties for others, he didn't often partake of the festivities.

"Bianca."

She jumped at Dean's voice. Once the door was latched, she turned to him.

"Didn't mean to make you jump." He ran his fingers along the side of her face. "Wear this dress, please. I want you on my arm all night. Meet me downstairs in ten minutes."

She took the miniscule dress from him and went to get ready. She hated it when he paraded her around like she was a prize he had won. But as always, she'd do what she had to. At least she could take care of Aurora. The last woman who had cared for Aurora had been rotten—downright mean. Aurora deserved better.

Once she was ready, she went downstairs. Two men had already arrived.

One of them let his eyes wander up and down Bianca's body. "Doc, she's a fine one. Is she partying with us tonight?"

Dean seized the man by the neck. "She's mine, Marty. Keep your paws off. There are plenty of others. Understand?"

The man nodded as best he could. Once Dean released him, he straightened his shirt and rubbed his throat.

Bianca took her place beside Dean and wrapped her hand around his elbow when he offered it to her. Over the next ten minutes, five more men showed up. Dean led them all to his office, and instructed Marty to close and lock the door.

A dining chair sat in the middle of the office. Dean said, "Colin, please take the seat of honor."

A tall, lanky man stepped forward. Sweat beaded on his forehead.

"Mick, come sit here." Dean patted a chair.

The man with the clock tattoo on his arm obeyed.

"Unfortunately, gentleman, it has become abundantly clear that Colin has no sense of duty, and our friend Mick here is also struggling with understanding his place."

Dean led Bianca to his desk. "Take my chair, dear."

She sat in the high-backed leather chair that swiveled. Why was she here? Knowing what was coming for Colin made her want to crawl under the desk, cover her ears, and cry.

Dean took a glass figure of an octopus off the shelf. "Do you know what this creature is called, Colin?"

He shook his head.

"It's a blue-ringed octopus. Its venom is strong enough to kill twenty-six men with only one bite. But it would kill you in less than thirty minutes." Dean put it back on the shelf and picked up a large orange and white shell. "The Cone snail is also an excellent source of venom as well." He walked over and held the shell out in front of Colin. "It can kill up to twenty men."

The room was silent other than Colin's and Mick's heavy breathing.

Dean put the shell back in its place and came back to his desk. He leaned on the side, arms spread wide and head hung. "Now, you see, you can mix just a tiny drop of each of those venoms, and that of a black widow spider. Add a little bit of drugs—you know the ones I have easy access to as a medical professional—and I have the perfect poison. It will kill you. And you will suffer."

Dean stood upright again and pointed at the drawer to Bianca's right. She opened it, and he withdrew a syringe and a small glass bottle of clear liquid. "I've already got it all mixed up for one of you." He inserted the needle and extracted the liquid from the bottle.

He tossed her the bottle.

She gasped and caught it, barely.

He winked at her and turned back to the men.

She replaced the bottle and wiped her hands on her dress.

"Mick, you've got two strikes against you already. One, you lost a very important kitten. And two, you can't seem to find said kitten. It's unacceptable. You are walking a thin line."

Mick swallowed so hard Bianca could see it. "I'll find her—"

"No. It's too late for that now. You will make up for it or this"—he held up the syringe—"will be your fate." Dean strode to Colin. "Now Colin here, he's done struck out."

"Sir, I can explain." He lifted his arms to defend himself.

Dean nodded to Marty and a linebacker-sized man. They came over and held Colin to the chair.

Dean continued his speech. "Everyone should take note of Colin's sins. First, he let one of his girls start using drugs. Luckily, it wasn't heroin. Second, he got too rough with a girl and broke her arm. Men don't want damaged goods." Dean inhaled deeply and walked away from Colin. The veins in Dean's entire body bulged.

Whatever Colin's third strike, it made Dean angrier than anything Bianca could imagine.

"And third." He turned and stormed toward Colin. "You knew exactly where my Angel was but didn't tell me."

Bianca jerked her hand to her mouth to stop a gasp from coming out. No wonder this man was going to die. Dean's deepest obsession was finding that woman.

"Imagine my surprise when I showed up at that fundraiser the other day and found her. And then compound that with my shock at learning she's been going to counseling in the same building where you are the janitor. For months."

"How did you ..."

"I'm a doctor, I can look up patients' schedules. I finally knew her name thanks to the fundraiser. Your car was in the parking lot. That means you saw her. Are you going to deny it?"

Colin didn't look at Dean.

Dean leaned down into Colin's face. "Tell me. Did you know she was there and not inform me?"

"I wasn't sure it was her."

"But you suspected it?"

Colin nodded ever so slightly.

Dean flipped the cap off the syringe and jabbed it into Colin's arm.

Bianca sank back into the chair. She wished the floor beneath her would swallow her up, chair and all. She didn't want to hear what came next.

The tension was thick in the room as everyone waited for the results of the poison.

Colin looked around, but a moment later his eyes bulged. He screamed. The most horrid, bloodcurdling scream anyone could release from their body.

Bianca squeezed her eyes shut, wishing she could do the same with her ears. But if Dean saw her plugging her ears, he'd yank her hands away and make her listen.

This is how he kept everyone in line. No one crossed or ratted on Dean Rockefeller and lived to see tomorrow.

The men holding Colin let go, and he fell to the ground, his entire body convulsing.

Dean set the syringe on the desk and came around to Bianca. Without a word, he motioned for her to stand. She obeyed, and he sat, then pulled her onto his lap.

No one else moved.

Dean held her close. She fought the instinct to break down at the horrific sounds coming from the dying man. Instead, she wrapped her arm around Dean and toyed with his collar to distract herself.

After more than ten minutes, he finally said quietly, "Is Angel's room ready for her?"

"Yes, sir. I freshened up the toiletries and washed the sheets."

"Good. I'm bringing her home tomorrow."

Bianca nodded. Would Angel actually be here again? Maybe this time Bianca would have the courage to open the door and talk to the woman. Maybe Dean would let her. Would he introduce her to Aurora yet? Too many questions, especially while the sounds of a dying man filled the air.

After another twenty minutes, Dean patted her rear-end, and they both stood. "I think you all understand what lies before you if you cross me. Let's go party. I expect an excellent crowd tonight, and there are two newer kittens to join us."

Bianca clenched her teeth to keep from releasing the sob that ravaged her insides. Would they ever be able to break free from this torture? If only she could do something. But what could she do? She was as much a captive as those children Dean kept locked in the basement.

Early Sunday morning, Jacq sat back against the wall in the bathroom. She'd woken up with the inability to keep her stomach acids down and had to make a beeline for the toilet. Nothing came out, but that didn't stop the retching. At least she felt a touch better now.

This was the worst queasy stomach she'd had all week. What was going on?

It couldn't be ...

She grabbed her phone off the counter, where she'd set it in her dash to the toilet, and opened the calendar app. Why didn't she keep better track of her cycle? Had she even had her period since she and Dylan got married?

Puzzling it in her head, she decided she hadn't actually. They'd been married for five weeks already. *Oh shoot.*

"Jacq?" Dylan called from the bedroom. "Are you okay?" A light rap sounded on the door.

"Come in."

He nudged the door open. "Feeling worse this morning?"

She shrugged.

"We can stay home from church."

She shook her head. "That's not necessary. It'll pass, and I'll feel better later. That's how it's been the last few days."

"But you're worse. Can I get you anything?"

"Can you run to the store and get a pregnancy test?"

"Sure. Wait, what?"

She gave him a cheesy grin that felt more rueful than joyous. "You think so?"

"Yeah."

He dropped to the floor in front of her. His attempt to tamper his enthusiasm distorted his face.

Jacq dropped her apprehension and laughed.

Dylan said, "Exactly. This is exciting."

"But so soon. We weren't going to try for at least a year. We had a plan."

"God's plans are always better."

"But Morgan and Gio. It's not fair."

Dylan sat back on his heels, catching the bitter side of the joy. "They'll be happy for us."

"I know. But they'll also be sad."

Dylan nodded. "They wouldn't want sadness for themselves to dampen our excitement."

"True. Go get the test, so we can know for sure. This conversation could be all for naught."

"Okay." He leaned forward and kissed her. "Go back to bed or take a shower, and I'll be back in a jiffy."

"Check on Harper first?"

"Of course." He met her lips with his again.

She reveled in his affection for a moment after he was gone before pushing herself off the floor. She hadn't even brushed her teeth yet. That man really did love her.

She didn't experience any morning sickness with Harper, but that pregnancy had been overshadowed by her recovery from the burns she'd gotten in the fire that killed her first husband, Sean. She didn't know what to expect from her body during a normal pregnancy.

After brushing her teeth, she jumped in the shower. As the water poured over her, she prayed for Morgan and Gio. Prayed a family would be something they could experience, whether through birth or adoption. She prayed for their hearts to hear the news she was sure a pregnancy test would confirm. She also prayed for wisdom for when and how to tell them.

They should wait to tell Gio and Morgan or anyone, she decided, until after Jacq was able to go to the doctor and confirm with complete certainty.

She was out and dressed when Dylan came home. She slipped into the bathroom and took the test while Dylan got Harper some breakfast. With a timer going on her phone, Jacq busied herself picking up their bedroom. When the three minutes were up, she called for Dylan.

He all but skipped into the room. She took his hand, intertwining their fingers, and they leaned over the bathroom counter together.

Positive. They were going to have a baby.

The last set of songs started, and Morgan stood and raised one hand in worship. Gio joined her on one side and Jacqui on the other. Morgan and Gio had spent a good chunk of time yesterday in prayer about how God would like them to be a part of Nicoletta's life. Their prayers had not revealed a clear *no*, so Gio even called Nicoletta's social worker and shared their interest in giving the girl a home.

It was exciting and overwhelming at the same time. And a little scary. One look at Morgan's past could make them say a resounding *no*. But that's exactly what she brought to the situation to help this girl.

Lord, give us grace and wisdom. I want to help her the best way possible, but I don't know exactly what we should do. I know what I want it to look like. But am I ready to adopt a ten-year-old?

Morgan raised her second hand and sang out the song of surrender.

During the final song, Gio slid his arm around her waist and raised his other hand. She loved worshiping her Savior beside her husband.

The song finished, and the pastor gave his benediction. Everything in Morgan wanted to turn to Jacqui and share the news about what they were thinking. But at the same time, Morgan knew if she told Jacqui or anyone, it would cement in her mind more, and she'd get too excited, which would lead to greater disappointment if it didn't work out. She needed to manage her expectations. She'd tell Jacqui soon, but now wasn't the best time.

The four of them exited the row and shuffled out of the sanctuary along with the other churchgoers.

Dylan went to get Harper, and Jacqui turned to Morgan and Gio. "You guys have plans for lunch?"

Morgan shook her head. "No. We'll probably grab something, though. Wanna come?"

"Wish we could join you. It's Dylan's parents' Sunday to have us over. While things are so much better with his family than I ever expected, I'd still rather spend my afternoon with you."

"Another week." Gio squeezed Morgan's elbow. "I need to go chat with the guys from Bible study real quick."

"I'll get the car."

He didn't let go. "Only if Jacq or Dylan walk with you, okay?"

"Of course, silly." She kissed him before he turned and went to talk to the guys.

Jacqui had a peculiar smirk.

"What?"

"It's just so surreal."

"No joke. I definitely couldn't have imagined any of this before." *Especially the idea of adopting a ten-year-old.* How she wanted to tell Jacqui!

Silence fell between the friends. It was not a normal thing for the two of them. But Morgan couldn't think of a single thing to say.

Dylan approached, and Harper propelled herself into Morgan's arms.

"Aunt Morgan."

"Hey, little one. How was Sunday school?"

"I caught five fishies." She held up a full hand of fingers.

"Good job, Harps."

Dylan asked Jacqui, "Ready?"

Jacqui looked to Morgan, who nodded. "We're gonna walk Morgan to her car on the way."

Dylan said, "Absolutely. Want me to take Harper?"

Morgan hugged the little girl a little tighter. "Not until we're at the cars."

As they passed near where Gio was talking with a man from his study group, Gio caught her eye and winked.

She bit her lip and gave her husband a little wave before he bowed his head to pray.

She walked out of the church beside her friends. Jacqui was being quiet, which, despite being a total introvert, was unusual for her. Was something wrong? Maybe she still didn't feel well.

Halfway to the cars, Dylan said, "Can't get Gio to use the handicap marker, huh?"

"Says to leave them for people who actually need the spots. He's like, 'It doesn't hurt most of the time. I'm fine.' I can't fight him on it."

Dylan smiled. "Neither should you. He'll come around if he needs to long-term."

"I worry about how he'll handle it if it becomes more long-term than he anticipates."

Dylan nodded. "I'm with you. It will be an adjustment, but his faith is strong. He'll lean into God. And with you there to support him, he'll be just fine."

"I hope so. I pray so."

"Me too." Dylan pointed down the rows of cars. "We're down a little farther since we got here late."

"I'm right there. Here, Harper, go to Daddy." Morgan handed Harper to Dylan.

Jacqui pulled Morgan into a hug. "Love you, friend."

"Love you too. I'll see you all later." She walked to her SUV, digging in her purse for her keys. She found them just as she got to the car. She turned and waved to Dylan and Jacqui, who had stopped their trek to watch her get to her vehicle safely.

They all waved, and her friends continued on their path.

Morgan hopped in the car, sliding the keys into the ignition, but she didn't turn it yet. What was going on with Jacqui? Morgan couldn't get her mind around it. Had she said something stupid? No. She didn't think so. It wasn't like Jacqui to be weird about that kind of thing anyway.

Whatever. She shoved the thought aside. She'd keep an eye out for them to get back to their mountain house that evening and check on Jacqui to make sure everything was okay.

Turning the key, she started the car. As she reached for the rearview mirror, movement froze her.

Duke.

In her backseat.

She felt a prick in her neck.

She needed to call for help, so she reached for the horn. But before she could touch the center of the steering wheel, the whole world went black.

Chapter Sixteen

Gio slapped his friend on the shoulder. "Hang in there. God's got it."

"Thanks. See you later."

They shook hands, and Gio, leaning heavily on his cane, went out the door.

Morgan wasn't at the curb with the car yet, but it hadn't been long.

Dylan drove by and waved.

Gio returned the gesture and searched the parking lot for Morgan. It was clearing out pretty quickly. *There she is.*

The car moved from the parking spot, but rather than driving toward him, she exited out the back to the side street.

Where on earth is she going?

He retrieved his cell phone from his pants pocket and dialed her number.

She didn't answer.

Is she leaving me? He shook his head. For once he knew that wasn't true.

Something was wrong. What was happening? The sick feeling spread from his stomach and up his esophagus. He tried to run after the car, but his knee failed to let him move faster than a hobble.

He dialed Dylan's number. As soon as he answered, Gio said, "Come back." He hung up and dialed 911.

The dispatcher answered with the customary greeting.

"My wife has been kidnapped."

She asked for all the information: his name, her name, location, vehicle. "Did you see the person who took your wife?"

"No, but I have a pretty good idea who it was."

"Did you *see* your wife taken?"

He heaved a sigh. "Not exactly."

"I'm sending a car your way."

"I want an APB put out for my vehicle."

"Sir, I'm not authorized to do that. The police will be there shortly and be able to assist you."

He hung up, and a moment later, Dylan and Jacq pulled up to the curb. They both jumped out and ran to Gio. Dylan asked, "What's wrong?"

The controlled voice he had used with the dispatcher was gone—just like Morgan.

Jacq slid up next to him and positioned herself under the arm that had been leaning on his cane.

Only then did he realize he was shaking.

"Where's Morgan, Gio?" Jacq squeezed his waist.

He raised his other arm and pointed where she'd driven away. "She's gone. Just drove off."

"She didn't ..."

"No. He took her or threatened her or something."

"Are you sure? She was acting off this morning."

Gio released a dry chuckle. "That's because she was trying to keep from telling you something we're thinking about. She's so excited and afraid if she tells you and it doesn't work out, she'll be too disappointed."

"Oh Gio, I'm sorry I assumed the worst."

"Her track record isn't stellar. She was too excited for this to be anything but Duke."

Dylan crossed his arms. "Or some other player we haven't even discovered yet."

Jacq said, "But we watched her get in the car. She was safe."

Dylan released a gust of air. "We didn't check inside. He could have been waiting for her there."

Gio leaned on Jacq more than he wanted to, but he needed the support. "It's also possible he got her phone number and called her with a threat."

Jacq nodded. "She'd do anything to protect you, Gio."

Did love really have to cost so much?

"Gio." Jacq looked up at him. "Can't you track the tag on Morgan's keys? We don't have to have official means to find her that way."

Relief washed over him. "Yes!" He pulled his phone out of his pocket and opened the app.

Dylan reached out. "Let me see if I can catch up and find her. You two stay here and talk to the cops. Chad's on his way."

Gio handed him the phone and straightened, his cane barely keeping him steady. Jacq took Harper out of the car before Dylan drove off.

The police arrived, and just as Gio feared, he had an uphill battle to get them to believe something nefarious was going on. How he wished Gabe Jacobs had been the officer to respond to the call. But Gabe couldn't always be the one.

The FBI would gladly take the case, but they needed cars on the streets looking for Morgan right now. So they needed the local cops. They needed a miracle.

Chad and Emma Harris, Dylan's brother and sister-in-law, arrived fifteen minutes into the conversation with the cop.

Jacq handed Harper off to Emma, and Chad joined Gio and the officer. Chad listened for a moment before getting in the cop's face. "Look. If you don't get patrols out looking for this woman now, I'll personally sue your tail off—you and your entire department. Do your job and stop arguing with the FBI."

The cop looked at Chad with a puzzled look.

"I'm Attorney Chad Harris." Chad let his name hang in the air until the officer's eyes grew wide, and he backed up a step.

Dylan returned and jumped out of the car. He lifted an evidence bag with Morgan's phone and keys.

Gio's chest caved in. "You didn't find her?"

Dylan shook his head. "These were in the grass just around the corner."

Chad turned to Gio and extended his hand. "You'll find her. We're praying. Let us know if you need anything." He went to his vehicle as Emma finished buckling Harper in, and they left.

The officer was more agreeable now and made sure everyone was out searching for Gio's SUV.

Gio hoped it wasn't too late. A lot could have happened in the last thirty minutes. He blocked his mind from running through all the vile possibilities. He didn't want to think about whether his wife was being raped or murdered or sold across the country. If Duke took her, the chances were he would hide her somewhere before doing despicable things to her.

Gio's knee collapsed beneath the weight of his emotions. But his cane didn't catch him, and he fell to the ground. His hand scraped across the concrete. Pain shot up his arm, followed quickly by humiliation.

He threw his cane across the sidewalk. Where was Morgan? Would she be okay? Could he find her before that monster hurt her? What if he couldn't?

Chapter Seventeen

Morgan rubbed her eyes in an attempt to dispel the fog in her mind. It didn't work. Where was she and what was happening? The last thing she could pull out of her memory was kissing her husband in the church lobby.

She pried her eyes open and absorbed her surroundings. She knew this room. No!

Duke had taken her. Somehow. But she couldn't remember. She hated not remembering.

Her heart raced. Her belly ached. Her body shook from head to toe.

Where was Gio? Was he okay? Would she be able to get back to him?

She bolted upright in the bed. She needed to get home. Gio would be devastated.

"Well, well, well. She's awake." A creepy voice came from the corner.

"Duke." She spat out his name.

He sat back in a chair, hands woven across his midsection. "You know better than that now."

"You don't deserve a name other than monster."

His eyes widened. "You've got a mouth on you now, huh?"

"My filter has just been loosened." She swallowed. She was so over playing games with men, but her past came charging back in. How many times had she been slapped over the years for her lack of ability to control her tongue? *God, I need your help. Please control my mouth too.*

She jumped out of the bed and moved closer to the door. "You need to take me back to my husband now. I refuse to be here. I told you I don't want to be with you. Why would you kidnap me?"

"That's not what you said that day with Ronan."

"I just wanted to get away from him. I was going to run first chance I got." *Please, God, don't let me say something that would make this worse.*

Duke stood.

Morgan's heart raced. What would he do to her? If only she had her memories from that missing time, maybe that would tell her something about how she should act now or at least what she was in for. Something deep within her feared the worst.

He strode over to her.

She wanted to run, but she wouldn't make it far before he caught her, so instead she stood tall, unwilling to be swayed by this man. What was that verse she'd studied about the proud being brought low? He'd get his in God's timing. But could she survive until then?

Duke ran his fingers into her hair, sending a chill through her body. She refused to react.

"I'll be back in a little while. There's a dress hanging in the bathroom just for you. I'd like for us to have a nice dinner this evening." He leaned in as if to kiss her.

She turned her head and stepped away.

Duke grunted and shoved her toward the bed.

She hit the edge and fell onto it.

"Be more cooperative this evening, and you might actually remember how much you loved me." He walked out the door.

A shudder shook her insides. That was not what she wanted to remember, but she needed to get back that missing time frame. What part did Duke play in it, and how long had she been with him?

She grabbed a throw pillow from the bed and smashed it against her forehead. *Remember, Morgan. You have to remember. Please God, give me something.*

An image flashed in her mind. Duke—no, Dean. A strange emotion accompanied the image—fear coupled with desperation but mingled with hope.

She dove headlong into the memory.

Half-naked, Morgan stood outside of the house she was normally trapped inside. Rain poured down, the cold numbing her sore body, which was bruised and battered. She'd let her mouth run again and was paying for it. In front of her, Rusty spoke with Dean. He'd come to see *her*. They'd had one rendezvous since the party. He had paid higher than normal for her time and was angry that, once again, she'd been high. But that was her normal state of being with Rusty.

Dean's voice was once again heavy with anger. Not explosive anger. No, this man was scary quiet when he was angry. He turned to Morgan. "Do you want to come with me?"

She looked from Rusty to Dean.

Rusty snarled at her.

Going with Dean seemed like the safer of her options at the moment. But why would he ask her?

She nodded.

His anger faded, and a smile graced his gorgeous face.

She tucked herself under his extended arm.

"You will never get any business from me again until you stop dosing your girls. I have other business channels. And beating them to the point they can't work is just bad for business." He tossed a roll of cash at Rusty. "That's all you get for her. Good luck making anything without her." Dean nudged her toward his car. "Get in."

Was she really free of Rusty? But how was she going to get her next hit? This guy clearly didn't want a girl to be on heroin. She'd gone through some withdrawals, and they weren't pleasant.

She sank into the leather seat of Dean's Rolls. The back of her leg hurt where Rusty had pushed her against the edge of wooden steps earlier. It was still bleeding—all over her rescuer's stupid-expensive car. Would he yell at her for getting rain and blood on the leather?

He got in.

"I'm so sorry." She tried to move in a way she didn't bleed on the seat.

"Leather is easy to clean. No worries."

He drove away. "I hope you didn't have anything special in that hell-hole."

She shook her head. Anything that had any value to her had been lost a long time ago. The only thing she clung to was the hope her heavenly Father hadn't completely forgotten her, but some days she doubted even Him.

Dean's hand settled on her bare thigh. "You'll be safe with me. I will take care of you and give you anything you could ever dream of."

Her heart tripped over itself. Was this guy serious?

"Wh—" She smacked her lips shut. Had she not learned her lesson? A sob slipped from her lips.

"It's okay. Say what you're thinking."

"You aren't going to beat me for speaking my mind?"

"Don't be stupid. I won't beat you for having a brain."

"What's the catch?"

"Catch?"

"You want to give me the world. I've heard that plenty of times before, but there's always a catch. How many tricks a night do you expect? Am I allowed to have Dr. Pepper every once in a while?"

"I want you to be my wife, not my money-maker."

"Wife?" Why did that sound even worse than his hooker? Did her past drive her to doubt him, or was there something deeper about this man that really was as terrifying as she felt?

"Doesn't have to be anything so formal, but I won't be selling you like that bozo."

Was she really no longer a prostitute? She didn't feel free.

A noise outside of the room pulled Morgan's mind out of the memory. Dean had actually saved her from Rusty. But what had happened after that? His wife? And what was his obsession with asking her if he didn't actually care about her answer. There was still too much disconnected. Why was she afraid of him?

One thing had become clear in her memory, though she couldn't pinpoint it yet. She only realized something was very wrong with this man. Even if she didn't know why, being afraid of him was the healthiest choice. He was not safe.

Gio gripped the door handle in the back seat of Dylan's Dodge Charger. It had been nearly two hours since he'd watched his SUV pull out of the parking lot, but they had finally located the vehicle.

The crime scene technicians had already dusted Morgan's phone and keys for prints. They'd been clean. Morgan's prints weren't even on them.

The weight of grief was crushing. He had to find her. He wasn't sure how he'd carry on with life if he didn't. God would sustain him, somehow.

The flashing lights of a squad car brought Gio out of his head. Dylan pulled behind a strip mall and parked his car in front of a dumpster. Gio's SUV was parked beside it.

Gio jumped out and ran as fast as he could with his cane.

Marty Denton, a uniformed officer Gio had interacted with in the past, hand raised, stood beside the vehicle.

"This is my car." Gio pulled out his badge in case Marty didn't remember him. "Is she here?"

Marty lowered his hand and shook his head. "I'm sorry, sir. Did find this, though." He opened the back door and pointed to a syringe.

Gio leaned forward. There could be anything in that syringe. "Is CSU on their way?"

Marty nodded. "And they don't want either of us touching anything before they get here."

Gio dropped his shoulders. The sun seemed to mock him with its brightness. He wished he could get his sunglasses from the console. He shielded his eyes as he turned back to Dylan and Jacq.

She looked as forlorn as he felt. His car being ditched like this proved Morgan had been taken. Not that he'd had any doubts.

Marty handed Gio a pair of gloves. "Do you want to get your sunglasses?"

"You a mind-reader, Denton?" Gio took the gloves.

Marty tapped the frames of his sunglasses. "I had to get mine too."

Gio opened the driver's door and reached into the console. Morgan's purse and Bible sat in the passenger's seat. A fresh wave of grief slammed into him. He grabbed his glasses and removed himself from the car before he collapsed under the surge.

They had to find his wife. He wasn't going to sit around waiting for CSU to do their job or the cops to stroll around town, hoping they find her. He knew exactly who had taken her. "We need to go knock on Dean Rockefeller's door."

He opened Dylan's back passenger door and slid in.

"I can't argue with that." Dylan nodded to him as he opened the driver-side door.

Jacq hopped in too.

Gio squeezed Jacq's shoulder.

She took his hand. "We have to find her."

"Yeah, we do."

No more words were exchanged between the three of them. Dylan did call their boss and requested a rush on a search warrant for Dean's house and office. Though Dylan made it clear he wasn't going to wait for the warrant to knock on the man's door.

Less than fifteen minutes later, Dylan pulled into the circle drive in front of the large house that, while not quite mansion-status, was close.

The three of them got out of the car, but Dylan turned to Gio as he came around the front. "You have to stay back."

"This is my wife we're talking about."

"Exactly. And you're on desk duty. But mostly I need this to remain calm." Dylan pointed at his wife. "I'm tempted to make you stay back too." She shot him a cheesy grin that fell flat.

Gio leaned back against the car and crossed his arms. "Go have your friendly conversation."

"I'm going to find your wife." Dylan gripped Gio's arm briefly before turning to the front door.

Standing back was a slow death, but Dylan was right, Gio was bound to say something unhelpful if he went to that door.

Dylan knocked.

Gio prayed. *God, please help us find Morgan. Protect her. Hold her while I can't. Remind her of Your presence. Give Dylan and Jacq wisdom in whatever conversation happens right now.*

Dylan knocked again.

Gio inspected the front of the house. Morgan wasn't here. Dean probably took her to some place that didn't show up on known records.

A curtain in a far window fluttered.

Morgan?

No. It was a little girl with dark hair.

"Jacq!"

She pivoted.

He pointed to the window, but the girl was gone. Had he actually seen her?

Jacq came to his side while Dylan knocked again. "What was it?"

"I thought I saw a girl."

"Does Dean have any kids?"

Gio shrugged. "Might be worth finding out."

Dylan walked back toward them. "No answer. Let's get the warrant and then just bust the door down."

"She's not here." Gio looked up at the window, but there was no sign of a little girl. "And if she isn't, Dean won't be either."

Morgan stood at the back wall of the room and stared out the large windows at the setting sun. The mountain ridges seemed familiar, but didn't all of the Smoky Mountains look the same? Or was she actually close to home?

The lock turned, the door opened, and Dean walked in.

She crossed her arms. "Come to release me?"

He snorted a laugh. "Not hardly." He closed the door behind him and strode toward her.

He had changed from the button-up and slacks he'd been wearing earlier in the day and now wore jeans and a T-shirt that fit snuggly across his muscular chest. No doubt in an effort to remind her how powerful he was, but she wasn't going to fall for that.

When he came close, she moved away.

"Playing hard to get."

"I'm done playing games. You can forget it."

Dean grasped her arm, yanked her back, and pinned her against the wall.

She swallowed. *God, keep my courage up. Help me fight him.*

Dean ran his hand along her face and down to her shoulder. "Then don't play, just let me love you." He leaned toward her mouth.

She turned her head, causing his face to go into her hair.

He smacked the wall beside her. "Angel, what on earth?"

"My name isn't Angel."

He gripped her chin and turned her face toward his. "You've never refused me in the past."

"Like I ever had a choice before. If I'd fought you then, Ronan would have done worse. I'm a survivalist. I do what it takes to survive to see another day. But I won't willingly break my vows to my husband."

Dean wrapped his fingers around her neck but didn't squeeze. "You'd rather die?"

"You don't want to kill me."

She fought to keep her heart rate slow. She didn't want him to know how afraid she was. Dying wasn't an option. What she wanted was to go home to Gio.

Dean slid his hand up beneath her chin, holding her head still, and planted his lips on hers.

She tightened her mouth and tried to move her head away. He was too strong. But she would fight with everything she had.

With all her strength, she pushed his body away, then drove her knee up fast and hard.

He yelped and doubled over, but not without grabbing her arm. He threw her onto the bed. His face grimaced with pain, but he charged at her. She tried to push herself away from him, but he caught her and climbed on top of her, pinning her hands down.

"So if I won't surrender willingly you're going to rape me?"

He hovered above her. "I would never."

"Isn't that what you're doing right now? It's all you've ever done in the times I remember. I didn't choose you when you threw money down on the nightstand."

"You always acted like you wanted it."

"You paid for a good time. I gave you a good time so I wouldn't end up beaten or dead. You're a bigger fool than I thought if you believed any different."

He released her hand and slapped her.

Her cheek stung, but a memory came rushing back.

This wasn't the first time Dean Rockefeller had slapped her. That had happened not long after she'd come to live with him. He had gotten her clean and given her a room much like this one. But she'd snuck out. She'd only been looking for a snack. Wasn't it supposed to be her home too? He'd been doing something—what, she couldn't remember—and he was mad. The memory became fuzzy except for the sting of her cheek; she'd talked back. Her mouth had always gotten her in trouble.

Dean lifted himself from the bed and straightened his T-shirt. "You will change your mind. You will choose better next time."

"I will choose what is right. And you will never be that." She was playing with fire. But she didn't care.

He glared at her before going around to the nightstand. He pulled out the snack food he told her was there before and carried it out of the room, slamming the door behind him. The lock turned.

Her stomach growled. Apparently, he was going to starve her into submission. She'd survive, even if she hadn't eaten since breakfast nearly twelve hours ago. At least he hadn't raped her.

Chapter Eighteen

Late that evening, Gio sank back into the couch in the field-office breakroom. He was sick of twiddling his thumbs, but he didn't know what else to do. *God, where is she? Is she safe? Has he ...*

Gio needed to not think about the possibilities, but they kept bombarding his mind. He knew too much. Dean was a man who got what he wanted and was willing to pay for sex. This was not someone who was going to leave her alone.

Leaning forward, Gio dropped his head in his hands. Exhaustion had overtaken his body and mind, but there was no way he was going to be able to sleep tonight.

The warrant they'd been fighting for all day had been rejected once again. No one wanted to touch Dean Rockefeller. They didn't have enough "proof" he was involved. The trace evidence from Gio's SUV was still being processed, and it could be tomorrow before they heard anything. Of course, tomorrow was only about an hour away.

They contacted every business in the strip mall where the vehicle had been found, but not one had surveillance that caught anything helpful.

It was a good thing he didn't have a glass in his hand. He'd throw it. Instead, he chucked his cane against the wall before a wave of grief consumed him.

He'd fought to free her, had promised to keep her safe, but he'd failed. Once again, she was imprisoned by a man with evil intentions.

God?

Gio ran his hands into his hair. His arms had never felt as empty as they did now.

The door to the breakroom creaked slightly, but Gio didn't lift his head.

"Crespi?" His boss, Warren Bridges, came into the room and picked up Gio's cane before sitting on the couch perpendicular to Gio.

Gio finally looked up.

"How are you holding together?"

"Barely." He took the cane his boss offered.

"I believe it. We've got your back and will do everything we can to find her. Maybe you should go home for the night, though."

Gio shook his head. That was the last thing he could handle right now.

"Then sleep here on the couch, but you need rest. I'm not going to keep you completely out of this investigation, but I want you to understand you are to go nowhere near Dean Rockefeller for any reason whatsoever."

Heat jetted through Gio's bloodstream. "But, sir—"

Warren raised his hand. "No buts. You're on limited duty as it is. It's as much for Morgan's safety as yours, and the rest of the team's."

Gio punched the seat beside him.

"I know."

"You didn't sideline Dylan when Jacq was taken."

"Don't compare."

"How can I not? He'd been shot, if you remember correctly."

"Yes, but barely. I'm not changing my mind. The wife of an FBI agent has been kidnapped. We will stop at nothing until she is found."

Gio nodded. "I know, but—"

"Listen, I'm not sending you home. You are helpful here, but right now I need you to think like the excellent investigator that you are, not a husband." Warren paused and softened his voice. "Your job typically is to be liaison to the family. This time, you and Jacq *are* the family. What would you tell someone else whose wife had been kidnapped in a similar situation?"

"To pray. But I know way more than most of the families know."

"True. What do you know about this situation that you can grab hold of to give you hope?"

"He's not going to kill her. At least not right away."

Warren nodded and opened his mouth, but before he could speak Gio cut him off.

"There are things worse than death. I don't know if she'll be able to come back from what he could do to her."

Warren rested his hand on Gio's shoulder. "We keep praying."

Gio nodded. His soul was in a constant state of prayer—if by prayer one meant pleading with groans that couldn't be expressed in words.

First thing Monday morning, Dylan, with Jacq and Matt by his side, entered the hospital where Dean Rockefeller had his office. They'd staked out his home and the hospital overnight, but while there had been no activity at the house other than a few lights going on and off, Dean had been spotted walking into his office at eight a.m.

If only they had a warrant.

But they would talk to him, hopefully corner him, and get him to say something incriminating. It's all they needed to get a judge to sign off on the warrant.

Dylan opened the door and held it for his partners.

He'd intended to bring Gio along, despite what Warren had said, and leave his friend in the car listening on the wire. Warren had roped Gio into something else when they were leaving, though, so the plan had been quashed. It was almost as if Warren had anticipated their plan. He probably had. He was a supervisory agent for a reason.

Matt pointed down a hallway. "This way."

At a reception desk they identified themselves and asked for Dr. Rockefeller.

"He's with a patient right now, but he can speak with you in just a few minutes. Please wait here."

Dylan sighed. Hopefully, Dean wouldn't just bolt. But then again, it might be suspicious enough to get that warrant.

Jacq closed her eyes as she leaned against the desk.

"Are you okay?"

"Have any antacids?"

Dylan shook his head.

Matt tilted his head to the side as he studied Jacq. "Are you pregnant?"

Dylan glared at him. "Why on earth would you ask that?"

"So yes?" Matt chuckled. "Jacq's been sick to her stomach for about two weeks straight. I know how these things work. My ex was terribly sick when she was pregnant, but it came and went like it's doing for you."

Jacq said, "Don't tell anyone yet."

"I wouldn't. And congratulations. But you do work with a lot of investigators. You won't be able to hide it for very long."

She shrugged and stepped closer to Dylan.

He put his arm around her.

Jacq said, "Now we really can't tell Gio, but I hate keeping it from him."

Dylan nodded. Before they could say anything else, Dean walked down the hallway in his white doctor's coat.

Dylan's muscles twitched at the sight of the man's cocky face. He wanted to smash his fist into that arrogant smile.

Dean approached. "Hello. To what do I owe the pleasure?" He stretched out his hand to Matt. "I don't believe we've met."

Matt did not shake his hand. Instead, he raised his badge. "I'm Special Agent Matt Olsen with the FBI. We'd like to ask you a few questions. May we speak in your office?"

"FBI? Are you two FBI as well?" He stared Dylan down.

"We are." Dylan showed his badge. "Special Agent Dylan Harris. And Special Agent Jacq Harris."

"Right this way." Dean led them into an office where he sat behind the desk. "I can't imagine why the FBI would want to talk to me. I am still willing to donate to your charity; it's just a matter of working the books to see how much I can contribute."

Dylan would have liked to spit in his face and tell him they didn't want any of his filthy money, but he kept his mouth shut.

Jacq's voice came out tight. "That's not what we're here to talk about. I'd like to know if you know where Morgan Crespi is."

"Who?" The man didn't miss a beat in lying.

Jacq took two quick steps forward, but Dylan caught her before she got any closer to Dean. Dylan shouldn't have let her come. He and Matt could have handled this.

Matt took charge. "Dr. Rockefeller, our fellow agent's wife has gone missing, and since you had a negative interaction with her a short time ago, we'd like to discuss that with you."

"I don't know what I can say, but I won't be saying anything more until my lawyer arrives."

"I assure you, sir, this is not an interrogation. We just have a few questions we'd like honest answers to."

"All the same, I'd like my lawyer present." Dean picked up the phone receiver off his desk. "Janet, please contact my lawyer and have him come down as soon as possible. Thank you." He replaced the receiver in its cradle and sat back in his chair, lacing his fingers across his middle. "Now we wait."

Dylan nudged Jacq and indicated with his head that she should sit. She read his mind and did so, but Dylan and Matt remained standing. And they would continue to stand until the lawyer arrived.

Shifting from foot to foot while they waited was unavoidable no matter how hard Dylan tried. Matt seemed to be able to stand without moving, but Dylan hated wasting time staring down a slimebag like Dean Rockefeller. After ten minutes of silence, Dean started shuffling through a stack of charts on the side of his desk.

Dylan was surprised at how many files he had sitting there. The rest of the office was immaculate. The bookshelf along the wall to Dylan's left held copies of medical books. He took a step closer and inspected the titles. They all had to do with internal medicine, which made sense for an internist. Something nagged at his gut. He'd half expected find an oddity on the shelf, but there was nothing. Just books and an off-white statue of an angel.

"Are you Catholic?"

"No. My wife gave that to me."

Dylan nodded and tried to pull information about Dean's wife from his memory, but they hadn't found out much.

"Tell me about her while we wait."

Dean met Dylan's gaze. The man had a strange look in his eyes. It wasn't grief, or was it? "I'm not going to talk about anything until my lawyer arrives. I don't want you spinning what I say out of context."

Dylan raised his hands. "Just trying to make small talk."

Dean shook his head and dove back into his charts.

Another ten minutes of total silence passed before the door to the office opened. Janet poked her head in. "Your lawyer is here."

Dean shut his files and restacked the pile. "Send him in."

Chad walked in and locked eyes with Dylan. The world seemed to pause. His brother represented this liar? With the connections Chad had to other traffickers in the past, Dylan shouldn't be surprised, but it didn't sit well.

Dean came around the desk and extended his hand to Chad. "It's good to see you, Mr. Harris. Thank you for coming down here on such short notice."

Chad shook his hand but glanced over at Dylan again. "Why is the FBI here? Is this trafficking related?"

Dean snapped back. "No. What on earth? Why would you ask that?"

Dylan stared at Dean. That was an awfully harsh reaction. Was that indicative of involvement?

Before Dylan could jump on it, Matt said, "We have a few questions regarding an interaction Dr. Rockefeller had with Morgan last week."

Chad's gaze darted between them all, then turned completely toward Dean. "I'm sorry, Dr. Rockefeller, but I'm going to have to excuse myself from representing you in this matter. Morgan is a close family friend, and I am not able to be impartial here."

Chad's breathing increased, and he stepped closer to Dean, pointing at his chest. "And if you had anything to do with it. You will go down."

Dylan crossed to him, put his hand on his brother's chest, and pushed him away from Dean. "Let's talk outside." Dylan turned back to Dean. "We aren't done. Find another lawyer immediately. Olsen, stay with him."

Matt nodded.

Dylan ushered Chad and Jacq out of Dean's office.

As soon as they were out of earshot, Chad turned to Dylan. "Did he take Morgan? Because I swear, I will rake him through the coals."

Chad owed Morgan for helping save his daughter from traffickers planning to squeeze him into compliance.

Dylan nodded. "But we don't have any proof. It's possible it was someone else, but we know from Morgan he's involved in trafficking at least as a john, and she was terrified when she ran into him last week."

"How do we nail him? What can I do to help?"

"I'm not sure yet. But maybe you can dig up whatever you can about this guy. Anything that might give us reason for a warrant. And any other properties that might be connected to him. We know he has a house in the mountains he's kept Morgan at in the past—that's probably where he has her now—but we haven't had any luck yet."

Chad clapped his brother's shoulder. "I'll find it." He pulled Dylan into a rare hug.

"Thanks, Chad." Dylan released his brother.

Before leaving, Chad gave Jacq a quick hug too.

She slid her hand into Dylan's. "I still can't get over how much he's changed in the last six months."

"I'm just glad it didn't take losing Anna to get him there."

Jacq nodded. "Can we leave Olsen here and go do something else?"

Dylan's phone rang before he could answer. "Agent Harris."

A quiet voice responded. "Hello? This is Peggy. We spoke the other day about my son and his cousin."

"I can barely understand you, ma'am."

"Sorry, but I don't want them to hear me. They are here right now, and I'm getting a sick idea about the supposed kittens they've been transporting. Please come quick."

"We'll be right there." He pulled Jacq along. He'd explain in the car.

Morgan turned the faucet off and wiped her mouth. Dean may not have given her any food but at least he hadn't turned the water off to the connecting bathroom, so she had plenty to drink. How long could someone survive on just water?

Dean had come in briefly that morning to see if she'd changed her mind. She'd spit in his face. That's when he'd killed the power to the room. Once she knew he was gone, she'd set to work trying to find a way of escaping. There wasn't one. The windows were impossible to open. The lock held fast on the door. She hadn't given up but had run out of options. Still her brain was thinking through the room. There had to be a way out. If there was, she'd find it. She'd rather die in the woods than at Dean's hands.

She went back to the bedroom. Even if he hadn't cut water, no electricity meant no TV, no lights. There were no books either. She'd tried to do the stupid puzzle books in the drawer of the nightstand but without a pencil it was pointless.

She just wanted Gio. She picked up a pillow and climbed onto the bed. Sitting up at the headboard, she hugged the pillow as tight as possible. She'd been trapped in this room for more than twenty hours. Gio would be going nuts worrying about her. Her heart hurt for him. God had knit their souls together, and neither of them could be complete without the other anymore.

"Help him, Jesus. Help Gio know I'm okay. Help him find me. Help me get back to him."

The tune of a worship song Gio had written started dancing in her mind. She leaned her head against the headboard and sang softly. She normally sang the harmony to the song while Gio sang the melody. It wasn't the same without him. But the praise of the song drew her to the Lord. And as much as she wanted to be with Gio, she wanted to be with the Lord more. He found her in this lonely room. And while Gio's arms couldn't be around her, she felt the Lord's surrounding her heart and holding her safe.

Dean could break her body and maybe even her spirit, but he wouldn't be able to break her soul. That belonged to Jesus, and He would never let her go.

She basked in His presence as the words seemed to build up a fortress around her, protecting her from the evil forces that permeated Dean's house. She hadn't noticed it before, but as she sang praises to the Lord, light filled her mind making the darkness evident. There was something very dark about this place.

A shiver coursed through her body. *God, what evil is here?* She was almost afraid to ask, but despite her hunger, she felt stronger.

Deep in her soul she sensed the Lord's nudging. **Remember.** "Remember what?"

She leaned in spiritually. "Jesus, help me remember what I need to know. Give me wisdom. I trust You to guide me."

An image came to her mind. It was fuzzy at first, but she saw a house, much like this one, but different. The view out the window was the ocean, not the mountains. Miami.

What happened in Miami?

She closed her eyes and let the memory return.

Morgan woke late one night, hungry. She rolled over in bed, but Dean wasn't there. Had he never come to bed? Why was her mind so cloudy? Her stomach so hungry?

She climbed out of bed and grabbed her robe. She could get used to this luxurious life. For the last few months Dean had treated her like his queen. She didn't mind him calling her Angel if he cared for her like this.

She padded out into the hallway, but something was amiss. Loud music came from the living room. Glancing around the corner, she noticed a few guys milling about. Before she could look further, she heard arguing coming from Dean's office. She snuck closer and listened.

A man said, "You promised to sell me one of the girls."

Dean's voice bit back. "I'm not selling girls to just be killed. What happened to the last one?"

"Look, man, she got sick. What was I supposed to do?"

"Get her treated. Bring her to me. You don't kill her." Cuss words filled the rest of Dean's sentence.

What on earth? Selling girls? Killing them?

Dean continued, "The price has gone up for you. These girls have a lot more money in them than you can produce. I won't see some beautiful woman floating in the bay because you can't keep them healthy."

"Aren't you the one that always says there's more where that came from?"

"Tell me why she was sick. Was it an overdose?"

Silence fell.

"You're done. No heroin. Out of my house. I won't do business with you ever again."

Her stomach churned. Was she in the pit of another trafficker? But he wasn't selling her. Why would she care?

It didn't sit right. This was wrong whether it was her or someone else. Yet she couldn't rock the boat. She couldn't risk losing favor in Dean's eyes. Too much was at stake.

The memory faded. Morgan was missing part of it. There was more. But she couldn't grab hold of it again. It was gone.

However, regardless of what detail was missing, she was confident of the truth now.

It would explain why Ronan had been so afraid of him, why Ronan let Dean control him. Dean Rockefeller was a trafficker. And not just any trafficker. An influential, deep-pocketed trafficker.

Chapter Nineteen

Gio took the cup of coffee Aliza offered him. Ten o'clock in the morning, yet he was a complete zombie. He hadn't been able to sleep at all last night. He might have dozed off a few times, but it wasn't sufficient.

Aliza perched her hip against the corner of his desk. "I'm not going to tell you to sleep, even though the motherly nature in me wants to. Instead, I'm going to tell you what Jacq just called to tell me."

He leaned back in his seat, more awake at the notion there was news from their teammates.

She told him about Dean's stonewall, Chad's arrival, and the phone call from Peggy about the cousins.

"They can't go work that case right now. What about Morgan?"

Aliza reached forward and gripped his forearm. "Gio, we are doing everything we can. Matt is staying with Dean. We will get answers from him and follow him back to wherever Morgan is if we can."

"It's not enough."

"I know. I'm sorry."

"It's not your fault."

Aliza narrowed her eyes. "It's not yours either."

"I didn't keep her safe."

"You did everything in your capability to do so."

"It wasn't enough."

"Of course not. You aren't enough. Only Jesus is, and you know it."

The words hit like an anvil to the head. Gio could never be enough. Only Jesus. He nodded slowly.

Aliza smacked his arm. "That's my friend. Now, caffeine up. No matter what Warren says, I'm taking you in the van to run the op. Let's go."

The first fieldwork since he was shot. He swung his pack on his back.

Warren's voice boomed through the bullpen. "You are not to get out of the van."

Gio tossed him a sloppy salute. "Yes, sir."

Fifteen minutes later, Gio and Aliza sat in the command van half a block from the house where Justin and Ron were sleeping, according to Peggy. Aliza was working hand in hand with the SWAT leader to run the op. These men were considered dangerous, so the plan was for Jacq and Dylan to go in with SWAT on their sixes.

Gio was nervous for his friends, but he wasn't sure why. Dylan had seemed to take extra care helping Jacq put her Kevlar on. They shouldn't still be going on missions together now that they were married. But Jacq's current goal was only to stay on until the end of the year, then she'd work at the mission full-time with Morgan.

With Morgan.

He pleaded with God again for his wife's safety and for direction in finding her.

It was a good thing he wasn't in charge. He was too distracted. Gio kept his eyes on the monitors in front of him.

Jacq and Dylan walked up to the front door and gave a slight knock. The door opened and Jacq ushered a portly older woman out of the house and back behind a squad car. *Good, Jacq's not in the line of fire.*

Glock at the ready, Dylan ran down the short flight of steps to the lowest level of the split-level home. Two men slept in the trashed family room, one sprawled on a twin bed, the other on a futon.

The SWAT guys came in and filled the space. An officer was ready to grab each man, when Dylan announced their presence.

Both men jumped up but were slammed back down to their beds and cuffed.

Dylan walked over to Justin and shoved a photo of the children in his face. "Where are these kids?"

"How am I supposed to know?"

"You're the one who brought them here from Miami. I personally saw you on that plane. You aren't getting out of this, but you tell us where the kids are, and maybe we'll cut you a little slack." *But it better be nothing more than a single-day sentence reduction. You deserve to rot.* How Dylan wished he could say all of what he was thinking.

"I'm just a lackey. They don't tell me where they go. I do what I'm told."

"How much money did you make bringing those two into the States?"

"I don't know what you're talking about. I was just a ... a host to travel with two minors. I didn't do nothing wrong."

"Hogwash. You're a trafficker. These two were kidnapped in Honduras days before you were photographed bringing them into the States. Do you really think your lies are going to get you out of this one?"

The man didn't argue. His mouth opened like he might try to, but apparently he was at a loss for a defense.

The cousin said, "He's gonna kill us."

"Keep your mouth shut."

Dylan put his hand on Justin's shoulder and pressed his thumb into his collarbone. "Who's going to kill you?"

He shook his head.

Dylan leaned over and got in the guy's face. "You talk, and it will only help your cause. Don't talk, and you're looking at some pretty stiff charges and extradition to Honduras. Now, I'm not sure, but I don't think their prison accommodations are as cushy as they are here in the States."

The guy looked down, and his eyes moved as if he was contemplating what to do. Then he shook his head and met Dylan's gaze. "A third-world prison is probably better than what *he*'d do to me if I ratted him out."

"The person you transported the kids for?"

Justin nodded. "He's powerful, and you don't want to be on his bad side. So take me in; do your worst. It'll be Candyland by comparison."

Dylan silently groaned and lifted the man from the bed to escort him out. He should be happy with the confession, but knowing there was someone worse out there …

Dylan asked, "Does this guy already have those two kids?"

"I don't want to answer any more questions."

"Just tell me if I can save the children."

Justin stopped at the steps and turned to Dylan. "They're gone, man. Even if he still has them, which he probably doesn't, they've already partied hard."

Dylan almost threw up. Children, young ones, sold for sex. It was sick and straight-up evil. He wanted to run all the way to Harper and never let her leave his sight. If anyone ever touched her, they'd wish they'd never been born.

Morgan rolled over in the bed. Her stomach ached. As best she could tell, it had to be Tuesday afternoon now. The sun was high in the sky for the third time since she'd woken up in Dean's cozy prison. She'd slept too much in the last twenty-four hours, but she didn't know what else to do. All of her energy was gone. Without food, she felt like she was withering.

She pushed herself up. Without a doubt, Dean would come in this evening and tempt her with food to act on his desires. How was she going to stay strong? She was so weak.

Lifting her voice again, she sang a song to the Lord. Praise was her weapon. Christ was her strength. *Fill me with Your presence, Lord. Help me. I believe You are with me. I believe You will rescue me one way or another.*

She continued to sing until she reached the end of the worship song. Then she sat in the silence of the Lord's presence. He was with her.

A few minutes passed before the lock on the door clicked. Morgan's heart rate shot skyward. Was Dean here already? She didn't want to fight. Not right now. The nagging idea that giving in to him would get her food tempted her. *No! I will not.*

The door opened. But Duke didn't enter. A young woman—no, a girl—came in and gave her a weak smile.

Morgan stared at the teenager who stared back at her.

The girl finally said, "Hi." She came the rest of the way into the room. A cloth bag hung from her shoulder.

"Hi." Morgan considered the teenager. Was she one of Dean's girls? Did he actively traffic? Her memory only remembered him as a middle man, but maybe there was more. No telling who else was in this huge house.

"He really did find you." A beautiful accent flowered the teenager's speech.

Morgan nodded. Something about her seemed familiar, but she couldn't place it. Did she know her?

"He said something that made me think he hasn't fed you at all." She dropped the bag from her shoulder to her hand. "So I brought you some food."

"Really? Why would you do that?"

The girl came closer. "Because ... honestly, I don't know. It won't end well for me if he finds out. But I hate him, so I kind of don't care anymore. He's been looking for you as long as I've been here. And I ..."

Morgan slid off the bed and gripped the girl's upper arm. "Thank you."

The teenager shrugged. She met Morgan's eyes and smiled.

Again, she felt like she knew her. "Have we met before?"

The teenager shook her head.

"What's your name?"

"Bianca."

"My name is Morgan." The name Bianca was familiar, but why? "Nicoletta. You're Nicoletta's sister."

"I had a sister named Nicoletta. But she's gone. Dead, I'm sure."

Morgan took the sides of Bianca's face in her hands. "No, she's not. She's safe. She thought you were dead and escaped because her traffickers said they'd killed you."

"Escaped?"

Morgan nodded. "Can you help me escape? We can go to her."

"But ... Dean."

An alert sounded in the hallway outside the room.

Bianca's eyes widened. "He'll ... if he finds me in here ... I can't escape today. I'll be fine. But I will help you if I can."

"You can't stay here. I will get you out of here."

"I have to stay. Trust me. For now." Bianca shoved the bag of food into Morgan's hands. "Hide it, don't eat until after he leaves you for the night." She pivoted and darted out the door, locking it behind her.

Morgan reeled. She'd found Nicoletta's sister, but why would she not want to leave? Morgan would have to escape and find a way to bring the team back and save Bianca.

Morgan glanced at the bag in her hand. She needed to hide it immediately. The bag crinkled when squished so she couldn't hide it near the bed just in case Dean decided he wasn't above taking matters into his own hands, so to speak.

She ran into the bathroom and hid it behind the towels on the bottom shelf of the little linen closet. She sped back into the bedroom and onto the bed, making it back just in time for the door to open again.

Dean's cocky smile met her.

She hugged the pillow and scooted away from him.

"That's not the greeting I was hoping for." He closed the door behind him and strode to the side of the bed. "Come here, Angel."

"Nope. I'm not your pet to obey your beck and call." She stood on the opposite side of the bed and tossed the pillow down.

"I just want to offer you some dinner."

"At what cost?"

Half of his mouth curled up. "I think you know the answer to that. Come to me, and you get a salad. Play along for a few minutes, and I'll give you a sandwich. Pleasure me, and I'll even give you dessert."

She crossed her arms.

She had food from Bianca and didn't need his food. But maybe she could play the game to gather information. She'd never pleasure this man again. Even if he went back on his promise of a salad, maybe she could learn something helpful before she escaped. Because she would escape.

He stepped around the end of the bed and opened his arms to her. "Come to me. Where's my girl who loved to snuggle?"

She wanted to run over and kick him where it hurt again, but instead she slowly moved toward him. Deliberating every step. She didn't want to betray Gio, but she needed to know his involvement in trafficking. Was he a pimp? A middle man. A dealer? Why did he have Bianca? Did he rape her? Hadn't Nicoletta said her sister was only fifteen? Was he raping an underage girl?

Morgan stopped shy of his arms. Her heart pounded in her chest. *Stay in control, Morgan.* She didn't need to give herself a pep talk. She needed to pray. *Jesus? Guide my words and actions. Help me.*

Dean reached out and stroked her hair. She fought the shudder that wanted to course through her. Instead, she stepped closer. Bile rose in her throat.

Reaching out she touched him but didn't walk into his arms. She turned him and pushed him to a seated position on the bed. It gave her a slight feeling of control over him, even though she knew he could overpower her with one move.

His smile reached as broad as possible, and he rested his hands on her hips. "Here's my girl."

She swallowed the urge to dry heave. "I have a question for you."

"Anything." Did he really think she'd give in to his demands for a piece of pie?

"My memories seem to be coming back."

"The good ones, I hope."

"Maybe. I do remember a conversation I overheard once between you and a guy with a raspy voice. Something about selling girls, not wanting them dosed with heroin or killed. Tell me. How deeply are you involved in trafficking of human flesh? Because it seems to me you're more than just a connoisseur."

His facial features tightened as did his grip on her hips. "You *would* ask that."

"And I did. I want answers."

"I have my own business ventures. They are none of your concern."

"You want me to choose to be with you. I'm not going into anything blind ever again."

His gaze narrowed. "Having a change of heart?"

"I'm hungry."

He pulled her closer to him. "Then lie with me, and we can talk details over dinner."

When his hands started to wander across her body, Morgan pushed back and slapped him across the cheek as hard as she could.

Dean's head jerked to the side, and he shoved her across the room.

Flying backward, she slammed into the dresser. She crumbled to the ground, pain radiating through her back.

He stood and marched toward her. Grabbing her hair, he lifted her to her feet. "How dare you." He chucked her onto the bed. "Why do you have to be so ornery? Don't you understand I want to give you the life you've always dreamed of?"

"You can't give me that."

"You want children?"

Pain pinched her heart. What could he know about that?

"I can see it in your eyes. You may not remember what we talked about, but I know the deepest desire of your heart. How you regret that abortion. How you long to hold babies in your arms. We can have that. We have."

She crawled to the head of the bed as far from him as possible. If she had a baby with him, she would never have left. Never. She buried her head in a pillow and hummed, tuning out every word he said.

The door slammed, and he was gone.

The emotions released, and she soaked the pillow. He hadn't denied the trafficking accusations, but neither had he admitted his type of involvement. She'd get the truth. But hopefully it wouldn't require too much of her.

Chapter Twenty

A DOOR SLAMMED AND Bianca jumped. She had noodled around in the kitchen while Dean had been in with Morgan—Angel as he called her. Bianca's emotions were all over the place. Why did she feel so weird about him being in there with Morgan? He'd been looking for her for years, and Bianca hated him, but it still felt so weird to know he was with someone else.

She scrubbed the island counter with more vigor.

Dean stormed into the kitchen.

Bianca tried to keep her body in check. *Don't react. Don't react.*

Dean yanked a stool out from under the island and sat down. She lifted her head, scared to meet his eyes, but doing so anyway.

His cheek was red. Had Morgan slapped him?

Bianca fought the smile that wanted to creep up from deep inside her. She'd love to slap the man too. But what had he done to Morgan in response? Bianca's urge to smile vanished.

Play the part, Bianca. She hated having to give herself these stupid little pep talks, but it was the only way to do what she needed to survive.

She tossed the rag at the sink and retrieved an icepack from the freezer. Strolling over to Dean, she gingerly touched his cheek while putting her body against his. Distracting him physically always calmed his rage.

"Can't have that showing at work tomorrow."

He pulled her close and let her place the icepack on his cheek. "Indeed. I'm not sure how to break her this time. That stupid husband has rotted her brain."

"She doesn't care about all you want to give her?" Bianca wanted to throw up at the thought. She didn't blame Morgan for wanting nothing to do with Dean.

"She doesn't believe me about Aurora."

How did Morgan not believe him? Aurora looked just like her. Bianca's brain searched for something that would help Morgan, even if it seemed like it was in Dean's favor. "Why don't you prove it to her? Take her to town tomorrow. I'll have Aurora all ready." If he brought Morgan there maybe once she saw Aurora, she'd be able to do something to get all three of them away from Dean. There was no way out of this house, but the town one was less secure and, at least, close to civilization.

Dean ran his hands up to Bianca's face. It took all her willpower not to bristle at his touch.

He said, "You are brilliant. She won't be able to deny me then. But the house in town?"

She ran her hands across his body, hating herself for knowing exactly how to make him listen to her. "Yes, of course. You can stay here tonight. I'll get Aurora all dolled up and make sure the house is spotless."

His hands coursed down her back. "But then I won't have you by my side tonight to make me feel better about Angel being so stubborn."

She wanted to cry, wanted to shove him off the stool so he fell flat on his back. But an angry Dean was a dangerous Dean.

Drawing her even closer, he kissed her neck. "I guess we'll just have to make do now and see one another again tomorrow."

"I need to leave to be home when Aurora gets there after school."

"She can wait. This won't take long."

Bianca squeezed her eyes shut, trying to override the tears that filled her vision.

How was it Tuesday evening already? Gio pushed his plate away, food barely eaten. He couldn't eat, not knowing where his wife was. What if she hadn't had any food?

Dylan's mom folded her napkin and set it on her dining-room table. "I'm so sorry, Gio."

The dinner had been stilted, no one knowing what to say. It had taken a lot of convincing on Dylan's part to get Gio to come, but getting out of the office was a good thing. Sort of.

Gio folded his hands on the table. "I'm sorry; I can't eat. The food is delicious. I just ..."

Mrs. Harris lifted her hand. "You don't need to explain. I can't even imagine how you're feeling. You all sit here or in the living room. I'll cover your plate and put it in the fridge, if you change your mind."

"Thank you."

Mrs. Harris and her husband cleared the table while Gio, Dylan, and Jacq went to the living room.

Harper, who had snuck off earlier to play, jumped up from the blocks on the floor and walked to Gio. She slipped her little hand into his and walked with him to the couch, climbing on his lap once he'd sat. He held her close.

How was this three-year-old so perceptive?

"It'll be okay, Unkwa Gio."

"Thanks, kiddo."

She wrapped her little arms around his neck, and he hugged her in return. She then hopped down and returned to her toys.

Other than the clacking of toys, silence fell in the room. They were all exhausted. At least they had two more traffickers in custody after yesterday's arrest. Those two may still be keeping their mouths shut about their evil boss, but they'd confessed to helping transport kids from different locations. Justin had not been out of the country, but instead had picked the children up at the airport from another trafficker.

There were too many moving parts to catch everyone. But Gio hadn't given up on getting the guy to crack on his boss and tell them where the kids might be. He hated the idea of putting a trafficker into witness protection, but Justin was small potatoes compared to the guy he worked for. In an interview earlier today, Gio had managed to get Justin to tell him the boss had an elaborate organization selling women and children across the globe. He kept children in his basement for parties before selling them off to the highest bidder.

Gio had built a rapport with Justin through a series of interviews in the last thirty-six hours, but he swore to Gio he wouldn't tell him anything about the boss's identity. It was too risky.

Jacq sat down next to Gio, yanking him out of his thoughts. She pressed a protein bar into his hand. "You have to eat."

"I can't, Jacq."

"You need to have some strength if—when we find her. You need to be ready to help her work through her trauma."

He opened the bar and nibbled on it.

Satisfied she'd accomplished her task, Jacq took Harper to get ready for bed. Not knowing when something would come in, Jacq and Dylan had decided Monday to have Harper sleep at his parents' until Morgan was home safe.

He forced the protein bar down. But his stomach ached at the food. He really hadn't eaten much at all in the last three days.

What could he do, though? Dean Rockefeller was walking around scot-free. No warrant had been issued. The conversation Matt had finally been able to have with him, once he had a lawyer present, had been completely unproductive. They'd even been ordered by a judge to leave the man alone. Dean still maintained he did not know Morgan Crespi beyond meeting her at the fundraiser a week ago.

Dylan brought Gio a cup of coffee and sat at the other end of the couch with his own mug and scrolled on his phone. Gio stared at nothing.

He'd run out of words to pray. He had faith God was sustaining Morgan, but that didn't remove the pit that had wedged itself in his gut.

A knock sounded on the door. Dylan rose and opened it. "Matt. Aliza."

Matt said, "Hey, we found something interesting I thought you might like to know."

Gio glanced up. He was grateful his friends kept working the case without quitting.

Aliza took a seat next to Gio on the couch. Putting her hand on his back, she asked, "You said you thought you saw a girl in Dean's window, right?"

He nodded.

"Well, guess what? He has a daughter. Most likely you weren't seeing things."

"Really? Do you have a photo?"

Aliza shook her head. "It would seem he's very private about her. No social media. The private school she attends doesn't post pictures of their students' faces anywhere because they have a lot of families who want the privacy."

"Why does it matter then?"

"Just a piece of information we've been able to gather. She lives at the house in town. A car brings her home but leaves immediately, then picks her up in the morning. Thing is, Dean's only been home once since Sunday."

Gio smirked. "And how would you know that?"

Aliza glanced at Matt.

He shot Gio a goofy grin. "Maybe a little unauthorized surveillance."

"No wonder he hasn't been to the house." Gio laughed, though it was tense and rueful even to his ears. "Anyone else coming and going?"

"Yesterday, a car left the house for about three hours before coming back just before the daughter arrived home from her after-school activities. It wasn't Dean. Didn't get a clear look at the driver, but it appeared to be a petite woman."

"The mystery wife perhaps?" Gio offered.

"Maybe. We haven't been able to find out anything else about her. She doesn't have a Tennessee license, so we could have her pulled over. But I'm not sure that would be the play we need."

Gio shook his head. "His wife and daughter aren't going to be the way to get to this guy. We need a tracker on him. Get him to take us to that mountain house."

Dylan, who leaned against the piano, chuckled. "Maybe we need to 'drop' one of your tracking tags into his car."

"That would be convenient, but the range isn't great."

Dylan shrugged. "I can just imagine explaining that one to the judge. 'Yeah, so my buddy's tag got stuck under the car. I have no idea how it was duct taped there.'"

Gio laughed with his friends. Laughing was a strange sensation in the middle of his heartache, but it felt good for his soul.

"So who's willing to take the fall?" Matt asked.

Gio shook his head. "You guys can't do that."

Aliza put her hand on Gio's shoulder. "Listen, Morgan is way more important than any of our careers. I will risk pretty much anything to save her."

A scared heaviness filled the room as each of them assessed the risk of what they were talking about. As officers of the law, federal agents, they'd be in more trouble for illegally tracking someone than a regular citizen. But what else were they going to do? The longer Morgan was missing, the greater the chance they wouldn't find her alive. If they ever found her at all.

Morgan flushed the wrapper of the granola bar and brushed her teeth. There was always a chance Dean would come back, and for Bianca's sake she didn't want her breath smelling like honey and oats.

She took a long sip of water from the faucet then wiped her face on a towel.

She hardly recognized herself in the mirror. Her eyes were red and bloodshot, sunken and puffy at the same time. *I feel disgusting. Maybe I should shower.* She was still wearing the same clothes she wore to church Sunday morning. She would put her dirty clothes back on. Dean had provided clothes, but she refused to wear any of them.

She prayed Dean wouldn't decide to come back now, not that clothes were enough to stop a man bent on rape, but she'd feel less vulnerable. After undressing, she inspected her back where she'd slammed into the dresser. Blue and purple marks were already showing.

Her outward appearance was nothing to the broken woman staring back at her. How was she ever going to heal if every time she turned around, she faced another moment of trauma?

Tears threatened again. "God, I just want to be free. Is that too much to ask?"

She turned the water on and stepped into the warm stream.

The interaction with Dean played back in her mind. Had she crossed the line in trying to get him to talk? Was that manipulation? Would it ever stop being her way of dealing with situations? *I don't want to be that person any more. But how do I deal with someone trying to manipulate me? Is there another way?*

She lathered her hair, even though she knew it would be a fluffy disaster later. As she rinsed the suds, Dean's comments about her being a mother echoed back in her mind.

She longed to hold a child of her very own. But how could she be a mother? She was a broken mess. How could she help Nicoletta work through her trauma? Morgan would never be enough to love children. Her tears mingled with the water.

"I need You, Jesus. I'm not enough, but You told me You are." Especially in this dark hour, she had to preach the truth to herself. If God ever gave her the opportunity to be a mother, it would be in His timing.

Despite the sobs that gripped her lungs she raised her voice once again in the song Gio had written. The words spoke of the freedom she had in Christ, of how death no longer held onto her, her place was with Christ, and restoration only came through Him.

She sang out "hallelujah" over and over again.

She had a long way to go, but Christ was working in her, and if she got out of here, He would continue to work on her. Children or no children.

Dean couldn't tempt her with lies and false hope. But as Gio's mom had said: hope in Jesus is never false.

Gio raised his cane to throw it across the breakroom, but Dylan caught it and yanked it from his hand.

"I really thought you were past throwing things in anger."

Gio grunted at his friend. It was eleven o'clock Wednesday morning, and there had been no sign of Dean at the hospital or at the house in town.

Jacq hushed them and spoke into the phone. "Yes, I'd like to speak with Dr. Rockefeller." She paused and listened to the person on the other end. "Oh thank you. Do you know when you expect him in?" Another pause. "Thank you so much."

She slid her phone back into her pocket. "He called in sick. Janet said he sounded pretty rough and doesn't expect him in at all the rest of the week."

"Convenient." Dylan groaned.

"Especially for a man who's not home." Gio took a sip of his coffee, his third cup already today. Sleep had once again eluded him last night, and it wasn't because he'd tried to sleep on the breakroom couch again.

Last night, dreams had plagued his mind. He couldn't remember anything specific other than two faces—mostly Morgan, but also a glimpse of the little girl he'd dreamed of before with her same purple headband.

Today he felt numb. Just walking through the motions of life. The anger he'd felt about not being able to drop a tracker in Dean's car had been the strongest emotion he'd felt all day.

Dylan put his hand on Gio's shoulder. "Come on, let's go back to the office and see what we can do legally."

Gio let his friend lead him out of the breakroom and down the hallway. In the office, he sat at his desk. The rest of the team worked at theirs, voices floating back and forth. But Gio didn't hear a single thing they said.

They were closing in on seventy-two hours since she'd been taken. Seventy-two hours—after that mark fewer missing people are found alive.

What if they didn't find her in time? The words hung in his mind. What if? God seemed to nudge him in that direction of thought. But he didn't want to go there. He didn't want to think about it. Could he survive the loss? Sure. But he didn't want to.

In his head, even in his heart, he trusted God had this. However, God's answer wasn't to always fix everything the way someone wanted. His will was bigger than human dreams.

Gio's faith was strong enough to know God was good even when life sucked. But it would be hard to trust Him if Morgan didn't come home.

Oh God, please bring her home. Please.

But what if she doesn't come home? Will you still follow?

I will always follow You, Lord. His heart ached at the question. He would follow God all the days of his life, but he couldn't move on from a loss. Life would never have the same joy Morgan brought.

But she's not your source. You must trust Me.

Gio wrestled with it. Was this what it was like for Jacob to wrestle with God that night so long ago?

Why was it so hard? He wanted to trust the Lord. He wanted to declare to the whole room he trusted God no matter what happened. Yet thinking the thought and feeling it in his soul were not the same thing right now.

But Lord, didn't You bring us together? Was it only for a short time?

Trust me.

Gio paused his thoughts and let the Lord's command flood his mind.

Trust the Lord with all your heart, and lean not on your own understanding. In all *your ways acknowledge Him and He will make straight your paths.*

Gio laid his head on his arms. *I trust You, Lord. Even if You don't bring her home. I submit to You, whatever You choose. We'll walk it together. Whatever path You take me down.*

Chapter Twenty-One

MORGAN STARED AT THE mountains from where she sat on the edge of the bed. Those mountains still looked familiar. Was it possible she wasn't that far from Jacq's property, from the little travel trailer ... from Gio? That's where her heart yearned to be. God had given her a home for the first time in her life. He was going to get her back there, somehow. This was not her end, somehow. God would carry on His good work in her until it was complete, somehow.

The door opened.

She closed her eyes. Part of her hoped it was Bianca, but that was unlikely.

"Good morning, Angel."

Definitely not Bianca. Morgan opened her eyes but didn't respond.

He crossed the room and perched beside her on the edge of the bed.

Containing her fear and disgust, she stayed perfectly still.

"I'm sorry, Angel. I've handled this all wrong. All you want is to be a mother. I intended to tell you our child is nearby, but you've just been so ... unhappy."

Her heart froze mid-beat. Child?

"And I needed you to love me for me. But I see it will have to come the other way around."

She turned her head toward him. *Don't believe him. He's just trying to manipulate you.*

He put his hand on her thigh.

She resisted the flinch and the urge to break every single bone in his hand.

"I'd like to take you to see our child."

"Where are we going?" If he took her from the house, maybe she could get away.

"Into town. I have another house there."

She considered him. Why would he lie to her about this? Did he really think she was so easily swayed? Did he really think her memories were that far gone? Well, they were, but he didn't know that, did he? She would never have forgotten her child. That's ridiculous.

"You are a mother, Angel. Let me prove it to you. Then we can finally be a family."

"You'll take me to meet this child?"

He nodded and ran his hand into her hair, lifting her face close to his. "Yes, and then you will see we belong together."

He stood and offered her his hands.

She took a deep breath and slid hers into his. Was he actually a child trafficker too? Did he find a kid that looks enough like the two of them to pass off as his own? The thought made her sick. But he'd found Bianca, and she looked remarkably like Morgan ... like Dean's wife.

Wife.

Where was the wife? The one who looked so eerily similar to Morgan and Bianca. This man had a type, to say the least.

He let go of one of her hands but maintained a firm grip on the other and led her out of the house and to a garage full of cars. He chose a modest sedan. Expensive but not one of his stand-out-expensive vehicles. This was a blend-in car. Half of the upper class had similar sedans.

Surely the FBI was looking for him, and if she were to guess, there was a good chance this car wasn't even registered in his name. While obsessive, he wasn't stupid. Unfortunately.

Morgan debated the entire drive down the mountain, which took about twice as long as necessary since Dean took every turn he could. And he'd succeeded in making it impossible for her to retrace her steps to the house. Almost anyway. She had driven that way once, and she recognized some of the roads to the mountain property. While she was a bit turned around, she made every effort to memorize as much as she could.

From what Morgan knew of Dean, he didn't carry a weapon. No gun. No knife. His mind was his weapon.

Then why was he driving her into Knoxville? That seemed like a really stupid move on his part. It would be the perfect opportunity for her to escape. She'd have to time it right. She needed to wait until they were all the way into town. But what part of town was he taking her to? If it was close to the FBI office or the police station, she should wait. Maybe it would be a place she recognized or knew better than others. But she shouldn't wait too long.

She needed to bolt when they were stopped, but if they were too stopped, he'd just jump out and chase her down. He was athletic with long legs. The two granola bars she'd eaten in the last twelve hours had not given her enough strength to make up for three days of not eating. And his legs were long. Even at equal energy, she'd never be able to outrun him. But she sure would try. If they had a stoplight in heavy traffic maybe she'd be able to open the door and bolt when the light turned green. Maybe ...

Maybe these doors have child locks. Weren't child locks only on back doors, though?

She'd have to unbuckle too.

Her heart raced. Hopefully he couldn't sense her anticipation. Although he might think she was falling for his ploys about a child.

She wanted to laugh. Did he really think she'd fall for that idea? But that hardly mattered at the moment. No, she needed to be on alert for the perfect opportunity. What would she do when she ran? She'd have to hide quickly. In plain sight was always the best option. Mix in with a crowd or something.

Where was she going to find a crowd midday on a Wednesday in October?

Dean turned off of the mountain highway and onto a city street. She would have to go for it soon. If he made left up here, they'd be headed back into an area that was only houses, and she needed more civilization.

Sure enough, he went into the left turn lane. Perfect. She'd dash out as soon as he started pulling away.

She slowly slid her hand toward the buckle release. *God, You're gonna have to help me. Distract him. Please.*

Dean started talking while looking out the opposite window.

She depressed the buckle release as slowly and quietly as possible.

The car started dinging the buckle was undone. *Shoot!*

Waiting until the light changed was no longer an option. She dropped the seatbelt and let it slide into its home. With one motion she flipped the lock mechanism and pulled the handle.

"What are you doing?"

She shoved the door open and jumped out of the car. Dean's hand grabbed at her shirt. With a quick glance back and forth, she bolted across the street.

Dean cussed, and she heard him slam the car door. He was following on foot.

Shoot.

She sprinted across the parking lot toward a large church building. No one seemed to be around.

Dean's footsteps fell behind her, but she kept running. Feet pounding the pavement; adrenaline making up for her weak state.

She slipped around some trees and darted behind an old house. Another yard met her on the other side. *Shoot.*

Fall leaves crunched under her feet as she crossed through to a circle driveway. Turning back toward the street, she prayed someone would step in and keep Dean from taking her.

She ran down the sidewalk away from Dean's car.

A police car appeared down the street. She frantically waved her arms. The police car sped up next to her and stopped. The officer jumped out.

"Morgan?"

"Gabe!"

He came around the car, and they embraced. She turned and pointed to Dean. He'd spotted Gabe too and had taken off back toward his car.

Gabe took off after Dean, but Morgan yelled, "You won't catch him. His car is right there."

Spinning back to his car, he said, "Hop in."

Gabe was in and moving the car before Morgan could get her seatbelt latched.

By the time they made it to the intersection, Dean was gone. Gabe called it in to dispatch, and Morgan relayed the information she could about the make and model of the car. If only she had paid more attention.

But that didn't matter as much as getting to Gio. She couldn't wait to see him, to wrap her arms around him, to kiss his grief away.

Chapter Twenty-Two

Gio stood in the breakroom, pouring himself yet another cup of coffee. As if the stress alone wasn't giving him an ulcer, the coffee was probably eating a hole in his stomach. Ever since his heart-to-heart with the Lord more than an hour ago, he'd had a sense of resignation. Not that he would ever give up looking for her, but more like the peace of knowing God was in control. Gio understood that truth, but walking in it was a lot harder than he ever imagined. After Eddie's suicide, Gio had walked through an extremely dark time, but if Morgan didn't make it home ... he couldn't quite put to words how dark this season would become.

"Gio!" Dylan's voice held urgency.

"What's wrong?"

"Gabe just called. Come with me. Leave the coffee." Dylan disappeared.

Gio groaned and set his coffee mug on the counter, muttering, "I'll be back for you." Leaning heavily on his cane, he hobbled to the door. His knee seemed even weaker today than normal. Probably due to his lack of sleep and proper nourishment. It hurt more today than normal too.

Dylan was waiting outside the door.

The elevator doors opened at the end of the hallway, and Gabe appeared. Beside him was a woman.

Morgan.

His knee buckled, yet he sustained his balance. His heart sped toward her, but he couldn't quite get his body to move as fast. He hobbled forward.

His foot hit the ground before he had the cane in place, and his knee gave out.

He caught himself on the wall and managed to not fall.

"Gio!" Morgan was beside him. She wrapped her arms around his waist, helping him stand.

"Is it really you?" He embraced her with all his might.

She smiled. "Yes, silly."

"I thought for sure I'd lost you for good."

"Nope." She leaned back and took his face in her hands. "Oh Gio!"

"Are you okay?"

She nodded. The movement released her pooling tears.

He leaned his forehead to hers. "Are you sure?" His mind raced with all the things that could have happened to her while she was gone.

"I'm fine." She stroked the side of his face, increasing his need to kiss her.

He seized her lips. She melted into his arms, kissing him back with increasing passion.

Dylan cleared his throat. "Maybe we should let them have a moment."

Gio released the kiss, and Morgan giggled. It felt so good to hear that sound again. He drew her back to his chest. "I would like a moment with my wife before we dive into what on earth happened."

Dylan and Gabe disappeared into the office, and Gio led Morgan into the breakroom. Once inside with the door closed, they resumed their kiss.

Was she really okay with this, though? What had Dean done to her? Had he violated her?

She pulled away. Her eyes narrowed, breaths quickened. "Are *you* okay?"

"I'm just concerned for you." He led her to a couch and tugged her down beside him. He laced his fingers between hers. "Part of me doesn't want to know the answer because it doesn't change anything, but tell me, before you go into the office and tell the team. Did he …?"

Her expression softened. "He wanted to." She laid her head on Gio's shoulder.

"So it was Dean." He released her hand and wrapped his arm around her.

"Yes." She snuggled closer. "Where's Jacqui?"

"I'm guessing she's on her way back here. She had an errand to run. Are you ready to go answer the questions we're all dying to ask?" He didn't loosen his grip.

"Nope. I simply need you right now."

"I can't argue with that." He slid all the way back into the couch, bringing her along. They cuddled close.

He couldn't believe it. She was back, alive and free. *Thank You, Lord, for restoring my wife to me. Thank You.*

He couldn't hold the emotion in any longer. Tears flowed from his eyes. His shirt became damp where Morgan rested her head. What had she endured? She made it sound like Dean didn't take advantage of her. But hadn't he, at least to some degree?

One day she'd tell him all of what happened. Wouldn't she?

They held each other until Dylan texted Gio to tell him Jacq had arrived back at the office.

"I have to see her." Morgan nudged herself off of Gio.

"Yes, you do."

They went to the office hand in hand. They had no more than walked into the room before Morgan dropped his hand and dashed toward her friend. The women met in a cacophony of squeals.

Gio laughed. The mood in the office was about to change, but for the moment they all seized the joy of Morgan breaking free from that monster.

Jacq found a sandwich in her bag and pressed it into Morgan's hands. She devoured the first half.

Gio cleared the corner of his desk, and Morgan perched on it with him by her side. As she nibbled on the second half of the sandwich, she told them what she remembered of being kidnapped and waking up in Dean's mountain house, in the same room where he had helped her get clean of the heroin months ago. She shared her memories of his involvement in selling girls, and his lack of denial.

Then she told them about the girl who snuck her some food. "I am certain she is Nicoletta's sister, Bianca."

Gio looked at her. "Didn't Nicoletta say they told her they killed her?"

"Yes, but she's with Dean, and based on what I remember about him in the past, he's not going to kill someone who could still make him money. More than that, she fits his type, even though she's so young."

Aliza asked, "Do you think it's possible Dean is the man who posed as their uncle, or did he buy them off of someone else?"

"All I can remember for certain are older girls. I have had a dream about kids. But most importantly, the picture Nicoletta drew reminded me of Dean." Morgan shrugged.

Gio rested his hand on her back. "Why don't we go talk to Nicoletta and show her a pictorial line up?"

Morgan's face stretched into a giant smile as he knew it would at the idea of seeing Nicoletta. "Perfect."

Aliza said, "I'll dig a little more. We never found record of Nicoletta's and Bianca's entry into the States, but maybe if we're looking for Dean, we'll find something. Just in case."

Gio nodded. "Sounds like a plan." He pushed off his desk and offered his hand to Morgan. "Shall we?"

While Morgan changed into a spare set of clothes Jacqui had, the team decided it would be safer to keep Morgan at the field office, and she wasn't about to argue. So the team contacted Nicoletta's social worker and foster mom. They brought her down to the office and met Morgan and Gio in the family interview room.

Nicoletta ran straight to Morgan's arms.

Morgan gave her a tight hug. How she wished she had a photograph to show the girl of her sister, so there would be proof it was the right one. Nicoletta would have to take Morgan's word for it.

"Let's sit. I have so many things to talk to you about. Some good, some not so easy."

"I threw away the picture you asked about, but I made a new one." Nicoletta dropped her backpack from her shoulder and unzipped it. She produced a paper and handed it to Morgan.

It was even more like Dean Rockefeller than the last one. She stared at the drawing, trying not to fly back into memories of the last three days.

"You know him, don't you?" Nicoletta's accent was still so thick it felt like music to Morgan's ears, anchoring her in the present.

Morgan nodded.

Gio pressed his lips together. "May I?"

She turned the picture toward Gio.

He sucked in a quick breath. "There's one way to confirm. You two keep talking, and I'll put together a photo lineup." He squeezed each of their shoulders before disappearing out the door.

Morgan and Nicoletta went to the couch, her foster mom and social worker hanging close by. Morgan winced as she sat down.

"Are you okay?"

"I'm fine. It's just been a tough few days. Let's just say I ran into your 'uncle.'"

Nicoletta's eyes grew wide. "You saw him?"

Morgan nodded. "I saw someone else." She could barely contain her excitement. Part of her worried she was wrong about this, but Bianca had confirmed she had a sister named Nicoletta. What were the chances?

Nicoletta pulled her feet up beneath her and waited. "Who?"

"Bianca."

Nicoletta's hopeful smile dropped. "There's no way. They said they killed her."

"They lied. I'm sure it was her. She thought you were dead too. When I told her you were alive and had escaped trafficking, she was elated."

"Elated?"

"Oh so happy."

Nicoletta smiled, but her eyes filled with tears. "She's alive? Vero?"

"It's true."

She threw her arms around Morgan's neck.

Morgan stroked the girl's back. Knowing her sister was alive was only somewhat comforting. She might be able to see her again; that held hope. But, at the same time, her sister was facing a terror few would understand.

Gio came back into the room a few minutes later with a couple sheets of paper. He sat across from them. "Nicoletta, do you think you can identify the man who claimed to be your uncle from a photograph?"

She nodded. "I remember exactly what he looks like." She slid her legs off the couch and sat on the edge.

Gio laid the two sheets of paper on the table in front of them. Each sheet had six photographs. Of the dozen pictures, Morgan quickly spotted Dean.

Her body involuntarily shuddered.

Gio gave her a sympathetic expression.

Nicoletta gravitated to one photo immediately but examined each of them. "Yep, it's him." She placed her pointer finger on Dean Rockefeller's photograph.

Chapter Twenty-Three

Morgan sank into the dining chair in their little RV kitchen. It felt good to be home. To be with Gio. To be free.

For months Gio, Dylan, and Jacq had been convincing her this was a safe place and no one would be able to track her here. And today was no different. Each one of them had assured her she was safe.

But she had hated to leave Nicoletta. It had also been hard to not tell her they were thinking about adopting her. It wasn't time yet. Morgan had to face the fact the increased trauma of having been kidnapped could affect their eligibility. How was that fair? She'd have to trust God. It was up to Him ultimately anyway.

Gio stood across the kitchen, making tea. Initially after their reunion, he'd seemed to have an insatiable need to hold her close. However, he had pulled back since they arrived home. Did he think her soiled like a dirty rag? She was tired though, so perhaps she was misinterpreting his behavior. Maybe he was acting normal, and her not wanting to be more than five feet away was a result of the kidnapping. She needed to stop psycho-analyzing the situation and enjoy being home with her husband.

Gio brought the tea over, and they sipped in silence until Gio let a yawn slip.

"You're tired."

He nodded. "I couldn't sleep without you by my side."

She set her teacup down. "Then let's go to bed." She stood and reached her hand out to him.

He gripped her hand and allowed her to lead him the three steps to the bedroom.

She pulled her shirt off and reached for her pajamas, which were exactly where she'd left them Sunday morning. "You didn't come back here at all, did you?"

She slipped her tank top on and turned back to Gio. His mouth hung open, jaw quivering ever so slightly. Her bruises. She'd forgotten to tell him that part.

"You haven't told me everything."

"He pushed me, and I fell into the dresser." She didn't want to admit she had touched Dean in an attempt to get information, but even more she didn't want to tell Gio Dean had touched her. "I'm fine. I slapped him. That's why he shoved me."

A smile peeked on Gio's lips. "That's my Morgan."

She shrugged and disappeared into the bathroom to finish getting ready for bed.

When she returned, Gio's expression was pensive. "My turn. I'll be right back."

"I'll be here."

His eyes relaxed. "Good."

She crawled into bed and curled up on her side of the middle. She wasn't all that sleepy, but she was weary. Her mind was processing so much, and her body was starting to feel the tiredness her brain was experiencing.

Gio came back, flipped off the light, and lay down on his side of the bed, giving her plenty of space.

She didn't want space. She didn't want to be clingy either, but right now she needed her husband. Did he think she was soiled because she'd been near Dean? She'd told Gio Dean hadn't raped her. She hadn't been intimate with the creep, so why was her husband staying away from her right now?

"Gio?" Her voice shook. She didn't mean it to.

He turned his face toward hers.

"Hold me?"

"Are you sure?"

"Do you not want to hold me?" A sob nearly escaped, but she caught it. Why was this so difficult? They had made great headway in their intimate relationship. Had they really lost ground even though Dean didn't touch her like that?

"I always want to hold you. I just don't want to upset you. Or hurt you." He moved his body toward hers.

"You could never." She reached out to him.

He slid an arm beneath her and tugged her close. Their legs intertwined.

She melted into his strong arms.

"I'm sorry I failed at protecting you."

"Oh Gio, you didn't. It wasn't your fault."

"I should never have let you go to the car by yourself."

"You know he was probably prepared for both of us to enter that car. He's not an idiot." She stroked his face. "You prayed for me. Knowing you were looking for me, praying for me, loving me even when I wasn't there, helped me stay strong."

He ran his fingers along her back, sending tingles through her body. Her desire for her husband heightened because of his tenderness and humility.

He kissed her forehead. "I love you."

"And I you." She kissed his lips. They both needed reassurance. They both needed the comfort only a husband and wife could share. They both needed to reconnect intimately.

Gio stepped out of the bedroom the next morning and found Morgan singing softly while she made breakfast. He leaned against the door frame and watched her.

She swayed to the rhythm as the melody filled the space around her.

It would be a challenge to ever let her out of his sight again. God had restored her to him, and he'd be eternally grateful, but he never wanted to experience that dread again.

What had happened in those hours she had been trapped in Dean's house? She hadn't told him everything, that much he knew. And the tears that had silently fallen in the middle of the night that she had tried to hide made him question if she was being completely honest with him about how far Dean had pushed her.

He walked over and reached past her for a mug.

She jumped. "Oh, morning."

"Didn't mean to startle you." He'd known better than to come up behind her and surprise her. That hadn't gone well the first time he had tried.

"It's okay. I just didn't hear you."

He tapped his cane on the floor. "Guess I need to stop trying to keep this thing quiet."

She giggled and slid her arms around his waist. Her eyes were still distant though.

"What's going on inside that beautiful head of yours?"

"I'm still trying to figure that out. Probably processing what happened. I'd rather just ignore it, but I'm learning that doesn't actually help anything." She let go of him with one arm and flipped the pancakes on the stove.

"I can help you process."

"I know. I'm not even sure what words to say, though. When I find them, don't worry, you're my go-to." She kissed his cheek.

He fixed his cup of coffee and helped her finish breakfast.

While they ate, Morgan asked, "Do you need to go into the office today?"

"I'm supposed to, though Warren gave me freedom to be as flexible as needed."

She nodded, but a sense of fear clouded her expression.

"Morgan?"

"I don't want to stay here by myself."

A rush of air escaped his lungs. "Of course not. I'm not sure what you'll do at the office, but you can come. We could call Jolene and see if she can squeeze you in today."

Morgan shrugged. "That could work. Still not sure I have the words to process."

"She can help you find them."

Morgan nodded.

He didn't want to push her. Frankly, he'd rather her process with him instead of the counselor, so she didn't fail to tell him something. Though perhaps talking to Jolene first would make it easier for her to share with him.

He also wasn't sure he wanted to go to the office today, but his desire to find Dean and dole out justice ... vengeance was tempting, however that was God's territory. Gio would have to be satisfied with bringing the law down on Dean's head.

Chapter Twenty-Four

THURSDAY MORNING, JACQ WAS an emotional mess. With the joy of the doctor confirming her pregnancy combined with the joy of Morgan's escape, one would think she'd be dancing in the clouds. But she hadn't been able to stop crying all morning—and it's not like she was a crier. Pregnancy hormones were no joke.

She walked out of the field-office bathroom, convinced she had washed away all of the lingering emotions. She needed to be her normal level-headed self. They had a mission today—to find Dean Rockefeller and lock him up until he rotted.

And even better, save Bianca and reunite her with her sister.

Jacq hated the idea of the girls being stuck in the foster system but finding someone to adopt them at fifteen and ten would be difficult.

She walked into the office where Aliza, Matt, and Dylan all sat at their desks. Jacq said, "Where are we with finding Dean?"

Matt leaned back from his computer. "He never went to his house yesterday. Morgan confirmed they were headed in the direction where his house is, but he didn't show. Don't blame him. The cops were sitting around the corner ready to pick him up once Gabe announced he was the number one suspect in a kidnapping."

Jacq settled at her desk. "Has anyone knocked on the door since? Talked to his wife or daughter?"

Aliza said, "Interesting piece about the wife. There's no record of her coming back to the country after they left for Italy nine years ago."

"So who else lives at the house with their kid?"

"I'm guessing a nanny."

"That would makes sense for how busy he is between being a doctor and a trafficker." Jacq wanted to roll her eyes. The man was probably hardly involved in his daughter's life at all. Unless she wasn't even his daughter ... no, he wouldn't pay for an elite private education for a child he was trafficking. "Has anyone checked to see if his daughter went to school today?"

Matt said, "The school won't release that type of information, even to the cops. The officer sitting on the house said the girl never came home from school yesterday though."

"Shoot, that means we've lost the opportunity to follow her to wherever Dean is."

Matt sighed. "True. In better news, though, the warrants came through. We have legal grounds to search his office, home, and any other property we have probable cause to believe he may be residing in."

"That's beautifully broad to include the mountain house." Jacq was relieved the warrant wasn't limiting.

"I worded it that way on purpose. The judge came through, since we had Morgan's testimony."

Aliza raised her finger. "I have more news connected to the wife." Gio and Morgan entered the room at that moment, so she paused while hellos were exchanged.

They both looked incredibly tired. The week had been stressful on them. A fresh wave of determination swept over Jacq. They had to find Dean in order for her two friends to fully rest and be free of the darkness trying to hunt them down.

Once everyone settled, Aliza tapped her pen on her metal water bottle. "Dean's wife's family is originally from Italy. She was third-generation in the States. But they still had a bit of family over there. Now, I totally went down a rabbit hole of genealogies. Dean was able to pull off the family-relation claim because it wasn't too far off. Obviously, he's not their uncle. Evangeline is the girls' third cousin at best."

Morgan hugged herself. "Really?"

Aliza nodded. "I've also been searching for other aliases Dean goes by, but I haven't had any luck in that department. If I could find the orphanage where the girls were, I might have a chance of working from that angle, but it's been a bust. Nicoletta was just too young to remember those kinds of details. I found their birth records but nothing beyond that."

"Is Bianca really only fifteen?" Morgan asked.

"Almost fifteen and a half. Do you know if Dean was having sex with her? Or selling her?"

Morgan shrugged. "I can only assume."

Jacq's stomach churned. At fifteen, she should only be worrying about who her friends were, not whether some creepy guy was going to have sex with her. Jacq hated how so many kids were robbed of their childhood.

"This is all good information. But where is Dean? How do we stop him before he hurts anyone else?"

Everyone stared at Jacq. She'd only said what they were all thinking. Those were the questions they needed answered.

Jacq stood. "I say we serve that warrant. Search the house from top to bottom. Maybe there will be a clue as to where he is."

Thirty minutes later, the team, save Gio, along with a host of FBI-jacketed agents and technicians, were at Dean Rockefeller's house. They knocked for a good long time, but with no answer, they entered by force.

They spread out through the house, different people assigned to different areas. The house, while not over-the-top lavish, was impressive. All of the finishes were topnotch but simple.

Jacq and Dylan went upstairs to help search the bedrooms. One was a large master suite. Something unknown pulled Jacq past that room and down the hallway. Another room drew her in. Someone lived in this room, yet it almost looked as if no one did. She didn't see clothes on the chair or slippers under the bed. No paintings on the wall. No vase on the dresser. None of the things one might put in a guest room. Wouldn't a nanny at least have a book or cell phone charger on the nightstand?

Jacq went across the room and entered the walk-in closet. Women's clothing, but it was on the small side. Not super stylish but not out of date either. She fingered a few pieces. Did Bianca live here? Why would Dean have her at the house in town? So he had access to her all the time?

Exiting the room, Jacq continued down the hallway and entered what was clearly his daughter's room. The opposite from the last one. The decorations of this room would put Pinterest to shame. Everything was pink. The bed was a literal castle, with a slide. A swing even hung from the ceiling next to a three-foot-tall dollhouse.

Jacq looked at Dylan who had joined her. His eyes were wide in wonder.

"Harper would be in heaven."

Jacq laughed. "Yeah, she would. I guess when your dad has limitless money, you can have extravagant."

"Maybe we could do a little bit of this for her."

"Not to this degree. No one needs all of this."

He nodded. "How long does it last for a girl, though?"

"That's a good thought. We never have discovered how old his daughter is. No need to. She must be younger than I was thinking. Either that or her dad hasn't admitted she's outgrown this."

"Did we have a specific reason for thinking she was a certain age?" Dylan opened the closet and revealed dozens of cute outfits for all occasions, including dressing up.

"I don't think so. But if the wife has been out of the picture for nine years ..."

"Who knows."

The two of them searched the little girl's room to see if there were any hidden clues. They took care to put things back, even though the rest of the house did not experience such care.

Morgan woke up early Friday morning, again just feeling off. She couldn't pinpoint the feeling, but she'd felt this way all week. What was wrong with her?

Gio wasn't in bed, so she rolled over and grabbed her phone. She checked the calendar. She still hadn't had her period since they had gotten married three weeks ago. Even her erratic cycle should have started by now. Was God going to answer that prayer already? That wasn't possible, was it?

Dean's words echoed back at her. "Our child." He'd been pulling her desperate leg, right? The abortion she was convinced messed up her body had happened years before she'd spent that time with Dean. Had her body not actually been as messed up as she thought?

What if she and Gio had been too quick to say *no* to any form of birth control?

Her heart bounded a little, but she was careful not to let it leap too high. No false hope in Jesus, so she'd put her hope in Him, baby or no baby.

Jesus, help me trust You in this, well, in everything, but this especially.

She climbed out of bed. Gio wasn't in the living area either. But there was a note on the table.

Good morning, beautiful Morgan. I'm out helping Dylan clear a tree that fell across the driveway. I'll be home soon. I love you. ~Gio

She smiled and tucked the note into her Bible.

Then she prepared herself some breakfast, but the idea that maybe she could be pregnant engulfed her mind. The week they got married Gio had bought a few packages of ovulation and pregnancy tests as an act of faith. She dug back in the cabinet and found the box. After extracting one, she considered the test. Should she take it? Should she get Gio first?

No. If it was negative there was no need to excite him.

She followed the instructions and set it on the counter. While she waited, she dressed for the day. But the more she thought about it, the more she beat herself up for taking the test. What was she thinking? Her stomach knotted up like a twisted pretzel. It was probably too soon anyway. Why had she bothered? It was a waste of a test she'd want later. But she might as well check it or at least throw it away.

She was headed back to the bathroom when her phone rang. It was Gio.

"Hey, you."

"Good morning. Dylan and I could use a couple more pairs of hands. Got a minute?"

"Sure, I'll be right there."

She went into the bathroom and paused. Fear seized her heart. The white plastic obscured the little window that would give her the answer. She couldn't bring herself to look at it. It was too soon. They weren't ready yet. *She* wasn't ready yet. She'd make a terrible mother. She was still too broken. Had too much healing to do. As much as she wanted, more than anything, to be a mom, how could she care for someone else? Gio was easy. But he made it easy. Didn't depend on her for every need. It was more like she depended on him.

Not that she wouldn't be ecstatic if it was positive, but surely it was negative anyway, right? Why put herself through the torture of disappointment or the fear of wondering if she'd ruin her child? Better to pretend she hadn't taken the test and move forward. Heal more. Then she'd be ready. Without looking at the little screen, she slid it off the counter and into the trash. Exiting the RV, she spotted Jacqui coming out of the house.

Jacqui said, "You got roped into helping too?"

Morgan nodded. "Apparently, they aren't as macho as they thought."

The women laughed. Morgan looped her arm with Jacqui's. She was grateful for her friendship, and the cherry on top was the proximity of their homes.

As they headed down the drive to find their husbands, the two friends chatted.

The men were hacking the tree as best they could. Dylan had an ax, and Gio a chainsaw. When he saw the women approaching, he cut the power.

Morgan could hardly contain her smile. What was more attractive than a man in jeans and a T-shirt with a power tool in his hands?

He winked at her.

She giggled. That was her husband!

Chapter Twenty-Five

Gio stacked the last bit of wood beside the road and turned back to the women. Jacq was busy convincing Morgan to come up to the house.

Morgan reached out to him. "Come with us."

"I have to take a shower first. Go with Jacq, and I'll join you in a bit." He wrapped his arm around her waist and met her lips.

Concern flashed in her eyes. What would worry her? She really struggled with being away from him for any time at all.

He kissed her temple. "Go with Jacq. I'll see you shortly."

She nodded and planted a kiss on his cheek before walking off with Jacq.

He wandered up to the RV, praying for Morgan and her healing and their future as he went.

In the bathroom, he inspected himself in the mirror and picked a few twigs and random wood pieces from his hair. He dropped them in the trash can and spotted a white stick with a pink cap. A pregnancy test?

Why was there a pregnancy test in their garbage?

Did Jacq think she was pregnant but didn't want to tell Dylan? That didn't make sense.

Morgan? Hope flitted in his heart.

Then slammed back down to earth. No. If it was positive, whether Jacq's or Morgan's, it probably wouldn't be in the garbage can. Right?

He didn't know what to think. And something in him felt pulling the test out of the garbage was wrong.

Trying to ignore it entirely, he jumped in the shower.

But as he washed his hair, he couldn't get the nagging feeling out of his mind that something was definitely out of sync.

How much hadn't Morgan told him? She was holding back. Had Dean forced himself on her?

He didn't doubt his wife at all. If she'd had sex with Dean, it wasn't of her choosing. But had that man taken advantage of her?

Then why wouldn't she have told him?

He rinsed his hair.

Maybe she was trying to protect him from the truth. That made more sense than anything he'd thought of thus far. She would do that. She'd proven herself to be one to protect him at all costs. That's how Ronan had kidnapped her. That's why Gio was still alive today. If she hadn't come back to protect him, he'd be dead and buried.

It's possible more happened physically with Dean than she'd told him.

What if she was pregnant? Was it possible the baby was Dean's? She'd throw the test away then.

His stomach twisted up on him like an over-wound guitar string. What if that was the truth? Would he be able to accept the child as his own? Because that would be the right thing. But not easy. His heart ached at the idea.

He wrestled with the thought as he dried off and got dressed, but the weight of it drove him to sit down on the couch on his way back to the bathroom to hang up his towel.

He wrung the towel in his hands.

Which was worse—the idea that another man violated his wife or raising said man's child?

Gio understood he was jumping the gun in assuming the worst. Wrestling with it before talking to Morgan, though, would make the worst possible answer easier to handle.

He dropped his head into the towel. *Heavenly Father, help me be the man You want me to be. The man Morgan needs. Help us face whatever comes our way.*

Resolution and peace filled his heart. He loved his wife no matter what, and any child she bore would be his as well, regardless of paternity.

Morgan searched for every excuse to slip away from helping Jacqui. She hated being that way, but what if Gio found the pregnancy test in the garbage can? She didn't even know what it said. What would he think?

"You're distracted." Jacq rested her hands on the papers she was folding.

"Maybe a little. I'm sorry."

"It's okay. Go be with your husband." The sing-song effect Jacqui gave to the word *husband* made Morgan laugh.

"This whole being married thing is still so strange, but strangely beautiful."

"That's the perfect way to put it." Jacqui gathered the contents of the informational packets they were stuffing for the women's center. "We can do this later."

"I do want to help you with it."

"Just not now."

Morgan nodded.

"I probably should get Harper ready for the day anyway." Jacqui sighed. "Only two and a half months. Then I'll be with her more than not."

"So you are going to quit the FBI?"

Jacqui nodded. "Yes, things are really coming together for the center to open, at least at some level, come January." Jacqui's smile widened. "This is actually happening!"

"I'm so excited."

"Good. Then get out of here."

Morgan stood. "We will do this, this weekend." She squeezed Jacqui's shoulder as she passed.

Keeping her steps at a steady pace, despite the urge to bolt across the clearing, Morgan strolled home.

She swallowed hard before entering the camper.

Gio sat on the couch. He looked up and set a towel on the little coffee table. Sorrow filled his eyes.

She gingerly closed the door behind her and stared at him. He'd seen the test. She should have told him before taking it. But she didn't expect him to be sad. It must be negative.

"You saw the test?"

He nodded.

Her heart fell. Even though she'd been certain it was negative, part of her still felt devastated. How'd she misread her instincts so badly? "I should have waited for you. Or just not taken it."

He patted the seat then slid back into the couch and rested his arm across the cushions.

She padded over and curled up next to him. "I guess the test was negative based on your reaction."

His eyes scrunched up. "You didn't look?"

"No. You called and by then I had convinced myself it was stupid to have even taken it. It's too early, even with my erratic cycle."

"I didn't look at it either. I thought maybe since you threw it away, you might think a baby would be …"

She considered Gio. What was he trying to say? "Dean's?"

He nodded.

She took his face in her hands and leaned in close. "I told you. He didn't. He didn't rape me. We didn't have sex. Why don't you believe me?" She let her hands fall from his face to her lap.

"It's not that I don't believe you. I was just worried you weren't being honest because you wanted to protect me. You aren't telling me everything."

She sank a little. This man knew her well, for which she was grateful and dismayed.

"I can't tell you how much it thrills me that he didn't violate you." Gio stroked the edge of her hairline.

"If there is a baby, it's yours. One hundred percent guaranteed."

"And if it wasn't, it wouldn't matter. Your baby is my baby."

His words overwhelmed her heart. Not that it was an issue, but for him to say it so freely …

"You are such a good man."

"Why don't you go find out what that test says."

She twitched to move but stopped herself. "No. I want to tell you what I wasn't saying before."

He took her hand and listened like he really cared, because he did. He loved her, and that gave her the confidence she needed to confide in him.

She told him about her attempt to work Dean over for information, how Dean had touched her, and that's why she'd slapped him.

Gio tried to stifle a snicker but failed. "I'm sorry you ended up getting hurt. But I bet slapping him felt good."

"You have no idea."

They laughed together for a moment before Morgan turned serious again. She proceeded to tell Gio about Dean's claim they had a child together.

"He was just trying to manipulate me. But a little piece of me wondered. And that sparked my mind to thinking maybe I can have kids. And if so, did that explain the off feeling I've been having all week?"

"Good chance the off feeling is a result of the trauma your body and mind experienced. You didn't eat for three and a half days."

"I know. And there's no way I could forget having a baby. I can't believe he would try something so absurd."

Gio chuckled. "He's pretty absurd."

"Do you think we'll ever catch him?"

"Hard to say. He's got resources beyond what we can imagine."

"He said he'd get Ronan a new identity and tickets out of the country."

"Then he really could be anywhere in the world by now."

Morgan nodded. "But for some reason, I think he's still really close."

"His obsession is a bit ..."

"Obsessive?" She winked at her husband.

"Exactly." He stood and pulled her up too. "Shall we risk a glance at that test? Just to know."

"Yeah." Wrapping her arm around her husband's waist, she took the place of his cane, and the two of them went to the bathroom.

She snatched the test from the trash can but didn't look.

Gio leaned against the sink and opened his arms.

Morgan rested her back and body against him, and he encircled her, resting his chin on her shoulder.

She turned the test over, but before she could see the results, she flipped it again.

"I don't know if I can do this. Even though I'm sure it's going to be negative, I don't want the heart hurt."

"It's okay to be sad. But no false hope in Jesus. He's got a plan for us, all we have to do is walk in it, even if we don't understand it."

She nodded.

"What are we looking for when you turn it over?"

"Two lines means pregnant. Only one line is a no."

Gio squeezed her waist and kissed her cheek.

She turned the test over.

No second line. Just one. Not even a hint of a second faint line. Nothing at all.

She knew that's what it would say, but it still felt like her heart had gone through the shredder. It wasn't final; it was only one test three weeks into their marriage.

But the emotions were too much. She spun in Gio's arms and buried her face against his chest.

"I know I shouldn't cry about it. This is stupid."

He stroked her back. "It's not stupid. You're processing a lot." He held her close and let her cry. "God has a plan. We trust Him."

She loved how Gio declared the statement for both of them. They would trust God. They did trust Him.

Chapter Twenty-Six

With Dylan by his side, Gio walked into the open prison interview room Friday afternoon. Warren had given him a short leash with field work, and Gio was ready to use every last inch.

Bobbi Fagon was serving time for trafficking, kidnapping a juvenile, kidnapping a federal agent, and shooting a federal agent. Never mind that he shot Dylan with his own gun, but Gio wouldn't bring that up now; it would upset Dylan. Warren had okayed Gio coming to the prison for a reason: no way would he let Jacq and Bobbi in the same room together. Dylan was bad enough, but he had insisted.

Gio would take the lead. With the support of his cane, he strode to the table the guards fastened Bobbi to.

Bobbi said, "It's true? Ronan really did nail one of you. Too bad it wasn't that one." He pointed to Dylan.

"One bullet hole is enough."

Bobbi shrugged. "I guess so. What can I do for you gentlemen today? Any chance I can tell you information that'll get me out of here sooner?"

Gio took a seat across from Bobbi. "There's a chance. But probably more likely to get you a few accoutrements. Make your life a little more comfortable in here."

"I'll take what I can get. I heard being a snitch worked out well for Daisy. Maybe it can work for me too." Bobbi leaned forward on the table.

Gio tried not to react to the name his wife used to go by when she was being trafficked. "Daisy is doing much better now. Trust me, working with us, not against us, will always be better for you."

"What do you want to know?"

Why is this scoundrel overly eager to help? Gio had two main questions he wanted to ask Bobbi. The entire way over, Gio had debated which he would ask about first. He'd settled on asking about Dean Rockefeller last.

Opening a folder, Gio pulled out a photo of the two kids Jacq and Dylan had seen in the airport. "These children were brought to the States by traffickers. We're hoping to find them, but our connections to child traffickers are limited. Do you have any names of individuals whose doors we can knock on?"

Bobbi distorted his face. "I'll never understand the kid thing. It's disgusting. Give me a woman, please. So unfortunately, I don't have many connections to that world. I'll gladly join in the lynching of the pedophiles."

Honor among criminals, huh? I guess everyone has a line they won't cross.

"Who are the knowns?"

Gio pulled out the mugshots of Justin and Ron.

Bobbi's shoulders slumped. "I'm not acquainted with either of those guys. Shoot. I really wanted to help you. I can ask around, though. See if anyone in here has anything."

"That would be appreciated." Gio scooped up the photographs and slid them back in the folder before retrieving another. "What about this man? We believe he deals in trafficking women. And he has his eyes fixed on someone we both know."

Bobbi stiffened. His mouth opened and shut a few times.

Gio slid the photograph closer to Bobbi.

He sat back, as if to put as much space between him and the photo of Dean as possible.

Why was he so afraid of Dean Rockefeller?

"Tell me about this man."

"Nope. I ... nothing. There's nothing to tell. Can't tell you what I don't know."

"Bobbi, I can tell there's something you aren't telling me."

"Nope. Nothing."

Gio leaned over the table and slid the photo even closer to Bobbi. His Adam's apple made a harsh rise and fall.

"Why are you scared of a simple doctor?"

"Doctor? I don't know what you're talking about."

"Bobbi, taking down this guy will mean everything."

"Let's talk about those kids again—" Bobbi cut himself off and sat up straight. "Actually no. You have all the answers you need about them." He eyed the photo of Dean again.

"Wait, are they connected?" Gio asked.

"You're the one asking me about both of them at the same meeting. I'm done talking, though. I've got all the accoutrements I need." Bobbi stood and looked back to the guard.

"You know something about this guy." Gio tapped Dean's photo. "Tell me anything."

Bobbi met Gio's gaze and shook his head. "No one is going to tell you anything about that guy. I'm sorry. It's just the way it is."

The guard led Bobbi away, and Gio grunted.

Dylan placed his hand on Gio's shoulder. "He told us a lot for not telling us anything."

Gio nodded and stood. They would wait until they got to the car, when they were out of earshot of anyone else, before they processed what they had learned ... and not learned.

Saturday morning had thus far been blissfully relaxed. Morgan and Gio had slept in and had a lazy breakfast. He and Dylan planned to go back to the office this afternoon, but she was reveling in the time they had.

As they cleaned up, a crunch of the gravel indicated today's visitors had arrived. Morgan glanced out the window. Sydney had come with her new baby, along with Lyla. The two women had been trafficked with Morgan, though they'd both gone by different names then—Stella and Lily.

"Go!" Gio took the towel from her hands.

She kissed his cheek and ran out the door and across to where they'd parked in front of Jacqui and Dylan's house. Lyla jumped out and engulfed Morgan in a huge hug. Lyla's round little belly got squished in between.

"Oh baby!" Morgan stepped back from the hug and cupped Lyla's baby bump, even though at five months pregnant, she was hardly showing. "How is everything?"

"As good as can be expected. Life is hard, but at least my baby is alive and growing."

Ronan had been Lyla's trafficker too, and if he had discovered Lyla was pregnant, an abortion would have been her only option.

Sydney lifted an infant car seat from the back. "Hey."

Morgan went around the vehicle and hugged the new mom. "How are you two?"

"Good. I'm finally making some breakthrough, and being this little guy's mom is helping."

Jacqui swung the front door open so fast the screen slammed against the side of the house. "Welcome!" She jogged down the stairs and embraced both the women she had helped escape trafficking.

They all went into the living room. Jacq had set the coffee table with tea, coffee, and scones fresh from the oven, though Morgan knew they came from the freezer first.

Morgan sat on the couch with Sydney, and the other two took chairs.

They chatted, sipped, and nibbled. God was really working in these ladies' lives, even if they didn't recognize it as such yet. Slowly and gingerly, Morgan and Jacq were able to turn the conversation toward the Gospel. It didn't stay there long, but Morgan prayed seeds had been sown and watered.

When Morgan placed her teacup down and settled back farther in the couch, she asked Sydney, "May I hold him?"

"Of course." She handed Morgan the newborn squish.

He was so tiny. Only six and a half pounds at birth, he was probably barely seven now at two weeks old. He looked like his momma, except his skin was a few shades darker. He curled right up against Morgan's shoulder.

Gio and Dylan came in and greeted the women. Gio came over to Morgan, his face beaming at the sight. He gently laid his hand on the baby's back while congratulating Sydney.

Gio kissed Morgan's forehead before righting himself. She could almost sense his thought—how natural Morgan looked holding the baby. She couldn't know for sure since he said nothing. But somehow she knew.

Too bad it might never happen for them.

She kissed the baby's head and got a whiff of his precious little baby smell.

Her mind jettisoned out of the room and into the past.

She was holding a baby—a little girl. Her little girl.

Beeps sounded in the room around Morgan. She was safe, but the terror filling her heart was beyond unsettling.

She looked down at the baby in her arms. Her little Aurora. She had chosen a name for the baby. How could one's heart be filled with so much love?

Her dark hair curled in little wisps. Her tiny fingers and toes were all perfect.

Morgan stroked the baby's soft skin. Also perfect.

Aurora had been three weeks early, but she was doing fine. They had prepared themselves for the chance she might end up in the NICU when Morgan's labor had started at thirty-three weeks. Fortunately, the doctors had been able to stop it with some medication. However, as soon as they'd stopped the medicine, she'd gone back into labor.

She'd done it, though. She'd given birth to a healthy baby girl. But how could she keep her safe?

She loved this baby with her entire being. For the first time she had a glimpse at the love she wanted to believe God had for her.

Dean walked into the room carrying a cup of coffee. "You're awake."

Morgan's heart trembled, and she held Aurora a little closer.

He put the coffee down and reached for the baby.

"She's asleep. You don't want to disturb her, do you?"

"I guess not." He stroked the baby's back. He was tender. Maybe he would treat Aurora different. Perhaps he would be a tender father who would always do what was best for his child. He treated Morgan better, after all. But what if he didn't?

Maybe it would have been better if neither of them had survived the nineteen hours of labor.

"Morgan." A hand rested on her shoulder.

Tears streamed down her face, and she snuggled the baby in her arms.

But it wasn't Aurora.

Her brain came fully back into the present. She glanced at Sydney, who looked concerned.

"I'm so sorry." Morgan gingerly handed the baby boy back to her.

She glanced around at all the faces before her. If only they had seen what she saw in her mind, then they wouldn't be looking at her with such confusion.

She stood and bolted from the room and the house.

The dream was so real. Had it really been a memory? Maybe. No. It couldn't have been. If she had a daughter, she never would have abandoned her. Never. Especially not to a man she feared with such intensity. But where did that fear come from? She ran along the edge of the clearing and down the little, well-worn path to the stream. Her favorite place to think and process was a flat rock by the water.

The rock was now covered with colorful leaves, some plastered on from recent rains.

She brushed a few off and sat, curling her knees up and hugging them close.

Footsteps fell along the path, and Gio appeared. "Flashback?"

She nodded and tried to capture a sob, but it broke free. He rushed toward her and pulled her against his body. He waited.

She wanted to tell him, to let him into her mind, to let him see it rather than her having to find the words to explain.

After entirely too long she found her voice. "Maybe it wasn't a flashback. Maybe my brain is playing tricks on me again. It couldn't be real. It just couldn't be."

"Tell me what you experienced."

Slowly she recounted the details she remembered about the pregnancy, the delivery, Aurora.

"You said he treated you better. That you hoped he'd treat Aurora better. Better than what?"

She searched her mind but found no answer. "I don't know. I must have known about the trafficking by that point. Did he treat me better than other girls? Then why was I worried about Aurora? I don't know."

"Answers may come in time."

"I'm not sure I want the answers. But I need to know what happened. I can't believe I would willingly leave my baby in his care. There's no way. It's not possible."

Gio stroked her back.

"I can never be a mother. I must have been a horrible one. If I had a baby, what happened to her?"

"Slow down, Morgan. Let's process and work through this, like we have with other resurfaced memories. And let's do a little research on this one too."

"He claimed to have a child—our child. Does he have my little girl? Or is it some child he bought to deceive me?"

"I don't know the answer, but we can find out. It's case related, so we have the FBI's tools at our disposal."

She rested her head on his shoulder. "I couldn't do this without you." She shifted her address heavenward. "Jesus, thank you. Help us find answers. Give me clarity about this ... memory. If it was a memory?"

Chapter Twenty-Seven

Gio held Morgan's hand as the four friends headed up the elevator of the FBI office Saturday afternoon. The plan had been to leave the women at home today, but Morgan's flashback had changed that.

It had taken a while for Morgan's sobs to subside while they sat out on the rock, but once they had, she had been able to go back inside and enjoy the rest of her visit with Sydney and Lyla.

Jacq hadn't pressed her about the flashback until after the other women left, but as soon as they walked out the door, Jacq asked. Morgan had Gio tell her—it was too hard to live through it again.

What Jacq said left Morgan reeling the entire drive down: "But Dean Rockefeller has a daughter."

Morgan hadn't spoken a word. Why didn't Gio think to mention that? How had he forgotten? Was it possible Dean wasn't lying to Morgan?

They walked into the office. Matt and Aliza looked up from their desks. With a flat tone, Matt said, "Yay for a full party. Best way to spend a Saturday."

Gio filled the two of them in on why Morgan and Jacq had joined them. Then he pulled out his chair for Morgan and stole another one from the other team's bullpen for himself.

After he sat, Morgan leaned close. "When I told you what Dean claimed, why didn't you tell me he actually had a daughter?"

He wanted to avoid her gaze but couldn't. Her eyes implored him for the truth.

"Honestly, I didn't remember. My wife was missing, I didn't care that the man who had kidnapped her had a daughter. It seemed irrelevant at the time."

"I guess that makes sense." Morgan wrapped her hand around his elbow. Her voice returned to full volume. "What do we search for first? The girl's birth certificate?"

"That's not as easy as you think."

"I thought they were public record."

"Only after a hundred years."

"Oh." Morgan's shoulders slumped.

"It's all right, though. Not sure what we'll be able to find today, but we can subpoena her medical records and discover what we need to know. It just might take a few days."

She nodded slowly.

How he wished he could fix it all for his wife. She was so forlorn.

From her desk, Jacq said, "I'm gonna search for Dean's daughter. If she isn't the right age that will give us an answer quickly. Did you do the math?"

Gio chuckled. Of course she had.

Morgan smiled. "Six, maybe almost seven. I don't remember when she was born."

"That should be enough to clue us in."

Morgan asked, "How are you able to find this information? If birth records are confidential, medical records are too, HIPAA and all."

Gio opened his laptop. "If someone is suspected of a crime or of being a victim of a crime, then medical records can be accessed by law enforcement. We won't even need a warrant."

"But it's Saturday."

"Exactly why we might not have answers today."

She nodded and stole some paper and a pencil from Gio's desk.

Gio sat back in his chair. "Aliza, Matt, you said the daughter goes to a private school. What grade is she in?"

Aliza shook her head. "Couldn't find that out. We discovered the daughter because there was a news release or something like that—right, Matt? It mentioned his daughter. Then the tail followed the car to the school. It's all circumstantial. We don't know much about her, really."

Matt said, "It was a few places, not just one. He seems to want to present himself as a family man, but there are zero pictures. We couldn't find her name or age."

Morgan asked, "No pictures in his office?"

Gio shook his head.

Morgan sighed and went back to doodling.

Aliza jumped up and pulled over the big whiteboard and uncapped a marker. "What do we need to find out? Obviously"—she wrote across the top as she spoke—"Where is Dean Rockefeller?" She turned back to them. "What else?"

"His daughter's name," Dylan said.

"Birth date," Jacq added.

Aliza wrote those things. "And once we know her name, we can find medical records that might shine light on whether Morgan is her mother."

Morgan said, "We also need to find the mountain house."

They brainstormed a little more and formed a plan. Gio would take Morgan to the doctor on Monday for an exam and to look into medical records. Jacq and Dylan would go to the girl's school and inquire after the Rockefellers.

Matt slapped his desk. "By George, Morgan, you said 'Aurora,' correct?"

She nodded.

"I found a press release from the school with a list of students who won an art competition. For the early elementary an Aurora Rockefeller won first prize."

Morgan sat up. "Is there a picture of her?"

Matt shook his head. "No, sorry, but there is a photo of a painting of a stellar butterfly."

Morgan slumped a little.

Gio rubbed her back. "We'll find one."

She nodded. "It can't be. I don't know that I want it to be. I just don't understand."

"I know. We'll figure it out." He really hoped they'd be able to. If only it was possible to find out today. But they couldn't. They'd exhausted just about all their options for the weekend. Their hands were tied until Monday. Unless for some reason Dean showed himself.

Gio hobbled up the steps to his old apartment with Dylan by his side. Before they headed home Morgan requested they stop by and pick up a few items, including her now very worn copy of *Redeeming Love*.

Dylan had insisted on coming with him. Gio had suggested they stop by on their way home, but Dylan wanted to leave the women at the office.

"You know Jacq could have protected Morgan in the car."

"Sure, but I didn't want them to be alone."

"Jacq is as tough as a momma bear. She's not gonna let anything happen to Morgan."

Dylan paused on the stairs.

Gio turned back to his friend.

Dylan's face was flushed.

"You know it's true."

"It is." Dylan pointed up the stairs. "Let's get what we came for."

Gio shot his friend a curious look before continuing up the steps. He pulled his keys out and went to insert one into the lock.

"Wait." Dylan put his hand on Gio's arm. "The lock." He unholstered his Glock.

The lock had clearly been picked and not by a professional.

Dylan said, "Test the knob—it might still be unlocked. When you open it, step back, and I'll go in first."

Gio nodded, leaned his cane against the wall, and pulled his own side arm. He reached out and twisted the knob. It was unlocked. He shoved the door in and stepped aside.

Dylan rushed in and swept his firearm to the right and then the left.

Gio reached in and flicked the light switch, illuminating the apartment.

The place was a disaster.

Working in sync as they had for many years, Gio and Dylan cleared the entire apartment in less than two minutes. Gio's knee only gave out on him twice, but both times he was close to a doorjamb or dresser and able to catch himself.

"And that's why you aren't on full active duty yet."

Gio holstered his Glock and waved off Dylan's comment. "But I didn't fall."

"To the ground anyway."

"I just want to know who trashed my apartment."

"As do I. What was going on in the kitchen? It didn't smell good."

They wandered from the bedroom and into the kitchen. The Dutch oven sat on the stove.

"Smells like smoke."

Gio looked into the pot. A pile of ashes indicated something had been burned inside, but not from underneath—more like paper with a match.

A photo frame sat next to the stove, glass smashed and scattered everywhere.

He knew that frame. It held their wedding photo and marriage certificate. No. He reached into the ashes. The pot was still warm, but nothing remained. Nothing but ash.

His lungs seized. *No.* His hands trembled.

"What is it?" Dylan stepped up beside him.

Gio pointed to the frame.

"Was that the display Mrs. Jacobs made for you?"

Gio nodded.

Dylan's hand rested on his shoulder. "I'm sorry."

"He was here."

"But why? And why trash the place?"

Gio moved out of the kitchen, careful not to trip on scattered dishes and papers and miscellaneous items from the shelves and drawers.

"Look at how it's scattered." Gio moved toward the bookshelf he kept by the kitchen table. "Every item pulled from the shelf was rifled through, not shoved off in one big sweep. He was searching for something."

"I concur. But what? Maybe the address of where you are staying."

Gio nodded. "That would make the most sense."

"Would anything in here give him that information?"

After Dylan retrieved his cane for him, Gio methodically thought through everything in the apartment. Did anything have an address on it to indicate where they lived?

He walked around slowly while Dylan reported the break-in. Everything seemed to have been searched and tossed onto the floor, but as far as he could tell, nothing was missing, and nothing would have given him information about the mountain home.

But he couldn't be sure. He needed Morgan to come look too.

Gio pulled out his phone and called Matt. When he answered, Gio said, "Are you still at the office?"

"I just left. What's wrong?"

He explained what had happened and asked him to bring Morgan and Jacq to the apartment.

Before Matt arrived with the women, the LEOs showed up and began their investigation.

Gio was talking to Detective Buckley, better known as Buck, about a pile of ashes and a couple of cigarettes they found outside when a hand snaked around Gio's waist.

He wrapped his arm around his wife's shoulders. Her forehead was deeply creased.

"He was here again?" Her quiet voice wavered.

Gio tightened his grip. "Yeah, I need you to look around and see if you can think of anything he might have found that would put you in more danger. Did we have the address for the property sitting around anywhere?"

"I don't believe so, but I'll think while I look." She kissed his cheek and left as smoothly as she had appeared.

"How do I keep her safe, Buck?"

The detective shook his head. "We catch the guy."

"That's easier wished than executed." How were they going to catch a man who seemed to fall off the radar constantly? A man of whom none would speak? What about him struck such fear? Dean Rockefeller had an air about him that said *don't mess with me*, but Gio didn't see why everyone he talked to seemed to be terrified of the man. As much as he didn't want Morgan to have to go through pulling back the memories, maybe if she remembered more, they'd have answers to those questions.

Chapter Twenty-Eight

BECAUSE MORGAN WAS STRUGGLING Sunday morning, they chose to stay home from church. Plus the idea of going to the place where Dean had kidnapped her only a week ago terrified her. Gio too. He had suggested they stay home when they had crawled in bed at midnight after the fiasco at the apartment.

She hadn't noticed anything that would have given Dean a clue about where they were living. Even so, Gio was ready to move the trailer to a campground or maybe even the FBI parking lot if they'd allow it.

But that wasn't the half of what was going through Morgan's mind. She'd had a baby. Though the memory was still fuzzy, it was becoming clearer. Very slowly. However, she was now convinced it was a true memory.

A little girl. Aurora. All she could remember was holding her baby in the hospital and small flashes of being in labor. Dean had actually been helpful, sort of. He had been present and had held her hand. But the nurse had coached her more than he did. That probably wasn't unusual.

Morgan snagged another tissue and curled deeper into the corner of the couch. Gio sat at the table engrossed in his Bible. She loved how he sought the Lord continually.

After tossing the used tissue in the garbage, she tugged the blanket up to her chin. She was feeling safe. Despite the confused tears that had fallen almost continually from the moment she woke up, watching the church service online had her feeling refreshed.

So, she dug into her memories. The part she wanted to remember most was also the most terrifying—why had she left her daughter? Dean wouldn't have been looking for her if he'd sold her off to some other schmuck. Why would she run without Aurora? Did something happen to the baby? Was she still alive?

Where was that memory?

If nothing else, she wanted to remember her baby more.

Flashes of memories began to return. Aurora's cries when she was hungry. Being dog tired. Dean was missing from the memories, sort of. She could remember feeling abandoned to care for the baby herself. She recalled her fear of him intensifying, but she couldn't recall why.

A decision. She would leave *with* Aurora.

What caused her to make that decision? She couldn't find the answer. Instead, the next steps came to her memory and played out in her mind.

As Aurora fussed in her bassinet, Morgan packed the diaper bag as full as she could without it being obvious she had more than normal. They'd leave right after Aurora's one-month exam. One blessing of Aurora being early was the doctors' insistence she go to her check-ups. Otherwise Dean might have refused. He'd only taken three weeks of paternity leave, even though the hospital where he worked would have given him more—another blessing. He wasn't home today.

Morgan needed to not set off any red flags. They needed to run, but she wasn't sure she'd be able to pull it off. Dean seemed to have eyes everywhere. She couldn't trust anyone.

Where would she go, though? Home? Could she find her brother? No, her family didn't want her.

She had to get as far away as possible. Maybe she'd aim for Iowa. She could get lost there, right?

Somehow she doubted there was a single place on the globe where Dean Rockefeller's grasp didn't reach. If only she knew how to fake their deaths. It might be better for them if they were dead, but as depressed as she was, she wasn't slipping into the danger zone of harming her baby. She could never.

With the diaper bag slung over her shoulder, Morgan scooped baby Aurora into her arms. Once in the car, she took Aurora to her appointment. It seemed to go well, and she tried to not act weird, but it was hard to conceal so much. How could she hide that she was with a psychotic man—one the community trusted and respected? Little did they know. How could she hide that she was depressed beyond measure? How could she hide that she was terrified of the life her daughter might face with her biological father?

She needed help. But a doctor was not trustworthy. She almost slipped up to the nurse but managed to keep herself in check.

No one could be trusted.

After the appointment, she drove north.

Stopping every three hours at the max made the drive seem to take forever. She finally stopped to sleep for a little while in a Walmart parking lot north of Gainesville. As soon as Aurora woke to eat again, they hit the road, continuing north.

Morgan was paranoid that Dean was following them, but as she drove along the interstate in the middle-of-nowhere Georgia, she didn't see anyone behind her.

She would never be able to live without looking over her shoulder. Maybe someone else could give Aurora the chance of living a normal life. Morgan couldn't.

A pit of despair opened beneath her, and she slowly slid into it.

What could she do? She'd been a prostitute for longer than anything. Without a driver's license or any identification, she'd never be able to get a job. And if she went and tried to get a license, Dean would just find her, somehow. Wouldn't that make her findable?

Aurora was better off without her. Maybe she could be adopted by a family who would love her and give her everything. A family where she'd never be at risk of being raped or trafficked.

The sun began coming up as she neared signs directing her to choose between Atlanta and Macon.

She chose Macon and drove toward the small-ish city.

Aurora was getting fussy yet again, so Morgan exited the highway and drove around looking for a secluded place to park.

She found a spot in a church parking lot. Could someone in the church take her baby and give her a good home?

Morgan fed Aurora as she debated, even prayed, about what to do. She didn't want to let go of her little girl, but she loved her so much she also didn't want her to grow up in the life Morgan could provide. She'd never be able to give her the stable home environment every child deserved. And who was to say that the next guy who came into Morgan's life wouldn't be as perverted as her step-dad. Hopefully, he was still rotting in jail.

Stroking her daughter's fuzzy little curls, Morgan worked to memorize every feature, including the little birthmark that peeked out from her hairline. The distinguishing mark might help Morgan recognize her when she was older, should their paths ever meet again. If only she could guarantee Dean was as disengaged as he'd seemed and wouldn't remember the mark.

She held the baby up to her shoulder to burp her. *God, I don't know why You'd listen to me, but please protect Aurora.*

Morgan's whole body shook. How could she abandon her baby? But what choice did she have?

She got out of the car and grabbed the diaper bag and car seat but kept Aurora tucked safely in her arms. She walked up to the church's front door.

There were other cars in the parking lot, but the door was locked. She pressed the button.

A voice came over the speaker. "How can I help you?" The southern accent was thick.

"I'm ... I need ... my baby needs a home."

"Miss, churches aren't a safe haven in Georgia."

"Oh." Morgan turned back toward the car. Maybe leaving her baby was the wrong idea anyway. But Dean. He'd find them.

The door opened behind her. "Miss?"

Morgan turned to see a stout older woman half-running, half-lumbering toward her.

"Is leaving your baby your only option?"

Morgan nodded, making tears slosh all over Aurora's head.

"Oh sweetheart, I think you have enough love to make this work."

Morgan shook her head. "It's not like that. I can't keep her safe. Please, where can I leave her with someone who can care for her and protect her?"

"Are you sure?"

"Yes." *No! No! No!* This was the last thing she wanted.

"How about I walk over to the fire station with you?"

"Please."

The woman took the car seat and diaper bag, giving Morgan the opportunity to focus on her daughter for a few more minutes before she surrendered her to the care of a stranger. But safe havens were supposed to be anonymous. Dean would have no way of tracking Aurora down.

Morgan followed her into the truck bay of the neighboring fire station.

An older Black man came around the end of the fire truck. "How can I help you ladies?"

The woman handed him the car seat and squeezed Morgan's elbow. "I'll be outside."

Morgan held Aurora tighter. "My baby needs a new home. A safe home."

The man's eyes watered. "How old is she?"

"Four weeks."

He nodded. "We can take her if you're sure that's what you want."

Morgan squeezed her eyes shut. "I have to."

The man's strong hand rested on her back.

"Do you promise to keep her safe?"

"Absolutely."

A hiccup stole her words. She lifted Aurora away from her chest and kissed the baby's pudgy cheeks. "I love you, baby girl. Maybe one day our paths will cross. May the Lord bless you and keep you."

She kissed her and hugged her one last time before placing her in the arms of the waiting firefighter.

He cradled the baby with tender care and tears slid down his cheeks.

"Please make sure she stays safe. Please."

"I will, miss."

Morgan tore her gaze away from her baby and bolted out of the fire station bay. She ran as fast as she could all the way back to the car, where she collapsed to the ground beside the driver's side door. She buried her face in her hands and wept.

The woman came to her side and sat beside her. She wrapped her arms around Morgan and cried with her.

She'd never hold her baby again. She'd just surrendered all of her parental rights in that one action. But she'd also stripped Dean of his. *Please, God, keep Aurora safe.*

Gio looked up from his Bible at the sound of his wife crying on the couch. He rose from his chair. She wasn't simply crying, though; she was weeping. A guttural, soul-deep anguish unlike any he'd ever witnessed. And with all Morgan had gone through in her life, she'd had to endure many grief-filled sessions to bring about her healing.

His heart broke, shattered for her. He sat beside her and pressed a tissue into her hands.

She looked up at him, a spark of understanding in her eyes. He'd pulled her from a memory.

He tugged her close, and she fell against his chest where sobs shook her body for a long time. He stayed silent. She'd tell him when she could.

As the sobs subsided, Morgan lifted her head and smiled.

He did not expect that. "You remembered something significant?"

She nodded. "I understand why I blocked the whole experience from my memory. Gio, I gave her up." The smile was gone. "I put her in the hands of a stranger to keep her safe." She told him the entire memory, and by the end he couldn't contain his own tears.

She'd given her baby up to protect her.

Gio held Morgan close. Zillions of questions flew through his mind, but he didn't want to rush out of this moment. Morgan needed to process remembering such a significant action.

She sat back and blew her nose again. "I wonder what happened after that. Did that man protect her like he promised? What happened to the woman who comforted me? Do you think we could find her?"

"I bet we could, especially if you can remember the name of the church or which fire station it was."

"I could probably figure it out. The memory was so clear. But I don't understand—if I remember leaving her, who is the child Dean has now?"

"That's a really good question."

"I need to see her."

He opened his mouth to reply, but Morgan jolted. Finger raised in the air, she jumped up, snagged his sketch pad from beside the couch, and sat right back down. She opened to the picture he'd sketched a few weeks back.

"What is it?"

Morgan ran her finger down the girl's hairline. "Why did you do this with her hairline?"

"It's what I remember seeing."

"But the only color you added was the headband. What about this?"

He closed his eyes and pulled up the memory of his dream. "A birthmark. It was a little red—maybe a port wine stain."

She gasped. "Oh Gio, this is my Aurora." Her fingers covered her mouth, and she stared at the sketch. "She's so grown up."

"When Dylan and Jacq go to the school tomorrow, I'll be sure to have them ask for a photo of Dean's daughter."

"Do you think the school will let them?"

"It's worth asking." He wrapped his arm around his wife, and she melted into him while continuing to stare at the sketch.

Surrendered to a safe haven, Aurora should have been protected from Dean's grasp. Maybe the child he'd claimed wasn't actually Aurora. If not Aurora, though, who was the little girl? Did she have parents somewhere looking for her? Or had Dean's tentacles reached in and grasped Aurora out of the safe haven? *Help us find answers, Lord. Please protect Aurora wherever she is.*

Chapter Twenty-Nine

GIO LEANED AGAINST THE wall outside the exam room at the doctor's office. The OB/GYN had been able to fit Morgan in first thing Monday morning. He'd come out a few minutes ago to wait while the female doctor examined Morgan.

It wasn't long before the doctor reappeared. She smiled at Gio. "As soon as Morgan is ready, come to my office. I'd love to talk to you both."

She seemed rather cheery for someone whose words made him think something was wrong.

He slipped into the exam room as Morgan was buttoning her jeans. "Is everything okay?"

Morgan shrugged. "She didn't say much, mostly listened. I talked the whole time and told her a lot. I made the long story as short as possible. She seemed sweet and understanding."

Gio picked up Morgan's purse from the chair while she set the exam cloth on the table. "Ready?"

She nodded and took her purse from him.

Hand in hand they walked down the hall and into the doctor's open office. The doctor motioned to the chairs. "Close the door and have a seat."

As Gio did what she asked, he said, "Thank you for seeing Morgan at such short notice."

"I'm glad to. Jacq has told me about you both, and I'm happy to help. Well, Morgan, you look really healthy. I understand your concern about getting pregnant, and obviously we'll have to run a few tests to see if anything else is amiss, but"—she paused—"I can say with certainty that you've had a vaginal delivery of a full, or at least nearly full-term baby."

Morgan's grip tightened around Gio's hand. "So it wasn't just my imagination."

"Definitely not. I searched medical records and was unable to find anything in Miami under the names you gave me. Is there anything else I can try?" She looked at Gio. "I know you'll be able to access what you need as FBI, but I thought it would be helpful if I could find exactly what you need to subpoena."

He nodded. "I appreciate that. Morgan, what did you say he always calls you?"

"Angel." She shuddered. "I don't know why. It creeps me out."

The doctor shook her head. "I didn't find anything under the name 'Angel' that could be Morgan."

"Wait," Morgan scooted forward in her seat. "He often called me his wife. It's what pimps do, though, claim to be our husbands. But what did we say his wife's name was?"

"I can't remember. Let me call Jacq. She can look it up, assuming they haven't left—"

"Just call Aliza then."

"Fair enough." He dialed Aliza's number. Once she answered, he kept the niceties short and asked for the wife's name.

"Evangeline Coffney Rockefeller."

"Ev*angel*ine—well, that makes sense. Thank you."

"Sure thing."

He hung up, then shared the name with the doctor. She punched it into the computer.

Morgan muttered, "Angel ... Evangeline ... why did he call me by his wife's name?"

The doctor said, "I found records." She told them the hospital's name and what exactly they'd need to request. "Once you look at them, let me know if they are actually yours, and if possible, pass them on to me. That could help me as your physician. I can see they are there but can't request them without Evangeline's consent."

Morgan nodded.

Gio thanked the doctor. As soon as they were in the car, he'd call Aliza back and have those medical records pulled along with Dean's daughter's.

Jacq stood quietly beside Dylan as they waited for the headmaster of the school to see them. She was grateful her stomach was holding steady this morning, unlike yesterday evening when she'd had to lie down instead of watching a movie with Dylan, Gio, and Morgan. She blamed it on Harper, but it had been the baby's fault instead.

Dylan elbowed her. "You okay?"

She smiled. "Better this morning." She let out a puff of air. "But I can't go any longer without telling Morgan and Gio. We need to tell them about the baby."

"But when? Timing feels off with Morgan's memory."

Jacq dropped her shoulders. "I know. But I feel like I'm lying to them, and I can't do that."

"Same. There's a chance Gio suspects something."

"If they didn't have so much going on, they would probably have already figured it out."

Dylan chuckled. "Most likely."

He rubbed her back briefly before letting his hand drop away. She loved working together, but maintaining a professional appearance was hard at times.

"Agents?" The school secretary came around the counter. "The headmaster will see you now. This way."

She led them down a short hallway and into an office lined with bookshelves. In the center of the room was a large, ornate desk.

A tall woman with short, white hair stood. "Welcome. I'm headmaster Heidi Boilan. How can I help you today? I understand it has something to do with one of our students. I'm not sure what business the FBI would have with any of them."

Jacq extended her hand. "I'm Special Agent Jacq Harris. It's more directly related to the father of one of your students as he's part of an open investigation."

Headmaster Boilan shook Jacq's hand and then Dylan's. "Oh dear. Please sit. How can I assist you?"

"We'd like to talk to you about Dr. Dean Rockefeller." Jacq let the name hang and watched Ms. Boilan for her reaction.

Her eyebrows rose to unnatural heights. "I can't imagine what involvement he would have with a federal investigation."

"Is his daughter in school today?"

"Aurora? No, she's been absent since Thursday due to a family emergency."

Yeah, if that's what you call hiding from the FBI. "That's unfortunate. Do you have an emergency contact for them? It's very important we reach Dr. Rockefeller."

"Agent Harris, we pride ourselves on our discretion. That's not information I can just hand out."

"Oh I understand, but we have a warrant for his arrest."

Dylan pulled the folded paper from the inside pocket of his blazer and handed it to Ms. Boilan.

"Dear heavens. Dr. Rockefeller? What charges could ..." Her voice trailed off as she read the warrant. "Kidnapping? False imprisonment? Good gracious."

Dylan added, "We are also very concerned for his daughter's safety."

"I am now as well."

Jacq asked, "Has anything ever given you pause about Dr. Rockefeller?"

Ms. Boilan shook her head. "He's perfect. A little too perfect, I've heard people say and would have to agree. It's always the handsome ones—present company excluded, I'm sure."

Dylan chuckled. Jacq agreed but rolled her eyes.

"Sorry, that was inappropriate of me. I'm probably old enough to be your mother. I'm just so off-kilter."

Dylan said, "No harm done. Does Miss Rockefeller have a locker or desk we could search?"

"Of course. Let me check the schedule. I'd prefer we do so when her class is not going to be around."

Jacq nodded. "That would be our preference too."

Ms. Boilan checked her computer for the schedule, along with contact information for Dr. Rockefeller. The latter produced no new information, but ten minutes later Ms. Boilan led them to the first-grade classroom.

Jacq tugged on Dylan's sleeve and whispered, "First grade. That's the age Morgan said Aurora would be."

Dylan pressed his lips together before saying, "We need to see a photograph."

They followed Ms. Boilan into the classroom. The decor was a strange mixture of ivy- league-style architecture and primary elementary posters.

"We'll have to wait until the teacher returns as I'm unsure which desk is Miss Rockefeller's."

Jacq nodded and strolled around the room. On one wall, class photos from the last few years were in frames. She skipped all of the others and focused in on this year's class of first-graders. She scanned the names along the bottom and found Aurora's, then she counted over the correct number of children until she found the little girl.

She gasped.

A tiny Morgan stared back at her.

"Dylan!"

He rushed over to her side.

"It's her." She pointed to the child with a purple headband. "Without a doubt."

Jacq pulled her phone out of her suit pocket and snapped a photo.

The headmaster joined them. "She's beautiful, isn't she?"

Jacq nodded and painstakingly reined in her emotions. She wanted to explode. How was it possible that Dean had Aurora? After the memory Morgan said she had yesterday, Jacq fully expected this kid to be some random child. But there was no denying this was Morgan's little girl.

Dylan was holding it together better. "Do you know much about her mother?"

"Unfortunately, no. I asked during their admissions interview, but all Dr. Rockefeller said was she'd been lost to them for years. And that was it."

A young woman walked into the room. "You were asking about Aurora? I mean Miss Rockefeller?"

Ms. Boilan said, "Yes, these federal agents would like to search her things."

The young woman stepped closer and extended her hand. "I'm Miss Arnet, Miss Rockefeller's teacher."

Dylan and Jacq each shook her hand.

"Aurora never talks about her mother, and I get the impression she's not allowed to. The other day she started to say something, but she cut herself off quickly and apologized repeatedly. It was a major red flag."

Jacq's heart cracked in half at the thought of what this little girl had to endure as Dean's daughter. There was a reason everyone seemed so terrified of him. And if she was apologizing for saying something about her mom, Aurora knew she was supposed to be afraid too.

Resisting the urge to grip Dylan's hand, she shoved hers in her pockets. How was she supposed to tell Morgan the baby she thought she surrendered to save her from Dean ended up back with him anyway?

Morgan sat on the edge of Gio's desk since the extra chair from Saturday had been reclaimed by its owner. She needed to go to the library, so she'd have a new book to read instead of twiddling her thumbs while everyone else investigated. Or she should take up Mrs. Harris on the idea of staying at their house during the day to help with Harper. But she needed to be near the office today, even if it wasn't normal for a wife or a victim to hang out there. It was probably only a matter of time before Warren sent her out the door.

Aliza's voice broke into her thoughts. "I have medical records for both Aurora and Evangeline."

Morgan hopped off the desk and darted across the aisle to Aliza. "Talk to me."

"Give me a second. I haven't even opened the files yet."

Morgan leaned over Aliza's shoulder, and Gio wasn't far away. He'd rolled his chair over to the end of her desk.

Aliza clicked on Aurora's file first. The first thing that struck Morgan was the date of birth. January fourth of the year Morgan had been with Dean.

They skimmed the records. The delivery lined up with what Morgan remembered. And the description of the baby: curly dark hair, olive skin, port wine stain birthmark at hairline.

This baby was the one Morgan gave birth to. But was the remainder of the file the same child? It couldn't be. She'd given her baby to that firefighter.

Aliza scrolled through the file. Nothing proved it wasn't the same child.

But the mother line on the birth certificate read Evangeline Rockefeller.

Aliza opened Evangeline's records. The woman was born eight and a half years earlier than Morgan. The records showed a disturbing past with drugs and alcohol. She'd been in and out of rehab on several occasions, primarily for the abuse of narcotics—heroin being her drug of choice.

Gio said, "I guess that could explain at least part of Dean's hatred of heroin."

Morgan could only nod. That poor woman. Heroin was a horrible drug to become addicted to. Morgan couldn't explain how she'd been able to break free of it so cleanly, but she had. However, that didn't mean the desire for the immediate effects of the drug didn't tease her mind on occasion. Addiction didn't disappear overnight. And while Dean was a horrible person, she was grateful to him for whatever concoction he had come up with that broke her bond to heroin.

But what had happened to Evangeline? If he worked so hard develop a detoxing regimen, wasn't she the first one he would have helped?

Aliza pointed at the screen. "Well, this is interesting." She quickly bounced back and forth between Evangeline's early records and Aurora's. "Someone's blood type doesn't change."

"Wait, what?" Gio leaned closer.

Aliza flipped to Aurora's records. She checked a couple of points. "Aurora has O negative."

Gio said, "That's significant."

Morgan asked, "Why is that important?"

"I think it typically requires both parents have O negative."

"I'm O negative." Morgan felt her heart rate slow way down. This could be proof. It seemed like her memories were enough, but proof could only help ... right? Yet she'd surrendered her daughter. "Sure, the baby had O negative, but what about the little girl who goes to that school?"

Aliza gripped Morgan's arm. "This test is only a few months old. She had some blood work done for a suspected allergy." Aliza pulled up Evangeline's records again. "But she's A positive. I doubt she's this girl's mom, regardless of what the documents show." Aliza scrolled through the records. "During the prenatal tests, blood work was done. And look. Out of the blue Evangeline is now O negative."

"These are real memories." Morgan sank back against the cubical half-wall, barely able to support herself. Part of her still hoped the memories weren't memories at all. But she'd really had a baby and then given her up. The equal parts exhilarating joy and crushing devastation ripped her inner self to shreds.

Gio reached for her, but the office door opening drew their attention away.

Dylan and Jacqui walked in. The expression on Jacqui's face, the intensity with which she met Morgan's eyes ...

"What is it?" she asked, skipping any pleasantries. She met Jacqui halfway.

Jacqui didn't speak a word but walked to Morgan and pressed a five-by-seven photograph into her hand.

"What's this?" She looked down at the photo.

A little girl. Her little girl. With a purple headband. No.

Her legs gave out under the weight, but Gio and Jacqui both caught her. She sank to the floor with them. Her little girl was in the hands of this monster.

She couldn't breathe, couldn't think, couldn't live. How'd she screw up so badly that the very thing she'd been trying to prevent came true?

Gio lifted the picture from her hand. "Oh Morgan."

She leaned into his chest. "This picture is exactly the sketch you drew."

He nodded, and when Jacqui questioned him, he explained the dream he'd had.

Morgan couldn't wrap her mind around it all. It was too much. More than before, she wanted answers. How did he get her back? That should have been impossible. Where was she right now? Was she safe? Had he hurt her? Had he let other men hurt her?

She pushed up from Gio's chest. "We have to find her."

Chapter Thirty

GIO WOULD DO ANYTHING necessary to find Aurora. But what did they have? Nothing. No idea where to even look. Dylan and Jacq's search of Aurora's school desk and locker gave them no information.

Except the photograph. Morgan sat on the floor beside his desk staring at the picture that Jacq had boldly asked the teacher about. Surprisingly, she had an extra. The school always provided the teacher a class photo and two of each student—one for the record and a second that was often tossed. The teacher freely gave it to Jacq.

What a blessing for Morgan.

A cruel blessing it seemed, though, since she was fixated now.

They had to find Aurora.

Gio's phone rang and he answered. Buck told him a canvas of Gio's apartment complex Saturday night had produced an interesting video, which he was sending to Gio's inbox right away. They had an ID on one of the suspects.

"One of?" Gio asked.

"Yep, it clearly shows two men. The tall one keeps his back to the camera, but the other guy's arm tattoo is significant."

Gio refreshed his email. A new message from Buck appeared. "Got it."

Gio pressed play, watching the security video as Buck let him know other details about where they were in the case. "No way."

"What is it?" Buck asked.

Gio motioned for Dylan to come over. "It's one of the guys we've been looking for since the beginning of last month." Mick, the guy with the clock tattoo, was talking to another man. Gio could tell the taller suspect was Dean Rockefeller, even though he didn't look in the right direction as he walked toward the stairs to Gio's apartment. Mick lit a cigarette and scanned the parking lot.

Dylan smacked Gio's shoulder. "Proof that Dean is connected to Nicoletta."

"And Mick is still in town." Gio switched Buck to speaker. "Do you have anything more on this guy? We need to find him."

Buck said, "You're in luck. Patrols picked him up last night on a DUI. It's like he was trying to get caught."

Dylan clapped. "Praise the Lord. Hopefully this guy will be a little looser with his tongue than the others have been."

"Only one way to find out," Gio said. "Thanks, Buck."

They hung up, and Gio leaned back in his chair. "I guess I'm supposed to sit this one out."

Dylan nodded. "It would be best. I'll take the firecracker with me. She'll break him."

Gio laughed.

Jacq stood up. "He won't know what hit him." She punched one fist into the other palm.

"Violence is never the answer."

"No, Jesus is the answer, but violence can be a handy solution." She winked at him.

He shook his head but considered Jacq. Something was a little different about her, but he couldn't place what.

After a late lunch, Dylan held open the interview-room door at the police station for Jacq. Ever since she'd seen the photo of Aurora, she'd been full-on momma bear, ready to take anyone down if it meant getting Aurora to her mother.

"Fancy seeing you again." Jacq took a seat at the table across from Mick.

"I've never seen you before."

Dylan walked into the room. "But you have seen me."

The man snarled.

They were *not* off to a great start. They needed this guy to cozy up to them and tell them everything they needed to know about Dean Rockefeller.

Dylan took a seat. "I should have led with the other foot. I'm Special Agent Dylan Harris, and this is Special Agent Jacq Harris. Look, we need your help. We want your boss, not you. Pretty sure you aren't the one who rifled through all of Gio Crespi's belongings."

He shrugged. "I don't know who that is."

"You don't make a point of knowing whose home you're breaking into?"

"I'm just the lock man. The lookout. The currier. Nothing more. I don't need to know anything else."

"You're confessing to picking the lock?"

"Whatever. That's nothin'."

"We can clear your DUI if you tell us where we can find Dean Rockefeller."

"You think I'd rather be on his hit list than have a DUI? You guys are stupid. I don't care about the DUI. I'm safer locked-up."

"Safer? What difference does it make if you're on his hit list? At least you won't be in jail. Surely you can escape his reach."

"There's no such thing as out of that guy's reach."

"How long have you worked for him?"

"Too long." Mick scanned the room. "You know he has eyes and ears everywhere, right?"

Dylan ignored the statement. "The arresting officer suggested you let yourself be caught driving drunk."

"Can't you take me to the FBI office to talk about this?"

"That's not how this works, but if you tell me what I need to know about Dean Rockefeller, I can pull some strings to get you into witness protection."

"You want him that bad?"

Jacq shifted in her seat. "You have no idea."

He shook his head. "The stories about how he kills people that cross him aren't fiction." Mick shuddered.

"Is that why everyone is so afraid of him?" Jacq asked.

"Have you met the guy? He carries himself with such intimidation because he knows how to suck the life out of a man in the most agonizing way possible."

Who were they dealing with? Was Dean Rockefeller even worse than they could fathom? *How does it get worse than trafficking women for sex?*

"Then what was he looking for in that apartment on Saturday?"

"You think he talks about these things to me? That's hilarious. I did catch something about finding another location."

"Come on, he talked a lot in that video we have of you two."

He sighed. Apparently he already knew about the video. "Mostly threats about keeping an eye out. He's gonna be furious that I didn't see the guy's phone in the window. That's my third strike. You will all be better off if he never finds out about the video."

Jacq opened the folder in her hand and placed the photo array they had shown Nicoletta on the table. "So you're saying one of these guys is your boss? The guy who trashed the apartment the other day?"

"He's done worse than trashing one guy's apartment."

Jacq tapped on the table. "Which one, Mick?"

"You know which one he is."

"Confirm for me we're talking about the same guy."

"The doctor." He firmly placed his index finger on the image of Dean Rockefeller.

"And you'll confirm he's involved in child trafficking? You brought Nicoletta here to him?"

"Wait, you—oh yeah, the airport."

"Exactly. You'll confirm though? You were bringing her here for him?"

He slumped in his chair. "I'm already dead, count my words. He will find me no matter where you put me, and you won't know what happened to me."

"If you're so convinced about that, why not just tell us everything you know? All his crimes. He's killed others?"

Mick's head slumped. "Oh yeah, and I'll be next."

"We can protect you."

He let out a huge gust of air. "I applaud your optimism. But you're right, I might as well tell you everything." He leaned over the table as far as he could and raised his pointer finger. "Promise me this: whatever you do, make my death worth it and take this guy down. Put a bullet in his head for the sake of the rest of humanity."

"Given the legal opportunity, I promise that is exactly what I will do." Jacq leaned forward on the table and met Mick eye to eye. "We will keep you safe. Tell me everything."

Morgan paced up and down the hallway between the office and breakroom. All the pieces were coming together, but she felt more lost than ever. She had a daughter, yet she had no way of getting to her. Six years gone. Six years missing the child of her womb.

"Hey, Morgan." Gio stepped out of the office with a laptop in his hand. "I got in touch someone you might want to talk to."

She paused and tilted her head. "Who?"

"Come with me. Let's find some privacy." He led her to the breakroom. "I found the firefighter."

"How is that possible?" She took a chair beside Gio.

"He still works at the station." Gio opened the laptop and placed a Zoom call.

The burly man whose arms she placed her baby into came on the screen. "Hello."

Morgan couldn't breathe.

Gio rubbed her back. "Thanks for being willing to talk to us, Captain Richards."

"My pleasure." He looked at Morgan. "It's good to see you again."

"You too." Her voice squeaked. "You remember me?"

"Don't run into your circumstances every day."

"Do you remember my baby?"

"Yes." He nodded and tucked his lips inside his mouth.

"What happened to her? I have reason to believe she ended up back with her father."

Captain Richards heaved a large breath. "That *is* what happened. About an hour after you left, the police arrived asking if we were the fire station where the baby had been dropped off. A man was with them, claiming to be the father. I fought for her, I promise. I told the cops the mother pleaded with me to keep her safe. The officer said the man explained the mother was suffering from postpartum depression and possibly psychosis."

"Convincing you I wanted you to keep her safe from *me*. I never said keep her safe from her father, did I?"

He shook his head. "I had a bad feeling, but I didn't know what to do. I followed up, though, and they demanded a paternity test. They didn't want to give her to someone who wasn't her parent."

"I understand." Morgan was crushed. How did Dean find her there? She would have been better off continuing to run with Aurora in her arms. Maybe she should have ditched the car sooner. Maybe he had put a tracker on it ... why hadn't she thought of that then?

"Miss? I did a little checking after your husband reached out to me earlier today. You should know the court order removing your parental rights was never filed."

"Wait, what? Really?" Could it be true? Could she fight for her baby?

"Yes, ma'am. I'm sure your FBI husband can confirm, but I have it on good authority." He hid his mouth behind the back of his hand and leaned close to the computer with an endearing twinkle in his eye. "My wife works in the courts."

Morgan and Gio both chuckled. They chatted with him for a few more minutes and promised to stay in touch.

As soon as Gio closed the laptop, Morgan collapsed back in the seat. Too many emotions. She couldn't pick which one to hold on to. Dean had their daughter, and she'd escaped, missing the opportunity to see her little girl again. Now he was on the run with her. Hiding only God knows where. *Jesus, help me find her.*

That's it. It was time to drive. "Gio, we have to drive and see if I can remember how to get to that house. I've been there multiple times. Surely, I can put it together."

"It's going to be dark soon."

"Then we need to leave. The first time I went was in the dark, maybe that will make it easier."

"It's worth a shot."

Fifteen minutes later they were in the car, and after swinging through the Chick-fil-A drive-thru, they headed out of town toward the mountains. She drove as Gio messed with the GPS on his phone. He planned to drop pins on the map for points where she remembered anything.

So they drove. She struggled to keep her mind focused on the task and not on all the parts of Aurora's life she had missed. What should she have done differently?

No, focus on the drive.

She turned down a mountain highway. It led in the same general direction to their mountain home, but it was the longer way to get there.

An hour later they had made a few turns and back tracks, but eventually they were headed down a road familiar to her.

A large gate loomed ahead. The one she'd been behind on a number of occasions, the one she'd been imprisoned behind only a week ago. She resisted the urge to stop. "That's it."

"Keep driving. Are you sure?"

"As certain as the red maple knows its leaves have changed to red." Was Aurora behind that gate? She wanted to turn around and bust the door down. "How far do I keep going?"

"Head home. I pinned it."

Her heart hurt to drive away, but she kept going and came to another road she recognized. "Wait a minute, how close to home are we?"

Gio put his GPS up on the dash for her. "Even closer than I realized."

They only had to go around another two bends, and they were at Jacq's property. Morgan turned up the long driveway. "I knew the mountains I saw out his window looked familiar."

She stopped at the gate and hugged herself. "I don't like that he's so close."

Gio reached over and placed his hand on her shoulder. "We'll get him. And we will keep you safe."

She nodded. "But Aurora. Is she really just over on the next ridge?"

"We will find her too. Praise the Lord she's so close for when the time comes to rescue her."

Morgan nodded. While Gio opened the gate, Morgan prayed. *Please, Lord, restore Aurora to me. Thank You for returning my memories. Bring back anything else You need me to remember. But above all, keep Aurora safe!*

Chapter Thirty-One

ONCE INSIDE THEIR LITTLE travel-trailer home, Morgan put on her pajamas and got ready for bed. It wasn't very late, but she was exhausted. When she came out of the bedroom Gio was on the phone, pacing the length of the living space.

He came back toward her, and she wordlessly questioned who it was.

He moved the phone away from his mouth. "Dylan. The guy who brought Nicoletta to Knoxville squealed like a kicked puppy."

Hope ignited in Morgan. "Does that mean we can get Aurora?"

"Maybe." Gio redirected his attention to Dylan. "Sounds good. Keep me informed."

He hung up.

"Well?" She waited with anticipation. Between her being able to identify Dean's property and the guy talking, maybe this meant they could move forward, storm the mansion, and bring it all to an end once and for all.

Gio stepped forward, leaned his cane against the table, and gripped her upper arms. "They're working on a plan. We just have to sit and wait. And sleep. It will probably be morning before things come together."

"I don't know if I can do that."

"A few minutes ago you wanted to go to bed."

"And I'm exhausted, but I'll get dressed if we need to go back and help."

"I'm still on limited duty. I can't do much on a sting."

"But ..."

"Dylan will call."

She fiddled with the buttons on his shirt.

"I can think of something that will pass the time." He slipped his arms around her and dipped her backward, meeting his lips to hers.

She reveled in her husband's passionate kiss. Until his knee gave out and they hit the floor.

Laughter bubbled from deep inside and burst out.

Gio scrambled to get up, but she pulled him back down to her.

"Where do you think you're going? I mean the bed would be more comfortable, but here works too."

Before they got too carried away, Gio pushed off the ground and pulled her up, then led her to the bedroom.

Bianca slid the plate with a brownie on it across the island to Aurora. The little girl's eyes sparkled with delight at the dessert. Bianca lifted her own brownie and raised it in a cheer. In unison they both took their first bite and giggled. Dean came around the corner with a smile stretched across his face. "Good brownies?"

They both nodded.

He looked at his watch. "I'm glad, but it's time for bed."

Aurora groaned.

Dean gave her a pointed look, and she quieted down and finished her brownie.

Dean ran his hand along Bianca's back and let it rest on her opposite hip. He leaned close to her ear. "Get her ready for bed as soon as possible."

"Yes, sir." Bianca finished her brownie too, though it didn't sit well with Dean's tone.

His phone rang, and he stepped away to answer it.

She was grateful for the space, but she listened closely to his conversation.

"What do you mean he got himself arrested?" He paused. "On purpose?" He listened to the person on the other end of the line. "Get him if you can and bring him up the mountain. This is strike three, and even if it wasn't ..."

He hung up and fumed in his quiet way.

Aurora's eyes widened.

Bianca rushed around the island and took Aurora's hand. "Time for bed."

They went upstairs as fast as Bianca could get them there. Aurora slid her pajamas on and asked, "Why was Daddy so mad when he was on the phone?"

"I don't know, Aurora. It's not our business." Bianaca wished they had some sleepy medicine for Aurora. She hated giving it to her, but at the same time tonight could become interesting if someone had earned their third strike against Dean.

She tucked Aurora in bed without too much hassle and wandered back downstairs since she didn't know if she had permission to go to bed yet.

She found Dean in his office mixing his poisons. She walked over to him, and when he'd set his materials down, she slipped her arms around his waist. "I take it everything is not okay?"

"You could say that. We will be leaving before daybreak. You should get some sleep; I'll wake you in time to throw a few of Aurora's things together."

"Before morning?"

"Yes." He pulled her close. "But we'll be together, so it'll be all right."

Bianca wanted to throw up. She didn't want to be with him. Morgan had said she'd get Bianca out if she could, but she wouldn't be able to if Dean took her away from this place. "Where will we go?"

"Probably Denver. It'll be a long drive. Go to bed." He led her upstairs and all but pushed her into her bedroom.

The lock slid into place.

How could she and Aurora escape? Why hadn't she thought to run sooner? Why did she always follow Dean's stupid rules? He never let her take Aurora anywhere, but he'd given her access to a car to drive back and forth on her own. She could have taken Aurora and driven straight to Morgan's husband at the FBI, then to Morgan. But Dean had men everywhere. He'd find her and kill her. If only she had a way to tell Morgan they were in danger of being gone forever.

Bianca shuffled to her bed and grabbed a pillow. She hugged it tight. If God existed like her nonna had taught her when she was little, would He listen to a girl who had never talked to Him before?

God?

Later that night, Morgan slept, but it was restless at best. Dreams haunted her. Roaming a house, looking, but finding nothing. Then, in her dream, she wandered down a hall until it ended abruptly at a bookshelf. Then the bookshelf opened like a door.

She knew she was dreaming, but it was different.

The boy. The man. Dean was in her face. "Why are you here?"

"I thought you said this was my house too."

"You shouldn't be down here."

He dragged her by her arm, back through the hallway and up the stairs. Once in his office, he shoved her into a chair beside his desk. The dream shifted; more people were there, and a man sat in a chair in the center of the room. It was the same man who'd crossed Dean about the woman he'd trafficked.

Dean spoke. "When I tell you something, I expect you to do it. When I tell you I won't do business with you again, you don't get to weasel your way around and try to undermine my business."

Morgan shook in her seat. The others in the room stood perfectly still.

Fear penetrated the space.

Dean picked up a syringe off the desk. He met her eyes. For a second he almost seemed to apologize that she had to be there. But his expression hardened just as fast. "I will be obeyed. I will not be undermined."

He turned and injected the man with the liquid from the syringe.

Morgan bolted upright in bed and screamed.

Gio flipped on the light. "What's wrong?"

"I remember. I remember all of it. I know why everyone is so afraid of him. And remember that dream I told you about? It wasn't a dream. It was a memory. That poor little boy. He'd been raped. And Dean facilitated it."

"Breathe, Morgan."

She was hyperventilating. She couldn't get the breaths to slow. Those children. They hadn't been a result of hearing stories about trafficked children. No, they were real kids with real faces.

She dashed out the door toward the bathroom at the other end of the trailer and lost the last bits of her fries to the toilet. Gio was a step behind her and held her hair back.

She wiped her face and collapsed against him. "There's more. I know why people fear him. He's cruel. Not only does he traffic little children, he murders the men who don't stay in line. And it is the most gruesome process."

She buried her head in the safety of her husband's shoulder. Memories seared her mind—the man thrashing and screaming in pain for nearly an hour before he finally died.

Gio held Morgan on the bathroom floor for a long time until her sobs settled enough for them to return to bed. She'd fallen asleep in his arms, but he struggled to go back to a solid sleep. When he finally did, his own dreams plagued his mind.

Aurora called out to him—to anyone who would hear. There were other children, but none of their faces appeared as clear as Aurora's. They were at the top of a hill in a cage.

But he couldn't reach the children. He couldn't reach Aurora.

He fought uphill as flaming arrows flew past his head. He picked up a shield and the arrows were extinguished as soon as they struck. His belt was slipping off, making it harder to climb. He fastened it tighter. A helmet rolled down beside him. He put it on.

He had to get to Aurora. "I'm coming. God will save you."

She reached her arms out to him, but he was still too far away. Monsters surrounded him, snarling and baring their teeth. Sticky, wet saliva dripped from their fangs.

He dug his hands into the hill to gain traction. But instead of roots he gripped the hilt of a sword. He pulled it free from the hill. He had to slay the monsters to save Aurora. He raised the sword and swung it with all the skill of a Roman legionnaire.

Angels appeared all around him, vanquishing the monsters. Opening the way for him to get to Aurora, Bianca, and the other children.

"Gio." Morgan shook him. "Wake up."

He opened his eyes.

Morgan sat beside him. "What were you dreaming?"

He sat upright and wiped the sweat from his brow. His chest heaved, panic filling his veins. He wheeled his mind around, trying to grasp on to what the dream meant. *God, bring clarity.*

As he told Morgan about the dream, the meaning became apparent. Aurora needed him, now.

"I have to go."

"Gio, I want you to get her, but there's probably a better way."

He stroked her hair and ran his fingers into it. "Maybe, but this is definitely an urge from the Holy Spirit. I have to obey."

"What are you going to do?"

"I don't know yet."

"Chances are good he has some pretty tight surveillance around that house. The room was impossible to get out of, and I bet the house is just as hard to get into."

"I simply need eyes inside. Confirm Aurora and Bianca are there."

"Bianca. She's probably there too."

He nodded his head. "I have to get them."

"Then I'm coming with you."

"No. I need you safe."

"Let's call Jacqui and Dylan—the team. You need backup."

"I need you to go to the team and work on a plan to come in." He got out of bed and dressed.

"Gio?" Morgan's bottom lip quivered.

He dashed to her, drawing her to his chest.

"I can't stand the idea of losing you. I'm so torn."

He held her as close as possible. "I know. I can't stand the idea of something happening to Aurora. I need to find her, protect her. I have to obey."

"But is this how? Gallivanting off without a plan, without backup?"

Gio reached his hand out to Morgan. "Heavenly Father, am I hearing you wrong? Give Morgan and me clarity, direction. How do we act on this prompting?"

He prayed through the Armor of God—that they would take up the shield of faith, sword of the Spirit, the belt, the breastplate, and all the rest. That God would empower them to fight the enemy, not just the one of flesh and blood but the true enemy. This was more than a fight to save a girl from a wicked father; this was a spiritual battle.

They sat in silence. Gio pleaded with the Lord quietly in his heart. They needed an answer, direction, discernment. But the urgency grew.

He opened his eyes and met Morgan's.

They spoke at the same time. "We have to go now."

Chapter Thirty-Two

JACQ REMOVED THE ICE tray from the breakroom fridge and threw a few cubes into her coffee. She needed the awake juice in her system as soon as possible. She'd stolen a few hours of sleep on the couch, but things were starting to come together for the raid on Dean Rockefeller's mountain house. Morgan's confirmation that Mick gave them the right address was exactly what they needed to get the operation moving. They'd bust down his door and arrest him in the morning. But there was an incredible amount of work to do before then.

They had to have everything lined up perfectly. If Aurora was there, plus any other children, they needed to be careful and keep the kids safe.

She exited the breakroom and was headed back to the office when Dylan came through the door. His face was ashen.

She nearly dropped her coffee. Was Morgan okay? "What's wrong?"

"Gio just called."

Her heart slammed against her ribs. It was Morgan.

"Morgan's fine."

Jacq slumped and let out a rush of air.

"But they're being stupid. I tried to convince Gio to wait, but he refuses."

"What are you talking about?"

"They're going to Dean's. Gio said he's going to try and sneak in. He had a dream, and he and Morgan prayed and feel a huge urgency to get to Aurora."

"What on earth? I mean, if Gio had a dream ..."

"Yeah, but it's stupid to go in there like this."

"I thought he said there was a gate and a really tall fence; good chance there are cameras and such too. How does he think he's going to get in?"

"He said, and I quote, 'God will provide a way.'"

Jacq grunted. "I don't doubt the truth of that statement, but it doesn't sound like a very good plan. Does he have coms with him? Is he going in armed? Please tell me he's taking more than his Glock."

"I don't know, but he's not going to want to risk hurting any kids. His goal is stealth and sneaking Aurora out."

"At two o'clock in the morning?"

Dylan shrugged. "I don't know, but our timeline just moved up. We need to gear up and get over there immediately."

"Agreed."

Gio needed them now. The little time they had was gone because of Gio's rash actions, but as much as that frustrated Jacq, Gio wasn't one to act on a whim. If he was going in tonight he had a good reason, even if no one else could understand what that reason was.

Dressed all in black, Gio used the closely growing trees for support as he trudged up the valley he had underestimated. It felt too much like the hill in his dream, but this was the shortest path to Dean's house. Thankfully, monsters weren't literally attacking him as he climbed the hill.

Morgan had driven him up to the point of the road Dean's house was on, but Gio didn't want to risk their car being seen on any cameras Dean had. He'd kissed her with every bit of passion he could before exiting the car.

She'd met his passion but hadn't mentioned how scared she was to have him traipsing into Dean's lair without backup, without coms, without heavy artillery. But he'd seen the fear in her eyes, felt it in her shaky touch. Still, he'd strapped a pistol to his ankle and his Glock to his waist. He'd contemplated taking an AR-15, and Dylan would be livid when he found out Gio had decided against it. He had calculated the risk, and it outweighed the benefit in this situation. The goal was to get Aurora out, not to engage in a fire fight.

He didn't know how he was going to convince Aurora to go with him, but he'd cross that bridge when he came to it. If nothing else, he'd hunker down with her until the FBI came in.

At the top of the valley, he only had a few hundred feet before he was at the edge of the woods by the front gate. An eight-foot wrought-iron fence circled the entire property, and even without his weak knee, he wouldn't be able to climb it.

Staying in the shadows, he looked for cameras. There was one on the call box at the gate. If there were more, he couldn't see them. That didn't make sense. They were probably well hidden.

What he needed was to have the lights on either side of the driveway out.

The shoulder was covered in gravel. Could he throw a rock and knock out the lightbulbs? Only one way to find out.

He picked up the first rock and hit his mark, shattering the glass on the outside of the light. He threw another. His aim wasn't as good this time. A third struck the lightbulb. One down, one to go.

His phone vibrated in his pocket. Morgan. He answered, "Hey."

"There's an old box truck coming your way. I bet it's headed to Dean's. Maybe you can sneak in when it goes through the gate."

"Perfect. God's got this."

"Be careful."

"I love you."

"You too."

They hung up, and Gio quickly calculated his options. If he ran across the street maybe he could jump on the back of the truck and ride it in.

Yep, that was his best option. He doubted he had time to take care of the other light, but at least it was twice as dark now.

He hobbled across the street. His knee gave out once, but he recovered quickly and was in the shadows before a truck that looked like an old U-Haul approached.

This would be easier than he'd feared. The truck was low enough that he could, stupid knee and all, jump on while it was moving.

It slowed to turn into the driveway. He pulled the hood to his black hoodie over his head.

Once the vehicle rolled past, Gio ran as best he could, grabbed the handle on the side, and hopped onto the bumper. He plastered his body against the back and white-knuckled the handle.

The truck came to a stop in front of the gate.

His heart pounded. Hopefully he could stay out of view of the cameras as he rode in.

The driver spoke to someone on the other end of the intercom. Then the gates made a faint noise.

The truck jostled forward, nearly knocking Gio off. He stood heavy on his good leg. But as he rode down the thankfully smooth driveway, his good leg grew tired. He didn't dare shift though. He couldn't risk making a sound or his knee giving out.

The truck slowed, and based on the growing light, Gio figured they were nearing the house. He had to make a jump for it.

The land was anything but flat, and the grass was too far.

This was going to hurt.

The truck swerved closer to the edge, and Gio leaped.

Tumbling to the ground, he rolled toward the trees and kept rolling even once the momentum of the fall ceased.

He scanned the area. The house stood about a hundred yards away. The towering and sprawling mansion was massive. The driveway alone was large enough to be called a parking lot.

Why on earth did evil men prosper? It wasn't right. Every muscle in his body twitched with the desire for vengeance. This house was bought with blood money—how many lives had not only been ruined but lost because this man wanted more money?

God impressed a passage from Psalm 37 on his mind: "Be still before the Lord and wait patiently for Him; do not fret when men succeed in their ways, when they carry out their wicked schemes. Refrain from anger and turn from wrath; do not fret—it leads only to evil. For evil men will be cut off, but those who hope in the Lord will inherit the land."

Yes, Lord.

Gio stayed prone, close to the tree line, and waited. The truck stopped by the front door.

Dean came down the front steps. "Finally. Did you get him?"

The driver of the truck appeared and shook Dean's hand.

Bile rose in Gio's throat. The driver was a police officer from Knoxville—Marty Denton. He lifted the back of the truck.

"I got him. I wasn't able to find out all he said to the feds, but he squealed like a rat all right."

"Get him out. He'll pay." Dean checked his watch. "We have just enough time for him to suffer. Get the kittens loaded up. We'll roll out of here by six at the latest."

The dirty cop jumped into the truck, then pulled Mick out.

Gio bit his lip to keep a gasp from escaping. This was not good. Mick had really told them everything. No wonder Dean was in a hurry to leave.

Kittens. He had children here, didn't he?

Gio waited until the men had gone inside, then pushed himself off the ground and hid deeper in the trees. He pulled out his cell phone and texted Dylan all he had heard. The FBI needed to be here long before six a.m.

Gio had to get closer to the house. He wasn't sure he could do anything to save Mick, but he would if he could. Maybe if he could see where they were taking him and if they left him alone. But Gio had a sinking feeling he wouldn't be able to do anything.

His first objective had to stay his priority: Find Aurora. She was probably sleeping on the upper floor, but how would he get there?

Gio darted across a dark area of the driveway and crept in closer to the house.

Chapter Thirty-Three

AURORA COULDN'T SLEEP. SHE didn't understand why, but she was scared. It was as if a deep darkness had come over the house. This house always felt a little dark, even with all the lights on. But right now, it was the middle of the night.

"Auntie?" she called out. "Bianca?" She preferred her name to Auntie. But Daddy might get mad if he heard. "Auntie?"

No answer.

Aurora sat against the wall at the top of her bed, clutching her stuffed unicorn in her arms.

"Daddy?"

A noise came from downstairs, but she wasn't sure what it was. Voices. Men. Why were people here in the night time?

She turned the light on beside her bed. No one was in her room.

Daddy yelled from somewhere in the house.

She clicked the light back off. She wasn't going to call his name again. But she needed somebody.

Gripping her stuffy as tight as possible, she climbed out of bed. It was cold, so she pulled on her plushy robe and slid her feet into her fuzzy slippers.

She turned the doorknob. *Yay, it's unlocked*. She opened her door as slowly as possible.

Daddy's yelling was so loud. And so many bad words.

She covered her ears and went to Bianca's door. It was locked. Daddy didn't like either of them wandering around the house. Why was Aurora's unlocked tonight?

She slid the hook out of the hole and turned the doorknob. Slipping inside, she called to Bianca. "Are you awake?"

"What are you doing?"

"I'm scared."

"Get over here." Bianca turned on a flashlight. "Why are you awake? Never mind, that's a stupid question. Climb up in my bed."

Another man shouted back at Daddy.

"Why are they so loud?"

"I don't know." Bianca wrapped her arm around Aurora. "Was my door locked?"

"Yes."

"Well, I don't care. Why don't we sneak down to the theater room and put a movie on? It'll drown out the noises."

"Do you think Daddy will be mad?"

"Hopefully he won't even notice. Sounds like he's got enough business to take care of."

Aurora nodded and slid back out of the bed.

After pulling on a sweatshirt, Bianca took her hand and put a finger from her other hand to her lips. "You have to be very quiet. We'll go down the back staircase."

Aurora nodded. She held Bianca's hand as tight as possible and let the older girl lead her out and down the hallway.

A man screamed. "Please don't. Just shoot me instead."

Daddy said, "You crossed me." His voice sounded like thunder. "You know what comes from that. You've seen it, and now you get to experience it."

Aurora turned. Down the stairs she could see Daddy holding a shot in his hand. She tugged on Bianca's hand. "What is Daddy doing?"

"Aurora, no." She dragged Aurora down the hallway toward the stairs. "Hurry."

"What's going on?"

Bianca scooped Aurora up into her arms and ran down the stairs.

The man was still screaming.

Aurora buried her face in Bianca's hair and hugged her with all the strength she had.

Bianca raced toward the basement.

What was going on?

Concealed, Gio peeked in through a window with a large shrub growing in front of it. A flash of purple in the hallway upstairs caught his eye before Dean leaned over Mick and shoved a syringe in his arm.

He shrieked.

Gio closed his eyes and leaned against the house beside the window.

The wails of agony were heart-wrenching, even knowing the man who was dying was a pedophile. Gio would never wish that kind of death on his worst enemy, not even Dean.

It took all of his restraint not to bust in the front door and put a bullet in Dean's head and another in the head of the suffering man.

Gio shut the screams out of his mind. That purple flash might have been Aurora. It had disappeared toward the back of the house.

Gio needed to find a way in there.

After sending Morgan and Dylan a quick status update, Gio snuck around the side of the house and down the hill. Maybe a basement door would be unlocked, and he could go inside. That was wishful thinking, but the Lord had provided so far. Somehow, He'd do it again.

Guide my steps, Lord. Where do I go? How do I find them?

Gio sneaked along the side of the house, staying in the shadows, darted from tree to shrub to the side of the house and so on.

He found a door, but it was locked. He wasn't sure that one led to much other than a storage area anyway. So he moved on quickly.

He rounded the corner of the house. It was totally dark. If there were cameras, they weren't going to pick up much unless they were set to night vision.

In the backyard was a massive pool and patio. The deck above covered a wide area of the patio. Pods of chairs and couches were spread out across the space.

Dean could have huge parties here.

A darkness settled around him, and Gio grabbed a pillar that held up the deck to balance himself. So much evil had taken place here.

Gio straightened, and with a voice, barely a whisper, he spoke the name of Jesus. "Jesus, You are greater than the evil done in this place. Banish the evil one from these grounds. Redeem the lives of those who have been violated here. Come, Holy Spirit, come."

The darkness seemed to flee at the name of Jesus. Gio couldn't explain it, but in his mind's eye he saw himself surrounded by a host of angels battling the demons that lurked out in the open.

Further proof this battle was bigger than just Dean Rockefeller.

He saw another door. He slipped toward it.

A light came on in what appeared to be a stairwell deep inside the house.

Gio darted behind a large pillar. Peeking around it, he saw a person appear at the bottom of the stairs. It was a small woman holding a child in a purple robe.

Gio scanned the area. No one else seemed to be present.

He ran to the glass and knocked.

Chapter Thirty-Four

Sitting in the SUV at the foot of their driveway, Morgan hugged herself. It had been five minutes since Gio's last text. She'd dropped him off nearly forty-five minutes ago, and the waiting felt like a slow death. But nothing could be as slow and painful a death as what that man was experiencing right now.

Jesus, I pray if that man ever heard about You he would repent and turn to You in these final minutes of his life, so that this is the worst thing he'll ever experience.

She really had come a long way. Until recently, she would have wished far worse for a man who violated women and children and sold them for sex to line his own pockets.

She drummed the steering wheel. Taking up knitting or crocheting might be a good idea, then maybe in the future she could do something productive with her nervous energy.

She'd tried reading and scrolling the internet, but she couldn't do it. She'd get out and pace but if Gio called and needed a quick getaway she didn't want to be anywhere besides the driver's seat.

A large black van pulled in front of her.

She screamed and hit the door locks. Jacqui jumped out of the back and ran toward her.

Morgan fumbled to unlock and open the door. As soon as she could manage it, she got out and fell into Jacqui's arms.

"Please tell me you brought more than one van."

Jacqui smiled. "Of course. We've got a full team and then some. They are setting up on the perimeter. You and I will sit in"—she pointed to the van—"the command center."

Morgan grabbed her phone and dashed to the van with Jacqui.

Inside she found mostly faces she didn't recognize. "Where's Dylan, Aliza, and Matt?"

From the front of the van, Warren said, "They're taking position to breach given the opportunity or necessity."

"First," a man with glasses said, "we hack into the security system Dean set up." He cracked his knuckles and started typing.

Jacqui said, "That's Foster. He's a pro hacker. Helped us find Marrissa."

Warren patted the back of a chair. "Morgan, take a seat. We'll get Gio out of there along with your daughter."

She smiled at him. "Thank you." She sank into the seat, wishing there was something more she could do. She could do the most important thing, though: she prayed.

Aurora spotted a man coming toward the back door, and he knocked on the window.

She took a big breath to scream, but Bianca slapped her hand over Aurora's mouth.

"Hush, Aurora. Don't scream."

"Scary man."

"I see him. Is that …?" Bianca walked to the door.

Aurora clung tighter, when Bianca tried to put her down.

"Let me put you down, so you can run if it's not who I think it is."

She made herself let go.

With a protective arm, Bianca hid Aurora behind her leg. She cracked the door open. "Are you ... who are you?"

"I'm Gio Crespi, FBI. I'm here to get the two of you to safety."

Fear surrounded Aurora's heart and made it hard to breathe.

"You are Gio." Bianca opened the door farther. "Ang—Morgan's husband. I've heard about you. Dean is out to get you, though. He's showing your picture to everyone."

The man dropped the hood from his head. He looked nice, but so did Daddy until he started yelling.

The man stared at her and smiled. His eyes were shining, but not in the creepy way some of Daddy's friends looked at her.

Aurora hid behind Bianca.

She stepped aside and pushed Aurora forward.

She resisted.

"It's okay, Aurora. This is your mom's husband."

"That doesn't make any sense. Mommy is supposed to be with Daddy when she gets away from the bad man." Anger filled her. "Are you the bad guy who's kept Mommy away all my life?"

"No, Aurora." He knelt down in front of her. "Let me show you." He pulled out his phone and opened his picture app. "Look, this is your mom. We just got married a few weeks ago."

Aurora took the phone and stared at the photos as he scrolled to new ones.

"Her name is Morgan, even though you've probably heard your dad call her Angel."

Aurora nodded.

"She's so happy." Bianca looked over at the pictures too. "See, we can trust him. I know. I talked to your mom. She'd want us to go with him."

Gio smiled at Bianca. "I want to keep you girls safe from anyone who might hurt you." He looked at Aurora. "I can take you to your mom. She misses you something fierce."

"I want to see her. But won't Daddy be mad? He wants to see her too."

Gio opened his hand to her. "I know, but your daddy is really mad right now, and it would be better to stay safe from the people who might hurt us."

She turned to Bianca.

"We're going with Gio," Bianca said. "Your dad has told you to obey me, right? This is an important time to do that."

Aurora nodded.

Gio slid his phone into the pocket of Aurora's robe. "Can you read?"

She nodded again.

"If we get separated, I want you to hide as best you can and call your mom. She's listed as Morgan in my phone. Can you do that?"

Aurora nodded once more.

Gio offered to pick her up, and she raised her arms to him. He held her tight but not too tight. He was protecting her. Why did it feel safer in his arms than anywhere else she'd ever been?

She wrapped her arms around his neck.

Gio turned to Bianca. "I want to get you girls out of here, but it'll be nearly impossible. Where can we hide that Dean won't find us?"

Bianca looked around. She pointed at the far wall.

"As far from there as possible."

Aurora asked, "Why away from the wall?"

Bianca rubbed Aurora's back. "Don't worry about it." She looked at Gio. "Dean's men know what's hidden over there—"

"Is that where Daddy hides the kittens?"

"Hush, Aurora. The pool house might be safest. If we can get there. But what about ..." she nodded toward the wall.

Gio touched Bianca's arm. "The FBI is coming. We'll get them too."

"Get them who?"

Gio patted Aurora's back. "Don't worry about it. We want to keep everyone safe. Let's go hide in the pool house."

"Okay."

The door at the top of the stairs opened, and two men were talking as they came down. One said, "Something triggered the motion sensors. We should check before we start loading the kittens."

Gio whispered in Aurora's ear. "Be very quiet."

She held Gio tighter as he and Bianca snuck out the back door.

She gripped her slippers with her toes, but one was falling off. It dropped to the ground. "My slipper fell off."

Gio said, "Shoot."

The men inside walked past the door but didn't notice it.

"I'll get you new slippers when this is all over." His voice was soft in her ear.

They hid in the shadows along the house, but it was a long way to the pool house.

Gio's heart pounded so hard she could feel it against her own chest. They came to the end of the shadows. Gio's arms squeezed her like a seatbelt when the car stopped quickly.

"Go." Gio's voice was more like a breath than words. Aurora tightened her grip, and Gio ran beside Bianca.

The deck lights turned on. How were they going to make it to the pool house?

"Hey!" a man called from the other side of the pool. He started running toward them.

"Into the woods." Gio ran faster, then turned.

Another man had appeared in his way.

Gio stopped.

A third man had blocked them. He said some bad words. "What are you doing?"

Gio held her tight, and Bianca stepped closer to them.

The men surrounded them.

One of them grabbed Bianca; another ripped Aurora from Gio's arms.

Aurora screamed. "No!" She reached for Gio. He was safe. She wanted to stay with him and go see her mommy.

Gio's face looked like his heart had broken in two. "I'm sorry."

"Gio!" She kicked and screamed, but the man threw her over his shoulder and stomped up the deck stairs. Would she ever see her mommy?

Chapter Thirty-Five

Gio died a little inside watching Aurora being carried away from him and up the deck stairs.

A fist met Gio's face. He lost his balance, and his knee couldn't catch him. He dropped to the ground.

"Gio!" Bianca shouted.

His face didn't hurt as much as the knowledge he'd failed to protect both girls. He wouldn't be able to live with himself if something happened to either of them. But he was certain Dean would have no intention of letting him live past sunrise.

The man who had punched Gio gripped a handful of his sweatshirt by the shoulder and lifted him to his feet. "You need to go see the boss."

"Did you check him for weapons?"

The guy holding him said, "Put your hands on your head."

Gio complied, and they took the Glock from his hip. But they didn't check him thoroughly and missed the Ruger on his ankle—not that it did him any good right now.

"Keep them up but move." The man shoved him forward to follow Bianca and her captor up the stairs where they'd taken Aurora.

Gio's group walked faster, and just as they reached the top, the man carrying Aurora entered the back of the house.

They followed.

The man carrying Aurora said, "Hey, Doc, we caught this guy trying to make off with these two kittens."

Dean swore. "Those aren't kittens. Put her down."

The man complied, but Aurora didn't run to Dean like Gio expected.

"That's my daughter, you imbecile. Who tried to steal her?"

The man behind Gio shoved him forward and into the living room where Dean stood over a writhing but no longer screaming Mick.

Gio's captor shoved him forward until he was closer to Dean. With a final push Gio's knee buckled, and he collapsed at Dean's feet.

Dean laughed. "Trying to be a hero, huh? Did your *wife* realize I was telling the truth about our daughter? How does that make you feel? Knowing your wife has slept with hundreds of men and has a child with someone else. She'll never be yours. I will own her forever."

Gio tried not to choke on the bile rising to his mouth. It didn't matter what Dean said. The past was gone, and Morgan belonged to the Lord and no one else—no human could ever own her.

Dean lifted his foot and pushed Gio over by his head with his expensive gym shoe. "Tie him up." He barked the command to one of his cronies.

He walked over to Bianca and grabbed her by the throat. "Were you complicit in helping him kidnap my daughter?"

Bianca lied and shook her head.

Good girl. Not that Gio wanted to encourage anyone to lie, but if possible, Bianca needed to stay with Aurora.

Dean narrowed his eyes. "Fine. Take Aurora to her room and pack a bag of her important things. The three of us leave in less than an hour."

Bianca nodded, and when Dean released her, she reached out to Aurora and took her upstairs.

Dean pointed to another of his men. "Lock them in the room."

The man followed. So much for them sneaking out again on their own. *God, please protect them.*

The crony Dean had instructed to tie up Gio came over, jerked him off the floor, and dragged him to a chair. He bound Gio's hands to the chair behind him with duct tape.

What was he going to do next? How far away was Dylan and the team? Gio could only hope and pray Bianca and Aurora would call Morgan, and Morgan would tell the team to hurry up.

Morgan hugged herself to keep from fidgeting and distracting the FBI.

Jacqui reached over and squeezed her arm. "We'll get in there as soon as possible."

"I know. My stomach is just turning over on itself with worry. I know I'm not supposed to worry, but I have an awful sick feeling."

Jacqui pulled Morgan into her arms.

Morgan held her friend. Her phone rang, and she let go of Jacqui. It was Gio's ringtone.

She fumbled to pick up the device, then finally pressed the green button and held it up to her ear. "Gio!"

Silence on the other end.

"Say something," a distant female voice said.

"Mommy?"

Morgan's heart froze. "Aurora?"

"Yeah, it's me. Are you really my mommy?"

"Yes, Aurora. It is so good to hear your voice. Are you okay? Is Gio there too?"

"Daddy is really mad. I think he might hurt Gio. I'm scared."

Morgan wanted to jump through the phone and hold her daughter.

The other female voice said, "Why don't you let me talk to her?" There was a slight rustle. "Morgan? It's Bianca. I'm with Aurora, but we're locked in her room. We tried to get out with Gio, but Dean's friends caught us. The FBI needs to hurry. I don't want to say too much in front of Aurora, but I think you know what Dean is capable of."

"Unfortunately, I do. As long as you're locked in that room, you're safe. Hang tight. The FBI is on their way." Morgan fought to hold it together. She needed to stay strong.

"Okay. Just hurry. He's worse than I've ever seen him. Dean's gonna ..."

Morgan was crushed. She could lose her family before they could even be together.

"Dean said we're leaving in an hour. That's all you've got, and Gio has less than that."

"We're coming."

Morgan hung up with the girls and, shaking, turned to Jacqui. She nodded and spoke to Warren. "We need to go in now."

"We aren't in position yet. We need more time."

Morgan sucked in a deep breath. "I can stall. Let me go. I can wear a wire, camera, whatever. Be your eyes and ears."

Jacqui grasped her arm. "Morgan."

Morgan took both of Jacqui's shoulders. "I have to. You know Dean wants me more than anything. If I go in there, I can stall him in so many ways. I need to go now before he injects Gio with his poison. Please."

Warren humphed. "As much as I don't like it, it's our best bet. Drive a few guys in too. That could work."

Morgan's heart raced. She needed to do this. She had to save Gio, but Dean terrified her. However, losing Gio would be far more horrific than facing Dean again.

Gio fought against the duct tape, but it was useless. Dean's crony had wrapped it so well it would take a knife to cut it. Breaking wasn't an option.

Gio prayed for Mick as he continued to writhe on the ground, dying the longest, most painful death.

Dean stepped over him and came closer to Gio.

"Oh you feel bad for that one, do you?" Dean's smile was a bit too large. "You'll find out soon enough exactly what he's experiencing. Actually, you know what? I think I'll change it up a bit. Anyone who would try to keep my Angel away from me needs to die the most agonizing death imaginable. I made it a little easier on Mick here. He'll be dead in another"—Dean checked his watch—"ten minutes max. Yes, there's the foaming mouth. Right on schedule."

Gio prayed it would end soon for the dying man. And Gio needed to get out of here, somehow, before Dean injected him with any kind of poison.

"I don't get it. How did you get her to marry you? I saw you walking with that pathetic cane. Which leg is it that gives you trouble? This one?" Dean pressed down on Gio's bad knee.

Gio clenched his jaw, trying not to reveal the pain. If he hadn't been running around without his cane it wouldn't hurt so much, but it was tender and angry at working so hard.

Dean laughed. "That's too easy." He straightened and paced away.

Gio tried to think through his options. He had no idea how far away the FBI was. If they were close all he needed to do was stall and keep Dean from killing anyone else. But if they weren't close, then escaping might be the only option. Too bad it seemed impossible at the moment.

"As soon as you're dead, I will find Angel, and then we can set up somewhere new. She won't even remember you." Dean snarled at Gio.

He laughed out loud. "You really think she wants to be with you?"

Dean jerked forward and grabbed Gio's neck. "She'd rather be with you?"

"That's what she said."

Dean's grip on his throat tightened, making it hard to swallow. He leaned down into Gio's face. "You think because you put a ring on her finger she likes what you do in bed better than me?" He loosened his grip enough to let Gio talk.

"She loves me. She never loved you. And I love *her* like you never could. It's not about sex."

His grip tightened again. "It's always about sex."

Gio shook his head.

Dean grunted and shoved Gio over. He landed on his side, and pain radiated through his body.

An alert sounded. Dean pulled his phone out of his pocket. "Now who's here?" He swiped something. And the scowl on his face lifted in a smile. "Well, I'll be. Come on in, sweetheart. Straight to the front door. I'll meet you there."

Gio's stomach sank deeper than the deepest trench in the deepest ocean. No. No, Morgan! *Oh God, protect her.*

Chapter Thirty-Six

Morgan pulled the SUV up to the front of the house, but carefully parked with the back close to the woods. Three FBI agents in full SWAT gear were lying in wait.

Keeping her eyes facing forward, she reached back and put the key fob in Dylan's hand.

He gripped hers. "Be careful."

"I will. Keep praying. And find my baby girl."

"You better believe it. Go."

She slid out of the SUV and tried to dig into her past to find the best way to distract Dean. She was not dressed properly for this role.

Her jeans were snug but not tight. Tennis shoes were not right either. And despite the coolness of the October night, she tossed her over-sized hoodie in the car. At least she was wearing a fitted T-shirt.

She swallowed and strode to the door. This was for Gio. For Aurora. For Bianca. She would get—no, God would get them out safely. *God, please don't let me have to cross any lines to keep Dean from hurting my family.*

She knocked on the door. Why hadn't she thought to put makeup on? She pulled her hair out of the ponytail and fluffed it.

The door opened, and Dean's cocky smile greeted her. "Hey, babe."

She put on her false smile and licked her lips. "Hey." She stepped inside. "I'm so sorry for running off on you." Fighting against her repulsion, which was stronger than a giant magnet, she stepped to him and ran a finger down his chest.

He took her in his hands, rubbing her upper arms. "I was beginning to wonder what had happened to you. I'm so ashamed of how you ran like that. You can't do that again. Do you understand?"

"I understand." Yep, the words were clear, but she wasn't about to stick with him.

She pushed past him seductively and scanned the room.

Gio! She tried to contain her reaction, but it was a good thing Dean was behind her when she looked at her husband. She wanted to run to Gio immediately, but he was alive and didn't look like he was suffering from Dean's poison. If that was so, stalling Dean, distracting him, was the most important thing she could do. *Forgive me, Gio, for what I'm about to do.*

Slipping a tiny device from her pocket, she turned back to Dean and reached out to him, clutched his belt, and pulled him close. She suppressed a shudder.

He released a delighted chuckle. "There's my girl. See Gio? She wants me."

Gio grunted.

Morgan hated this. It was a careful balance of playing the part but not disassociating. She had to stay in control completely.

She ran her hands around his waist and found his phone in his back pocket where he normally kept it.

She pressed her body to his. Sliding her hands into his pockets, she slipped the device into one while giving his rear a little squeeze to cover her movements. The device was supposed to jam his phone so the FBI could breach the front gate without setting off the alerts. Foster was still working on accessing the cameras in and around the house when she left the van. Another device in her pocket should help Foster piggyback into Dean's network.

Dean leaned over and nuzzled her neck. His hands roamed freely.

She forced a giggle and ran hers up his back to his chest, then to the sides of his face. "I'd like to see our daughter." *My daughter.* He didn't deserve her.

"Of course. We're finally all together. The way it should be." He stepped away, letting his touch slowly slide from her hips.

She took a shaky breath and tried not to show her repulsion, though she wanted Gio to see it. Would he understand why she was doing what she did? Even if he did understand, would he still be angry? Could he ever forgive her for acting the part of the slut she used to be?

Dean called up the stairs to one of his guys.

She had hoped he would go, so she could cut Gio free.

Dean smiled back at her.

She gave her eyebrows one quick flutter. Why was it still so easy to play this part?

A little girl appeared at the top of the stairs, Bianca behind her.

Morgan's heart felt like it was going to pound right out of her chest. Her baby really stood there in the flesh.

"Mommy?" Aurora raced down the stairs and across the living room. Her hair flew back showing the birthmark along the side of her face. It was her.

"You know who I am?"

Aurora jumped into her arms. "Of course. Daddy showed me pictures."

There were photographs. Morgan held the little girl for a long moment before setting her back on the ground and kneeling in front of her.

Morgan dropped her voice low. "I need you to listen to me. Daddy isn't safe. You and Bianca need to get out and run. The FBI is waiting outside. If you can't get out, open your curtains and put something purple in the window, so they can see where you are."

"What are you saying to her?" Dean's voice boomed.

Morgan threw him a scowl. "Just how much I love her and have missed her. You robbed us of a life together."

"I did no such thing. You're the one who ran away and gave her up."

"Mommy?"

"All I wanted was to keep her safe."

Dean shouted, "Aurora, upstairs."

Aurora looked back at Morgan.

Morgan touched her forehead to Aurora's. "I love you, Aurora. Can you do what I said?"

She nodded and added, a little extra loud, "I love you too, Mommy."

Morgan stood as her heart walked away with Aurora. Bianca caught Morgan's eyes and wordlessly Morgan tried to tell her to escape. Bianca nodded as if she understood, took Aurora's hand and led her upstairs.

Morgan wanted to crumble onto the ground in a heap of ashes, but she had to deal with Dean and free Gio.

Dean strode toward her. He didn't look happy. "How dare you speak that way in front of her?"

"I'm sorry." She looked down at the floor in faux contriteness. "I've just missed her."

"I thought you didn't remember her." He put his fingers under her chin and made her meet his gaze.

"I didn't, but as the memories have come back, so has the grief of being without her."

"And me?"

"Of course."

"You hesitated. How much do you remember? Everything?"

She shook her head. "No. There are lots of blanks still. But I now remember having her."

He considered her with narrow eyes. Gradually his expression softened to something less angry and more sinister.

Her skin crawled.

He ran his hand into her hair and drew her face near his.

The one thing she told herself she wouldn't do was kiss him, but what was she supposed to do if *he* kissed her? And in front of Gio? She might throw up in his mouth.

Morgan turned slightly, and he kissed her cheek. Drawing her close to his body, he kissed her neck. All she wanted to do was thrust her knee up and make him sing soprano.

Dean shouted, "Everyone out!"

A few men emerged from the shadows.

"And take the dead guy with you. I think he finally gave it up. Set the *husband* upright but leave him here." He spit the word *husband* out.

Oh no. What is he planning to do?

Morgan fought to maintain her breathing, but she was on the verge of a full panic attack. Where was the FBI?

Dylan crouched low and shifted through the trees with the two other agents who followed close behind on either side of him. So far, he'd spotted two men working in the back of a medium-sized box truck and another two roaming around. How many men did Dean have?

The front door opened.

Dylan held up a fist in the air.

Two more guys came out carrying Mick's limp body.

They moved in the opposite direction of Dylan and his men, so he motioned for them to continue around the house. It had been nearly ten minutes since Morgan had gone inside. Hopefully, she'd been able to deliver the message to Aurora and Bianca.

Once he was sure Dean's men were out of earshot, he reported their presence to command.

As the first wave of agents on the premises, their primary objective was recon. Secondary objective was to secure Aurora. Once they were certain Morgan had the jammer close enough to Dean to keep their entry concealed, another team would approach.

A voice came across the radio in Dylan's ear. "We have visual inside. Crespi is bound to a chair."

Dylan closed his eyes for a second. He wanted to bust in the front door and save his friend. But that was not the plan. As an agent, following the mission plan was imperative. Sometimes it went awry, and then you had to act differently, but as long as things were moving along—and Morgan hadn't indicated she needed them—they'd continue to scout and find Aurora.

They continued forward.

The agent to his right tapped his arm.

He looked at the agent then up to where he pointed.

In a window on the second floor, light shown through open curtains. They had been shut. Two girls, one young and one a teenager, appeared. The older girl helped the younger slip out of her robe and hang it in the window. "Objective located." He described the location as succinctly as possible.

Warren answered, "Find for a point of entry."

"Affirmative."

They'd scale the side of the house, if necessary, but perhaps there was an open back door they could sneak in.

Gio fought against the duct tape. If Dean was sending his men out, was he planning to rape Morgan? Though he probably didn't see it that way. She was playing a good game with him. But Gio knew better. At least he thought he did. His flesh continually wrestled with his spirit. He was sick to his stomach, watching his wife press her body against another man. A man she was terrified of. A man she'd had sex with more than Gio wanted to think about.

How far would she let this go before she called in reinforcements? She did have backup, right? He prayed she hadn't come in on her own.

Dean led Morgan to the couch. He sat and tried to pull her onto his lap.

"Not in front of him." Her voice was not normal. "We wouldn't want him to enjoy it."

"I don't think he'd like it very much. He thinks you'd rather be with him than me." Dean chuckled. "Isn't that ridiculous?"

She laughed. But it wasn't her normal beautiful laugh that made Gio's heart soar. No, this one was tight and manipulative.

Gio wiggled his arms again.

Dean chuckled harder. "See, we're upsetting him." He tugged on her hand again. "Come on, babe. At least a little lap dance."

She yanked her hand free and walked away. "We don't have enough time, do we?"

"Playing hard to get isn't your style, Angel."

Morgan bristled but managed to smooth it over before turning. "I need to know something. What happened to Evangeline?"

It was Dean's turn to bristle.

Gio prayed harder than he'd prayed all night. *God, help.* Had Morgan ignited something that would take them both down?

Dean stood. "You are my Evangeline now."

"My name is *not* Angel. I'm not your wife. What happened to her?" Morgan took a few steps back. Her eyes told Gio she was searching for what to say. "I need to know so I can take better care of you. I can't make things right if I don't know."

Dean softened.

She'd said the right thing. Gio breathed a touch easier.

"Heroin."

"She OD'd?"

He nodded. "In Italy. That's where I buried her."

"And that's why you hated it when I was on heroin?"

Again he nodded. He reached out to her.

She walked to him. "I'm so sorry."

"How could someone poison their own body like that?"

"But you enjoy poisoning others to the point of death. That's different?" She ran her fingers along his arm.

Morgan really liked to dance with danger. Normally, Gio admired his wife's gumption, but right now he wanted to yell at her to shut up. Doing the tango with the devil himself was deadly.

Dean snorted. "Touché. It is different. My poison is a one and done. Heroin keeps you running back, doing things you'd never do simply to get another hit. It poisons your mind, not just your body. Everyone who gets my poison deserves it."

"Naturally. What's in your poison?"

"A combination of things." He went on to list a variety of drugs and animal venoms. There would be no surviving once injected with that concoction.

Morgan bit her lip like she always did when she was debating what to say. "What a horrible death." Her disgust showed despite her attempt to flirt with him.

"You have nothing to fear, my dear. He, on the other hand"—Dean nodded toward Gio—"has everything to fear. I know you were a little attached to him, but you're with me now."

Was this man really that arrogant he didn't see through Morgan's act? It was rather convincing, but it was inconsistent with how she'd reacted to him before. Didn't he see that?

"I am, but why bother killing him? Let's just leave. No one will ever find him tied up in this house."

"You've always been a softy." Dean cupped her chin and kissed her cheek. "Just trust me. Come. Let's get things ready."

"I'll be more use for you here making sure he doesn't try anything."

Dean chuckled. "Smart girl." He smacked her rear end and walked away. "I'll be right back."

As soon as he disappeared down the hall, Morgan bolted to Gio. She was distraught.

"I'm so sorry, Gio. Can you ever forgive me for acting like that?" A shudder rocked her entire body.

"Nothing to forgive. I know why you did it. I do want to throw up, though." He nodded toward his bonds. "A little help."

"Of course." She whipped a knife out of her pocket.

He sat as still as he could.

"There is so much duct tape. I don't know if I can cut it fast enough."

"Just do your best. At least get it good and started before he comes back."

"I really am sorry, Gio."

"I know, Morgan." He understood how much hearing her name meant. He could sense her absorb him saying it.

"I'm gonna make it up to you."

"You already did, earlier this evening." Remembering their time together helped to block the image of her leaning into Dean.

She giggled. That was the sound he loved to hear.

She continued to cut at the tape. "I can't get it."

"Start the other side too. I'll keep working at it if he comes back. Just don't let him inject either of us."

"The goal is to all live to see the sunrise."

"Absolutely."

"Is he coming?"

Gio looked down the hall as far as he could see. "I don't see him." He turned to glance at Morgan.

Dean stood behind her. His eyes flamed with fury. He held a syringe in his right hand.

Morgan's gaze didn't leave Gio's, but her eyes widened.

Gio's hands still weren't free. He hadn't had a chance to tell Morgan to get the Ruger on his ankle. *God, we need those angels in here now.*

Chapter Thirty-Seven

Morgan couldn't move. Dean stood behind her, and she could feel the rage emanating from him. She slipped the knife into Gio's hand.

"Stand up." Dean's voice thundered like a tornado about to ravage the prairie.

She stood, keeping her eyes locked with Gio's. He wasn't telling her what to do. Did Dean have the syringe? Was it open and ready to strike? Would he kill her?

She wanted to say he wouldn't, but she couldn't guarantee that. His obsession with her only went so far.

To Gio she mouthed, *I love you.* Then she turned around and faced Dean. A new confidence filled her being. It wasn't the fleshly confidence she could pull off when acting the sexy role. This was deeper, truer, and outsourced. This was the confidence of the Holy Spirit. She was a child of God, redeemed and restored.

She'd face whatever Dean could throw at her, and she would fight back, but not to save her own life. No, to end Dean's reign of terror.

She was no longer afraid of the man who had terrorized her so much she'd forgotten her own daughter.

"How dare you turn on me?"

"How? You want to know how? I dare because you're evil and need to be stopped. You're a fool if you didn't see I was playing you."

He fumed, but she was only getting started.

"I won't go anywhere with you and neither will Aurora."

With an eerie calmness for a man who looked like he was going to blow a fuse, Dean set the syringe on the mantle.

Morgan prayed she'd cut the tape holding Gio enough that he'd be able to break free.

Physically, she'd been trying to get stronger, but she was no black belt. Dean could take her out without much effort. Still she would fight him to the bitter end. For Aurora. For Gio. For the rest of the children.

Before she could even move, Dean grabbed her by the neck.

She scratched and clawed at him, but he lifted her from the ground and threw her at the couch. She hit with a thud, knocking her elbow on the hidden wooden frame. Pain blazed in her arm. She tried to get up before he could do anything more, but the couch was too soft.

Dean came down on top of her, pinning her legs under one of his. He choked her again with one hand and smacked her face with the other.

Her cheek stung. Fear crept back in as her oxygen was limited. *Fight, Morgan.* She tightened her body and thrust her fist into Dean's side.

His grip on her neck loosened. She punched his side again and again. The motion distracted him enough that she was able to push him off.

He tumbled to the ground.

She rolled off the couch and ran toward Gio, but Dean caught her by the hips and threw her back.

She kept her feet under her, but Dean swung his fist at her face. It made contact and her footing was gone. Pain shot through her cheekbone, and she collapsed to the floor.

Chapter Thirty-Eight

DYLAN CREPT UP THE stairs. He held his Glock in front of him. The agent next to him aimed his AR-15 straight ahead. The final agent kept his muzzle pointed down. They'd made it into the house through a basement door off the pool. One tiny purple slipper had been on the ground holding the back door open. They'd made their way up the basement stairs and at the top found another staircase that led up to the second floor.

They reached the top, and Dylan held his fist up. They stopped. He inspected the hallway.

The sound of a struggle echoed through the entire house.

On his coms, Dylan said, "Crespi needs assistance in the living room."

Matt, who led the team on the ground, responded. "Halfway there. Booking it as fast as we can."

Move faster. He kept it to himself. They would get there as soon as they could. But they'd have to go through all of Dean's henchmen.

Dylan counted doors to determine where Aurora and Bianca were. But the man, with no visible gun, leaning against the wall at the end of the hall pointed them to the right one. Dylan told his men to stay, then dashed across the hallway into a bathroom. He tapped the barrel of his pistol against the wall and quickly holstered it. Just as he'd anticipated, the man left his post to check out the sound.

Dylan waited. As soon as the man walked past, Dylan grabbed him from behind, covering his mouth. Dylan's partners joined him, and they tied him up, gagged him, and put him in the bathtub with both doors closed. Hopefully, he wouldn't make too much noise.

With long strides, Dylan made it to the room and flipped the lock out of its place. Who locked a door from the outside?

Dylan turned the knob. "FBI." He kept his voice soft.

He rounded the corner and found a child's room much like the one in Dean's other house, expect slightly less over-the-top.

"Aurora, Bianca? My name's Dylan. I'm Morgan and Gio's friend."

Two heads lifted from the other side of the bed.

Aurora stared at him, and he could only stare back. She was an exact replica of Morgan.

The girls stood, and he motioned for them to come to him. "We're going to go down the backstairs and out the basement."

Aurora froze. "That's where they got us before."

Bianca hugged the younger girl. "We have to try again."

Aurora lifted her arms to Bianca, who picked her up.

Dylan asked, "Are you okay carrying her out?"

Bianca nodded and pulled Aurora's legs tighter around her waist before wrapping her arms around the six-year-old.

Dylan confirmed with his team they were ready to move. He got the affirmative and indicated for Bianca and Aurora to follow. Dylan went behind them. He reported their status over the coms. They were getting the girls out.

Unable to get the knife at an angle to cut the tape more, Gio fought against it. Still, despite Morgan's efforts, it would not give. That last punch had sent Morgan to the floor, and she was struggling to recover. Gio prayed her cheekbone wasn't broken and she'd have the energy to keep fighting.

Dean reached down and grabbed Morgan's hair and pulled her up. "You will learn your lesson. You will never cross me like that again."

"You'll have to kill me. I will never cooperate with you. I will never be what you want me to be." She spit in his face.

Dean flung her across the room like she was a rag doll. She hit her head on the arm of the couch, narrowly missing the corner of the end table.

"Morgan!" Gio jerked against the duct tape. He needed to distract Dean. Get him to stop hitting her. "Dean, keep your filthy paws off of my wife."

Dean snarled. "You're both fools. I will not stand for such insolence."

"Your reign of fear is over. You will go down. You fall tonight."

Dean faced Gio and stepped toward him.

The man Gio had always thought would keep his cool was about to blow his top. Veins bulged, and he breathed with the force of a steam locomotive.

No matter how terrifying the contents of that syringe were, Gio wasn't afraid of Dean. He wasn't afraid of dying. He wasn't even afraid of losing Morgan. He had confidence the host of heaven was on their side right now. Even if they lost all their lives, Gio knew deep in his gut today was Dean's last. The man was so irate, it was unlikely he'd let himself be arrested without a fight that ended in death.

Morgan kicked the back of Dean's knee. Gio kicked the other.

Dean buckled and hit the ground.

Morgan bounced to her feet but wobbled as if she were dizzy. She gained her balance in time to avoid Dean's arm sweeping toward her.

Gio met her eyes. "Run."

"No. I'm done running." She avoided another attempt by Dean to grab her legs.

Dean made it back to his feet and charged her.

She avoided him, darting behind the couch, but he caught up to her and slammed her against the wall.

Gio fought against the duct tape. He had to get to her. He couldn't let Dean hurt her.

Dylan scanned the area as they crept through the trees toward the front of the house. According to the communications over the radio, only four of the six men spotted outside had been apprehended. Two more. At least. It was reasonable to figure there were more.

They made it past the front of the house but stayed in the woods rather than venture to the driveway. Once they were out of visual range, they'd move to the easier-to-traverse asphalt.

Leaves and twigs snapped underfoot. The concealment of the woods didn't come without its own risks.

A twig snapped out of sync with his team's and the girls' steps.

His heart jumped. But there was no time.

The butt of a rifle struck him upside the helmet. The helmet absorbed the concussion, but Dylan lost his center. His attacker grasped his pistol, disarmed him, and dropped him to the ground.

"Run."

It was too late.

His teammates were also tackled to the ground, and a fourth man scooped up Aurora and took off running toward the house with her over his shoulder.

She screamed.

"No!" Dylan fought against his assailant, but the man smashed his head to the ground. He was pinned.

Chapter Thirty-Nine

MORGAN STRUGGLED AGAINST DEAN, but he had her completely trapped against the wall.

"Why do you keep fighting me?" A string of nasty words assaulted her ears.

"It's not like you to stoop to vulgarity and violence. You've lost control of this situation, and you know it."

He slammed his fist against the wall beside her head. His hand then went back to her throat. She hit him, trying to punch him in the sides, but he was immune to her attacks. He didn't even flinch.

Dear God, help!

The front door opened. Dean swore. "What do you—"

A man walked in with Aurora over his shoulder.

"Put her down," Dean yelled.

Aurora fought the man as he complied. He held on to her wrist, not letting her get away.

Dean, hand still on Morgan's throat, pointed the finger on his other hand at Aurora. "What were you doing? You naughty little girl."

Her countenance fell. "Why are you hurting Mommy?"

"She's been very naughty too. You both need to be punished."

"Sir?" the man holding Aurora asked.

"What?" The bite in Dean's voice made Aurora flinch.

"We captured three FBI agents trying to kidnap her."

Dean's eyes widened. A new string of cuss words flew from his mouth. "Aurora, come here." He indicated the floor beside him.

She obeyed.

Gripping Morgan's throat, he flung her at the other man. "You hold her."

Morgan slammed into the linebacker's chest. His giant hands grabbed her wrists and clamped them together behind her back.

She glanced over at Gio. He was still struggling to get his hands free, but it wasn't working.

Dean picked up Aurora and, to the linebacker, said, "Bring her and follow me. We need a new escape plan."

Linebacker held her hands with one of his, and the other he gripped the back of her neck. He pushed her forward.

Dean led them to his office. The man was smart enough to know if he controlled Aurora, he controlled Morgan. She would do anything to protect that little girl—her daughter.

How were they going to get out of this? It would take a miracle.

Linebacker shoved Morgan onto a squared-off chair in the office and maintained a hold on the back of her neck.

Dean put Aurora down. "Go to your mother and sit on her lap."

Morgan opened her arms, and Aurora ran to her. They hugged one another.

Dean said to the linebacker, "Don't let them move."

"Yes, sir." He pressed down on her shoulders.

Aurora leaned close to Morgan's ear. "I'm sorry. I did what you said. I went with the man who said he was your friend. But Daddy's friends got them."

Dylan! "Was Dylan hurt?"

"I don't know. He was on the ground."

Morgan hugged Aurora tighter and prayed for her friend, for her husband, for all of them. God could, somehow, get them all out of this alive. She had faith, but it was hard not to fear.

Dean went to the fireplace and flipped a switch. Flames flew up from the base. He then pulled a few books from his desk and started ripping pages out and throwing them in the fire.

The linebacker said, "Not to question your methods, sir? But this is going to take too long. If one team of three FBI was inside the gate, isn't it likely there are more? We don't have much time."

Dean grunted. "You're right." Dean laid the books he wanted to destroy on the floor in front of the fire and, using a stack of pages he'd ripped from the first one, ignited one of the books.

He snatched a bottle of liquor from a shelf beside the fire and chucked it into the center of the blazing book.

It crashed and burst into flames.

Morgan shielded Aurora and continued her prayers.

Not knowing what was happening down the hallway infuriated Gio. He had to break free. He tried the knife again, but it was useless; he'd only managed to cut his arm. He dropped the knife and tried to move in different angles. But the tape would not give. If anything, it seemed to tighten.

The front door was still cracked open. Where was the FBI? Were his friends okay? Who had tried to extract Aurora and gotten caught? Were they even alive?

The door opened in painfully slow increments until finally a face appeared.

Bianca.

"What are you doing?" He kept his voice as low as he could.

"Where's Aurora?"

"Dean has her and Morgan down the hall."

"He hasn't given you an injection yet?"

Gio shook his head.

"That's a miracle."

She darted across the living room and went straight for his bound hands.

"That's a lot of tape."

"There's a knife."

"Found it." She started cutting at the tape.

"Why are you helping us?"

"I hate Dean. He's the whole reason my sister and I were separated. He wanted me, but not her. I'm sick of being his slave. But I love taking care of Aurora. She reminds me of Nicoletta."

"Let's get out of here in one piece, and we'll take you to Nicoletta." He wanted to tell Bianca they were thinking about adopting Nicoletta, and they would take her in too, but it wasn't the right moment.

She got his left hand free.

He brought it around and shook it. It tingled as it regained feeling.

"Bianca, how many children are hidden in the basement?"

"Unless more have moved that I don't know about, I believe there are twelve."

The number smacked Gio in the chest. Part of him wasn't surprised and almost expected it to be higher. But at the same time, even one child being imprisoned as a sex slave was too many.

His other hand was free. He shook it and rubbed his wrists.

"What do we do?"

"*You* don't do anything." He stood and took Bianca by the shoulders. "I need you to stay safe."

"But I want to help. I won't get out of here to see my sister if you don't succeed."

Gio considered how she could help without putting her at risk. He didn't know how many men still roamed outside. He didn't know where the FBI was. He didn't know what Dean was up to or when he'd come back. Too many unknowns.

A sound down the hall made Gio spring to action. He glanced around the room. The curtains on the giant windows bunched on the ground. He pushed Bianca toward them. "Hide behind the curtains. Given the opportunity, get Aurora and bolt out the front door and hide in the bushes."

She nodded, darted to the curtain, and hid.

Gio crouched down to retrieve his Ruger from his ankle.

Dean came around the corner.

Gio leaned too heavily on his bad knee, and it gave out. Instead of drawing his firearm he caught himself on the floor.

Dean's voice boomed. "What the—"

Gio lifted his head and caught Morgan's eye. She had Aurora in her arms. The linebacker was behind them with his massive hand on the back of Morgan's neck.

The terror in his wife's eyes crushed him. She had been fearless before Aurora came back in, before Dean had said or done who-knows-what down the hall.

Dean stormed toward him.

Gio reached for his Ruger but glanced over at Aurora. He did not want her to see him kill her dad. But Dean was a threat to them all. He hesitated too long.

Dean kicked him in the side.

Gio rolled away and jumped to his feet, being sure to put most of his weight on his good leg.

Dean darted to the mantle and grabbed the syringe.

Gio reached down, drew his Ruger, and pointed it at Dean.

The linebacker said, "Drop it." He held a knife at Morgan's throat.

Gio set his gun on the floor.

Dean said, "Kick it away."

Gio did so but in a direction that kept it just as far from Dean. If Gio couldn't have it, neither could he.

The cool steel of the knife pressed slightly into the side of Morgan's neck above Aurora's arm.

Aurora's tears saturated Morgan's shoulder.

She stood still. Dean held the syringe of deadly poison about fifteen feet away from her husband, whose gun was now across the room.

The curtain beside the window closest to the front door fluttered. Fingertips barely showed on the edge of the curtain as it shifted. A partial face appeared that only Morgan could see.

Bianca. Was she how Gio broke free of the duct tape?

"Aurora," she whispered just loud enough for the little girl to hear, "I'm going to put you down. Run to the curtain by the front door and go with Bianca. Run and hide."

"I love you, Mommy."

"I love you too. Now go."

Aurora slid from her arms and took off.

Dean yelled, "Where are you going?"

Aurora didn't turn back to look at him.

Bianca appeared and the two of them darted out the front door.

"I'll get her." The linebacker dropped the knife away from Morgan's neck and moved toward Aurora.

"No. Keep *her*."

Gio rushed at Dean.

"No!" Morgan's insides twisted up. *Lord, protect us all.*

With the knife no longer at her neck, Morgan needed to act.

She calculated what to do. There was only one way to overpower a man so much bigger than her. With all the force she could muster, she swung her arm. Her fist hit him squarely between the legs.

He let go of her neck and doubled over.

She bolted to a marble statue on the end table, lifted it, and swung it around, smacking the linebacker upside the head.

He slumped to the ground, but he wasn't completely out.

Gio and Dean struggled in the living room. She looked down at the statue still in her hands. It was heavy, but she could throw it.

"Hey, Dean!" She spun around and launched the thing into the living room.

Chapter Forty

As the statue crashed on the floor two feet shy of Dean, Gio grasped the wrist of the hand holding the syringe.

Dean tried to bend his arm to get more leverage, but Gio held it straight and out to the side. He stepped forward, angling so he had more force, and grasped the back of Dean's neck to control his movements by keeping his own arm close and stiff.

Dean snarled and maneuvered his feet to counter Gio's strength. A triangle of space formed between them as they vied for the dominant position.

He needed to make Dean drop the syringe. That was his first objective. But ultimately, Gio had to take Dean down. Not even for the sake of his own life, but for Morgan. Aurora. Bianca. The children. For every man, woman, or child he had taken advantage of or killed.

The sound of Morgan's struggle with the linebacker met his ears, but he tuned it out. He couldn't let himself be distracted from his fight with Dean.

Dean repeatedly punched Gio in the side.

He grunted as pain radiated through him but maintained his hold on Dean. Thankfully, none of the punches had been directly to his liver.

Pulling Dean forward wouldn't bring the man to his knees. They were matched in strength and size, even if Dean had about two inches on him.

Gio tried a different approach. He tried to hook his foot around Dean's but lost leverage in the process. He snapped back to his stance before Dean gained the upper hand.

Dean jerked his arm around, trying to break his wrist free. Gio would lose it soon.

Gio eyed the triangle of space between them. It was narrow, but maybe enough.

He released Dean's head and spun until his back slammed against the other man. He maintained his grip on Dean's wrist until his forearm was secure under his arm.

The syringe came close to his chest but not close enough.

Dean fought, but Gio had control of his arm completely.

Gio jabbed his elbow into Dean's solar plexus three times and stomped on his foot before slamming the back of his hand into Dean's face.

Dean stumbled backward, but Gio didn't let go of his forearm until, finally, the syringe dropped from his hand.

Gio spun and with a quick burst of movement, seized Dean by the neck and slammed his head down into his good knee.

His questionable one maintained its strength. After a final slam of Dean's head into his knee, Gio glanced at his other one. The light seemed to shine on it, almost as if it glowed. Had angels held him up? Is that how his knee had stayed strong throughout so much of the night?

He tossed a disoriented Dean to the floor.

Gio needed to restrain him. Turning to fully face him, Gio stepped closer, but Dean wasn't as disoriented as he thought.

Dean swept a leg at Gio's and knocked him to the ground. He landed on his back. The wind rushed out of his lungs. Before he could get oxygen in he rolled toward the syringe and smashed his arm against Dean's.

But Dean already had a hold of the syringe. He thrust his body toward Gio and grabbed him from behind, pinning Gio down.

Gio pressed off the floor.

Dean flicked the cap of the syringe. Gio needed to get control of Dean's arm or get away. Neither seemed possible. But death wasn't an option.

The syringe with its bare needle came straight at him.

Chapter Forty-One

HEART POUNDING, JACQ LEAPT out of the van that had driven them part way up the long driveway. Dylan still hadn't responded on coms. But they saw Aurora being dragged back into the house on the video Foster had hacked. At that point, Warren had made the rest of the team—the final wave—enter the premises.

Only Warren and Foster remained in the van.

They needed to get inside that house. They needed to find Dylan and his team. They needed to end this once and for all.

Her team of six formed a line and ran down the driveway toward the house. The van was parked in a way to block the truck from escaping, in case that came into play.

Matt was on the far left of the line, two people down from Jacq. He ran to the tree line. His counterpart at the other end did the same thing.

As they neared the house and line of sight, they split into two groups of three and slipped into the woods on opposite sides of the driveway.

Matt let out a shrill whistle. She and the agent between them followed the sound.

Three agents were strapped to trees.

Dylan!

She ran to untie him. Then taking his face between her hands, she plastered a kiss on his lips. When they'd dropped contact, she'd been terrified she'd lost Dylan. She kissed him with all the relief she felt. But it had to be a quick one, so she released him.

"I can't lose you. I can't be a widow again, so you'd better live through this."

He kissed her. "I know. That goes for you too. You should go back to the van."

"I can't. We need everyone on this."

"This is why agents aren't supposed to get married."

Matt put his hands on their shoulders. "Especially when they go making babies. Both of you need to be extra careful, but let's get Gio and Morgan out."

They all sprang back into action.

Each of Jacq's team handed guns off to Dylan's. The six of them, now armed, found four of Dean's men and were able to subdue them, cuff them, and move on. When Jacq and company emerged from the woods, they spotted the other three agents from their initial team make it to the truck. Those agents took out two more of Dean's cronies.

Screams came from inside the house.

But they still had to secure the outside.

God, please protect Morgan and Gio!

A rustle in a large bush beside the house caught Jacq's attention. She raced to it, Glock at the ready.

She circled the bush and jumped toward the figure hiding.

But it wasn't a single figure. "Aurora! Bianca!" Jacq holstered her Glock.

They looked up at her, scared.

"I'm Jacqui, Morgan's best friend."

Aurora bounded up and bounced into Jacq's arms.

Jacq sat behind the bush with the girls. She'd protect them right here. She pressed Aurora's head to her chest and covered her other ear. This could get nasty.

Morgan fled into the kitchen after throwing the statue at Dean and snagged the largest knife she could find.

The linebacker, angry beyond words, followed her. He chased her around the island. The same island she'd sat at the first time she'd come out to this house for a night with Dean. Her skin crawled at the thought of what she'd had to do with that man so often in the past. But she'd be free from him tonight, whether she was dead or he was.

Butcher knife still in hand, she darted the other direction around the island.

Linebacker scurried over the top of the island and came straight for her.

She screamed and bolted out the opposite entrance than she'd come in. She ran through the dining room and toward the stairs.

Then she skidded to a stop.

Flames licked the shelves of Dean's office.

The house was on fire. It was just a matter of time before the whole thing was ablaze.

Smoke billowed out and attacked her lungs. She coughed.

The linebacker ran up behind her.

She turned, knife out. He didn't stop fast enough. The knife punctured his chest. It caught on a bone, slipped off, and sank deeper between his ribs. With a gasp, she let go and stepped back.

He reached for the knife.

"No! Don't!" Morgan shouted, but he pulled it out anyway.

Blood poured from the wound, and he began to cough and spit blood.

She stepped back farther. "Oh God, I'm so sorry." She hadn't meant to kill him.

He collapsed to the floor.

The heat behind her singed her back. They needed to get out of this house immediately. She had to call the fire department. If they didn't get the fire under control as soon as possible, the entire mountain could be set ablaze.

And it could spread to Jacq's property, to their home.

The children!

She searched her mind. The house she'd seen in her dreams had been Dean's house in Miami, not this one. He hadn't shown her a secret room here.

She dashed down the stairs to the basement. It was probably there, dug into the side of the mountain. Maybe.

Chapter Forty-Two

Gio held Dean's hand away, but the syringe stayed pointed at Gio. He shifted his weight. They had made it back to a standing position as they fought and struggled. Dean whipped around, and wrapping his arm around Gio, Dean tried to jab the syringe into Gio's chest. Gio's hands shook against the pressure of Dean's arm trying to stab him. But he was the only thing between Dean and the syringe.

Wriggling his whole body, Gio tried to buck Dean off his back, but it wasn't working. The man was a raging lunatic.

Gio's knee gave out, but instead of bracing himself to keep from falling, he used it.

Momentarily maintaining his grip on Dean's arm, Gio swung down and out, away from Dean's body. As soon as he was clear, he released the pressure that had been keeping Dean's arm from jabbing into Gio.

The shift in pressure sent Dean's arm flying toward him.

The needle plunged into Dean's chest. He stumbled backward.

Gio regained his balance and turned fully to Dean.

They both stared down at the syringe. Somehow in the midst of it stabbing Dean, the plunger had been depressed.

Dean had taken the full amount of poison he'd intended for Gio.

The effects were quick. Dean's muscles started constricting and seizing.

He screamed. Then he raged. A string of horrid words escaped his mouth before he lunged at Gio.

Gio glanced toward where he'd kicked his gun. He dove for it, narrowly missing Dean's enraged grasp.

Gio gripped his Ruger and rolled away from Dean, who continued advancing.

Dean's eyes were more crazed than they had been before. His body twitched. The pain must be excruciating.

He grabbed the largest half of the broken statue and came for Gio.

Gio raised the Ruger and fired. He unloaded all seven rounds before Dean finally dropped the statue and collapsed to the ground.

Dean was dead! Duke's reign was over.

Gio caught his breath and switched the Ruger's magazine for a loaded one.

He jumped to his feet, rubbed the ear ringing from the gunfire, and looked around for Morgan. Where had she gone?

Fear gripped his heart again.

The front door swung open.

Dylan and two more fully geared guys came into the room.

"*Now* you get here."

One of the agents secured Dean's body.

Gio said, "I don't know where Morgan is."

Dylan nodded. "Let's find her. Which way?"

Gio shrugged but headed toward the hall.

Smoke assaulted his nostrils. The house was on fire. How had they not noticed?

Dylan radioed it in.

Gio spotted a figure on the ground but through the smoke couldn't tell who it was.

He pulled his collar up over his nose and ran to the body. It was the linebacker. Blood covered the front of his chest. He was dead too.

But where had Morgan gone?

The fire was spreading into the basement. The smoke wasn't too bad though.

Morgan searched but couldn't find where Dean might have hidden the children, or "kittens," as he called them. She had to locate them before the fire overtook the house completely. What if the hidden rooms were on the side of the house already on fire?

She ran her hands down empty walls and checked every piece of furniture for a hidden lever like she remembered in her dream. She couldn't find one.

Jesus, guide me to the right place.

A boom sounded near the stairs, but it wasn't just one. It continued.

She hid inside the theater room and peeked through the crack she left in the door.

She finally identified the noise as footsteps.

Four shadowy figures appeared at the bottom of the staircase.

"Morgan!" one of the figures called.

Gio! She burst out of her hiding place.

All four raised guns in her direction.

"It's me." She continued her course, and they lowered their weapons.

Gio ran toward her, and they slammed into one another, arms encircling the other.

"You're alive." She couldn't believe it—no, she could. God was good. But even if Gio hadn't survived, God was still good. He'd been extra good to them tonight. *Thank you, Lord.*

Gio loosened his grip and ran his hands into her hair, cupping the sides of her face. He was breathless and without words.

He kissed her deeply.

Dylan tapped them. "I get the reunion—just had one myself—however, we need to get out of here."

Gio let go of her face, and she seized his hand.

"We have to find the children. I know there's a secret room, but I can't locate it."

Gio pointed. "Bianca said it was over there."

The five of them bolted across the room, away from the fire, and down a short hallway.

At the end of the hall was the bookshelf Morgan remembered from her dream. "That's it." She ran to it and pulled on a book—the lever that opened the door.

The bookshelf clicked and came forward. She pulled it open.

Anyone searching the house who stumbled on the hidden door might think it opened to a tiny panic room. That wasn't what this was.

She felt the wall and found the switch that opened another door. A short hallway offered three doors.

If this was like the Florida home, the children were abused in the two rooms on the right, with a small bunkroom on the left.

She opened that one.

Children scattered like scared mice.

"It's okay, boys and girls, we're here to get you out of here."

Slowly, they started shifting toward her.

Dylan called, "We need to hurry. The house is engulfed."

She encouraged the children to follow the agents out. "They will get you to safety."

As the kids formed a line and moved through the door, Gio pulled two aside. "Pablo and Marta, we've been looking for you!"

The little girl smiled up at him. "Go see Papa?"

"Yes, we will take you to your Papa."

Her grin grew, as did Gio's and Dylan's.

The kids continued to file out. Twelve children followed the two agents out the back door.

As the last child walked out, a boy of about eleven, Morgan asked him, "Is that everyone?"

"I don't know. There are thirteen of us. At least what I counted earlier today."

They were missing one. Morgan, Gio, and Dylan searched the room until Gio found a little girl of about four hiding underneath one of the bunkbeds.

Morgan got down on her knees. "What's your name?"

"Ida."

"Come here, Ida. It's not safe. We'll get you out."

The girl scooted forward and jumped into Morgan's arms. The four of them exited the hidden passageway. The smoke had thickened, and flames invaded the downstairs.

Gio put his hand on Morgan's back, and they ran outside. They went up the hill and around the house. Once at the driveway, Morgan scanned the gathering agents and criminals they had apprehended.

Where was Aurora? She'd held her daughter for less than ten minutes. Would that be all she ever got?

The sound of wailing sirens met her ears before the lights from the fire trucks penetrated the dark of the forest.

After the first fire truck passed, Morgan's eyes met Jacq's across the driveway. Another fire truck went by, and Morgan found Jacq again.

Bianca stood next to Jacq, and in Bianca's arms was the most precious little girl Morgan had ever seen. Aurora!

But she couldn't just put Ida down.

Morgan rushed across the driveway and introduced Ida and Jacqui. The little girl went to Jacqui, and Morgan turned to Aurora and Bianca.

Morgan looked in Bianca's eyes first. "Thank you for everything."

She nodded and bit her lip. Aurora sprung from Bianca to Morgan. With arms tightly wrapped around Morgan, Aurora cried.

Morgan didn't ask why. The emotional release of the tension of the last few hours would make anyone cry. "I'm so glad you're safe and we're together now."

Her daughter leaned back and looked Morgan in the face. "Did Daddy die?"

Morgan's heart broke. She had no idea what this little girl's opinion of her father was. Had Dean actually been a decent dad? He seemed to have given her everything she asked for, but that didn't make for a good father.

Morgan had heard the gunshots; they were hard to miss. She'd been so afraid Gio had gotten hurt, she hadn't thought about how the alternative would affect Aurora. "I think so." Morgan watched her face.

She looked down, but the girl's expression didn't change. She wasn't overcome with more sobs. "I thought so. He shouldn't have tried to hurt Gio or that other guy. Is Gio okay? He said he was your husband."

Gio came up behind her. "I'm just fine, Aurora."

She turned in Morgan's arms and reached out to Gio, placing her hand on his chest. "Good. Because I like you."

Morgan, Gio, and Bianca all laughed.

Gio said, "I'm so glad. I can't wait to get to know you better."

Morgan's heart swelled. Could this be happening? Did they really have a family?

She watched Bianca, who stayed close to them. Could Bianca and Nicoletta be part of that family too?

Gio slid his arm across Morgan's shoulders. They were safe, including Aurora and Bianca. Plus Pablo and Marta from Honduras.

Gio had thought for sure those two had ended up across the country and would never be found.

Thank you, Lord, that we will be able to get these children back to their father. Help us find the parents of the other kids. Thank You for Your provision and protection tonight.

The house blazed, and firefighters worked to keep it from spreading to the trees.

FBI vans arrived to transport the children to Knoxville. A prisoner bus was filled with the men Dean had hired to do his dirty work, including the corrupt cop who had kidnapped Mick and delivered him to his death.

As agents loaded the children, Bianca stayed close to Morgan and Gio. An agent approached and said to Bianca, "Come on over here, and we'll give you a ride in the van."

Bianca didn't budge. Her lips were tight with worry.

Gio lifted his hand. "It's all right; she's going to ride to Knoxville with us."

Bianca's entire countenance lifted. Her eyes scrunched a touch, but she smiled.

Gio said, "It'll be a bit of a walk to the car."

Morgan giggled. "Not so much. I drove it in full of agents. The question is, did it get too close to the fire?"

Gio turned and saw his blue Kia sitting between two firetrucks. "Looks okay." He turned back to Bianca. "You all right hanging with us?"

She nodded.

"Good. We all like you."

She chuckled.

The four of them went to the SUV and piled in. Morgan sat in the back with Aurora and offered the front seat to Bianca.

Morgan touched his shoulder. "Wait, Dylan has the keys."

Gio held the keys up. "He gave them to me. Let's get out of here."

Bianca turned to them. "Where are we going?"

"At the moment, we'll head to the FBI field office in Knoxville, and from there we'll call Nicoletta's foster mom and case worker. And in a few hours at most, we'll reunite you."

"Then what? I join her in the system?"

Gio nodded. "Unfortunately, but just until you get adopted, or we can work something else out." He looked back at Morgan. They hadn't talked yet, but he was pretty sure he knew what she was thinking.

Bianca nodded. It was hard not to tell her their plan, but he didn't want to set her up for disappointment if it didn't work out.

Gio drove and prayed for Bianca and Nicoletta. He prayed he and Morgan would be able to adopt them, and, more than anything, that they would have the opportunity to share Christ with them. *Heal them, Lord, of all the trauma they've been through. Morgan too, and Aurora.*

As they left the property they turned east for a moment. The sky in the distance was growing light. Truly the brightest sunrise was after the darkest night. The past few hours had been dark, but light rose on the horizon. The Lord's promises were up ahead, and the girls in the car were the fulfillment of the words his mom had spoken a month ago. Hope in Jesus is never false.

Chapter Forty-Three

MORGAN SAT ON THE breakroom couch at the FBI field office, Aurora snuggled up on one side and Bianca on the other. All three of them had been dozing on and off, but the girls were both out now. Morgan wasn't sure how she was awake, though her adrenaline was still running high.

Only four days ago she didn't even know she had a daughter. She wanted to berate herself for not remembering, but she had good reason. Trauma did that to a person. The pain of not having her had been so intense her brain had blocked it out.

The little girl curled up against her didn't have the life Morgan had hoped. Dean had swooped in and stolen her back. The only thing Morgan could figure was he'd been tracking her while she ran and saw her drop off the baby.

What kind of life had Aurora had with Dean? Had he been cruel? Kind? Aloof? How do you ask a six-year-old if she was violated by a man? Answers would come.

She had more questions now than would fit into an entire book.

Where would they live? Their little trailer was only big enough for two. Not three, let alone five.

Would they even be considered fit enough to adopt Nicoletta and Bianca? Would the girls want that?

The breakroom door opened, and Gio walked in. He had his cane again but didn't seem to be using it.

Morgan yawned.

He nodded. "Me too. But I just got a call. Nicoletta will be here in about fifteen minutes."

Bianca stirred. "Really?" She sat up and rubbed her eyes.

Morgan ran her hand along Bianca's back. "For real. I can't even begin to imagine how happy she will be to see you."

"Will we be able to stay together? Or will they separate us?"

Gio stood on the other side of the coffee table. "We will fight for you to stay together. You have my word. I will do whatever it takes."

"I can't believe I'm going to see her."

Morgan squeezed her shoulder. "I'm so excited for both of you."

Gio went to the coffeemaker, fixed Morgan a mug, and brought it to her just the way she liked it.

He looked at Bianca. "Do you drink coffee?"

"Not really."

"Fair enough. Hot chocolate?"

She nodded. The false maturity she'd been forced to live with seemed to melt away before their eyes, and she was a little girl again.

Gio fixed three hot chocolates and a cup of coffee for himself before settling onto the other couch.

Aurora woke up but didn't move away from Morgan's side.

It wasn't long before Aliza entered the room, followed by Nicoletta, her foster mom, and her social worker.

For a second, Nicoletta and Bianca could only stare. Then, without wasting another instant, the sisters were clasped in a hug. The embrace lasted a long time, only breaking long enough to pull back and search the other's face.

Then the talking began. Initially, the girls jabbered in rapid Italian.

Morgan would have to ask them to teach her.

The girls sipped their hot chocolate as they caught up. Eventually, they switched to English and included the others in their conversation.

Gio asked, "How long has it been since you've seen each other?"

Bianca looked to the side as if calculating. "About a year or so."

They all continued to visit, but after a while, the social worker asked Gio and Morgan to talk to her on the other side of the room.

Aurora was hesitant to let Morgan venture far but accepted Bianca's comfort. The little girl needed Bianca as much as Bianca needed Morgan and Gio.

Morgan's heart pounded in shaky vibrations. What was the social worker going to say?

Gio beat anyone to talking. "These girls need to be together. Is Nicoletta's foster family willing to take Bianca too?"

She nodded. "Yes, they are." She took a deep breath. "And Aurora as well."

Morgan's body seized.

Gio gripped her arm. "No, she's Morgan's biological daughter, and she's coming home with us."

"Ideally, yes, but we have to establish—"

Gio cut her off. "We'll get the maternity test done today, and we'll get it rushed. We have all the proof you'll need."

"If we get it established today, she won't need to leave with anyone else. But she stays here or goes with this family, if not."

Morgan slumped against Gio. This couldn't be happening. What if there was a hold up getting the DNA done? These things took forever, didn't they?

Gio took in a sharp breath. "What about adopting the girls?"

"Both of them? I know you were interested in giving Nicoletta a home, but a fifteen-year-old too?"

"Absolutely." Gio looked at Morgan.

They hadn't had the chance to talk about it, but she wasn't surprised to learn they were on the same page.

Morgan said, "One hundred percent."

"I'll have the paperwork together for you this afternoon then. I don't know if you'll get approved, but there are special considerations. You will definitely need a bigger home. A two bedroom apartment would have been fine for adopting just a ten-year-old. But now you are asking about having three children in the home."

"We'll find a new one by this afternoon."

Morgan held in a gasp. That was a bold statement on Gio's part. He had a giant mound of paperwork to do, she still had to give her statement, and neither of them had slept much.

Gio kissed Morgan's temple and whispered, "God's got this."

Indeed He did.

Jacq took each of the kids' hands as she led Pablo and Marta into the airport. The morning had been spent identifying the children, learning their stories, and searching for their families.

Upon returning to the field office, Warren had immediately called his contact down in Honduras. The parents had booked the first available flight to the States.

Jacq felt honored to be the one to reunite these children with their parents. They clung to her hands. The little girl's lip quivered, and the boy hugged Jacq's hand with both of his, ready to retreat behind her should anything upset him.

They went to the designated meeting location near baggage claim. Looking around, she could hardly believe this was the same place where she'd met Nicoletta. Over lunch, Gio and Morgan had shared their intent to adopt both girls. God had blessed them beyond measure, and Jacq prayed all of the adoption hoops they would have to navigate would be easy and quick. Bianca and Nicoletta needed a stable situation, and there was a lot of trauma to work through. Who better to help them than Morgan?

Jacq sat in a chair, and Pablo and Marta stayed as close to her as possible. Dylan smiled but remained standing as a lookout for their contact.

He checked the flight status again. "It's landed and deplaning. Just a few minutes, kids."

Their English was minimal, but they seemed to understand exactly what Dylan meant. They both sat up straighter and studied the crowd.

Pablo spotted them first. He jumped up and dashed away before Dylan could reach out to grab him. The boy disappeared into the crowd, Dylan following.

The girl stood, and then climbed on top of the chair. She searched the crowd.

"Papa!" She launched from the chair and took off.

A Honduran man in his mid-thirties appeared and held open his arms. He squatted and the girl hit him with such force he almost fell over backward.

Dylan and a woman with long black hair appeared. Pablo was in her arms.

It was beautiful. All these kids had had to endure in the last two months broke Jacq, but to see them back with their mother and father was marvelous. If only everything they had gone through could be erased from their minds and bodies. *Jesus, heal these children.*

Jacq joined the family. Both mother and father hugged her and Dylan profusely.

They had just been doing their job. But how could it ever be enough? As long as society continued to distort sex, the demand for flesh would persist. This wasn't new; she understood mankind had been corrupt since the fall in the garden. Rape and sexual abuse had been rampant since Noah's day.

But maybe, just maybe, God could use Jacq, Dylan, Morgan, and Gio to help rescue a few and point them to Jesus—Jehovah Rapha—God the Healer.

Marta pulled on Jacq's shirt sleeve.

She leaned down and looked the girl in the eyes.

"Muchas gracias. Thank you."

"You're welcome. I'm so glad you're back with your momma and papa."

The little girl put her arms around Jacq's neck.

Jacq pulled Marta into a hug and silently prayed over her.

Gio restrained a grunt. *God, I still need your help.*

He was frustrated with all the obstacles in their way. And he was exhausted.

Morgan came into the office and placed a hand on his back. She set a cup of coffee in front of him.

"You are too good to me. Where's Aurora?"

"Sleeping on the sofa in the breakroom. Aliza's in there with her. She's missing Bianca something fierce. How's the paperwork?"

"Mostly been working on FBI stuff. I got the paperwork for the adoption, at least the first parts. We have to do some training, and then the home study." He was overwhelmed.

"That's it?"

A dry chuckle escaped. "Feels like a lot to me. We don't actually have a home to have studied yet."

A wide smile stretched across his wife's beautiful face.

"What?" He narrowed his gaze at her.

"I just got off the phone with Chloe." Chloe was Gabe Jacob's sister, who was a realtor. "She has a client who is closing on their new house on Thursday, but they're still looking for renters for their three-bedroom, single-family home."

"Neighborhood?"

"Same as Dylan's brother. And this is a foster family, so the house itself is up to snuff for DCS." She pulled her phone out of her pocket. "It's perfect, Gio."

Lord, give us wisdom and discernment.

She handed him her phone, and he scrolled through the pictures. "It's gorgeous, but how much?"

She clicked the screen back to the listing info. It wasn't much more than his two-bedroom apartment.

It could work really well. *Is this where You want us, Lord?*

He returned her phone, then pulled up the budgeting app on his and considered the numbers. They could swing it and still move toward building the house up in the mountains. It would be tight, but that was okay.

"Call her back and say we want it."

"We have to go see it, silly."

"If necessary, then fine. But ..." Gio paused and waited for the Lord. He knew the answer. "It's where we're supposed to be. I'm confident."

"Yay!" She called Chloe as she walked away.

He laughed. Not only was his wife adorable, but that was one burden off his shoulders.

He glanced at his cell phone. It needed to ring with the results of the DNA. They had a private company do it and were paying a pretty penny to get it rushed. But they needed the proof before they could leave for the day. For some reason the State had to put their nose in and couldn't see how obvious it was that Aurora was Morgan's flesh and blood.

He tried not to roll his eyes. Theoretically, they had Aurora's best interest in mind, but it felt ridiculous.

Refocusing his thoughts, Gio dove back into his paperwork. When Morgan got off the phone with Chloe, she came over and reported they had an appointment to see the house and possibly sign papers tomorrow afternoon. Morgan pulled up a chair to his desk and filled out the adoption papers, while he continued working.

About a half hour later, Aliza and Aurora came into the office. Aurora let go of Aliza's hand as soon as she spotted Morgan and ran into her mother's arms.

If only they could leave. They all needed to decompress and get some solid rest. Plus, dinnertime was approaching quickly. They also needed to go to the store. Aurora didn't have much. He wanted to try and get as many of her belongings from Dean's Knoxville house as possible, but it was still tied up as evidence. If only life could wrap up neatly, and they could fade into their happily ever after. But that wasn't real life. They were going to face hurdle after obstacle after hoop to get to any semblance of normal.

Dylan and Jacq arrived back at the office, bright smiles stretched across their faces.

Before anyone could say anything else, Jacq said, "Did anyone find little Ida's parents?"

Aliza leaned back in her chair. "Her mom and aunt are driving from Mississippi as we speak. Poor thing was kidnapped while on vacation in Florida—just lifted from the beach back in June."

Aurora tapped Gio's shoulder and moved closer to him. "My daddy didn't really have kittens in the basement, did he?"

Gio glanced over Aurora to Morgan, who nodded with a sober expression. It was her way of saying *tell her the truth*. "He did not."

"Those kids were down there? Why did daddy hide other kids? Didn't he love me?"

Gio put his arm around Aurora. How did he answer those questions? As horrible as Dean was, Aurora knew him as her father. "Yes, the children were hidden in the basement. But some of those questions are hard to answer. I believe your daddy loved you though. He wasn't trying to replace you."

"It's hard to understand because I'm little?"

Gio nodded.

"Okay. Gio?"

"Yes, Aurora?"

"Are you going to be my new daddy?"

"I'd like to be."

"Good." She crawled up in his lap and put her arms around his neck.

Tears glistened in Morgan's eyes.

Gio winked at her. Now if only they'd hear back about the DNA so DCS would let them take their daughter home.

His phone buzzed. With one arm securely around Aurora, he reached for the device with the other. He answered it and held it to his ear.

"Mr. Crespi, we have the results. I'm sending them to you and DCS, but I wanted to call you with the results too because I know you're anxious to get them."

"Yes, we are. Thank you for calling."

"As you suspected, it is conclusive that Morgan Zalman Crespi is Aurora Rockefeller's biological mother. The information is in DCS's hands, so you shouldn't have any problems from them."

"Thank you." Gio hung up with the gentleman.

Morgan's grin was so big, he was afraid her cheeks would split.

"Shall we go home?" Morgan asked.

Gio met Aurora's eyes. "What do you think? We'll be moving to a bigger home soon, but are you ready to go see one of the places your mom and I live?"

She nodded.

Gio hugged the little girl and thanked God for His grace and favor.

Saturday afternoon, Morgan carried another box into their new house. Everything was happening so fast, but she enjoyed riding the wave with her husband and daughter.

One week ago, she'd remembered she had a daughter. Tuesday evening she'd taken Aurora back to the apartment she'd sworn she'd never sleep in again, but that was when Dean was still a threat.

While he'd left behind wounds, he could no longer kidnap or kill them.

Aurora had struggled for the first two nights. Nightmares woke her, and she was confused about where she was. A strange blend of grief about her dad being dead combined with what almost seemed like relief.

They had made a point of seeing Bianca and Nicoletta almost every day, and that seemed to help the transition. Aurora adored Bianca, and she and Nicoletta were getting along great too.

Morgan was having a wonderful time getting to know her daughter. The kid was sweet, spunky, and a bit sarcastic. How could she be so much like Morgan when they hadn't been together until now?

After setting the box down in the master bedroom, Morgan poked her head into Aurora's room, where she sat on the floor playing with Harper. "You two having fun?"

Both girls glanced up from their dolls and smiled. Aurora said, "Yep."

"Good, keep playing. We're still unloading boxes."

"Okay, Mommy."

Morgan's heart wasn't quite sure what to do with the sound of Aurora calling her mommy. She'd probably get used to it eventually, but part of her didn't want to. The wonder and gratitude that filled her heart at the sound was refreshing.

She went back downstairs and found the other three adults in the kitchen. She put her arm around Jacqui. "Our daughters seem quite taken with one another."

"I'm so glad." Jacqui took a deep breath. "That makes me think of something." She smiled up at Dylan.

What was going on? "What?"

Jacqui bit her lip. "We're pregnant."

Morgan squealed. "Oh that's so exciting!"

Jacqui nodded, and the women embraced, as did Dylan and Gio.

Morgan pushed Jacqui to arms' length. "Why didn't you tell me sooner? You've known for a bit haven't you?"

Jacqui shrugged with one shoulder. "I was so nervous to tell you. Here we were planning to wait for a bit, and the two of you weren't sure if you would be able to."

"Rubbish. We're ecstatic for you. God's got His plan all worked out. Our hope for our future, both children and eternity, is in Jesus. And hope in Jesus is never false."

Chapter Forty-Four

ON MONDAY EVENING, MORGAN'S heart was full as Nicoletta and Aurora ran around the house, giggling and playing like they'd always been sisters. Hopefully, soon they would be. Morgan scraped the leftover peas from dinner into a smaller container and put them in the refrigerator.

Bianca handed her the dish of leftover rice.

"Thanks for helping."

"It's nice to not be responsible for it on my own."

"No doubt."

"Most of the time, it was just Aurora and me I needed to make dinner for, but sometimes he was there too."

"Where did you learn to cook?"

"My mom always had us in the kitchen with her before she died, so I remembered a lot from that. But the internet mostly."

"I'm glad you remember your mom. How old were you when the car accident took your parents?"

"Nicoletta's age. Ten. We were in the orphanage for two years before Dean came and swept us away."

"Did you think it would be a good thing he came, that he was going to give you a new home?"

Bianca nodded and rolled her eyes. "Sure, but it was stupid. Life was fine in the orphanage; we would have been okay, but Dean offered a lot. We were excited."

Morgan placed her hand on Bianca's forearm. "I'm so sorry."

"It didn't take long to figure out it wasn't all he had painted it to be."

"I can imagine."

The two sat at the table, and Gio came around the corner. "May I join you? Or is it girl talk time?"

Bianca giggled. "You can join us. It's your house."

"But I want to give you space to process things with Morgan that you might not want to talk about in front of me."

Bianca squished her nose around like she was trying to keep from crying. "Please sit. I wanted to talk to the both of you."

Gio pulled out a chair and sat, eager to hear what Bianca had to say.

Morgan loved this man. He was always ready to listen to others.

Bianca appeared hesitant.

Morgan said, "I have a question for you, that's not about you. Would you like me to ask that first?"

Bianca nodded.

"I hate to ask it because part of me doesn't want to hear the answer, but I need to know how best to help Aurora. Did Duke ever …" Morgan let out a huff of air. "Did he ever abuse her or let other men … touch her?"

"Oh no. She was his little princess. He was hard on her and wasn't around much, but as far as I know no one was allowed to be near her. Not that Dean's friends didn't ask, but that often ended not so great for them. I still don't get how he could think it wasn't okay for others to touch his daughter, but if it was any other kid, it's fine." She shook off the anger consuming her.

Morgan reached out and squeezed her hand. Bianca squeezed back and stared at their clasped fingers.

Morgan wished she could reach in and know what Bianca wanted to tell her without the teenager having to come up with the difficult words. "What's going on?"

"I'm pretty sure I'm pregnant."

The words hung in the air, heavy like a thundercloud in the Tennessee summer just waiting to unleash its torrent. This child was going to have a child.

"I don't want to be a mom yet. I just want to be a kid again, a chance to be a teenager. But I don't want an abortion. My dad taught me a baby is a baby from conception and abortion is wrong." A sob slipped out.

Morgan scooted her chair closer to Bianca and put her arm around the girl. "First, you can take a test and know for sure."

Bianca nodded. "I'm sure it'll be positive." She met Morgan's eyes. "Nicoletta seems to think you are going to adopt her. I don't know why she thinks that, but I want to know if you'd adopt my baby."

Morgan was hit with a flood of emotions and didn't even know where to start to reply to her. "Nicoletta thinks that because it's true. I'm sure Aurora has heard us talking and told her. But we don't just want to adopt Nicoletta. We want to adopt you too. Would you like to be our daughter?"

Bianca's lip quivered. "Really? Me?"

Gio said, "Absolutely. You are an amazing young woman. Smart, resourceful. You are worthy of love and a family. We want you to be a part of our family, to be our daughter. We would absolutely love to adopt the baby too."

"The baby could be my little brother or sister instead of my child? I would like that very much. After all, the baby is Aurora's biological sibling."

Morgan wanted to ask if she was sure, but she also didn't want to think about how many men this young woman had had to endure.

"I know it's Dean's because he kept me for himself for the last year. He said he noticed how I took care of the other kids and asked if I wanted to move upstairs and take care of him and his daughter. It was such an improvement. He had already stopped letting just anyone pick me at parties and had started keeping me for himself."

Morgan shook her head in disbelief. "I'm so sorry. But I'm glad that was a turnaround for you."

"I felt horrible, though. Nicoletta was gone to that horrid man. I didn't know if she was still alive. And here I was living a much easier life. Dean even had me driving around by myself. I don't know why I didn't run, but I didn't know where to go."

Morgan said, "I understand that. I had a lot of supposed freedom with my trafficker, especially the last one, but I literally thought there was no other option. The chain he had around my neck wasn't near as long as it looked."

Morgan could sense the bond with Bianca increasing in depth. *Lord, please help me know how to minister to Bianca. Help me point her to You.*

One month later, by a miracle of epic proportions only possible by a work of the Almighty, Gio and Morgan were moving Bianca and Nicoletta into their own rooms. It was really happening. The adoption was going through with very little hassle, and what they did have was manageable. It wasn't final yet, but close enough to have the girls move in.

Everyone was over-the-top excited. The buzz in the house as they spent all day Saturday settling the girls in was electric. Dinner rolled around, and they ate together as a family. Tomorrow after church, they would go pick out a Christmas tree together as a family. Then they would decorate and talk about the Christmas story together as a family.

And in half a year, the five of them would become six. Bianca was indeed pregnant and doing surprisingly well. Being a teenager was hard enough on its own, but stack on the trauma she was working through and the added hormones of pregnancy, and Gio was surprised she was holding it together at all.

But maybe she wasn't and could hide it well.

Lord, help Bianca. Help her know this is a safe space where she can work through all the things. Help her to be open and honest and to come to us with anything she needs.

Gio struggled to know how to parent a fifteen-year-old whose experience with men over the last three years had been anything but healthy. He knew daughters needed affection from their fathers, and he found it simple enough with Aurora, but she didn't have the same trauma as the other girls.

Aurora snuggled up to him, jumped on his lap, and climbed on his back like any six-almost-seven-year-old would.

With Nicoletta, he'd found he shouldn't touch her back at all. It scared her every time. But she loved holding his hand when they walked through a parking lot or across a street.

Gio cleaned up the kitchen while Morgan took the two younger girls upstairs to get ready for bed. Bianca, though, hovered nearby.

Gio caught her eye as he closed the dishwasher. "You okay?"

She shrugged.

He pushed the start button, then grabbed a towel to dry his hands.

She slipped out of the kitchen, but before he could set the towel down, she came back into the room.

"Dad?" A smile toyed with her lips.

Warmth filled his heart. He never expected her to call him that. But he loved it.

"I can call you that, right? It's not weird."

"It's an honor. Definitely not weird." He leaned back against the counter.

"I have an odd request." She inched closer.

"Shoot." He braced himself, not knowing how odd it could be.

"I really need a dad hug."

He raised his arm. "That's not an odd request at all."

She slipped up next to him and under his arm. Staying at his side, she wrapped her arms around him.

He rested both of his hands on her opposite shoulder and leaned his head on top of hers.

She sank into him. "Thank you."

He squeezed her shoulders. "Any time." He held her until she loosened her grip.

She slid out of the hug and swiped at her eyes. "Ugh. I'm so sick of being so emotional."

"I don't think that ever actually stops."

She chuckled. "Part of being female, I guess." She took a deep breath. "Thank you for taking Nicoletta and me in."

"We love you girls and are delighted to have you as part of our family. I'm still trying to figure out what our relationship looks like, though, so be sure to talk to me. This dad-thing is new, in general." He shrugged.

"I think you're doing a great job. Thanks, Dad." With a giant grin, she practically skipped from the room.

He chuckled and watched her skip through the living room and up to Morgan, who was headed to the kitchen.

"Good night, Mom." Bianca gave Morgan a hug that matched her smile, then bounded up the stairs.

Morgan called after her, "Let me know when you're ready for bed, and I'll come tuck you in."

Bianca leaned over the railing. "Really? Tuck me in?"

"Sure, unless that's weird."

"No, it's perfect. I'll let you know." She disappeared.

Morgan came into the kitchen, shaking her head, smile as large as Bianca's.

Gio wiped his face dry and opened his arms to his wife. "Hey, Mrs. Crespi."

She walked into his embrace. "What did she need?"

"A hug—a dad hug."

"Oh Gio, we have three amazing girls. How did that happen?"

"God. It was all God." He touched his forehead to hers. "How are you doing?"

"My heart is so full. Didn't know it had this much capacity. But it feels like the broken parts are healing up and being restored. The Lord is using you and these girls in my life in ways I could never have dreamed of. It's like He's taking me right out of the ashes and letting me bloom in a way only He could."

Gio cupped her jaw and drew her lips to his.

She slipped her arms around his neck, and her soft curves melted against him.

He moved his hands to her back and drew her even closer. The electricity and passion that melded them together sizzled like it did the first time they'd kissed in that hospital hallway while hiding from Dean. But even more now. They were husband and wife.

She ran her fingers through his hair and broke the kiss with her hands on either side of his face.

"I love you, Morgan."

"I know, believe me, I know." She threw her arms around his neck again and hugged him with all her might.

What had he ever done to deserve this amazing woman's love? She fit him perfectly. God knew what He was doing when He brought them together. And while the past reared its traumatic head from time to time, it had no bearing on their present or their future. They would face the challenges set before them with grace and humor. And above all with the guidance of their heavenly Father.

Christmas morning arrived, and Morgan could hardly contain her excitement. Today was huge for all of them, but the girls didn't even know.

This was the first Christmas Morgan had celebrated in thirteen years, and she had gone all out decorating and baking all the goodies. She was going to gain another twenty pounds easily. She giggled. She had gained weight since escaping the trafficking life, and Gio didn't seem to mind one bit. But she was the healthiest she'd ever been.

She padded into the kitchen in her fuzzy slippers and fleece robe.

Gio must not have been able to sleep for the excitement either because she found him there with a pot of coffee ready to go, and the cinnamon rolls she'd prepped the night before in the oven.

"Hope you don't mind that I got them started."

"Not at all."

He poured her a cup of coffee. She took it and doctored it.

"Are you ready for this morning?" she asked.

"Absolutely."

The timer went off, and Gio pulled the rolls from the oven. They smelled heavenly.

The patter of little elephants echoed on the floor above signaling that the girls were up.

The three of them had had very different experiences for Christmas. Morgan had taken the time to talk to each girl, so they could all get on the same page as far as expectations. Aurora had experienced overly extravagant Christmases with hundreds—if not thousands—of dollars being spent on her. The other two had only ever received small, mostly homemade gifts. And nothing at all since their parents died. But they all agreed having a family was the most important thing this Christmas.

Morgan wasn't big on gifts in general after years of gift-giving being about manipulation, but this was different. She had taken each of the girls to the store individually and learned what they liked and wanted. Then she went back and bought a gift she knew they would be excited about.

But the best thing was the surprise that waited for the whole family. All three girls rumbled down the stairs, stopped in front of the tree, and huddled together. Morgan pulled her phone out of her robe pocket and snapped a picture of them.

Gio ran his hand across her shoulders as he passed her and met the girls at the tree. Morgan took a few more photographs. She never wanted to forget this moment. God had restored her life tenfold. *Thank You, Lord!*

"Mommy!" Aurora ran toward her.

Morgan exited the kitchen and met Aurora halfway, swooping the little girl up into her arms. She joined her family and exchanged greetings of "good morning" and "Merry Christmas."

Nicoletta met Morgan's gaze. Her wide eyes sparkled with the twinkle of the Christmas lights. "Can we open gifts?"

"Soon. The cinnamon rolls need icing first."

"Can I help?" Nicoletta bounced.

"Of course. To the kitchen." Morgan raised her pointer finger.

Aurora dove for Gio, and he hugged her close.

Morgan took Nicoletta's hand. They skipped into the kitchen where they iced the rolls and fixed a few more breakfast goodies.

They all sat at the table and enjoyed their breakfast as Gio read the Christmas story from Luke chapter two. It was so magical.

After breakfast they settled on the floor by the tree and opened presents.

Morgan's heart pounded harder and harder as they waited to the end for the big surprise. The girls were all so happy and grateful for their gifts.

Aurora displayed a hint of disappointment, but she didn't complain or whine. It had to be hard for a kid who was used to getting above-and-beyond to only get a few things. But that's all Morgan and Gio could afford.

Bianca pointed at a final present in the corner. "That one doesn't have a label."

Morgan couldn't sit still. "That's for all of us. Go ahead and grab it."

Bianca pulled it over and set it in the middle of the five of them.

Gio nodded. "Open it."

The three girls set to ripping the paper. They pulled out three rectangles wrapped in tissue paper with each of their names on them. Bianca passed them out according to the name on the label.

In unison, they unwrapped them. Bianca and Nicoletta read the paper Morgan had put in each of their frames. They both teared up.

Aurora tilted her head. "What's it say?"

Gio motioned to her toward him. She crossed the circle and sat in his lap. He struggled to keep from getting whacked in the face with her new fairy wings.

"It says, 'This is a frame to put your official adoption paper in after we get them at the courthouse on *Monday*.'"

"Me?" Aurora looked up at Gio, her face scrunched up tight.

Morgan couldn't help but chuckle.

Gio answered, "Yep, I'm going to officially adopt you."

"So for real, you'll be my daddy forever and ever?"

"Forever and ever."

She threw her arms around him as Nicoletta and Bianca rushed Morgan, and they nearly fell over in a pile of hugs and giggles.

They were a family forever and ever.

A Future Chapter
An Extended Epilogue

Because we all want a glimpse into their happily ever after

And frankly, I couldn't bear to stop writing about these characters

Extended Epilogue

JUNE – TEN AND A HALF YEARS LATER

At five o'clock on a Friday morning, Dylan held his Sig at the ready. The team lead, who was active law enforcement, counted down.

It had been five years since Dylan left the FBI. When they had wanted him to transfer, he'd refused, unwilling to shift the work at the women's center in any way. God was moving through all the effort Jacq and Morgan were putting into the place. They'd grown it from the ground up, and tomorrow they would celebrate ten years of ministry and 150 lives changed through it. And that didn't include Morgan or her children and the way the center had been God's tool in their lives to bring healing and restoration.

But resigning from the FBI didn't end his mission to rescue those enslaved in human trafficking. When he left the FBI, he'd joined a private organization whose sole purpose was to end human trafficking. And that's what they were doing now. In coordination with local law enforcement, they were going to take down yet another brothel.

"Go."

The team rushed in at the command. The first wave of agents and officers pulled men out of the rooms of the supposed massage parlor and took them out one end of the building. The second wave, of which Dylan was a part, went in and extracted the women, leading them out the same way the team had gone in.

Dylan took the arm of a young woman, twenty at the oldest. He spotted a long leather jacket, grabbed it, and draped it over her shoulders before leading her and another woman about the same age out the door.

He led them to the parking lot and had them sit on the curb next to the building.

He hated that the routine was to put these women in cuffs. But too often they were hostile and didn't understand the team was actually there to help them escape this hellish game and find a better way of living.

Another team member came along and slipped the zip-cuffs on each of the girls.

Dylan squatted down in front of the young women he'd helped bring out. "I'm sorry about the cuffs, ladies. Give us time, and we'll get them off as soon as possible."

The girl with the leather jacket gave him a slight smile but quickly redirected her gaze to the ground.

The other girl spit at him. Her saliva barely missed its mark.

He ignored the gesture and took the clipboard offered by another team member.

"What are your names—your real names, not the ones your pimps gave you—and ages?"

The spitter snarled. "Why would I tell you that?"

"So I can help you."

"Help? You're kidding, right? If you wanted to help me, you wouldn't have busted in when I was right in the middle of making a few bucks."

"And how much of that money do you have to hand over to your pimp?"

She scrunched up her face and snorted at him.

The girl with the jacket said, "Oh come on, Nellie. You know you have to hand it all over. We don't get to keep a single bill." She met Dylan's eyes. "My name is Beth. I'm nineteen."

Nellie said, "Look who's lying."

Dylan raised his eyebrows at Beth.

"Fine, I'm only seventeen. He'll kill me for telling you the truth, you know."

"We'll keep you safe. But you have to work with us to make that happen. My wife runs a center for women breaking out of this life. I can see how many openings they have right now."

Nellie asked, "Seriously?" Her tone sounded like he'd lost his mind, but her eyes pleaded for it to be true.

"I'll see what I can do. But there will be a few requirements."

Nellie shrugged her shoulders. "I'll never be able to meet requirements."

"I think the requirements will surprise you, but for now, how old are you?"

"I'm actually nineteen. So of consenting age. And quickly approaching the statistic, I'm sure."

"Four years in the life?"

"Yep, ran away at fifteen, hoping for a better life. Didn't get very far."

"What about you, Beth?" Dylan asked.

"I was kidnapped after school about a year ago. Pretty sure everyone thinks I ran away, though."

Dylan's heart ached for these girls and their families, who had no doubt been worried about their little girls.

Gio, who also worked with the private organization, came over. He still walked with a cane ready at his side. Even though he'd made good strides in gaining strength back, his knee never fully recovered from the gunshot wound. After two months back at active duty, he'd decided it was time for a change. So less than a year after getting shot, he'd left the FBI. The Bureau called on him occasionally to do a sketch, but they both loved focusing solely on hunting down traffickers and breaking people free from slavery.

Gio said, "The transports are ready." To the women he asked, "Are you ladies doing okay? Do you need medical attention in anyway?"

They both shook their heads.

Another girl down the line decided to get nasty with the officers. She'd be headed to the police station, but the two young women in front of Dylan didn't need to go there.

Dylan asked, "Would either of you like to call home?"

Beth looked up eagerly.

Nellie let out a humorless chuckle. "They don't want to hear from me."

"I think you'd be surprised." He turned to Gio. "Put these two on transport to a safe house."

"Perfect." Gio copied the names and ages the girls had given Dylan onto his own clipboard. "Follow me, ladies. We'll cut your cuffs by the van."

They stood. And Nellie said, "I've been shoved in a van full of girls before."

Dylan gently touched her shoulder. "This one's different. I promise."

Not that he expected her to believe him. He would find her parents, though. She'd been fed lies for years that no one back home would want her after all she'd been through. But while some might be much like Morgan's family had been, many parents of runaways just wanted their babies back.

Jacq poured herself a cup of coffee, excited for what this Friday would bring, even though Dylan hadn't been beside her when she woke up this morning. But hopefully they were busting some traffickers and helping more women break free.

She set the pot back on the coffeemaker, turned, and leaned back against the counter, inhaling the warmth of the black liquid.

Feet pounded on the floor above.

"Welp, so much for enjoying a little quiet." She doctored her coffee.

For three years, she and Dylan had housed women upstairs until a larger facility could be built. Now their kids had bedrooms on the second floor. All three of them. God had blessed them abundantly. Between their amazing family and the success of the women's center, Jacq's heart overflowed with gratitude.

Though not without its share of difficulties, the ministry was worth every struggle. Running a nonprofit like this in the middle of the mountains was expensive. And not only was she challenged by the work, raising a family in the midst of it was sanctifying too.

Squabbling echoed from the second floor. Jacq sighed. If only children didn't fight about everything.

Footsteps pounded faster down the stairs than seemed humanly possible. The screen door slammed.

"Alex!" Jacq strode to the front door.

Her almost-ten-year-old son turned on the front steps.

"Where are you going?"

"To play with Eddie."

"And I assume by 'play with Eddie' you mean eat breakfast first." She loved that Alex and Eddie were best friends, really more like brothers growing up next door to one another and being so close in age.

Alex huffed and marched back up the stairs and into the house.

"And I'm guessing an apology to your sister might be in order."

Fourteen-year-old Harper stood in the kitchen getting a bowl of cereal.

"Sorry," Alex spit at her.

Harper scrunched her face and gave him a stink-eye.

Jacq shot her a pointed glare.

Harper sighed. "I'm sorry for shoving you out of the bathroom."

Alex finally looked at his sister. "Yeah, sorry I didn't leave when you asked nicely."

It took Jacq entirely too much self-control to keep from saying, "Now isn't that better." But she didn't.

Thump. Thump. Thump.

Something was getting dragged down the stairs. Jacq went to investigate. The eyes of a very sleepy six-year-old met Jacq's. Josie was dragging her stick horse by the bottom of the stick. The head hit every wooden step as it came down.

"Morning, Josie."

"Hi, Mom." She held her hands out three steps up.

Jacq took Josie in her arms.

After making sure all the children had eaten, gotten dressed, and were off to Aunt Morgan's house, Jacq took the golf cart over to the main area of the center, which was now separate from the two families' homes. The center, in fact, was on the property that used to be Dean Rockefeller's den of evil.

The Lord had burned the house to the ground, and after months of prayer, the center had bought the lot at auction. Then after years of prayer over the land, they had broken ground for the first building, then a second, and tomorrow at the ten-year celebration, they would dedicate the third.

The first building held the offices for the center and a remote office for the organization Dylan and Gio worked for, which was dedicated to breaking women free from the game. It also held a large meeting room, several small meeting rooms, and the counselors' offices, which used to be dormitory rooms. They had set up the new buildings in little pods with rooms and kitchens, created to feel more like a home environment and help the women prepare for returning to the outside world.

Jacq walked down the hall and greeted everyone she saw. It took so many people to make the ministry function. How had she ever thought she could do this on her own? She laughed at herself. She wouldn't have been able to get things off the ground without God's hand, Dylan's support, and a multitude of others contributing in hundreds of ways. God was using this place in mighty ways, and she prayed it would continue well past her lifetime.

Jacq entered the large meeting room where they held their daily chapel.

One of the newest volunteers, Kimberley Lyons, straightened the chairs.

"Good morning, Kimberley."

"Hi, Jacq." The sorrow in the woman's eyes was a constant. Her daughter, Penelope, had run away four years ago. Best they could tell, she'd been sucked into the trafficking life despite her desire to make it big in the music scene.

"It looks great in here. Thank you." Kimberley had really taken the room up a notch in the decoration for tomorrow's celebration.

She smiled and came over to Jacq. Though she could see the question in Kimberley's eyes, she wouldn't ask. But as Gio and Morgan always said, hope in Jesus is never false. Jacq prayed daily they would find Kimberley's daughter.

Dylan stuck his head into the meeting room. "There you are. Got a minute?"

"Sure." Jacq squeezed Kimberley's arm. "See you later."

Kimberley nodded with a smile.

In the hallway, Jacq gave her husband a kiss. "How did the bust go?"

"Well enough. But they never feel like enough, it's like a hydra ... cut off one head ..."

Jacq wrapped her arm around her husband's waist, and they walked to the offices.

He said, "There were a couple of girls I think are really good candidates for here."

"Aren't they all, Dylan?" She paused and looked up at her husband. How she longed to be able to take in every survivor.

Dylan took the sides of her face. "There are only so many beds. Some of them have to go other places."

She nodded, and they continued.

"Gio is helping process them, find their identities, et cetera. One of the girls was only seventeen, the other nineteen."

"So young." They'd had to make decisions over the years of who to take in. And while Jacq wanted to accept all the children, and young men too, that wasn't the demographic God was calling them to at this point. Their focus was helping young women ages sixteen to thirty-five, approximately. "Bring them home."

Dylan gave her a toothy grin, kissed her forehead, and dashed to his office.

She giggled. She loved that man more every day. The last eleven years hadn't been easy but had been absolutely worth it.

Gio sat in the Knoxville FBI field office conference room, sketching the face of a trafficker. Even after all these years, it still took prayer and concerted effort to keep his emotions in check as he put faces to the scumbags who took advantage of their fellow human beings. As Beth gave him a detailed description of the man who had kidnapped her as she had walked home from school one day, she told him parts of her story. He wanted to chuck the pencil and pad across the room. But that wouldn't change what happened to her.

Lord, let this man be found and brought to justice under the law. Keep him from hurting other young women.

Gio set his pencil down and turned the sketch around to Beth.

"Yep, that's him. That's the man who kidnapped me."

"Thank you, Beth. I know this is hard, but you've done a great job."

She shrugged. "Now what?"

"The agents are trying to contact your parents. When we connect with them, you'll be the first one we tell."

"I just go home and forget this ever happened?"

"No, we want to help you. We'd like to offer you a place to live and work though things with trained counselors."

"For how long?"

"It depends on what you need. You're young, and from what you've told me, it sounds like you have a strong family to go home to, so maybe not too long. But I can't say a specific timeframe. Too many variables."

Beth said, "That makes sense."

"Hang in there; it will all come together."

She stood and left with an FBI agent.

Gio stifled a yawn and looked at his watch. The hours had gotten away from him. He'd been up since one-thirty for the five o'clock raid, but the day wasn't even close to done.

He grabbed his phone off the table and checked the progress of Bianca and Nicoletta's flight. The two girls had gone off to Bible college two years ago. Bianca had taken a few years after high school to give herself time to slowly enter adulthood. Then the girls chose the same school to attend together, where they were roommates and growing by leaps and bounds. He couldn't believe they were twenty-six and twenty. Time had flown. He wished they had had more time with the girls under their roof, but God had worked in their lives and brought them both to a saving knowledge of Jesus a little over a year after they'd become his and Morgan's daughters.

Their flight was actually running ahead of schedule. He needed to leave.

He packed up his art supplies and headed toward the door.

Matt Olsen stopped him. "Gio."

He turned.

"I haven't been able to find Nellie's parents. I'm going to arrange for her and Beth to get to the center this afternoon."

"Perfect. Thank you."

"I'm headed to tell Beth we talked to her dad. They're driving up from Atlanta to meet her at the center."

Gio's heart lifted to the ceiling. "That's fantastic. Praise the Lord."

His phone dinged. A text from Bianca. "Girls have landed; I've got to run."

He said goodbye to Matt and rushed to the airport as fast as he could. After parking, he headed toward baggage claim. The girls hadn't been home since Easter, and he couldn't wait to see them.

He leaned on his cane and scanned the crowd. A text came through.

Headed down the escalators.

He immediately spotted them.

Nicoletta waved with all her normal exuberance. She hadn't lost a touch of it in the process of growing up.

Bianca's smile reached from ear to ear.

The escalator was full, so they couldn't rush down it like he could tell Nicoletta was itching to do. But as soon as the crowd disembarked the moving stairs, she bolted toward him, Bianca half a step behind.

"Dad!" Nicoletta shouted.

He took three steps forward and braced himself on his good leg. Nicoletta slammed into him, and Bianca's arms wrapped around the two of them.

"Welcome home!" He hugged them and kissed both of their heads before releasing them.

"I have a zillion things to tell you, Dad. But I have to do one thing before we leave the airport."

"Of course."

Nicoletta walked away, her exuberance exchanged for somberness. She did this every time she flew into the Knoxville airport.

Bianca wrapped her hands around Gio's elbow, and the two of them followed her sister. Nicoletta stood in front of the trash cans where Jacq found her nearly eleven years prior. She closed her eyes and swiped away the tears that fell as a result.

The first time she had done this, he had walked over with her, holding her hand, and she had prayed a prayer of thanksgiving for all God had done from the moment He had pushed her to run from her trafficker. She had told Gio how she'd felt as if someone had been talking inside her head yelling the word *run* over and over again. It wasn't until she met Jesus personally that she recognized that voice she had heard in the airport. It was Jesus.

She opened her eyes, and the brightest smile possible graced her face. "Let's go home."

"Let's get your luggage first."

Bianca laughed. "Minor details. Now tell me, is Mom having a boy or a girl? I must know. The wait is killing me."

Gio laughed. "I'm not at liberty to say."

Bianca stomped her foot. "It's not fair."

"Your mother wants to tell you herself. I can't get in the way of that."

Nicoletta put her face to his shoulder. "We can act surprised."

"You know she'll know. Ain't gonna happen." He made a motion of zipping his lips.

The girls both slumped in defeat.

He chuckled and helped them find their luggage. He couldn't wait to see their reaction to the surprise.

Morgan cradled her growing belly as she leaned over the table helping her eight-year-old son, Anthony, better known as Tony, with his math. He was nearly an exact replica of his dad. The poor kid took after Gio with his math skills too. Give Tony a pencil and all he wanted to do was draw a picture—a stunning one, but it wasn't his math. It had taken nearly two years of trying to get pregnant, but God had blessed them with Tony as their first biological baby.

"Mom, I can't figure this out." Henry, thirteen, sat across the table from Tony.

"I'll be right there."

Henry and his sister, Talia, who was seven, came to their family four years ago, after Gio rescued them from a container in a North Carolina port. They'd been sold by their father who didn't want to raise them anymore. Gio had known instantly they needed to be a part of their ever-growing family. A few hoops had to be navigated as far as locating biological relatives, but no one had wanted the children. Except Morgan and Gio. The trauma of their experience had been a lot to work through, but about two years ago they made a major breakthrough and both Henry and Talia were flourishing as Crespi children.

Seventeen-year-old Aurora walked around the corner from the living room with their littlest, Greta, in her arms. "Mom, she won't let me finish my work."

"Come here." She took the three-year-old from her sister's arms. Homeschooling so many children was no joke. She and Jacq split the responsibilities to school all of their children, but Morgan took the bulk of the task so Jacq could put in more hours running the center.

"Thanks, Mom."

"Yep, go finish. Your dad will be home soon."

Aurora's face lit up. She adored her older sisters.

Morgan distracted her other biological child with a book on the couch. They had never tried to prevent pregnancy, and while three pregnancies, not including with Aurora, proved it was possible, it had never been a given. But God had been so good.

Her phone alerted her to a text message. Gio and the girls were five minutes out. She finished reading the book to Greta and called the other children. "Drop the books and come to the living room. School's done for the day."

After putting their books away, all eight other children, including Jacq and Dylan's three, joined Morgan and Greta in the living room. Eddie and Alex, the "twins" from other mothers, needed an extra call before they actually showed up.

Morgan shook her head. The two of them would be ten next week, their birthdays only three days apart. And they would forever be partners in all sorts of mayhem.

Eddie, Gio's brother's namesake, was the biggest surprise in all of their lives. He looked nothing like Dean but strangely like his biological half-sister, Aurora. He was the kindest child Morgan had ever met, always caring for the younger children and all the animals he could find. He was never without a dose of encouragement when someone was having a tough time. He had also been the youngest of all their children to declare Jesus the Lord and Savior of his life. And he preached it to everyone he met, even the cats that lived under Jacq's porch.

Morgan and the kids had all settled when the front door swung open, and Gio and the oldest girls walked in. Everyone erupted with excitement and jumped up. Hugs and squeals were exchanged.

Morgan gave each of the girls a hug then turned and raised her arms. "Everyone sit. I can't wait to share the news any longer!"

Gio placed his hand on her back. "You aren't going to wait for Jacq and Dylan?"

She bit her lip and heat filled her cheeks. "They already know."

He shook his head then kissed her.

Half the kids groaned.

Gio said, "Just tell them."

"Raise your hand if you think the baby is a girl."

Of the eleven children in the room eight raised their hands. Tony sat on the floor with his arms crossed, a scowl deeply etched into his face.

Morgan could hardly contain the laugh that wanted to bubble up. "How many think the baby is a boy?"

Tony raised both arms, fingers on both hands crossed.

Morgan covered her mouth. Five children voted for a boy.

Gio laughed. "That doesn't add up."

Aurora smacked Harper's arm. "Can't you tell she's carrying the baby like she carried Greta not Tony?"

Harper crossed her arms and shook her head with a coy smile. She was one of the ones who had voted for both. Aurora would no doubt call her a cheater.

Gio couldn't stop laughing. "Just tell them."

"But it's way more fun making them sit in suspense."

A chorus of "Come on, Mom" filled the room.

She smiled at Gio and pulled two strips of ultrasound pictures from a book on the shelf. "Baby A is a girl."

Cheers erupted.

Tony's bottom lip quaked.

Morgan knelt in front of him. "And baby B is a boy."

Tony's eyes widened, and he flung his arms around Morgan's neck.

The cheering cut off.

Aurora jerked her head toward Morgan and Gio. "Wait, twins?"

"Yep. Crespi number nine and number ten will be here in about four months. It would seem God has truly blessed us tenfold!" To have ten children after suspecting they wouldn't have any was more than Morgan could process.

Two hours later, after much celebrating and then sending the children off to play, Morgan, Gio, and Bianca walked into the administrative building of the women's center. Two new girls had just arrived, and Morgan was anxious to meet them.

All the way over from the house, Bianca had been telling them about school, but she became quiet and stopped just inside the building.

Morgan turned to her. "Everything okay?"

Bianca's cheeks filled with a rosy color.

Morgan knew that expression. "What's his name?"

"Owen." Bianca looked down at her hands that she had clasped in front of her. "He seems really great, but ..." She raised her gaze to Morgan then to Gio. "How do I know if he's truly like Dad or is actually like ... Dean?"

She rarely mentioned that man's name. None of them said it unless they needed to.

Gio set his hand on Bianca's shoulder. "It's hard to know. But does the Spirit in you see the Spirit in him?"

"Yes. Either that, or he's putting on a really good show."

Morgan said, "The Spirit doesn't lie."

"Exactly." Gio added, "Bring him home, and I'll put him through the wringer."

Bianca smiled. "Maybe Uncle Dylan can interrogate him?"

They all laughed, then Morgan took Bianca's hand. "In all seriousness, the most important thing we can do is pray. If you are steeping yourself in God's Word and spending time in prayer, you'll hear from Him. You've got a good head on your shoulders too."

Cane hanging from his arm, Gio punched one fist into the other palm. "And if he knows what's good for him, he won't mess with my daughter."

Bianca grabbed his hand. "Dad!"

He winked at her, and they continued into the building. They went to the office for Gio and Dylan's organization first.

Dylan was sitting behind his desk, two girls across from him.

Morgan walked up beside them. "Hi, ladies. I'm so glad you're here. I'm Morgan. I believe you've met my husband, Gio. And this is our daughter Bianca." Even after ten years it would never get old calling her *daughter*.

The young ladies gave them shy smiles.

Morgan met the eyes of one of the girls. She'd seen those eyes before.

But before she could place where, Dylan introduced them. "This is Nellie and Beth."

Beth asked, "Have you heard when my parents will be here?"

Nellie shifted uneasily in her seat.

Morgan said, "I'm sorry I haven't. We can find out, though."

Gio winked, meaning he would take care of it, and left the room.

Dylan said, "Paperwork is done here. Want to show them around?"

Morgan said, "I'd love to. Maybe we can find your rooms and everything."

This was the hardest part for all of them. The girls were uncertain and not sure if these people were trustworthy. Morgan just wanted to spill her story and tell them how Jesus had worked in her life. It could easily be a bit too much for someone who had been on the move since who-knows-what hour last night. But Morgan looked forward to getting to know these girls and sharing her testimony at some point.

Bianca engaged Beth in conversation as they walked to the main office of Shepherd's Heart Center for Women.

There they got the girls' welcome bags, which included toiletries, basic clothing, a homemade blanket that had been prayed over extensively, and a few other items they had found to be helpful for the transition. Within the first week, each woman was given her own Bible, but they were sure to make it more personal than stuck in a bag of things.

As Morgan handed Nellie her bag, their eyes connected, and she knew she'd seen them before. She didn't let go of the bag. "Nellie—short for Penelope."

Nellie nodded.

Her suspicion grew, but instead of saying anything, she led the girls back into the hallway.

Jacq came running toward her, a paper in her hand.

"Penelope Rand?"

So it was true.

Nellie turned to Jacq and tilted her head.

"It's really you?"

Nellie nodded.

Jacq showed her the piece of paper. It was the "in search of" paper they had pinned on the bulletin board in the lobby. "Your mom has been searching for you for years."

"Really?" Nellie's eyes narrowed in disbelief.

Morgan squeezed her arm. "It's true. I thought I recognized your eyes."

"You know my mom?" Nellie asked.

Jacq and Morgan both nodded.

Morgan spotted movement down the hall. It was Kimberley. Morgan waved her over, and then tapped on Nellie's arm.

The girl turned and took a step backward. "How could she ever forgive me for running away? For all I've done? She must be so ashamed."

Morgan took the girl by the shoulders. "That is all lies. Your mom loves you no matter what has happened."

Nellie looked back toward her mom.

Kimberley stood there, hands covering her mouth.

"Mom."

"Oh Penelope."

They ran to one another and embraced.

Seeing families reunited was one of the most beautiful things in the entire world. Morgan had never reconnected with her mom. Not because Morgan hadn't tried, though. Her mom had written off Morgan completely. They had talked once, but her mom lived her own life, and when Morgan's stepdad was released from prison, her mom took him back in again. That was the end of it. Her brother, Nate, didn't speak with her anymore, either. They both kept praying she would come around, but she'd cut them out, and there wasn't anything else they could do.

Morgan felt no bitterness in her heart, just joy at seeing Kimberley and Nellie reunited after four very long years.

Gio joined them, sliding his arm across Morgan's shoulders. "Beth's parents should be here within the hour."

All the tension in the girl's face released, and her eyes fill with tears.

Bianca put her arms around Beth and pulled her close. Beth sobbed and none of the rest of them could maintain dry eyes either.

Morgan leaned into Gio. "Why are we so blessed to get to see God work?"

The next day, everything for the ten-year celebration and building dedication fell into place, even though there was a snafu with the caterer and Dylan's parents had a flat on the way.

Almost everyone was there. Most of their friends and family. Dad and Mom—Leo and Sarah Crespi—were there since they had moved to Tennessee years ago to be near the grandchildren. Her brother, Nate, and his family were in from Ohio. Nearly all of the 150 women who had come to this place post-trafficking to then find Jesus and walk out into the world a new creation, ready to face a new life. Many of them now had husbands and children. Many others had gone home to live with their parents, who had missed them terribly while the evil world of trafficking had enslaved them.

God had done the work in this place, in each of their lives, in Morgan's life.

When it was her turn to walk up onto the steps of the new building, she was so overwhelmed with gratitude, she could barely breathe.

She shared her story, not mincing words about how low her life had been at times. "But in the darkest dark, the light shines the brightest. Jesus is our hope—and hope in Him is never false. He will change your life in ways you could never imagine. No matter how many wrong turns your life has taken, He will use them for His glory and your good. Because He is good. Ask me how I know."

Morgan met Gio's eyes and couldn't continue. No more words could be said, no more needed to be said. Jesus deserved all the glory. All of it.

Gio and the kids came up and stood around her. Dylan and Jacq and their children joined them, and together they cut the ribbon for the newest building for Shepherd's Heart Center for Women. A building where more women could find hope, a new life, and joy everlasting.

Morgan turned her face toward her husband's.

He smiled at her. "I love you. And I'm so proud of you."

"Don't be proud of me, just thank Jesus with me. Thank you for letting Him use you in my life. Thanks for loving me at my worst, through all my wounds."

"To God be the glory." Gio kissed her forehead.

"To God be all the glory."

Author's Note

Phew! What a series! It's been a wild ride, y'all. I never expected this series to become what it has. When the idea first popped into my head, I didn't even see Morgan and Gio as characters in the story. When Gio opened that door to Dylan and Jacq in book one, I had no idea he would become one of my favorite characters of all time. And Morgan wasn't even in the first draft of that book. But then she stole the entire series. HA!

People often ask me how I came to write about human trafficking. They wonder if I have any personal connection. I do not, not that I know of anyway. But with how pervasive trafficking is, I honestly wouldn't be surprised if I actually know someone (or more than one). However, that is not where this came from. It was totally from God.

I definitely couldn't have done this without Him. It has been a very challenging series to write, but I wouldn't change it. I'm honored that God would give me this assignment. My prayer is that I showed an honest glimpse into the hard stuff without crossing any lines. It was definitely a challenge. I pray God has used this series in your life to draw you closer to Him and to open your eyes to a true crisis of our times.

Thank you for reading this series, for sticking with me to the end. I pray you will place your hope in Jesus, because hope in Jesus is *never* false! If you haven't put your hope in Him, I beg you to do so. Visit my website at lizbradfordwrites.com/hope to learn how.

If you don't know the saving power of Jesus, please reach out and let's talk. He loves you and wants to be in a relationship with you.

Blessings,
Liz

Keep in Touch

Be sure to sign up for Liz's newsletter. By signing up you will have a short story delivered to your inbox. You'll also be able to stay up to date on release dates and sales!

Sign Up for Liz's mailing list by going to:
https://subscribepage.io/lizbradford

You can also find Liz at:
www.facebook.com/lizbradfordwrites
www.pinterest.com/lizbradfordwrites
www.goodreads.com/author/show/18532678.Liz_Bradford

Also By Liz Bradford

The Detectives of Hazel Hill

A FRIGHTFUL NOEL - Prequel - Christmas Novella
NOT ALONE - Book One
PURSUED - Book Two
ON YOUR KNEES - Book Three
A SHOT AT REDEMPTION - Book Four
GIANTS FALL - Book Five
Book Six is in the works

Knoxville FBI

REVENGE IGNITED - Prequel - Christmas Novella
INTO THE FLAMES - Book One
UNDER FIRE - Book Two
SMOKY ESCAPE - Book Three
OUT OF THE ASHES - Book Four

Tracking Danger – A K9 Search and Rescue Series

TOO LATE - A Novella - Book One (previously in the Winter Deceptions Collection)
SWEPT AWAY - Book Two (previously in the Small Town Danger Collection)
More books to come with Josh, Chloe, and Poirot

Hazel Hill Police & Fire

ABANDONED - Book One (previously released in Stay with Me – the Summer Heat Collection Vol.1) – Rerelease coming later 2024

Acknowledgments

First and foremost, I must thank my Lord and Savior, Jesus! Thank You for the gift of story and allowing me to pen words. I hope and pray that You will use them to touch hearts and draw readers closer to You!

Thank you, Ken for being so supportive as I pursue my dreams and make the voices in my head earn their keep.

Thank you to my daughters for doing your school work without complaint eventually and helping me by not fighting not killing each other while I'm working.

Thank you, Mom for always being just a text or phone call away when I get stuck on a medical issue, a word, or whatnot.

Thank you to my partners in crime and dearest friends, Crystal Caudill, Angela Carlisle, and Voni Harris for your accountability, wording advice, and general mayhem fun. This book definitely wouldn't have happened without all y'all support, advice, and prayers! Love you, girls!

Thank you to my friends on Discord! May your sprints always be productive and GIF filled.

Thank you, Teresa for helping me make my story all that it could be!

Thank you, Sharyn for catching my wording errors (and my readers thank you for your ruthless cutting of the word that)!

Thank you, Emilie Haney for an incredibly beautiful cover!

Thank you, ACFW-Louisville Chapter for being my monthly dose of encouragement and writerly friendship.

About the Author

Liz didn't always know she a writer, but she was. Before she even knew it, God was plotting out this path for her. From her earliest days, stories were a natural part of her imagination. In high school, she toyed around with writing, but it was nothing more than a secret hobby. But one day, when her middle daughter was a little over a year old, a story idea crept in her mind and wouldn't leave her alone. So, she started writing. She would stay up late after everyone else was in bed and frantically write the words that brought her characters to life.

That first novel lives buried deep in her hard drive, and maybe one day it will see the light of day, but that would take a LOT of editing. About the time she couldn't figure out where that first book would end, another idea persisted in her mind. That was Becca and Jared's story, book one in *The Detectives of Hazel Hill* series. Before she knew it, what started as a single novel turned into a trilogy... but wait, there's more. In that series, she now has six stories published (including the prequel novella) and many more percolating. She also has several more ideas for the characters of Hazel Hill, North Carolina. The *Knoxville FBI* series is now complete. Her *Tracking Danger* series currently has two books out with more coming. Liz also has numerous other series forming in her mind!

Liz is a member of Faith, Hope, & Love Christian Writers, American Christian Fiction Writers, and ACFW Louisville Chapter. Her heart longs to live in North Carolina (where she was born) or Tennessee and that is why she set her stories there. But, for now, she and her husband live in Southern Indiana where she homeschools their three daughters.

Made in United States
Orlando, FL
19 February 2024